ARROWS OF LONGING

Arrows of Longing

VIRGINIA MORICONI

Duckworth

First published in 1985 by
Gerald Duckworth & Co. Ltd.
The Old Piano Factory
43 Gloucester Crescent, London NW1

© 1985 by Virginia Moriconi

ISBN 0 7156-2069 X

British Library Cataloguing in Publication Data

Moriconi, Virginia
  Arrows of longing.
  I. Title
  813'.54[F]   PS3563.0871644

ISBN 0-7156-2069-X

Photoset in North Wales by
Derek Doyle & Associates, Mold, Clwyd.
Printed in Great Britain by
Billing & Sons Limited, Worcester

To Anna Haycraft

1

There was a star-shaped flaw in the mirror at Dufresne Hall; a proliferation of slender fissures radiated outward from the crack at the centre of the star. Gretchen deplored the damage, which defeated her purpose. As the survivor of an ordeal which had severely strained every article of her faith, she had been prepared to see a meaningful alteration in her face – in consequence of the ordeal – she had counted on a mirror for proof of the alteration, she had meant to study the proof – if she found it – before she wrote to her mother. Some record of what she had undergone should, it seemed to Gretchen, be signed on her flesh.

But staring at the havoc in the mirror she was unable to verify a trace of any modification in her image. Indeed, she could scarcely distinguish her face; from her eyebrows to the point of her chin it was overlaid by clusters of splintering rays.

Her old reflection, the reflection she remembered, had been smooth, unlined. Sometimes, by scowling, by smiling, she had deliberately ruffled it, she had made it ripple like the surface of a pond. But the ripples had always raced away, leaving it clear as ever. Ten days earlier it had been merely a limpid testament to her youth; as of the present writing it would hardly be so ingenuous any longer – of that she was certain – even though the broken mirror could confirm no change. Vexed that she had nothing visible to note or to describe, she turned back from the insubordinate glass.

'Nevertheless I *am* changed,' she said to herself. 'Whether I can prove it or not.'

Yet she was convinced that there, in the mirror, behind the shattered star, lay the impress of the harsh experience she had so unhappily endured.

'I was *naïve*,' she said, feeling sorry for her blameless shade. 'In fact, ten days ago I was the girl next door. Whereas now –'

Now she had added miles and miles – not to mention an interminable night – to her brief history. She had had to contend with a mob of harassed, embattled strangers, some of them hostile,

7

she had been condemned to alien companionship.

Now, she supposed, she was fledged, but had she forfeited every vestige of the innocence she had been so eager to supplant with an informed *savoir-vivre*? Although it was true that she had been searching for a peak on Darien, she had been a long way from seeking a rarefied – and precocious – cynicism. All told, she could not help but wonder if she had not been better off in her circumscribed, best-of-all-possible worlds.

Now, in a manner of speaking, she had arrived. But where? She was lost, she was on foreign ground, between innocence and disenchantment, another stranded immigrant.

Doubtful that she could express as much – and somewhat doubtful of her high-glown sentiments – she stood at the window, looking out on the afternoon, on the grey clouds, heavily shifting, on the dark, heavy waters of the harbour below. Then, impatient with the ugly weather, with the unquiet moment, she moved away from the troubled view. Lost or found, she was loving, she was bound to let her mother know that she was somewhere – more or less safe – that her journey was behind her.

Rapidly she filled six sheets of writing-paper with an account of the tribulations which had shocked her into sudden sophistication or, at least, into a sudden distaste for the age of excursion, into sudden, grim suspicions of brotherly communion. Finally, dissatisfied with her report – everything that had happened to her was grotesque in her reconstructions – she scribbled a postcript.

'Perhaps it's just that I've simply grown up,' she wrote. 'If so, I almost wish it were yesterday again, I wish my illusions were still part of me. I may be wiser than I was but I don't feel wise. Only diminished.'

Yet even the hard-won philosophy – 'Perhaps it's just that I've simply grown up' – of the postscript brought her no peace of mind. Her recollections remained as keen, as intolerably raw as they had been when she had unburdened herself to Dr Donovan, when she had told him everything about the tormented flight across the Atlantic. On that occasion Donovan had been patently bewildered by such a torrent of dismay.

'What were you expecting?' he said.

'Rapture,' said Gretchen, and waited for mockery.

'Instead, you discovered yourself at disagreeably close quarters with your fellow man?' said Donovan.

'It was as if hundreds of unclean lives were rubbing off on me,' she said.

'Rapture's in short supply these days,' said Donovan. 'To be frank,

I can't think of anyone in search of it recently.'

'Well, *I* was,' Gretchen said.

And so she had been. Up to the day she had set out on her own her world had been restricted to the perimeters of her family, her friends at school or in college, and her reading. Her dreams were untested, her visions unfounded on practical knowledge. As artless as her confession must, she supposed, have sounded to Dr Donovan, rapture was precisely what she had expected since, to her, the airplane was the glorious symbol of the twentieth century and she had envied every one of her contemporaries who knew what it was like to be lifted into the archways of the sky.

During her childhood on the quiet Pennsylvania hills she had never longed for escape given that she had never conceived of herself as a prisoner. During the years at the university, sheltered by ancient trees, surrounded by broad reaches of opulent lawn, she was aware that she had yet to travel very far from her beginnings. Then, intermittently, she was fretful, hemmed in; she had had a sense that she was regularly rehearsing the same attitudes, the same postures – for lack of touch with any other models, any other society.

'If you come right down to it I'm unfinished,' she had said to her mother. 'I'm nearly twenty-five, I've got my B.A., I've got my M.A., in another couple of months I'll be ready to write my thesis and even so what am I but a grab-bag of odds and ends?'

'I hope you'll continue unfinished,' said her mother. 'A good life is a becoming. Which is not to say that a wider horizon would do you much harm.'

'A wider horizon would cost money,' Gretchen said.

'On your twenty-fifth birthday,' said her mother, 'you'll inherit five thousand dollars.'

'Five *thousand* dollars?' said Gretchen. 'From whom? Five thousand dollars? I could go to Tibet.'

'It's cold in Tibet,' said her father, from the doorway.

Gretchen's Tibet had no existence in an atlas. It was – as both her mother and father had understood – her word for a country too distant to touch on the frontiers of her own, a country which was other, a country in which she could try herself against unfamiliar customs, unfamiliar points of view.

'If, at her age, she weren't curious,' said her mother to her father, 'you and I would have something to worry about.'

'I'm curious,' said Gretchen. 'So you have nothing to worry about.'

'There's always something to wory about,' her father said. 'Cyrus is limping around on three legs. If you'd run him up to Dr Welles I could get on with the milking.'

'She'll have to use the pick-up truck,' said her mother. 'The battery's dead in the Plymouth.'

'Cyrus won't ride in the front seat,' said Gretchen.

'Cyrus is quality folk,' her mother said. 'He was born to a limousine.'

'Put him in the back of the truck,' said her father. 'And bring Anna or David along to hang onto him.'

'I'll get David,' Gretchen said. 'He's reliable.'

'Take Cyrus' mattress,' said her mother. 'The back of that truck is hard on old bones.'

Alone by evening, walking over the fields in a lake of twilight, Gretchen – drunk on the powerful aroma of affluence, out of her element on waves of unbridled exhilaration – had already slipped away from the present, was already reaching toward the arcane landscape of the future. From the moment her mother had divulged that, upon her arrival at the age of twenty-five, a legacy was waiting for her, she had been startled into an awareness that money could buy more than everyday necessities, she had instantly appreciated that – at least for a limited length of time – it could buy freedom.

She had not chafed at the disciplines of learning; as much for her own sake as for the sake of the parents who were so proud of her, she had committed herself to win – and to continue to win – the scholarships which could set her on the highroad to academic distinction. But five thousand dollars meant to Gretchen that, once she had completed the necessary research, once she was ready to write her thesis, she could leave home – for possibly as much as a whole year, if she were prudent and thrifty – she could find modest lodgings on the same earth which had belonged to Yeats, to Joyce, to Synge.

Not once had she confessed to anyone that, although she was willing to live to teach – which was what so much higher education might prepare her to do – she wished that she could live to write. Such an ambition seemed almost as improper to Gretchen as it would have seemed to her mother or her father; she had not been brought up to indulge in inflated self-esteem, to believe herself endowed with any singular talent. From the fifth winter of her life, when she had learnt to read, she had been taught that diligence was its own reward. Dilegence was what .had been expected of her, was still expected of her; had she admitted that she required something

10

different, something more from herself, her parents would, at best, have thought her immature, at worst, vainglorious. Secretly she sometimes dreamt of a row of bound volumes with her name on every spine, but all the while she knew that she had no talent for story-telling or for the cadences of poetry.

'You have a first-rate critical intelligence,' one of her professors had said to her.

'Is that an asset?' she had said. 'Would it get me a job as a cashier in a supermarket?'

'It's a rare gift,' the professor had replied. 'Cultivate it, cherish it, and it will lead you almost anywhere you want to go. Your thesis will be a stepping-stone –'

The hills had been stained a dusky violet, the clouds had been tipped with a golden light, emanating from the sun's benevolent farewell; slowly the light and the benevolence had faded, a crescent moon had risen, cold and prim, darkness had come upon the valley while Gretchen, sitting under a maple tree was fast in contemplation of the life before her. At last she rose, a little stiff, and chill in her summer gingham.

'Why shouldn't I go to Ireland?' she said to the thin moon, as soon as she was standing up. 'After all, my thesis is concerned entirely with Irish letters.

'I *will* go to Ireland,' she said, to a night-world rasped by crickets. 'And when I come home maybe I won't be unfinished any more. Maybe I'll know who I am, maybe I'll *be* who I am –'

With only a sliver of moonshine to guide her homeward, she missed her footing twice and fell. In the morning it was her mother who remarked on her bruises. Gretchen herself had not noticed them.

She could not immediately mention Ireland to either of her parents since she was quite sensible enough to be sure that, to her father or her mother, Ireland was the contemptible runt of what had once been the British Empire, a miserable island teeming with shiftless men and women – most of them alcoholics, all of them slipshod Catholics – perennially in arrears with the rent or behind with the chores. Not even Yeats could have redeemed the Irish in her mother's eyes, while her father would not have heard of him. But when her mother had gone to Knightstown to do the weekly shopping, when she had the house – and the telephone – to herself, she could call Aaron.

'I have a problem,' she said.

'If you'd married me you'd be scrubbing floors and putting my winter clothes away in mothballs,' said Aaron. 'You wouldn't have time for a problem.'

'I'd rather have you as my best friend forever than as my ex-husband,' said Gretchen. 'Do you know if there's an Irish tourist board or a centre for information about Ireland in New York?'

'There must be,' Aaron said. 'Have you decided to go to Ireland?'

'I'd like to write my thesis there,' said Gretchen.

'Then I'll call Mother now and tell her you need a bed for a couple of nights,' said Aaron.

'You're the daughter-in-law I've always wanted,' said Mrs Isaacs. 'Even if you aren't descended from the tribes of Israel.'

'I'm not ready to get married,' said Gretchen. 'And Aaron never will be. He's not on the look-out for a wife, he's on the look-out for a doormat.

'Did he tell you I came to New York because I need to learn something about Ireland?'

'He did,' Mrs Isaacs said. 'So Ephraim's bringing his secretary, Rebecca, here for a drink before dinner. She spent her vacation last summer in west Cork.'

'Are you well-heeled?' said Rebecca?'

'In September I'll have a little windfall. I want to make the most of it,' said Gretchen.

'You can't go to Dublin,' Rebecca said. 'It's too expensive. Decent lodgings would eat up your windfall in no time and cheap lodgings would be in dangerous quarters where you wouldn't be safe on the streets at night. You must go south where your money will last and you can make friends everywhere you turn.'

Before Rebecca left, Gretchen had the name and the address of a woman who ran a guest-house – open the year around – in a small town called Ralston's Cove.

'Go to her,' said Rebecca. 'You won't regret it. Dublin's a third-rate tourist trap.'

'Gretchen, you've only just arrived,' said Ephraim Isaacs at the breakfast table the next morning. 'You can't leave Helen and me on such short notice.'

'I'd love to stay on and on,' said Gretchen. 'But I've got to get to the end to my research before the fall. As it is I'm a year behind my own schedule.'

'Were you troubled for source material?' Mrs Isaacs said.

'No,' said Gretchen. 'I still have quantities of material. My favourite professor's speciality is Ireland – Irish history, Irish writers, poets, playwrights. I've had the run of his library for so long that lately he and his wife automatically put me out when they let the cat in for the night.'

'Are you still living in a dormitory?' said Mr Isaacs.

'Fortunately not,' said Gretchen. 'I'm a boarder in a house on the campus.'

'Do you realise that ever since Aaron went off to architectural school he's had no one to sew his shirt buttons on when they're hanging by a thread?' Mrs Isaacs said. 'For four years he's been lost without you.'

'We really were happy together in the undergraduate days,' said Gretchen. 'When and if my thesis is written I'll teach him to sew on his shirt buttons all by himself.'

'Of course you'll keep in touch with us,' said Mr Isaacs.

'Of course I will,' Gretchen said.

By the end of August – after spending long mornings with her professor, briefly reviewing everything she had read – Gretchen concluded that her research was done. Her notes alone filled a suitcase.

By the end of September she was twenty-five, whereupon her grandmother's legacy was hers. Since her grandmother – her mother's mother – had died twenty years earlier, the original five thousand dollars, wisely invested, had almost trebled. Until she came into her inheritance Gretchen had been used to thinking in terms of small sums like twenty-five or thirty dollars. A hundred dollars had seemed a fortune to her. But if she was dazzled it was not by the money, which she thought of as a grave responsibility. As for Ireland, the loom of genius, she had – temporarily – stopped thinking about it. Somehow she would find the spiritual strength to live up to its majestic ghosts, to lay her best work in one of its shrines. A week before her leave-taking what was dazzling was the imminence of the journey, high above the enormous ocean, on wings made for man.

'I think I have a Daedalus complex,' she said. 'There's something magical about flight, isn't there?'

'Your feet haven't touched the ground since you booked your passage,' said her mother.

'A plane ticket wasn't necessary,' her father said. 'She could fly the Atlantic under her own steam.'

'I can't wait to be airborne,' said Gretchen.

The adventure for which Gretchen could not wait turned out to be, as she characterised it for Dr Donovan, an 'exercise in distress, discomfort, and disgust'.

Distress met her face to face the instant she was inside the airport, which was so crowded that she feared the breath would be crushed out of her lungs in whichever stream of travellers she chanced to join. After a time of anxious indecision, she stood on tiptoe, she craned her neck and, at last, her eye lit on what she prayed might be the check-in counter which corresponded to her flight. Anxious indecision gave way to panic while she struggled to manoeuvre her five suitcases, her typewriter, and her purse – whose shoulder strap kept slipping along her arm – towards the goal. Feverishly she tussled and shoved as, inch by inch, she made an awkward progress forward to the airlines desk. Yet the relief which flowed into her once she had presented her ticket and surrendered her luggage – all of it, save for the typewriter – was quickly succeeded by a panic even more acute when, without an inkling as to the whereabouts of the passport control division – her next objective – she wandered into the awful labyrinth beyond the check-in desks. Reckless by then, she followed a purposeful couple, brandishing their own passports. They brought her straight to authority in uniform but – that hurdle cleared – she was helplessly swept on, through lounges, past duty-free shops, until she was utterly disoriented. Every few paces she disengaged herself from the flux, she strove to catch sight of an indication, a signpost which pointed to the departure gate. Ultimately she glimpsed a train of arrows overhead, she found the gate; ultimately her flight was called but, when she was safely on board, she was too spent for rejoicing.

Nothing miraculous occurred as the plane lumbered toward the runway, nor was there anything to see but flares, at intervals. Presently it took off, roaring directly into the blind night. Quite shortly after take-off the pilot, via the loudspeaker, announced to the passengers that they were entering an 'area of turbulence'; the Fasten Your Seat Belt sign remained alight and, for over an hour, there was virtually no activity in the body of the aircraft.

Gretchen was disconsolate. The very act of breathing grew forced, unnatural, wedged as she was between a restless teenager on her right, whose matted hair lay lank on his shirt-collar, who knocked her shins as he continually crossed and recrossed his legs, and the vast hulk of a man in the aisle seat, whose bloat, oozing past the confines of the arm-rest, threatened to engulf her on the left. The soft cradle of the fat man's blubber revolted her, his attentions – the chewing gum he offered, the puffed and dimpled hand dangling above her knee, the familiarity with which he declared that he was gonna hafta get-ta-know her – left her outraged. Resolved to ignore him, she was obliged to turn her gaze elsewhere; however, when it came to rest on the boy's face, she dropped her eyelids immediately, startled by the glimmering of a diseased spirit leashed within his narrow skull, behind the sockets of his narrow, furtive eyes. Meanwhile the fat man, offended, listed invidiously closer, so that she was all but immobilised by his nearness, in his spreading flesh.

As for flight the great winged ship semed no more than a clumsy, climbing bus. Far from the ecstasy she had anticipated, an ecstasy generated by limitless power and piercing speed, by a triumphant defiance of the limited, substantial earth, she had to make do with a drunken lurching, while the huge invention, quite failing to manifest its omnipotence, was cruelly buffetted in the blackness of the celestial sea. If she was overwhelmed, it was not by the tumult in the clouds or by a high delight, but by an acute discomfort, by the steaming mass of the passenger on the aisle, by an intuitive dread of the haggard boy at the window.

Painfully cramped, at constant risk of contamination – what she thought of as creeping infection brooded on her right and on her left – she craved instant release, space, a fresh wind, liberty. The girl who had yearned to fly might never have existed; in her place a novice in a purgatory of her own, unwitting election, suspicion of, repelled by the company she was keeping.

As the minutes passed she grew numb in her confinement; she composed herself to wait – for nothing but the end of the trip. Long before that the Seat Belt sign was switched off, the cabin crew sprang into life. Without enthusiasm Gretchen watched the advance of the bar trolley, while she decided that she was not thirsty. Pushing the trolley, the approaching stewardess bestowed on the most manly of the captives pining for refreshment a glassy rictus, an enamelled smirk which, once, accidentally settled on Gretchen. Caught unaware, Gretchen shivered. She wondered if the automaton behind the automatic smile ever so far forgot herself, when she was off duty, as to turn the lacquered grimace on a transient lover and whether, if she ever had, he had been transmuted into stone.

An hour went by. The uneasy boy guzzled a beer, the fat man nursed a double whisky. Then dinner was served. Gretchen was momentarily diverted by the plastic trays with their neat assortments of small, plastic containers. But when she had tasted the synthetic food in one of the containers, she sank back into misery, she ate nothing but the roll – which was stale.

After the trays had been collected she tried to read Virginia Woolf's *Moments of Being*, but Virginia Woolf could not hold her own

15

against a Goliath, swollen with food and drink, and a sickly David, repeatedly changing his position, repeatedly bruising her ankles with his sharp, pointed boots, and driving his bony elbow into her ribs.

Some time later – she had rejected the headset, having rightly concluded that the film was trash – she was lulled by the darkness in the cabin. She lapsed into a clouded sleep. She drifted just above the incontinent howls from the baby across the aisle, above the sweet, spoiled odour of the fat man, the beer-charged breath of the young hoodlum at the window. She dreamt of a warm animal nestling on the inside of her right thigh. In the dream the animal moved nearer and nearer to her groin.

Suddenly she was awake. In a violent spasm she grabbed the boy's left arm and flung his hand back against his chest. At that, he sullenly averted his head and Gretchen, flooded by a killing rage, could do no more than to sit bolt upright for the rest of the journey.

The plane touched ground in a light mist, lightly speckled with rain. Slowly stumbling toward the exit, Gretchen had time for a searching look at the emptying interior of the aircraft, at the carpeting, the wisps of curtains, the seat coverings. Everything was worn, everything was seedy, and so, she thought, with a tremor of revulsion, was she. Worn, seedy, disenchanted – and defiled.

Time came to a stop in the airport at Shannon; there she pieced out a whole morning cat-napping and fretting. The flight which she had booked for Dublin was delayed since, at Dublin, the airport was fog-bound. Had Dublin been her final destination, a late arrival might have been a trifling matter; but from Dublin she was to fly to Port Ferris, where she had planned to catch a bus. In spite of friendly reassurance that there were hourly flights between Port Ferris and Dublin, Gretchen was on edge. Friendly reassurance was welcome, but what she needed was deliverance – deliverance from airports and airplanes and fellow travellers. By two o'clock, when the Dublin flight was called, she felt hollow, apprehensive, and immeasurably tired.

Landed at Dublin, waiting in another departure lounge, she was so light-headed that, for some minutes, she feared she might faint. Slow in its coming, a nearly overpowering homesickness slowly unnerved her; she realised that she was ignominiously close to tears, she was horror-stricken at her weakness, she fought to collect what was left of herself. When she embarked for Port Ferris she was stiff with self-control.

Rough winds met the plane head-on as soon as it was off the ground,

16

reminding Gretchen of the beginning of her odyssey. Sharp as if they were present, she remembered the boy and the fat man. Intimations of some deep, private loss assailed her and were abruptly superseded by others of deeper, more pressing trouble. In point of fact, there was a ringing pain in her neck and a long-stretching ache from the small of her back right down to the calves of her legs. Passionately she repudiated the possibility that there was anything the matter with her. She, to whom a rare cold was an event, she, almost invariably strong, confident, she, Gretchen, could not allow herself to fall, alone and unremarked, by the wayside in a strange nation.

So she braced herself but, although she had meant to take a bus from the airport to Port Ferris, when she had assembled her five suitcases and her typewriter, she crawled into a taxi – a wicked outlay of her precious hoard.

'Please, could you help me?' she said, and heard such a pitiful voice that she hardly believed it was her own. 'I must get to Port Ferris and find a bus for Ralston's Cove.'

'Where did you say, then?' said the driver.

'Ralston's Cove,' said Gretchen.

'That's where you're bound?' the driver said.

'I've got to get there,' said Gretchen.

''Tis late,' he said.

Gretchen had seen as much. An angry dusk was deepening. A dirty fog rolled ahead of the cab.

'You'd be lucky to catch the last bus, I'd say,' said the driver.

'Oh, do hurry,' said Gretchen.

'Conditions are not favourable,' he said. 'I'll do my best, of course.'

Before they reached Port Ferris Gretchen was swept by a shaking chill. To her astonishment she heard her teeth chattering. She clamped her jaw to keep them from falling out of her head. More than ever it was imperative to catch the bus. As ill as she felt, she must complete the last lap of her journey. Like a crippled vessel she must make port.

Port Ferris was dark when they rattled through the outskirts.

'How much longer?' said Gretchen.

The driver made no reply. However, shortly afterward, he turned to speak to her.

'Well, you've a charmed life, I see,' he said. 'There's the bus now. It might have been waiting for no one but yourself.'

'Don't let it start without me,' said Gretchen.

But for the taxi-driver she could never have managed to board the bus

17

with her baggage. He arranged her suitcases while she collapsed into a seat at the front.

'You're very kind,' she said, wondering if her voice was too frail to carry.

'I'd have taken you along myself,' said the taxi-driver, 'only that the wife's down with gallstones and Ralston's Cove is a good four hours – there and back.'

The bus, with just a scattering of passengers, rumbled away from the depot. As it throbbed into motion's Gretchen's head went spinning. Desperately she fixed her eyes on the travellers across the way – a child with an emerald green scarf around its neck, a stout woman in peacock blue – and, to her anguish, she began to see them as if she were looking into a kaleidoscope. Fragments of green, scraps of blue swirled into patterns, patterns dissolved in brilliant chaos, chaos erupted, spattering scraps and fragments, fragments and scraps fell into new patterns, new patterns wheeled before her. So giddy that she stiffened every muscle to keep herself from being flung, like a bundle, into the aisle, she covered her face with her hands to blot out the whirls of green, the whorls of blue.

Vigorously the bus battled against the city, braking with a remorseless jerk before countless stop-lights, then thrusting ponderously forward, swaying and shuddering as it gained velocity, wheezing as it slowed for crowded intersections. Searing pains flashed at Gretchen's temples, locked in her wrists, sped through her legs, while she quivered like a hound in a freezing rain. But just as each of her torments seemed to be ascending to an explosive climax, the bus turned out of the city onto the smooth band of a darkened road.

Easy now, the engine raced steadily; gently she was rocked, gently the fingers clenching her head loosened their grip. She lowered her hands, went limp in the envelope of her coat, and rested on the verge of sleep. After a long time the bus coasted to a halt; Gretchen was roused by one or two departing passengers, then it moved forward again. Every once in a while it rolled to another standstill only to start over. Finally it came to what she sensed might be a definitive arrest; opening her eyes she saw that she and the driver were alone.

'You wanted Ralston's Cove?' said the driver.

'Yes, I did. I mean, I do,' said Gretchen.

'You've arrived,' he said.

Gretchen rose, clutched back of the seat, and gave him a drowning stare.

'Not keeping too well, are you?' he said.

'I must find a cab,' said Gretchen, although she was afraid that she was too weak to get off the bus.

'Myself, I doubt you'll do that,' he said.

Hopeless, she kept on looking at him; of the two of them only he had the force to alter the balance of adversity.

'All the same,' he said, 'we're pulled up before the hotel. Someone inside will help you, sure.'

'The trouble is,' said Gretchen, 'I don't think I can get my luggage there.'

At that he got to his feet, unwilling but competent.

'I'm not allowed to leave the bus,' he said. 'Never mind, I'll give you a hand.'

Three pieces at a time he carried her suitcases and her typewriter away. Twice he disappeared and returned. Then, baffled by her immobility, he seized her elbow, all but dragging her toward the exit. Once he looked back.

'Did you mean to forget your hand-bag?' he said.

Gretchen gasped.

'Right on,' said the driver. 'I'll fetch it for you.'

She had no idea where she was, but she knew she was neither in the bus nor out on the street; she recognised a circle of light, of which she seemed to be the core. With what she believed might be a last effort, she compelled herself to concentrate on the near distance before her. She saw a counter with a panel behind it, from which two rows of keys were hanging; more important, she saw the figure of a woman between the counter and the rows of keys. It was the woman whom she strove to bring into her liquefying focus.

'I'm sorry to bother you,' said Gretchen.

'Not at all,' said the woman.

'I need to find a guest-house,' Gretchen said.

That much elicited no response; the woman was silent, patient. Gretchen understood that, if she were to receive any help, she must somehow explain herself.

'The guest-house belongs to a person named Mrs Griffey,' she said. 'Mrs Griffey is expecting me.'

'Oh, my dear,' said the woman, whose outline wavered, who was dwindling into nothing more than a voice, 'I'm afraid you're out of luck. Mavis Griffey's had a stroke. She's past expecting anyone.'

The words were nonsense to Gretchen; all she could do was to stand and listen – for more, if more were to come.

'Don't you follow me?' said the voice. 'No one can go there. The house is closed.'

A last instant was left to Gretchen.

'Closed?' she said. 'It *can't* be –'

Absolute defeat rose up to meet her, she took one backward step and fainted.

There had been ground and then there was none. She was floating, she was clasped, she was rising. Then she was dipped; there was new ground, high ground, soft ground, and two people close to her. One of them was a man.

'She'll have to be put to bed, Eileen,' he said. 'Could you undress her?'

'I could try' – that was a woman's voice which Gretchen had heard before. 'Will I lend her a nightgown, or will I search her things for one of hers?'

'Lend her one of yours,' said the man. 'And a shawl for her shoulders.'

'You'll be back, of course?' said the woman.

'I'll be back,' he said. 'I'll just nip into my office and see what I can find for the occasion. Meantime, do what you can to get her into the bed.'

Gretchen was proud to be helpful. Coaxed and supported, she slipped her arms out of the sleeves of her coat – a considerable achievement.

But there were other sleeves, forgotten sleeves.

'Now for your dress,' said the woman.

Those sleeves were tighter. The woman was wheedling and pulling. Gretchen pulled too.

'That's lovely,' the woman said. 'I can do the rest.'

Gretchen was rolled, she was peeled, she was naked, she was trembling violently, she was frozen. She moaned.

'We're almost there,' said the woman. 'I've only to slide this nightie over your head.'

She was grabbing Gretchen, she was handling an arm, she was handling the other, she was far too near, she was exuding a dark smell of damp armpits. Gretchen retched and gritted her teeth. Presently she was heaved up, something rough tumbled over her shoulders.

'There we are now,' the woman said. 'I'll get you under the covers.'

The ground was dragged away from underneath. Then it rolled up again, right to her chin, and she was lying on a sheet of ice.

Something terrible was going to happen. Gretchen knew what it was. She nerved herself to tell the woman that she was about to be sick, but no words came. Grimly she bit back her vomit and soon she understood that the woman had gone away. She believed herself

20

alone and then she was not alone. The man was bending over her.

'I'll have to take your temperature,' he said. 'Keep the thermometer under your tongue. Don't bite it or you'll have a mouthful of broken glass.'

Gretchen lay very still and did her best not to bite the thermometer.

'Now,' said the man, 'I want to listen to your chest. It won't take long, I promise.'

Further interference was more than Gretchen could bear. If she had had the strength she would have fought him off, but she had no strength at all and, once again, she was turned and pushed and shifted, once again she was naked and perilously cold.

'One moment more,' the man said, 'while I check your blood pressure.'

Then she was covered and restored to herself.

'Dizzy?' said the man.

Gretchen nodded.

'I'll lift you a little,' he said, 'and give you a small pill with the ginger ale Eileen sent up for you. Swallow it for me, like a good girl.'

She thought she could do that much for him, given that his touch was so sure, his voice was so gentle. She raised her head, quite by herself, and his arm was around her. Blind, she took the glass, took the pill; when she had swallowed it he let her lie back. Directly afterward she was falling, soon she was revolving as she fell. One hand struck out for anything to grip, anything to save her from the fall, the hand closed around his. As hard as she could she clung to him.

2

Although within half an hour Dr Donovan had withdrawn his hand from hers, Gretchen's hold on him was established before the evening was over. At first, sitting by her bed, he was simply pleasantly aware that this last errand marked the end of his daily round. Most of Ralston's Cove had long since gone home to supper, only the lonesome sweep of an occasional automobile or an occasional dissonant refrain, infused with whiskey, interrupted the stillness of the street under the windows and he, Clement Donovan, was comfortable in the dim electric glow, in the quiet hour. After some minutes he discovered, with a rare twinge of self-recognition, that he was not just comfortable, he was glad to be where he was, keeping watch over Gretchen, lending his hand to her convulsive clasp. He had a curious sense that his place was there, that he belonged in that lamp-lit room, in that time, that he belonged, in short, not to the world at large, but certainly and peculiarly to Gretchen. Somehow she made a silent appeal to his soul – the soul which, when he had outgrown his childhood, he had come to see as a merely sentimental attribute, a romantic fiction and, accordingly, rejected. But could a man without a soul pretend to a belonging? Might a soul, unclaimed for the better part of fifty years, surrender itself to the unconscious possession of a stranger?

No sooner had he considered the question than he pulled himself up sharp, embarrassed by its specious glamour. The truth, he reflected, was that he was no longer young, that he was – quite naturally – grateful for a respite after an unusually hard day. Yet he was reluctant to reconsign himself to his astringent professional responsibility while, in fact, he was enjoying a brief, vagrant interlude. Little by little the most insistent of his peripheral preoccupations – what was to be done with the ghost of Janet Sullivan's husband who, so the old woman said, smashed her crockery and boiled her kettle dry, how Pat Reardon, well into his sixty-third year, was to be prevented from lashing his child-bride to a bed-post every time he left the house – ceased to prey on him. Then and there he was context to be with Gretchen whose hand, though it still lay in his, had slowly relaxed.

She had been sleeping for a while; the small pill had offset her nausea, her giddiness; her face was tranquil, where it had been pinched and strained. But Donovan knew that when she woke it would be troubled again by her fever. Abruptly he was visited by an overmastering desire to take her in his arms, to hold her illness at bay by encircling her with his own body. The wanton surge aroused in him as much astonishment as chagrin. A lifetime in medicine had taught him never to let himself be too closely moved by suffering; without a measure of sternly cultivated detachment he could not have continued to care for the sick, week in, week out. Yet here he was, inexplicably, inexcusably longing to interpose his physical self between Gretchen and her disease.

'This won't do,' he said to himself, and carefully disengaged his hand from Gretchen's. Gretchen opened her eyes.

'How do you feel?' he said, and was thankful to find that the ordinary words had the immediate effect of reinstating him in his proper capacity, that Gretchen would recognise him for no more than what he was, an ordinary practitioner.

'Every bone in me is broken,' said Gretchen.

It was merely a statement; it asked for no pity, no relief.

'But you're not so dizzy, I think?' said Donovan.

Gretchen thought about that earnestly.

'I'm not nearly so dizzy,' she said, after what seemed to have been a searching retreat to the interior.

'Good,' said Donovan. 'I'll give you another pill which will mend your bones and let you sleep again.'

He offered her the glass with the ginger ale and a large capsule.

'That should do the trick,' he said.

'I'm terribly cold,' said Gretchen.

Donovan drew down the coverlet of the second bed, pulled off two blankets, and tucked them around her.

'You'll soon be warmer,' he said.

'Will I be all right in the morning?' said Gretchen.

'No,' said Donovan. 'But, with any luck, you'll be on the road to recovery.'

An hour later he had finished a cold supper. His housekeeper was out, consoling a newly-widowed sister, there was no one under Donovan's roof to come between himself and the image of Gretchen. He could see her face – her broad forehead, her sharp, rounded cheek-bones, her short, shapely nose, the gentle arch of her mouth, her skin, as delicate as the lining of a shell – so distinctly that she might have been opposite him at his own table; he remembered her as if she had been lodged with him always. For a few minutes she was fixed in his remembrance, stilled and changeless in sleep. Then, for a moment, memory summoned up another Gretchen – awake and wary – her serene image wavered, clouded over. He recalled her expression while he was examining her, the anguished, mutinous, incredulous expression of a child betrayed by a force beyond its comprehension. The force beyond Gretchen's comprehension – entrenched as it was in her renegade body – had obviously, in her feverish reckoning, brought her inconceivably low and, obviously, although she was too feeble for speech, she was storming against herself. From the inner tempest she had flashed him a wild look of outrage as he approached her with his stethoscope; that look had reminded him of something at the time, and now, teased by retrospection, he strove to join the fugitive impression to a memory which eluded him. Momentarily his head was as empty as his empty plate; a long-case clock in the corner of the room began its formal strike, to which he listened with impatience, still stupidly staring at the dish. The glazed lilies-of-the-valley bordering its rim took his

23

fancy, soft clear skies and sunshine vaguely skimming across the surfaces of irrelevant recollections, when a forgotten instant snapped into his mind's eye and he made the connection with sudden, surprising ease.

On a Sunday in August he had spent the afternoon with a couple much younger than himself. When the baby of the family – hardly two years old – had wakened from his nap, his mother had led him out into the garden where she had encouraged him to run to his father. Intrepid, he had started out gleefully but, half-way across the rough grass, he had tripped and come a-cropper. The misfortune had loosed a howl of protest and, on the little boy's face – which was blurred by tears – rage, rebellion and incredulity had been marvellously intermingled. As the baby's expression merged, in Donovan's invention, with Gretchen's, he rose from the table, mildly pleased by the link he had so effortlessly forged between the two luckless adventurers. Then, almost as quickly as it had been fabricated, the link gave way. After all, there could be no such coupling, no firm conjunction which would hold. Gretchen was not a child; she had gained her independence, she was beyond paternal patronage, beyond the protective reach of paternal benignity. For reasons which Donovan could not explain to himself, that was a fact which bothered him until he fell asleep.

In the morning he woke to an extraordinary thrill of expectation; then he remembered Gretchen. Directly he had had his breakfast, he stopped at the hotel.

'If you ask me,' said Eileen, 'I think that girl is crazy.'

'What has she done?' said Donovan.

'Not only has she had a bath,' Eileen said, 'she's washed her hair. To tell you the truth, she even washed my nightgown – sick as she is.'

'How sick is she?' he said.

'Good and sick, I'd say,' said Eileen. 'I brought her up a cup of tea. It was then that I saw her head was sopping. Naturally I fetched her my hand-dryer. She was so weak she could barely manage it.'

Gretchen was leaning back against the pillows. A shower of sunlight from the window gilded the dry-sherry colour of her hair. Her hair flowed over her collar bones, which rose above the boat-neck of a plain, sky-blue flannel nightgown – far more becoming, far more suitable than Eileen's gaudy, hot-pink nylon.

'You've been up to mischief, so I'm told,' said Donovan.

'I had to get clean,' she said. 'There was so much to wash off –'

'Let's take your temperature and listen to your chest again,' he said.

As he had before, he noticed her lovely shoulders, her small, young breasts; but what touched him, while he bent over her, was the pale fragrance of soap and talcum powder which hovered on her nakedness. He was used to the rank odours of most of his adult patients, and yet he had never been quite hardened to the stench of human filth.

'Your chest is clear,' he said. 'But you're running a fine fever. I daresay you appreciated that?'

'Well, was that my fault?' said Gretchen.

'I won't make a moral speculation,' Donovan said. 'However, I will tell you that you are not to get out of this bed – save to obey a call of nature.'

To which, aching all over though she was, she gave him a wicked, swift smile. 'There's no need for me to get out of bed any more,' she said.

'Swallow this capsule with that bit of cold tea,' said Donovan. 'Eileen will bring you another one at twelve o'clock and another at tea-time. She'll also bring you some ginger ale, from time to time, and some toast and broth. Drink as much as you can. I'll be by this evening.'

It was after eight o'clock when he came back.

'Is this what it's like to die?' said Gretchen.

'I've never died,' Donovan said.

That night Donovan had a dream in which he sustained a loss so shocking that he clearly recalled it an instant after his alarm clock imperiously woke him. He dreamt that, with Gretchen in his arms, he had climbed a stairway. At the foot of the flight her weight had been almost too much for him but, as he mounted, it grew lighter with each step he took. By the time he reached the top of the stairs he was carrying no load at all, and when he looked down at his arms, still outstretched to support his burden, he saw that they were empty; he was holding nothing. The awful discovery had astounded him while he slept; once awake, amazement had given place to a sense of acute bereavement.

'I must be losing my mind,' he said to his razor, which slipped and cut his chin.

That morning Gretchen's fever was still high, she was still miserable.

'I wish I knew what's the matter with me,' she said.

'Shall we say you have the 'flu?' said Donovan. 'For lack of a more sophisticated diagnosis?'

25

'I've never had the 'flu,' Gretchen said. 'Does it last forever?'

'Right to the grave,' said Donovan. 'If the sufferer persists in disregarding the doctor's orders.'

'I had to take a bath,' she said.

'Another one?' said Donovan.

'Another one,' said Gretchen.

'It will be a pleasure to lay you out,' Donovan said.

Ridicule appealed to Donovan as – possibly – the only antidote to Gretchen's indefinable spell, which had been reinforced by the glimpse of her.

'What would you say if I told you that I have a female patient with a fetish about personal cleanliness?' he said to Mrs Mullin, when he walked into his office.

'I'd say she never came from Ralston's Cove,' said Mrs Mullin.

'The odour of sanctity is certainly very strong in here,' said Donovan. 'Does no one ever think to air the waiting room?'

Donovan kept office hours in the afternoons, but he was apt to stop by his office in the mornings to let Mrs Mullin know what housecalls he was about to make and where – as accurately as he could guess – so that she might reach him in case of an emergency.

'I didn't expect to see you today,' said Mrs Mullin. 'Seeing as it's Thursday.'

'It happened that I was just across the street,' said Donovan.

Each Thursday he drove to Port Ferris to see his patients who were in hospital there – such of them as were too ill for the cottage hospital in Ralston's Cove. Dr Reilly did the same on Tuesdays. Every Tuesday Donovan covered for Reilly; Reilly returned the favour on Thursdays.

'Ask Dr Reilly to look in on Alice O'Neill,' Donovan said. 'She's not coming along as fast as I'd hoped.'

'I'll see to that,' said Mrs Mullin, and wished him a good day at the door.

As soon as Ralston's Cove was at his back Donovan gave himself up to the luxury of two hours of uninterrupted solitude. He knew the road so well – each hill, each narrow bridge, each curve, each gate, each meadow – that he felt quite irresponsible every time he drove it; he could virtually leave it to the car itself to find the way. Often if he was pressed or out of sorts he found the trip restful; often he looked forward to it – it was, almost infallibly, escape. Sometimes he could even escape the tyranny of thought.

On the whole he was not inclined to introspection. For a long time he had been used to think of himself simply as a means to other people's ends, as an object in a landscape, a bridge between distress and solace, pain and relief, sickness and health. To be sure, over the years, a number of his patients had failed to complete the crossing; but those, in the main, had been too old to survive under any circumstances. Prudently he had learnt not to dwell on defeat; he believed that he was useful, he knew that he was not irreplaceable. The two convictions were the sum of his creed.

But if he was not inclined to introspection, he was unequivocally disinclined to revisit the past. What had happened had happened, what was done was done, the past was in hard covers; like the Xenophon he had been required to read at school, it was not a book which he was tempted to reopen. However, unlike his copy of the *Anabasis*, it was not lost and, once in a great while, it announced itself, it declared itself as irrefutably his property – not even successfully mislaid. Ralston's Cove was scarcely out of sight before a rise of ground came into view and there, against all reason, acting on a naked impulse, he pulled over to the weed-wild shoulder of the road and cut the engine.

Seen from the highway, the little hill was nothing but a meagre patch of ragged green. But Donovan knew that, over the crest, the south flank widened as it dipped, and flowered in the springtime. On that sheltered inclined, invisible from the road, billows of untended meadowlands rose and fell over the long descent to the distant sea, in an age-old stillness swelled by leaf and breeze. There, on those slopes, he had picked buttercups and daisies with his mother – the radiant foreigner whom Ralston's Cove had neither touched nor changed. It was his fifth birthday and, deep in the neglected hillside, where she could not be overheard by any native alien ear, she had told him that she was leaving his father, that she was going back to France. Before he could begin to cry, before he could snatch her skirt to keep her close, she had promised that, once she had found a house for the two of them, she would send for him. Thereafter he had waited for a summons – he had waited for days which had seemed like weeks, weeks which had seemed like months, months which had lengthened into years. No message ever came.

When he was old enough to venture away from Ralston's Cove on his own he had secretly, every so often, gone back to the fields where his mother had been next to him where, sometimes, he could catch an echo of her. It was there – during the summer before he was due to enter the university at Dublin – that he had spent anxious, lonely hours seeking out the particulars of his identity, facing the necessity for distinguishing a shape of sorts within himself, accepting the necessity for a decision as to his future course. Looking back over his childhood – while clouds gathered overhead and lingered until the wind chased them to the eastern horizon, or the sun sank in the western dusk – he had felt that his life, up to that point, had not been meaningful either to himself or to anyone else. Nor had he expected it ever to assume a strong personal significance, accustomed as he was to the insignificance of the unwanted.

Indeed he had been schooled to find himself intrinsically worthless. After his mother had abandoned him, and his father, a peevish alcoholic, had proved unfit to provide a home for him, he had been brought up by a great-aunt to whom he had been a notable inconvenience. As a growing boy he had come to understand that he counted for nothing so far as his parents were concerned; nor did his great-aunt encourage him to put any solid value on his existence, much less to see himself as someone with a special purpose. Thus, during that pivotal summer when he had gone, many times, to his unsuspected sanctuary in the meadows, when he had looked ahead, when he had considered the possibilities which were open to him, one seemed as arbitrary as another. At last, for want of a driving ambition, he had reasoned that he might as well go into medicine. Once he had settled the matter in his own mind he felt that, at least, he had made a positive resolution; good physicians, he had supposed, did not live in vain.

At the university he had been too busy – and usually too tired – to doubt his choice of a profession; when he had built up his practice his life was, effectively, no longer his to lead. Every day was predicated on the demands of the sick or the infirm, frequently even the nights were not his to spend as he pleased. He took it for granted that he had forfeited – to his employment – the soul which he had already denied, while he hoped that his conscience was never in jeopardy. Yet even after he was well established in Ralston's Cove, even after he had inherited his grandfather's house – and with it a stout front door which could be shut against intruders – he had retreated, once in a while, over a holiday, to the fields where the memory of his mother still lifted in the timothy grass and the clover. That he had done, not to revive the past but because, in the heedless countryside, he had always been able to make his peace with the present.

Halted by the road that Thursday, Donovan gazed at the barren northern flank of the hill and imagined himself over the rise, wandering through a green and tender April with Gretchen. Nineteen years earlier, when he was thirty-one, he had gone there with a shy but wilful girl who had prowled into his life like a famished cat and, drunk on the breeze, on the songs of larks, he – all too impetuously – had asked her to marry him. Impetuous herself, Melissa had agreed. Six months later there had been no more magic left to work on either of them.

'We don't love each other except in bed,' she had said, astutely enough.

When she had been delivered of a still-born son, Melissa had slid into an agitated post-partum depression. Once she had cut her wrists, once she had swallowed a bottleful of sleeping tablets. On both occasions her life had been saved – to her fury. Then one evening when he came home she was gone; almost five years had passed without a word from her. He had very nearly forgotten her when, just before a savage Christmas, she had turned up as if the wind had whipped her to his doorstep. Where she had been, how she had lived, he had never learnt. Only a week had gone by before she was dead of a leukaemia which she had, apparently, chosen to ignore.

It had been so long since Donovan had thought of Melissa that he could hardly recall the look of her – her black, tangled hair, her black, starving eyes. She had been the only person to whom he had ever shown his blossoming landscape; never, not even in a careless moment, had it occurred to him to share it with Dolly Marsh, although he had been on intimate terms with her since Melissa's death.

Before Melissa's death Ronald Marsh, an old friend of his, had been killed in a motor accident. Donovan had stood by the widow, who was childless; regularly, once a week, he had called on her in her bungalow in Port Ferris. By unhurried stages his ready sympathy had been replaced by a comfortable affection for Mrs Marsh. Then Melissa had come home to die and Mrs Marsh had sympathised with him, although what he had felt for his dying wife was neither love nor grief, although he had been no more than vaguely saddened by the waste of a life. However, sympathising with each other, Donovan and Dolly had recognised that they were both lonely and both relatively young. Within a few months they had slipped into a relationship which had nicely suited them. Every Thursday, when Donovan had done his stint at the city hospital, he had gone on to Mrs Marsh, dined with her – she was a good plain cook who liked to feed a hungry man – spent the night with her, and left early enough to be back in Ralston's Cove by nine o'clock the next morning.

Not once had Donovan's conscience – the conscience which he had always hoped might never be in jeopardy – given him the least dismay. However, there, by the uneven slope of the northern hillside,

watching the lank grass bend under an irritated wind – his conscience
was alive with injury.

'I'd no excuse to disappoint Dolly,' he said to himself, and started
the car, stepped hard on the accelerator, and tried to race away from
guilt. But guilt was a passenger all the way to Port Ferris.

From Donovan's point of view, ever since the death of Melissa, the
arrangement between himself and Ronald Marsh's widow had had a
great deal to be said for it. There was no one in Ralston's Cove with
whom he could let down his guard; in the town whatever anyone said
was broadcast within seconds of its utterance – and a doctor's
utterance was a prize snatch of gossip. But he could talk to Dolly
Marsh sure that no random observation would fly past her trim lace
curtains and, eventually, return to him, overblown with a swelling
passage from mouth to mouth. When he had something to say she
listened; when he had nothing to say she could embroider a silence
with the sociable remarks of unforced companionship. Beyond that,
she could give him the bodily release he could never have risked in
Ralston's Cove, where tongues continually thrashed like worms on
fish-hooks. Release, repose, refreshment were he expected to find in
her tidy parlour or in her ample bed. And yet, indebted though he
was to her, that very morning he had fobbed her off without a
thought for the empty day which, through his dereliction, must now
loom ahead of her.

'Dolly,' he had said, when he telephoned, 'I won't be there this
evening. I've a patient here in critical condition and I shall have to
get back from Port Ferris in jig-time.'

Mile upon racing mile he abused himself; angrily he ripped past
every vehicle on the road until an agate rain baffled him, compelled
him to slacken speed. But all the while no soft, self-deceptions had
muffled the soundless voice in the accusative. He knew that he had
sacrificed Dolly because, preposterously fascinated as he was by
Gretchen, he could not allow any other presence to superimpose
itself on her image, particularly not the staunch, faithful presence of
Dolly Marsh – which would have separated him from Gretchen as
surely as a shutter closing between the light outside and the dark
within. What he could not comprehend was how he could have
cheated Dolly of the pleasure which she had had every right to
anticipate and every reason to deserve, when Reilly could have gone
to Gretchen in his stead and reassured her quite as well – or even
better – than himself. Nevertheless, despite the insistence of remorse,
when he glanced at the dashboard clock, it was not to reckon the
hour of his arrival at the hospital, but to calculate the space in time
which would keep him from Gretchen until the end of the day.

On the way home in the twilight the remorse still weighed on him, but it was stunned, inert. What was quick to him was the suspicion that he was not in charge of his own affairs, that his private promptings were wholly involuntarily, subject to no effective control and, worse, that whatever he might do would be ill-judged. For the first time in his life he mistrusted himself, and the sensation, for all its uneasiness, was delicious. The knowledge that Gretchen was waiting for his return intoxicated him while, at the same instant, he was disturbed by the threat to his habitual composure which she embodied, by the turmoil she had precipitated in his orderly inner world. As fast as possible, he thought – as fast as she was out of bed and able to fend for herself – he must forget her; in all common sense he must remember that she neither had nor wished to have a position in his life. She had happened – how he could not imagine – to catch him off-stride, as it were; but shortly he would recall her as he might recall a passing moment in a dream. In fine, she would wear off.

'What I am,' he said to himself – here a word which had not occurred to him since his boyhood leapt to his recollection – 'what I am is banjaxed. That's all there is to it. But none of this will last.'

Banjaxed, he sped into Ralston's Cove and stopped the car before the hotel with a powerful, if tremulous, sense of home-coming.

3

After Dr Donovan left her, while Donovan was on the road to Port Ferris, Gretchen lay, fevered but still, staring at the nearer window. The light from the sky was dull as lead. However, it was sufficient to show the dirty fleece of dust on the window panes and, as she had mindlessly done during most of the day before, she gazed at the writing embedded in the fleece. Some earlier guest, with a thick forefinger, had traced the words 'Wash Me Quick' on the dense, greasy film which veiled the glass. For so long as there was enough light to catch each sprawling letter Gretchen remained wearily transfixed by the message. Then, as near-darkness accumulated beyond the window, a burst of rain fell suddenly, straight yet violent, and she could no longer decipher the injunction. The curtains of grey water seemed like layers of her recent experience, layers which could not be cleft or penetrated, through which she was unable to pass. Instinct called her home, called her back to a time could rely on; but that self was irrecoverable since – so she felt – she would never find a way back to innocence or safety.

Recollections of her journey continued to break over her like a rushing nightmare from which there was no awakening and even, she said to herself, if she could struggle free of the nightmare, she would still be encaged by four discoloured walls, trapped in a rancid bed, committed to an unsleeping despair.

It did not cross her mind that her despondency might be – at least in part – an outcome of her illness. The illness, as she saw it, was the outcome of the journey, was only an extraneous offshoot of desolation, while the desolation itself was proclaimed and reiterated in her surroundings. Over and over she reviewed each of the squalid discoveries she had made since she had been confined to the wretched room, given that each of them had contributed to her malaise, and now the sum of them rose to become the scaffolding of her dejection.

On the first morning, before she had washed her hair, she had set out to make the bed. Stripping it, she had seen that the sleazy cotton blanket spread over the mattress was spattered with venerable stains, some of them semen, some of them blood. Disgusted, she had stripped the other bed, but the covering there was impregnated with the same histories. When she had put both beds to rights – both were cheap and ugly, both were made of slick, varnished deal but, although they were similar, they were not a pair, the one being lower and wider than its mate – she found that the sheets, which appeared to have been laundered in dirty rain-water, were a good eighteen inches too short for the lumpy mattresses. As for the worn blankets, bleached stiff, they were not long enough to tuck in at the foot of either bed, and the pillows were so thin that she had appropriated all four of them for her own.

Once she had dealt with the beds she had thought to put her underclothing – which Eileen had draped over a broken-down chair from which two of the struts were gone – in the chest of drawers. But however she tugged not a swollen drawer would yield, and the interior of the mottled wardrobe – where she had planned to hang up her coat and dress – stank of rot. In the end she had opened one of the suitcases, neatly folded all of her clothes, and laid them on the top of her other belongings. Before she had gone into the bathroom she had glanced about to see if – after her valiant efforts at order – the room looked any better for being neat. But no amount of housekeeping could have effaced the deep scars and cigarette burns on the night-tables or sealed the cracks in the shrill brown leatherette which upholstered the squat metal frame of the armchair, or filled out the gaps in the withered fringe which looped aside the bile-green curtains – shrunken curtain which missed, by a foot, the trodden, defiantly flowering carpet.

In the bathroom she had been further disheartened. There was no mirror; the tumbler on the ricketty shelf over the rust-entinctured wash-basin was so incrusted with a hard, chalky deposit that she could not bring herself to use it; the tap in the bathtub, turned on full, discharged such a weak trickle of tepid water as to make it almost impossible to rinse the lather from her hair; there was no bathmat; and the grimy towels were not much bigger or thicker than ordinary table napkins.

'Is this what I came so far to find?' she had said to herself.

Twice during the first day she had got out of bed to pour the broth, congealing in its own scum, down the lavatory, so as not to hurt Eileen's feelings by leaving it evidently untouched. And, throughout the day, she had had to force herself to drink the lukewarm ginger ale while, hour upon hour, she had craved something sharp and cold.

'So this is Ireland,' she had said, and the words had played in and out of her fever, were still playing after a whole night and another dawn.

Abruptly as the rain had begun to fall it stopped. Gretchen leapt up, opened a window and leaned over the sill, hoping to forget everything at her back, hoping to see a different, new-washed, shining Ireland waiting before her.

But there was no shining in the dispirited world outside. Two tight, grey rows of decrepit houses, huddling askew, straggled down both sides of the crooked street, each of them disfigured by a tawdry storefront, none of them boasting so much as a geranium to meet a morning or delay the glow of a setting sun. Stunned by such deliberate misery – for there was no sign that a single house had risen from a graceful inspiration or even from a good-natured builder's hands – stricken by half-delirious visions of the destitute lives therein immured, of bony wraiths waiting in their rags for a final summons, of obese phantoms stealthily moving on padded feet behind the sullen windows, Gretchen drew away and crept into the bed.

'I've brought you some more soup,' said Eileen, putting a battered tin tray on Gretchen's knees.

Gretchen shot a glance at the opaque yellow liquid and sobbed.

'Is patience fretting on the monument?' said Donovan, after he had driven home to Ralston's Cove from Port Ferris.

'I'm not on speaking terms with patience,' Gretchen said.

'Well,' said Donovan, 'what have you been doing all day today? Renovating the premises?'

'If I had been renovating the premises,' said Gretchen, 'you'd see a change in here.'

33

Donovan took her temperature, noted that it was a degree higher than it had been in the morning, sat down by the bed, and sat back as though he had time on his hands.

'Cleanliness, no doubt, is next to godliness,' he said. 'I can't complain about the bath you took this morning. Good habits are as hard to break as bad ones. But yesterday you severely overtaxed yourself. Not only did you take a bath, you washed your hair. Could you possibly tell me why, when you were so sick, you had to get yourself, your hair – everything, even to Eileen's nightgown – so clean, so soon?'

'I'd had a bad trip,' said Gretchen.

'Literally or figuratively?' said Donovan.

Gretchen, brought to the border of what, to her, was unutterable, hesitated.

'Literally,' she said, before the pause had lengthened into discourtesy.

'Then you can talk to me about it,' said Donovan.

'No, I can't,' she said. 'I just can't.'

Donovan waited and so did she. While she waited a flood-tide was building up; shortly cataracts of distress, spiked with fury, began to pour away from her and, when the flood had spent itself, she had told him all she remembered about the flight.

She told him about the brutal throngs in front of the check-in counters at Kennedy Airport; she told him about the passengers idling in the departure lounge, remarking that she had studied their faces –

'– and not one of them had a mind behind it,' she said.

'Some minds don't travel,' said Donovan. 'My own deserts me whenever I fly.'

She told him that the journey through the night had been like a laboured passage through a tunnel in a hearse replete with the living dead – and overrode Donovan's mild objection to the extravagance of the metaphor. She told him about the vile interior of the plane, the foul seat-coverings; she told him about the crew of robots, the celluloid food, the depravity of the film – which she had glimpsed even if, without a head-set, she could not hear the sound-track. She told him about the fat man and about the boy in the darkness with the feeling hand. At the back of every smallest detail there was an intensity which confounded Donovan, an intensity which, he thought, had its origins in the depths of herself, although – very likely – only a fever could have lent her the passionate energy to give it voice.

'What were you expecting?' he said.

'Something other,' said Gretchen.

When she added that she had felt as if hundreds of unclean lives were rubbing off on her, Donovan understood that she might indeed have been driven to wash her sleepless recollections away. But how, he wondered, was he to leave her easy for the rest of the evening?

He had made one or two quips to which she had responded shortly. However, it was evident that something more studied was in order.

'One can well imagine that you were shocked by such a trial,' he said, at last. 'But you aren't making any allowance for its aftermath. You've been acutely ill. Illness distorts perception. Once you're yourself again you'll make light of the whole experience. You'll put it down to life. You'll expunge it.'

'I won't expunge it,' said Gretchen. 'I could never expunge it.'

Donovan had no answer to that and Gretchen shrank in the vacant silence.

'I'm not usually so vehement,' she said. 'Truly I'm not.'

'And I'm not usually taken aback by vehemence,' said Donovan. 'It's a much abused Irish indulgence.'

'Yet you're taken aback by me?' said Gretchen.

'A shade,' he said. 'I've not before had the privilege of being face to face with a noble savage.'

'I'm not noble,' said Gretchen. 'But I was different from anyone else on that plane.'

'You had nothing in common with humankind?' said Donovan.

'I was different,' she said.

Donovan, sure that her sense of proportion must be warped by the 'flu made no effort to contradict her.

'Perhaps she is different,' he said to himself, after he had left the room. 'But she's nothing to do with me.'

The cruel admission racked him; as the lonely evening wore on, his whole body ached with the conviction that she was was everything to do with him, while his conscience – still very much awake, still charged with reproach – insisted otherwise.

Whether she was or was not different from run-of-the-mill humanity was not his affair. She was not his ward nor his mistress nor his friend; she was – and that not even of her own choosing – his patient. One day she would be well. She would be ready to go her own way, and when she was he would be duty-bound to let her go. For what – if he came down to a finest .point – had he to offer her? What was he but a besotted fool, past his prime and suddenly longing for rejuvenation? Whereas Gretchen –

He could hardly bear to think of her – so young, so proud, still so mysterious to him. At the same time it was impossible not to think of her. Thinking of nothing but Gretchen he fell asleep in his armchair by his own hearth. When he awoke, the fire had burned low, he felt cold and be-numbed, coldy equal to renounce his every natural impulse, to resolve that the moment Gretchen could do without him he would do without her. Such – before the night was over – was his best intention; an intention which – within less than a week – chance defied.

That he came to know her better and better was – as he frequently reminded himself – none of his doing. Nor could he flatter himself that it was any of hers. For, although five days later Gretchen was well enough to quit the hotel, although he had taken his leave of her formally, quite as though it were out of the question that their paths should cross in any foreseeable future, she was in need of medical attention again and perforce – for over a month – he took care of her. During that time he discovered that she was, as she had said, different.

But while she was still confined to the hotel he had yet to learn if he were or were not off the mark, he could only resolve to steel himself against her, and there were still some days to go – days which were to reveal to him how difficult it could be to put an exemplary resolution into practice – before he left her with what he meant her to interpret as a last good-bye.

4

On Friday, the fourth day of her first week in Ireland, Gretchen, though bedridden, was recovering. In the morning Donovan had found her greatly improved. In the evening her door was ajar; before he knocked he saw that she was reading.

'I'm all better. I'm cured,' she said, and when Donovan had taken her temperature he agreed that she was on the mend.

'So I can take up my bed and walk?' said Gretchen.

'You could take up your bed for a couple of hours tomorrow and sit in this chair,' said Donovan. 'On Sunday, if you're up to it, you might go for a little walk. But it's early days to think of running – which is what you doubtless had in mind.'

'It wasn't running that I had in mind,' Gretchen said. 'It was lodgings. I was supposed to stay with a Mrs Griffey. Now Eileen says the guest-house is closed.'

'So it is,' said Donovan.

'I've got to get out of here,' she said.

'You've been very ill,' said Donovan. 'You won't get out of here for another few days – unless you want to go courting a relapse.'

'Don't you understand that I can't possibly afford to stay in a hotel?' said Gretchen.

'We'll see about that,' Donovan said, and walked out of the room.

'If it were up to myself,' said Eileen, 'I'd gladly keep her on the Q.T. But it would be as much as my job is worth if Port Ferris ever got to hear about it. However I'll tell you what I could do. I could bill her for a single room without a bath – that would come lower than what she'd have paid at Mavis Griffey's – and, as of this minute, she's owing almost nothing for her meals, seeing as she's hardly had a morsel to eat. All the same, she'll have to leave within a week since, after the wedding, Saturday next, I'll be shutting up shop for the winter.'

'That's generous of Eileen,' said Gretchen. 'I've been terribly worried about what every hour here was costing me. The question is –'

'I think I know of a place for you,' said Donovan.

Gretchen understood that the words were kindly meant. She also understood that, for the time being, Donovan might be her only resource in her hour of need. Nevertheless she was used to looking out for herself, she was proud to be twenty-five and independent.

'You make me feel like a parcel marked "Unknown at this address. Return to sender",' she said.

'Would you prefer to be returned to sender?' said Donovan

'I'd prefer to take the responsibility for myself on myself,' said Gretchen. 'I was a little weak in the knees during the last few days but –'

'Hardly any guest-houses in Port-Ferris stay open all year around,' Donovan said. 'The game's not worth the candle when the tourists are all gone. But if you'd rather I left you to shift for yourself –'

'Do you really known of a place where I could stay?' said Gretchen.

'Leave it to me,' said Donovan.

'I could never pay you back for such a favour,' said Gretchen.

'Perhaps you'd allow me to take my dinner with you in your room tomorrow evening,' Donovan said.

The instant the words were out of his mouth he knew he had overstepped himself. It was true that Gretchen was all alone and barely convalescent in a foreign country, but that was not his reason for proposing to dine with her. It was merely his excuse for the gratification of an ungovernable desire, a desire to be close to her, watching her, listening to her, memorising her. In rude terms he meant to take advantage of her misfortune, her illness; she had no choice but to welcome him. None the less he had not earned the privilege of her company; he was – in rigorous truth – too old to pretend to it. Left to her own devices it was most unlikely that she would ever have a second thought to spare for him. So he argued as he was walking home. But the justice of the argument did not prevent him from being prompt to the engagement on Saturday evening.

'Well,' said Donovan, 'we've eaten the inedible, and when Eileen brings the coffee we'll be drinking the undrinkable. You've a good constitution to have survived for nearly a week here.'

'I could bear to leave,' said Gretchen, who was convinced that, in the hotel in Ralston's Cove, she must have explored the very pit of Ireland.

'Not,' Donovan said, 'that a change will necessarily be for the better.'

'Eileen's been thoughtful,' said Gretchen. 'But I honestly can't imagine that any change could be for the worse.'

'Ever since I saw your luggage,' said Donovan – and forbore to mention that he had carried most of it up the stairs – 'I've been wondering why you came to us, whether you were planning to establish a civilisation in this county. Why did you come? What do you mean to do in these back-waters?'

'Work for my doctorate,' said Gretchen. 'I have a thesis to write and I need to be somewhere all by myself to get it done.'

'Did you pick the Emerald Isle out of a hat?' Donovan said.

'Oh, no,' said Gretchen. 'My thesis is entitled *Irish Writers: The Written Word and the Spoken Word*. I *had* to come to Ireland sooner or later.'

'You *had* to come to Ralston's Cove?' said Donovan.

'Not exactly,' Gretchen said. 'But I met a person who had spent a happy month here with Mrs Griffey. She told me that the guest-house was cheap and, what was more, it was open all winter.'

'Now you have your mournful face on again,' said Donovan. 'Don't worry. I'll find you a Petit Trianon where you can finish your work in peace.'

'I'm much to *gauche* for Versailles,' said Gretchen.

'Marie Antoinette's life was a study in *gaucheries*,' said Donovan.

'She was a queen,' Gretchen said. 'She could set her own style.'

38

'Perhaps you'll set yours in Port Ferris,' said Donovan.

'I'd prefer to live and let live,' Gretchen said. 'I may be earnest, but I'm shy.'

Gauche was not, in Donovan's opinion, the word for Gretchen. Even in sickness she had preserved a certain proud formality, even quick with indignation – as she had been while she reconstructed the chapters of the flight – she had maintained a certain distance between the two of them. Her blazing indignant sincerity had burned no barrier, the walls which defended her essential self were still intact, however much she might have felt them threatened by an ignominious adventure, by strangers, or by an alien land. From the moment he had laid eyes on her Donovan had been moved to shield the native chastity he suspected in her; his joke about a Petit Trianon had been quite inappropriate.

'It's a convent she wants,' he said to himself – and wondered how he could believe that anyone living in the present day was chaste. What she was – she had said it herself – was different. That much he was already almost prepared to believe and the hospitality he sought for her might just be sufficiently bizarre to accommodate a 'difference'.

Early the next afternoon he went to visit her.

'Do you think a baronial hall – fallen into great disrepair – would suit your purposes?' he said.

'To live in?' said Gretchen.

'To live in,' said Donovan.

'It might suit me,' she said, 'but it couldn't suit my budget.'

'For five pounds a day you'd have a room to yourself and three meals,' said Donovan.

'Is it true?' said Gretchen.

'Absolutely true,' he said. 'In fact it's all confirmed. You'll be physically safe at the Hall, although I must confess you might come to feel that your sanity was endangered.'

'What have you found for me?' said Gretchen. 'A madhouse?'

'Unofficially – yes,' said Donovan. 'It belongs to a clan called Dufresne. You've heard, I presume, about the Massacre of St Bartholomew?'

'I've heard of it,' she said. 'I didn't know it happened in Ireland.'

'*Touché*,' said Donovan.

Edouard Dufresne was one of the few Huguenots who, on the night of August 24th, in 1572, escaped from Paris. Connected by birth to power and to affluence, he had gone to London. Some years later he had turned up in Ralston's Cove, then no more than a hamlet. Seven miles from Ralston's Cove he had discovered what was, effectively, a broad inlet of the sea. Thereafter he had gone back to London in search of a wife with a substantial dowry. When he had found her he returned to Ireland, where he had purchased a vast woodland acreage giving onto the inlet – which became known as Dufresne Bay. There, on a point looking south over the placid harbour, he had built the Hall – two tall structures joined by a long, walled walk-way, roofed over.

'It's a most uncomfortable lay-out,' said Donovan. 'The dining-room is on the ground floor of the east tower, the kitchens are on the ground floor of the west tower. Some thirty yards of bleak corridor separate the kitchens and the dining-room so, as you may imagine, the food is stone-cold by the time it reaches the table. However no Dufresne has thought to interfere with the original arrangement.'

Since the seventeenth century every first-born Dufresne son had been christened Edward and each Edward – without exception – had married English wealth.

'*Not* Anglo-Irish wealth,' Donovan said. 'Every single one of them went to England for a bride – and a Protestant bride at that.'

In the reign of William and Mary a wing had been added to the east tower; in the reign of George the Third another had been added to the west tower.

'The whole thing's a great ungainly mass,' said Donovan. 'The situation is lovely and when the gardens were kept up it was considered a handsome estate. But there's no money in the direct line now and the place is badly run-down. The west wing is uninhabitable, nobody's been able to live there for years – if one excepts the grandchildren who used to come and camp on the bay in the summers.'

In 1905 providence had played a scurvy trick on the family. Only one child was born to the marriage of the last Edward and the child was a girl.

'That child,' Donovan said, 'has always been called Miss Nellie. She'll be your hostess at the Hall and, since she brought disgrace on the Dufresnes, you'd best be warned about the hoary scandal before you find yourself under her thumb.'

Miss Nellie had been very pretty when she was young; her parents had hoped she would make a distinguished match. But she had had a mind of her own; at sixteen she had fallen in love with one of her father's grooms. When she was four months pregnant there was no disguising the disaster; her father and mother disowned her, hence she fled to England – to Leicestershire, where her lover, whom she married, found work as a stable-hand. His name was Seamus Taylor.

'Seamus did well in Leicestershire,' said Donovan. 'He made his name as a trainer. But for so long as her parents lived Miss Nellie was forbidden the Hall. Her mother died some time in the late twenties, her father survived till the late thirties. It wasn't until after his death that Miss Nellie came back, with Seamus, to Dufresne Bay. By then Seamus had changed his name to Taylor-Dufresne, in order not to break completely with Miss Nellie's line, in order that their children should be, in part, Dufresnes.

'But what you should know,' he said, to a most attentive Gretchen, 'is that Miss Nellie was not received by the Anglo-Irish here until after the last war, until towards the end of the forties. Until that decade nothing was forgiven her and nothing has yet been forgotten – although customs and conventions are changed entirely.'

Miss Nellie and Seamus, with four children – Edward, Randall, Catherine, and Quentin – had come home to find that Miss Nellie's father had squandered most of his own and most of his wife's inheritance; the Hall, which had once boasted an immense staff of domestic help, gardeners, grooms – and magnificent thoroughbreds in the stables – was sadly reduced.

'She's shrewd, Miss Nellie,' said Donovan. 'She keeps herself and Seamus by selling off land – parcel by parcel. She's seventy-four, Seamus is eighty-one or eighty-two. They'll last out and, of course, the children are long since on their own. All of them left Dufresne Bay years ago. But if I were you I'd shy off Lady Chatterley for the duration of your stay in the west tower.'

Gretchen, who had been so bored by *Lady Chatterley's Lover* that it would not have occurred to her to discuss the book with anyone, agreed to make no mention of it.

'It's only fair to warn you,' Donovan said, 'that Seamus weeps on the least provocation. Don't let his sobs upset you. Seamus is an angry man. An angry Irish peasant miscast as an aristocrat. But Miss Nellie keeps him on a short lead, so he spends his rage in drink and tears.'

That Miss Nellie who, since she was sixteen, had had a mind of her own, should allow her husband to drink surprised Gretchen.

'Years of experience have taught her that Seamus is much easier to handle drunk than sober,' said Donovan. 'Sober, he can be very destructive. Drunk, he cries. Make no mistake, they're devoted to each other. Never more than when they quarrel – which they do, night and day.'

'Why are they willing to take me in?' Gretchen said.

'Miss Nellie would walk seven miles to Ralston's Cove for half a quid,' said Donovan. 'For thirty five pounds a week she'd take you into her bed, if need be. To be sure, she can't offer you ideal accommodations. On the other hand, while Mavis Griffey's a good soul, she's bog-trotting Irish. I doubt you'd have had a moment's peace there. She'd never have left you to yourself. Whereas, at the top of the west tower, you'll be – wholesomely, I hope – neglected.'

'I'd like to be neglected,' said Gretchen. 'By the way, for four hundred years of Dufresnes you've stuck to the direct line. Aren't there any other branches?'

'Hugo Dufresne and his wife live in the east tower,' Donovan said. 'He's Miss Nellie's first cousin – he still has quite a bit of money. Hugo and his wife are mad as hatters, but they rarely mix with Seamus and Miss Nellie.

'Wouldn't it be fun to take tea with a mad hatter?' said Gretchen.

'In the east tower you'd be far more likely to get a pink gin,' said Donovan.

On Sundays Donovan seldom made a housecall. However, that afternoon he was worried about Alice O'Neill whom, on Thursday, he had recommenced to Dr Reilly's attention. He left Gretchen at sunset. Twenty-four hours later he was not surprised to find her up and dressed and sitting in what he had come to think of as his chair. She rose when he came in and, standing, challenged him.

'How soon can I go to Miss Nellie?' she said.

The following day – against his better judgment – Donovan drove her to the Hall after lunch.

'You *will* run before you can walk,' he said.

'Now I can do both,' said Gretchen.

The road wound past humps of fields were cattle were still grazing, although the pasturage, in October, was scanty. Gretchen was silent until, almost at the end of the trip, Donovan turned left and stopped the car at the head of a hill so steep that Gretchen exclaimed over it.

'We're at the top of Dufresne Village,' said Donovan.

Gretchen stared at the road leading downward. Small houses – each with a small patch of lawn – bordered both sides of it.

'All that you see sprang up in the last seventy-five years,' said Donovan. 'Most of the people here make a bare living by letting rooms – they advertise bed and breakfast – to the English who come to Dufresne Bay for the sailing in the summer. A few have built cottages just for themselves – the lots are cheap – on their retirement.

There's a decent pub on the right, half-way down and, directly opposite, there's a post-mistress to whom you can give your letters.'

'The drop's dead sheer to the bottom,' said Gretchen, peering through the windshield.

'Oh, it's not quite so bad as that,' Donovan said, and put the car in gear.

'It's half a mile,' said Gretchen.

'Nearly,' said Donovan.

Slowly they coasted to the foot of the hill where a majestic marble horse with a majestic rider was standing on a colossal block of marble, which stood on a limp island of turf. Donovan swung round it and picked up the road again, now on the level.

'Ahead of you,' he said, 'are the gates of the Hall.'

'One of them's off its hinges,' said Gretchen.

'It's been that way since I was born,' said Donovan, driving through the gateway.

Forty yards further on they arrived at the west tower, which commanded the sweep of Dufresne Bay.

'Is the front door always open?' said Gretchen.

'Always – except in the worst weather,' Donovan said. 'Neither Miss Nellie nor Mary McDaid can be bothered to answer the bell. They assume people will walk in and shout. Or blow the horn – if they come by car.'

Donovan's horn brought a tiny figure to the entrance and Gretchen had her first sight of Miss Nellie. At a glance Miss Nellie's clothing was arresting. She wore a rose-pink dirndl with a rose-pink bib and wide shoulder straps. Under the bib she was wearing a mauve pullover with long sleeves, her legs were stockinged in ribbed, shamrock-green wool, her feet were in scarlet ballerina slippers. For a few seconds Gretchen saw nothing but Miss Nellie's costume; then, as Miss Nellie advanced, she noticed her shrivelled face – sharp nose, sharp chin, eyes like marbles, round, bright and scalding blue, under a froth of palest yellow hair. Donovan, meanwhile, was making the introductions.

'So glad you could come,' said Miss Nellie.

'It's very kind of you to take a chance on a stranger,' said Gretchen.

Ten minutes later – she and Donovan had carried her luggage up three flights of stairs – Gretchen was alone in her room. Donovan had said good-bye and wished her luck. Miss Nellie had said, 'Tea in the drawin'-room on the dot of five', and the two of them had gone downstairs together.

Gretchen moved to the window, looked across the bay, and

listened to Donovan's car, turning, accelerating, receding. When the car was out of earshot she felt lost without him and not a little frightened.

'I wonder if I'll ever see him again,' she said to herself and, at the remembrance of his kindness she was suddenly destitute and forlorn.

5

What had sustained Gretchen during her confinement in the hotel at Ralston's Cove was a sense that she was somehow, accidentally marooned on an island in no way connected to a mainland, that the squalor of the hotel, that the excrescence which was the town were grossly irrelevant, that beyond the draggling street below the windows lay the Ireland of poets and princes and martyrs, the country of legendary enchantment. Where she was to go to discover the enchantment was the problem which had bedevilled her until Dr Donovan had proposed the Hall; from that moment on, although she had believed him when he assured her that the Hall and its lands were long since gone to seed, she had looked forward to a fragrant ruin.

What she saw, when Donovan had left her alone in her new-found realm, was the ugliest room she had ever seen, as shabby, as neglected as the room in the hotel and the more wretched for its blatant pretensions to a splendour which the frieze of plaster nymphs and garlands, choked with grime, the massive proportions of the chest-of-drawers in oak, the tarnished loops and scrolls of the huge brass bed wholly failed to substantiate.

At first she had eyes only for the room itself. She glanced at the baseboard moulding which ran around the walls, off-true toward whichever compass point it staggered, at the peeling wallpaper, sporting heavy purple bunches of grapes, at the mustard ceiling, splotched with damp, at the hanging bulb with a red silk shade, draped in white netting, which shielded the observer from the naked light. Then, already discouraged, but still intent on her surroundings, she studied the particulars more thoughtfully.

The south wall was interrupted by two pairs of French windows leading out onto a balcony. It was from that vantage-ground that she had looked across the bay. One pair was so stiffly closed that she was unable to open it; the two doors of the other were loosely held together by a loop of wire. A sharp rain which had just begun lashed against the windows, and shortly Gretchen watched a dribble of water sweeping through the pair which was so insecurely fastened. Slowly the edge of the carpet darkened as it soaked up the widening stream.

Curtains of mustard brocade, bled by summer sunlight and deeply frayed at the edges, hung at the sides of both pairs of windows; the same brocade disguised what appeared to be an alcove to the west of the windows. On the west wall there was a small hearth, its tiles blackened by ancient fires, its grate rusted, its coal-scuttle laced with spider-webs. Above the mantelshelf was an enlarged studio photograph of Edward VII in an elaborate gilded frame; on the mantel-shelf was a scallop shell, a curling iron on a stand, a china shepherdess, a shoe-horn, a miniature carriage clock – missing the minute hand – a wrench, and a bon-bon dish filled with thumbtacks.

On the north wall the bedroom door gave onto a broad corridor; cheek by jowl with the door stood the great dark chest-of-drawers – a chest-of-drawers which, on account of a broken foot, rocked and lurched whenever a drawer was opened or shut, as Gretchen was to find out for herself. On the east wall the bed was centred and was flanked by two gangling commodes, each with a liver-coloured marble top, a drawer and a little cupboard. The bed was covered by a rumpled maroon bedspread. Above the bed hung a painting, a pre-Raphaelite head of a girl, the flesh-tones as yellow as the skin of a plucked chicken, the staring eyes swimming in what seemed – on first glance – to be uncooked white of egg. A faint hymn of thanksgiving welled up in Gretchen when she realised that, lying in bed, she would be facing not art but royalty.

Unhappily she wondered if Yeats had been accustomed to rooms like this one; more unhappily she wondered if she could endure to live in it now that Dr Donovan was lost to her, now that he would never come by before lunch or after supper to put new heart into her.

'I'll have to make do with Your Majesty,' she said to the portly monarch above the mantel.

As yet she had not taken off her coat, as yet she had not made the least attempt to settle in; she was still gazing at the king and remembering the rumour that he had infected his queen with a venereal disease when she heard a slow thumping on the stairs, followed by thumping steps approaching her door. A moment later she was confronting a woman – no taller than a ten-year-old child – round and soft as a ball of dough, with a high colour inflaming her round face, a shining scalp showing through a pitiful network of sparse grey hair, blunt, reddened hands and enormous legs rolling into fat cuffs at the tops of her sensible, work-a-day shoes.

'I'm Mary,' said the woman. 'You'll be the writer person, of course.'

45

Gretchen, not anxious to lay claim to any special status, was about to confess that she was no more than an amateur of letters, but before she could say a word Mary was off on her own.

'The room's only partially ready for you,' said Mary. 'I'd no sooner made the bed than it was 'Mary this' and 'Mary that' the whole morning long. She won't get it through her head there's only just the one of me. Just the one, but she never left me a minute to dust the place at all, and that's the truth. In the meanwhile you'll be wanting to put your things away.'

So saying she ran the flat of her hand roughly over the chest of drawers and was instantly enveloped in a floating film of dust while Gretchen sneezed.

'A fine state of affairs, wouldn't you say?' she said. 'And the room's thick with it. As for the drawers, I'll be bound they're full to the brim and you needing them.'

The drawers were not full, but neither were they empty; and the dust was everywhere, as Mary had remarked.

'Still and all,' Mary said, 'many hands make light work, as the old saw has it. I'll fetch what's wanted from me broom cupboard whilst you could begin by tackling all the junk in here – if you've the patience.'

'I'll find the patience,' said Gretchen. 'But where shall I put what I take out?'

Mary led her to a cubby-hole of a room down the corridor, unfurnished but for an iron bedstead with a thin mattress and two straight chairs.

'Just dump the lot on the bed,' said Mary. 'No one'll ever be the wiser. As you can see this is the back of beyond.'

Returned to her own room, Gretchen had no compunction about meddling with the bottom drawer of the chest, for it contained nothing more intimate than standard items of a gentleman's wardrobe, long ago put by. In three trips to the room down the corridor she quickly made three neat piles of dress shirts, white evening scarves, silk handkerchiefs, all yellowing and fragile with age. The moth-eaten shawls in the middle drawer provoked no misgivings and, although she was reluctant to handle the whalebone corsets, she made short work of those too. But over the top drawer she hesitated, loath to touch the personal articles scattered at random therein, at the same time fascinated and slightly revolted by many of them.

She stared at a haphazard collection of spats, two tortoiseshell side-combs stuck into two blond rats, a crumbling jeweller's box in red leather, a moulting fox's brush, a pair of duelling pistols, a gilt starfish studded with rhinestones, a riding crop, a little case with opera glasses in mother-of-pearl, a pack of Tarot cards, an ivory snuff box, a black satin choker, a monocle on a black ribbon; but she made no move until she heard Mary tramping up the stairs. Then, gathering up as much as she could, she went swiftly down the corridor. There she endeavoured to put her gleanings in a tidy file at the foot of the bed while, in her haste, the jeweller's box fell to the floor. It had fallen on its side and, in falling, had opened up and gaped. Gretchen knelt to retrieve it and gave an involuntary shriek when she saw a complete set of false teeth – for the upper and the lower jaws – reposing, slightly askew after the tumble, on deep green velvet.

'Have you hurt yourself, so?' said Mary, in a loud voice.

Gretchen rapidly righted the teeth, closed the box, laid it on the bed, and joined Mary in the other room.

'I barked my shin,' she said. 'It's nothing.'

With which she began to sweep up what was left in the drawer, even though she winced as she put her hand on the fox's brush.

When she returned, under Mary's direction, they pulled the bottom drawer out of the chest, turned it upside down, shook and pounded it vigorously, and put it back in place.

'Don't give a thought to the carpet.' said Mary. 'It may be Persian, as she says, but it's outlived its usefulness. As have all the carpets in the Hall. There's holes in some of them you could put a melon through.'

'We *have* made a mess,' said Gretchen, looking down.

'Don't fret over it,' Mary said. 'I've the Hoover outside the door.'

The middle drawer was dustier – if that were possible – than the bottom drawer.

'It's the woodworm does it,' said Mary. 'The entire house is in the same condition.'

When they turned over the top drawer two small objects which Gretchen had overlooked fell onto the carpet. She bent to pick them up.

'I've never seen a scissors like this,' she said, holding them out to Mary.

'Haven't you then?' said Mary. 'Sure they're to trim a gentleman's moustache.'

'And what's this?' said Gretchen.

'That's useful, that is,' Mary said. 'That's a corn knife. Dull, I've no doubt, or I'd take it for meself. I don't expect you suffer from corns at your age.'

Gretchen put the knife aside, gave Mary a hand with the top drawer, shaking and beating it, and then, between the two of them, it too was pushed back into position.

'There we are,' said Mary. 'I'll line this chest fresh for you so. Then you can get to your unpacking.'

She left Gretchen for an instant and returned with an arm-load of newspapers, which she proceeded to fold and fit to the bottom of each drawer. When she finished, her hands were black with newsprint. Gretchen made a silent vow that, if she could not find clean shelf-paper to line the drawers properly, she would never unpack, even if it meant living out of suitcases for as long as she remained at the Hall. Mary, however, was quite satisfied with her efforts.

'So that should take care of all your odds and ends that lie flat,' she said. 'Next we'll see what's to be done about anything that wants hanging up.'

She marched across the room and twitched back the brocade which hid the recess in the west wall, thus revealing an array of elegant clothing – swallowtails, two morning coats, two dinner jackets, three smoking jackets, a shooting jacket, a Burberry and, folded on a shelf above the hanging bar, a number of pairs of trousers.

'Well, it's the back of beyond for all of this,' said Mary and together she and Gretchen emptied the alcove, thus securing for Gretchen ten frail wire hangers – not one of them stout enough for her overcoat which, earlier, she had thrown over the foot-rail of the bed.

'Downhearted, are you?' Mary said, shooting a shrewd glance at Gretchen from eyes which might have been beads of jet. 'Or tired out after your sickness?'

'A little tired,' said Gretchen, ashamed to admit that she was more depressed by the grandiose room at the Hall, abandoned to the inroads of time, than she had been by the shoddy room at the hotel, abandoned to the ill-bred and the unwashed.

'Twill pass off,' said Mary. 'Now be a good girl and slip out onto the balcony whilst I fling this duster around.'

'It's raining,' Gretchen said.

'To be sure it is,' said Mary. 'Well, we'll forget about the balcony. You go out into the corridor – there's a bench down a few steps from your door you could sit on.'

Gretchen dutifully sat on the bench while Mary, lustily chanting three or four choruses of *The Rose of Tralee*, attacked the furniture with a stiff, scorched tea-towel, flapping it over the brass curlicues of the bed or screwing it up and rubbing it over the chest of drawers and the two bedside commodes.

'You can come in again,' she said to Gretchen, when the job was done, the dust redistributed.

The next moment she was fiercely running the Hoover in all directions over the carpet as Gretchen perched on the bed, keeping her feet well above Mary's ferocious thrusts.

'That's that,' said Mary, shutting off the machine and wiping her hands on her grubby apron. 'I'll just give a last flick to the towel rack and then I'll show you where you can find your towels or anything else you fancy.'

Gretchen followed her along the corridor to what Mary called the 'airing-cupboard'. It was no cupboard. It was a fair-sized room with shelves on all four walls and a light bulb hanging from the ceiling.

'You'll find the towels on your left,' said Mary. 'Sheets and pillow-cases there ahead of you. You're to change the bed regular on Wednesdays, in time for the laundry pick-up from Port Ferris.'

Gretchen hardly heard her. Her eye had lit upon one long shelf with eight or ten heaps of linen on it. On every heap was a small card with the word 'Rag' printed on it in large letters.

'If I were ever in need of a rag,' she said, 'could I take one or two?'

'You could help yourself,' said Mary. 'There's far too many of them cluttering up the place. As for towels, you're to have one big and one small one once a week she says.'

Back in Gretchen's room she hung two towels on the bars of the wooden towel rack.

'Now for a word to the wise,' she said. 'They never go to bed until after eleven o'clock news. Up to eleven o'clock you can turn Catherine wheels in here, if you've a mind to. But don't walk about past half eleven for this room's directly above the master chamber and they wouldn't stand for any disturbance once they're abed.

'And another thing – while I'm at it – pay no heed to the noises in the night. It's only the rats in the walls. She will have it 'they're nothing but mice and it never pays to argue with her. But rats they are and big as terriers. Just the same, they're not in the room with you, if you take my meaning. They're just creating behind the walls.'

At the thought of rats overrunning the very structure of the Hall a *frisson* of disgust raced through Gretchen.

'Rats scare me stiff,' she said. 'Why haven't they been exterminated? When you think of the diseases they carry, the infections they spread –'

'It's early days for you to be finding fault with our rats,' said Mary. 'Come along with me now and I'll show you the bathroom.'

The bathroom was on the floor below; Gretchen gazed at it in awe. The lavatory – whose seat and cover were made of wood, badly swollen – stood below an overhead tank in green cast-iron. Raised lettering on the tank read, 'Charles Cutter & Sons, Cork, 1887'. A chain was suspended from the tank. Mary gave it a masterful tug and waited. Nothing happened.

'You'll have to buy yourself a nice bucket,' she said. 'I've only just the one for all the chores so I can't give you the loan of that.'

'Won't the lavatory flush?' said Gretchen.

'That depends,' said Mary, 'upon whether or not it's herself to pull the chain. It works a charm for her – and she won't hear a word against it, mind you. But neither himself nor me, nor any of the lads, if they chance to be here, can persuade a drop out of it. I'm only telling you this for your own good, I'm only warning you to make no mention of it. But with a bucket to fill from the tap in the tub you'd be in grand shape. You'd have to be careful, of course, for if she caught you coming or going with the bucket in hand she'd be none too pleased – that I can promise you.'

The wash-basin, hardly any larger than a gravy-boat, was bolted to the wall. On each side of it stood two low tables covered with a great assortment of hair-brushes, tooth-brushes, shaving-brushes, drinking glasses, bottles of pills, bottles of cough syrup, bottles of lotions, jars of cold cream or lanolin, tubes of toothpaste, tubes of liniments, nail scissors, nail files, tweezers, hairpins, hairnets.

'You've to bring your own soap in here,' Mary said. 'She's very near with soap so don't you go touching hers on any account.

'Now the tub behind you –' said Mary.

Gretchen turned and stared at a long bathtub standing on claw feet.

'I'll not go so far as to say it's clean,' Mary said. 'What I will say is that one hundred years have not improved it. I'm supposed to look after it, but I've told her time and again when me back's paining me it's the most I can do to get me shoes on or off, let alone bend over to scrub out the bath.

'As for hot water, we've not had a thimbleful in a week. Billy O'Connell's been and gone three times in three days but he has yet to make any impression on the boiler.'

'Perhaps he doesn't know his job,' said Gretchen.

'Wiring's only a sideline with Billy,' Mary said. 'But Saturday nights see him – without fail – at his speciality.'

Mary went back upstairs with Gretchen to pick up her vacuum cleaner.

'By the bye,' she said, 'there's a potty in that little chest by the bed. A potty's a comfort during the night, isn't it?'

Gretchen opened the chest, took one look at the plenitude of amber crystals coating the sides and the bottom of the bedroom utensil – which was sweetly enlivened by rosebuds – and closed the cupboard.

'I very rarely get up at night,' she said.

'You're young,' said Mary. 'There's no gainsaying that. So I'll be off then. Your door won't shut – the latch is gone – but you've nothing to worry over. There's no one but yourself up here at the top of the tower.'

'I hate to bother you with anything more,' said Gretchen. 'But I do write – there's my typewriter – and I can't work without a table.'

'The same thought struck her this very morning,' Mary said. 'You're to have the table from the larder. I can spare it and it's sure to fit between the windows. I'll get Kevin to bring it up to you when I lay eyes on him next.'

'And then I'd need a chair,' said Gretchen.

'A plain chair?' said Mary.

'Oh, perfectly plain,' Gretchen said. 'Just so it's not too high or too low for the table.'

'Try one of those from the back of beyond,' said Mary. 'If neither of them suits Kevin could take you through the west wing tomorrow when there's plenty of light. You'd be certain to find something there.'

'Tell me one last thing before you leave me,' said Gretchen. 'Miss Nellie spoke of tea in the drawing-room at five o'clock.'

'On the dot,' Mary said. 'She's punctual, you'll find. And she expects others to be the same.'

'Where is the drawing-room?' said Gretchen.

'Down two flights,' said Mary. 'You can't miss it, for it takes up the whole floor.'

Gretchen waited until she could no longer hear Mary's footsteps on the stairs before she stripped the newspapers from the drawers in the chest, refolded them, took them down the corridor to join all the other things discarded there, and slipped them under the iron bed. Then she went back for the potty and it, too, was shortly out of sight, hidden beside the newspapers. After having handled the potty and the papers she badly wanted to wash her hands but there was one more little cupboard in the other commode to inspect and each commode was fitted with a small drawer. In one of the drawers she found several pairs of ladies' gloves, a fan, three or four stubs of candles and a Church of Ireland prayer book; in the second was a magnificent coiled switch of long, burnished, chestnut hair. Beneath

51

the hair in the drawer, the cupboard was full to bursting of empty bottles of Irish whiskey. Gretchen's courage all but failed her until she reminded herself that Mary was an ally, that Mary would stand up to Miss Nellie if Miss Nellie were to take account of the transformation of the room down the corridor, demand to know who had plundered the chest of drawers, the alcove, the commodes without a by-your-leave. Relying on Mary, she trotted up and down the corridor, laying out the gloves, the fan, the prayer book with the teeth and the starfish, placing the hair gently under the shawls, and stowing the candle stubs and the bottles under the bed next to the potty.

At last she believed she was entitled to feel slightly cleaner, she opened a suitcase, immediately found her soap – in the plastic soap-box for travellers which her sister Anna had given her as a going-away present – picked the smaller towel off the towel rail, went downstairs to the bathroom, saw the door ajar, and washed her hands in icy water. Going back upstairs she made a detour to the so-called airing-cupboard for a pile of rag before, once again, she rummaged in the suitcase – this time for a pair of scissors. Carefully she cut the rags – which were largely cast-off sheets, too threadbare for further use – to fit the bottoms of the three drawers in the chest; next she cut three companion lengths to cover her clothing when it was unpacked.

Close to the scissors in the suitcase she had seen her alarm clock, and that she placed on the commode to the left of the bed. The hands stood at half-past four. With thirty minutes ahead of her before she must join Miss Nellie for tea she had time to make a start at putting her things away, but such a lassitude overtook her that she lay down on the bed and shut her eyes.

'I've only myself to blame if I'm stuck in this rotten country,' she said to herself. 'But could I, could any reasonable human being have expected anything so vile as that hotel or so foul as these quarters at the top of this tower –'

On the stroke of five Gretchen stood timidly on the threshold of the drawing-room, not bold enough to come forward until Miss Nellie – who was in colloquy with Mary – noticed her arrival.

It was an immense, high-ceilinged room with five pairs of French windows on the south side overlooking Dufresne Bay and a huge fireplace on the west wall in which a sulky fire – newly lit – was petering out. The whole room was done in chintz, was a veritable explosion of chintz, since seven or eight quite different patterns were each at odds, the one with the other. There were winsome chintz curtains – patiently fading – chairs of all styles, all periods, covered in several sprightly designs of chintz, which were grouped together in twos and threes around spindly tables, and one vast armchair in a vast exuberance of chintz was placed by the fire. Between two of the windows stood the tea-table with Miss Nellie seated behind it, her back to the view, and Mary bending toward her, speaking in a shrill tone. Presently Miss Nellie rose imperiously – if petulantly.

'Drat the man,' she said, in a high squeak of a voice which sounded to Gretchen's ears like someone tearing silk. 'I shall have to go down to him, of course, but I shall make it quite plain that I see tradesmen by appointment only.'

It was when she had risen that she caught sight of Gretchen.

'There you are,' she said. 'Will you take my place and pour? I've an unexpected visitor but I shan't be long.'

Before Gretchen was established in the chair Miss Nellie and Mary had left the room.

Directly opposite the table, close to the opposite wall, was a gigantic television set running at full volume. The set largely obscured a man sitting in a wing chair – also chintz-covered – who was watching the screen, but from where Gretchen sat she could just make out a pair of legs in corduroy and a pair of feet in carpet slippers. Unable to raise her voice to the level of the blast bounding from the television, she rose and approached the man, who was dressed in a checked woollen shirt, open at the neck to reveal a stained woollen undershirt, whose head sprouted an angry shock of white hair, and most of those face was prickled with a coarse, white stubble. Since he appeared neither to have seen nor to have heard her, Gretchen put a hand on his shoulder.

'How do you like your tea?' she said, in an unseemly yell, when he turned to look at her.

'I don't take tea,' said the man who, Gretchen was certain, must be Seamus Taylor-Dufresne, Miss Nellie's husband.

For an instant he glared at her. Then his eyes were suddenly full of tears. The tears rolled down his cheeks, and Gretchen quickly backed away.

'Don't you come pestering me again,' he said, on a rising sob. 'If I've said it once, I've said it a thousand times. I don't take tea.'

Appalled by the exhibition of such distress, Gretchen moved further off, putting the television set between them so that they were all but invisible to each other. At the west end of the room she waited, stricken, for Miss Nellie's return. When Miss Nellie did return she bent one exasperated glance at the tea-table, so obviously undisturbed.

'What's this?' she said, more than loudly enough to vie with the television.

Gretchen drew closer.

'I asked him – it's Mr Taylor-Dufresne, isn't it – how he liked his tea,' she said. 'He said he didn't take tea, and then – and then he broke

53

down.'

'Just showin' off,' said Miss Nellie, who had taken her seat behind the table and was manipulating the tea things. 'Would you be so good as to take this cup over there and put it down beside him? And turn off the television. It's not allowed at tea-time.'

'I couldn't do that,' said Gretchen. 'He doesn't know me. And this is his house.'

'It's not his house and it never was,' said Miss Nellie. 'Seamus,' she said – her voice far more powerful than the voice in the box – 'turn that thin' off immediately. Else there'll be no programmes for you after dinner.'

There was a scraping noise – Seamus pushing his chair back so that he could rise, Gretchen thought – and at once the room was silent.

'Do give him his tea,' said Miss Nellie – who seemed to be thoroughly irritated. 'He makes a dreadful fuss when it's cold.'

Gretchen, not daring to look at him, set the cup and saucer down on a pie-crust table at his elbow. Coming back to the tea-table, she found Miss Nellie deftly buttering bread and spreading it with honey.

'Brin' that to him too, if you would,' she said, handing Gretchen a small plate. 'He always stops cryin' when he has somethin' to eat. He can't do both at the same time, you see.'

Quite soon she had arranged a plate of bread and honey for Gretchen and ascertained that Gretchen wanted milk but no sugar in her tea.

'Take these thin's over to the big chair where it's nice and warm,' she said, superbly unaware that the fire was quite dead.

Gretchen obeyed, putting the plate and the cup and saucer on a small oval table beside the chair before she sat down. When she sat down the bottom springs gave way and she found herself folded up like a jack-knife, her rump on the floor, her knees almost touching her chin.

'Oh, fudge,' said Miss Nellie. 'Seamus, get up this instnat and give the girl a hand.'

Seamus, a diminutive man on his feet, with a distended paunch, shuffled across the room, wheezing as he went. With both hands he grasped Gretchen's wrists and – so it seemed to Gretchen – with surprising strength for a man so short-winded, he pulled with all his might. But all his might went to no avail; Gretchen remained a prisoner, bent double, locked into an enormous padded vice of chintz.

'Turn the chair over,' said Miss Nellie, 'and she'll fall out. That's the way Captain Hargreaves extricated the vicar this summer.'

Seamus dropped Gretchen's wrists and stumbled around behind the chair. Suddenly Gretchen felt a violent shove, the chair overturned and her head struck the floor.

'Now use your arms as if you were swimmin',' said Miss Nellie, 'and you'll be loose.'

Gretchen, whose arms were disengaged, did try to propel herself forward, but the chair held her in its plump, upholstered grip.

'Have you never learnt to swim,' said Miss Nellie, whose voice, when she was impatient, was sharp enough to cut glass.

'I've never done it on dry land,' said Gretchen.

'You'll have to get out of there,' Miss Nellie said. 'If you don't, you'll miss your tea.'

'Call Mary,' said Seamus. 'Perhaps the two of us can pull the chair away off her.'

'Well, I never,' said Mary. 'Did nobody think to warn the poor child about that old wreck?'

'I encouraged her to sit in it,' said Miss Nellie said. 'After all, I paid Dennis O'Rourke a young fortune to shore it up and I had his assurance it was sound.'

'Don't you take on,' said Mary, easing herself down to a squat so that she could speak to Gretchen. 'One way or another, please God, we'll get you out of this.'

'Come along then,' she said to Seamus, and the two of them seized the legs of the chair, now upended, and heaving and panting they tugged at it, while Gretchen struggled to dislodge herself.

Abruptly, with a jolt, she was free. Seamus and Mary staggered backwards, the chair rocking in their grasp, while Gretchen, unsteady but determined, stood up.

'No bones broken?' said Miss Nellie.

'Oh, I don't think so,' Gretchen said.

'She's a mortal bruise on her forehead,' said Mary.

'Go upstairs and lie down,' said Miss Nellie. 'Your tea will be brought up to you directly.'

Gretchen climbed the stairs a little uncertainly. She had hardly sat down on the bed than she saw Miss Nellie herself carrying a tray.

'This is a fresh cup,' said Miss Nellie. 'The other was cold.'

'I never meant to give so much trouble,' said Gretchen, but she had had just time enough to discover that her head was aching and that she was trembling with rage.

'Before the sun sets tomorrow,' Miss Nellie said, 'Dennis O'Rourke will wish he'd never been born.'

The tea was excellent, the honey delicious. Gretchen carried the tray down to the drawing-room when she had finished with it and noted, with surprise, that Miss Nellie – who was still clasping the poker – the coaxed the fire into a roaring blaze.

'Very good of you to spare us two flights of stairs,' said Miss Nellie, when she saw the tray. 'Just put it down wherever you please. Dinner's at eight o'clock sharp. You needn't be mindful of your watch, for Mary rin's the gong at five minutes before the hour.'

'I hope I can find the dining-room,' said Gretchen.

'Nothin' to it,' Miss Nellie said. 'Come all the way down to the ground floor, turn left into the corridor. That will lead you straight into the dinin'-room.'

'Thank you,' said Gretchen. 'I'll be there at eight.'

By the time she was in her own room again Gretchen had herself well in hand. She would unpack slowly, carefully. No hasty dispositions – simply to get the suitcases out of the way would do. If she was to stay in the Hall all through the winter she would make herself comfortable, she would be mistress of her own domain. An hour later she had laid out the contents of three suitcases on the bed and was puzzling over how best to arrange them in the chest-of-drawers and in the alcove when she heard a knock. Turning, she saw a long, thin table, painted a sticky bright blue, just outside her door with a boy behind it.

'Did you carry that all this way upstairs by yourself?' said Gretchen.

''Twasn't so hard,' he said. 'It's quite light for all its size. Will I put it in place for you?'

'We can do it together,' said Gretchen.

The table fitted nicely between the windows and Gretchen was grateful to see that, although it was narrow, its length ensured ample space for her working paraphernalia.

'Are you Kevin?' Gretchen said.

'Yes, I'm Kevin,' said the boy.

'It was awfully kind of you to bring the table up to me,' said Gretchen.

'Mary told me to have a look at two chairs here at the top of the tower,' said Kevin. 'Just a look to see if either of them will do.'

Gretchen took him down the corridor. There was no light in the little room but the light from the hallway allowed Kevin to study the chairs, first by picking one up and turning it over in his hands, by doing the same to the other, and then by sitting in each of them.

'They're only fit for the fire now,' he said. 'Tomorrow morning when the sun's up I could take you through the west wing where you might find something that would do you better than either of these.'

'I'd love to see the west wing,' said Gretchen.

'It's not much to look at,' he said. 'I sleep there, so I'm quite familiar with it.'

'How long have you been there?' said Gretchen.

'Going on for a month now,' he said. 'She gives me my board and lodging. I do whatever she wants me to do – mostly fixing broken things. Everything in this place is broken.'

'I'm beginning to see that,' said Gretchen. 'I'm also beginning to notice a smell all over the house – like the smell of a dog with infected ears.'

'That's Solomon,' Kevin said. 'He's canker in both ears and wild with it. She takes him to the vet, I'll say that for her. But the vet does no good. No good at all.'

'We have a dog at home who had canker,' said Gretchen. 'Our vet gave us an ointment, an antibiotic ointment. It comes in a large tube with a very fine nozzle – for sticking up into a cow's tit if she has mastitis. Our Cyrus was cured in six weeks and he's never been troubled with canker again.'

'Is that a fact?' said Kevin. 'Odds are you'd have to find a veterinary supply shop for anything like that.'

'Naturally,' Gretchen said.

'But with all the cattle roundabouts there's sure to be a chemist in Ralston's Cove with veterinary medications for sale,' said Kevin. 'If I could find the ointment I could do Solomon's ears myself – and she'd never know the first thing about it.'

'I could help, if you'd like,' said Gretchen. 'I'm used to it.'

'The only thing is,' Kevin said, 'I've got no money. She gives me no wages, you see.'

'I'll give you the money in the morning,' said Gretchen. 'Right now I've got to put my mind on stowing all these things away in good order.'

'Then I'll go along,' said Kevin. 'Mary'll give me a call whenever you're ready for the west wing.'

Alone again, Gretchen put all of her clothing into the chest of drawers or hung it up in the alcove. The other two suitcases, full of books and notes and yellow pads and typewriter paper, could wait until after dinner. Indeed, just as soon as she had everything cleared off the bed, she heard the dinner gong which someone – presumably Mary – was beating with frenzy.

'Only the dead could sleep through that,' she said, putting her hands to her ears as she went toward the stairs.

Following the passage leading from the west tower to the east tower Gretchen dallied, for the walls on both sides were hung with portraits – doubtless of Dufresne ancestors. She paused before bearded men in ruffs, their arms in billowing sleeves, frilled at the wrists, their breeches fastened by ribbons at the knee, women in farthingales, men

57

in doublets embellished by jewelled buttons, women in stiff collars, women in ruffs, men in loose, furred sleeves and broad-brimmed hats.

For no reason that she could have defended she stopped, stock-still.

'Perhaps my brain was damaged when I was so sick in the hotel,' she said to herself. 'Because none of this is what it's meant to seem. I'm sure of it. But I must be mad.'

Once again she started for the dining-room, past men in coats tight-fitted to the waist and flaring to the knee, men in wide-sleeved velvet coats, women in redingotes, women in slender, Empire frocks, women in hoop-skirts, men in double-breasted dress coats and long, striped trousers, a judge in his robes.

'Surely you heard the gong,' said Miss Nellie.

'I'm awfully sorry,' said Gretchen. 'I was so taken by the portraits in the corridor I forgot about dinner.'

Plainly mollified, Miss Nellie rose from her high-backed chair at the head of a table some fifteen feet long and, taking Gretchen by the arm drew her toward a small table in the embrasure of a window curtained in crimson satin, much worn and dulled.

'This will be your place,' Miss Nellie said. 'In the daytime, when the curtains are opened, the window overlooks the courtyard of the east wing – the William and Mary wing.'

Gretchen remained standing until Miss Nellie was once again seated in her grim and lofty chair. Then she, too, sat down. A napkin in a blackening silver napkin-ring lay before her, the fork and spoon and knife were equally tarnished, a slice of bread had been put on a thick kitchen-ware plate, a chipped stemmed glass full of water completed the setting. Presently Mary trudged up to the table and laid a magnificent Spode dinner plate in front of her. On the plate were two hunks of what Gretchen supposed was beef – and soon discovered that it took all of five minutes to chew one mouthful fine enough to swallow – two dry, boiled potatoes, two large, boiled carrots, unscraped and looked as if the soil were still clinging to them, and a stiff mound of what might have been a purée of peas. It was all she could do to eat the potatoes – washing them down with water. Fortunately Miss Nellie, at a regal remove, was talking to Seamus, on her right, in an undertone, and paying no attention whatsoever to Gretchen's corner. When Gretchen had dispatched the potatoes she laid her knife and fork on her plate and scrutinised the room.

The great table, the great sideboard, the high-backed chairs – all of them in oak like her chest of drawers on the third floor – bore carvings of grotesque creatures with cruel, misshapen heads and open jaws. Overhead a tremendous chandelier, fitted with electric bulbs in the form of flames, cast a glare which inexorably illuminated the patches in the crimson curtains on the south wall, picked out the crumbs which had fallen to the scruffy carpet under and around Seamus' chair, and gleamed harshly in the stately mirrors facing each other – one on the west and one on the east wall. A splendid fireplace – like the fireplace in the drawing-room – occupied most of the north wall.

'So that's how you keep your figure,' said Mary, frowning at the plate which Gretchen had hardly touched.

'I was too tired to eat much tonight,' said Gretchen.

'It's fluffy semolina pudding for dessert,' Mary said, exchanging the Spode dinner plate for a coarse glass bowl which might have come from a village hardware store.

'I don't want fluffy semolina pudding,' said Seamus, suddenly.

'Nonsense,' said Miss Nellie.

Coffee was served in the drawing-room and, like the tea, it was very good indeed. Gretchen commented on both the tea and the coffee.

'All our coffee comes from Port Ferris,' said Miss Nellie. 'Our tea comes from Dublin – from an importer who caters to a few old clients.'

A black and white spaniel which had been dozing by the fire roused himself and shambled over to inspect the newcomer, Gretchen. Gretchen twice warned – by the smell of the dog himself and by Kevin – was carefuly not to touch him near his head. Instead she fondled his chest and, within a moment or two, Solomon had rolled over on his back in blissful submission.

'We called him Solomon,' Miss Nellie said, 'because as a puppy he looked so wise. When he was grown he was not wise at all. We were quite misled.'

'I like spaniels,' said Gretchen. 'They're so sociable.'

'They're undiscriminatin',' said Miss Nellie. 'Sloppy with their affections. Still the Dufresnes have always kept spaniels.'

Gretchen had noticed how rapidly and economically Miss Nellie could abort a complaint or a conversation. Her 'Nonsense' to Seamus over the pudding had been effective – Seamus had eaten it – she had neatly closed the chapter on coffee and tea, she had dismissed spaniels in a brace of adjectives, even if she had gone on to recognise them since the Dufresnes had always kept them. Gretchen would have liked to stretch out a minute or so with Miss Nellie; she would, for instance, have liked to ask her if the Dufresnes had always

59

kept newspapers – since there were untidy mounds of the *Port Ferris News* on the floor by each of the windows, on the love-seat, on most of the small tables, and stacks of it on both sides of the hearth. But keeping spaniels and hoarding newspapers seemed to Gretchen two different sorts of idiosyncrasy. It was not impossible that Miss Nellie was vain of the one and touchy about the other. In which case –

All at once she fell asleep. How long she slept she had no idea, but when she woke up the television set was on, Seamus and Miss Nellie were sitting in front of it, holding hands. Waking, Gretchen was shocked by her rudeness; she hoped she had not fallen asleep over one of Miss Nellie's pronouncements and, at the same time, she realised how tired she was. Solomon had gone back to the fire, Seamus and Miss Nellie were watching the television, she could easily slip off to her own room. Rising, she found herself – once on her feet – facing Seamus directly. His whole attention was claimed by the screen, while large tears gushed, unchecked, down to his chin and he sobbed gently with each breath he drew. Just before she silently turned away, Gretchen saw Miss Nellie blot his face with a handkerchief. But neither of them – it appeared – had a word to say to each other.

Softly Gretchen took the stairs, automatically committing each riser to memory by the size and the position of each hole in the stair-carpet. She remembered that, before she went to bed, she had meant to unpack the suitcases with her books and papers. But she was too played out for any more unpacking. It was all she could do to brush her teeth and put her clothing away before she got into the bed. Just before she slept she thought of Dr Donovan. How relieved he must be, she said to herself, to have seen the last of her, to be able to look forward to long, uninterrupted evenings in which he would be free to please himself.

At that moment Donovan was far from pleasing himself. He had had his supper; he had retreated to his library, where he had sat down with a whisky and soda. At the far end of the room his grandfather, in a meticulous portrait, watched him – a more than usual reproach in the cold eyes.

'It's quite true,' Donovan said to the old gentleman, 'that Alice is dead. But she was ninety-three, and if I'd been damned fool enough to have put her in hospital she'd have died within minutes of the admission. I've discussed it with Reilly and he agrees with me. We did what was suitable. In spite of that we lost her. However, she died in her own bed, which was what she wanted.'

Nothing was altered in the portrait after his angry speech, and

Donovan had a very real sense that his grandfather was not waiting on the chronicle of Alice O'Neill but on an accounting of himself – himself and his attachment to Gretchen.

'What more can I do?' he said. 'I've left her at the Hall. I won't be back with my hat in my hand and my heart on my sleeve. I swore that when she was well I would never trouble her again. It will be a trifle awkward, of course, when you think that I was in the habit of dropping by for coffee every ten days or so, but Miss Nellie and Seamus can get on nicely without me.'

If possible his grandfather's gaze was more obdurate than ever.

'I will concede,' said Donovan, to the inflexible painting, 'that at my age infatuation is obscene.'

With that he lay back in his chair and looked up at the ceiling. Sensible arguments, arguments which would have elicited his grandfather's approval, rose to his mind and rigorously connected themselves until his most aberrant inclinations were interwoven with an inexorable chain of reasoning.

He was not in love; that he could rule out at a stroke. There was no such thing as unrequited love; what was thought of as love unrequited was merely a painful bedazzlement – in itself not only worthless but a prodigal self-indulgence as well. Love – the genuine article – was intimate, wordless, reciprocal knowledge. Love was a steady, profound, experience of another, love was a mutually elected bondage and he, Donovan, was not bound. Gretchen was beyond him, Gretchen had not, would not require him to disclose his intrinsic self. Nor was she, he was sure, under the slightest impulsion to disclose her own. As much, perhaps, as twenty-five years lay between them; his life – his active life – was realised, it was approaching its completion; Gretchen's was scarcely begun. Why should she beckon, across the canyon of a generation? How could he possibly respond – fully, appropriately – if she did?

'I am not in love with her,' he said to himself.

But although he was not in love with her, he could not sleep for a long time that night. Fitfully he wondered if she was comfortable at the Hall, if Miss Nellie had been kind to her, if Mary had tried to make her feel at home, if she had already forgotten him entirely –

6

The next morning Gretchen woke to immediate chagrin. Mary was standing, holding a breakfast tray, at the foot of her bed.

'How long have I overslept?' said Gretchen, sitting up at once.

'You've not overslept,' said Mary. 'By her orders you're to have breakfast in your room at half past eight every morning.'

'But surely,' Gretchen said, 'I should come downstairs for breakfast.'

'Even Seamus Taylor-Dufresne takes his breakfast in his bed,' said Mary. 'She'll not tolerate company in the dining-room – and himself is not excepted from the ban – until she's had her coffee.'

'At least I could have come down to the kitchen for the tray,' said Gretchen.

'She'd never put up with a stranger on the prowl at this hour,' Mary said. 'Mark my words, you've no call to go rewriting the rules and regulations in this house.'

At that Gretchen acknowledged to herself that the rebuke was justified. Holding her peace she rose from the bed to take the tray from Mary, who suddenly regarded her with a rush of horror.

'God bless us and save us, what's happened to you?' said Mary.

Hastily she slammed the tray on the long blue table from the larder and jerked the covers off the bed. Both the top and the bottom sheets were generously stained with blood, as were the pillows.

'By all that's wonderful,' Mary said, 'sure you're covered in it too.'

Gretchen, who had been staring at the sheets, fixed her eyes upon herself and saw that the left side of her nightgown, from the shoulder to the waist, was as deeply stained as the bed clothing.

'But it's impossible,' she said. 'There's nothing the matter with me.'

'Only that you've been bleeding like a stuck pig all through the night,' said Mary.

'Where?' said Gretchen. 'Where am I bleeding?'

'Step out of that gown and we'll see,' Mary said.

As soon as Gretchen had lifted the skirts of her nightgown – preparatory to pulling it off over her head – Mary pounced on her.

Never mind about the nightie,' said Mary. 'Just have a look at your left arm.'

Gretchen let the short nightgown drop to her knees again and glanced at her arm. At once she saw two gashes running from just below her shoulder to her elbow. The wounds, which were fierce and ugly, had hardly clotted.

'What on earth –' she said.

Mary yanked the bottom sheet loose, disclosing a thin, and badly blood-stained, cotton blanket, protecting the mattress. That, too, she pulled back and, when the mattress was bare, Gretchen saw that one of the springs – apparently broken off and away from its coil deep within its housing – was sticking up sharply, a good three inches of it showing through the ticking.

'And you never felt a thing all night long?' said Mary, as both of them gazed at the wicked spike.

'I was just tuckered out when I went to bed,' said Gretchen.

Somehow, by mid-morning, things were more or less put to rights. Mary had left Gretchen to her breakfast of bread and honey, and the pungent coffee Gretchen remembered from the evening before. No sooner had she finished than she heard Mary's laboured tread in the corridor.

'Now then,' said Mary, 'we'll have all the time in the world. For I've told herself that I'm off with a letter to post so we'll enjoy the peace and quiet we need and I've a change of bedding here.'

Together she and Gretchen turned the mattress, saw that the underside was intact, and made up the bed with the clean linen. Just as at the hotel, both the sheets and the stiff, worn blankets were too short for the bed; Gretchen refrained from any comment on that since Mary did not appear to find anything amiss either with her sheets or with her blankets.

'Next we'll bind your arm,' said Mary. 'Else when you're dressed your clothes will rub against your scratches.'

'Please, not yet,' said Gretchen. 'First I must take a bath – if no one's using the bathroom.'

'There'll be nobody in the bathroom,' Mary said. 'But the water's cold as ice.'

'I've pioneer stock in me,' said Gretchen.

'Then here's what we'll do,' said Mary. 'I'll take all these bloody things away with me and put them down in a big tub of water. Then when Paddy McClure comes to pick up the laundry for Port Ferris – which he will, seeing as it's Wednesday – I'll just shove the lot in with the rest of the wash and she'll be none the wiser till next week when she sees the bill.

'In the meanwhile you take your bath and soak your nightgown while you're at it. Cold water's what the doctor ordered for blood stains. Mind you be as quick as you can, for she'll never believe I spent the entire morning posting a letter and I'll have to nip up here again to bind your arm before you dress.'

Gretchen's fingernails were blue after the icy bath, but her pioneer stock had stood her in good stead. She was clean from head to foot; she had washed the blood out of her nightgown and washed the stockings she had worn the day before. Mary was waiting for her and,

with a length of rag from the airing-cupboard, bound her arm –
which was bleeding again slightly – and fastened the bandage with
safety pins.

'Now take a hint from me and keep mum,' said Mary. 'Will I tell
Kevin to come up for you in ten minutes or so? He's his eye on a
chair in the west wing he thinks should do you nicely.'

'Yes, please tell Kevin to come for me,' said Gretchen. 'And don't
worry about Miss Nellie. I won't say a word to her.'

'She'll have a word or two to say to myself,' Mary said. 'Seeing as I
can't write and she knows it – besides I've no one to write to – she'll
be straight out of her mind wondering whatever I was doing
dawdling about with the post-mistress.'

For half an hour Gretchen explored the west wing with Kevin –
Solomon trotting at their heels.

'How can you sleep here?' she said, at the last.

'It's a bit of a luxury for me,' said Kevin. 'At home there was four
of us in the one bed.'

'Even so –' said Gretchen.

''Tis a sorry sight,' Kevin said. 'Still, my door's barricaded against
the rats.'

Everywhere he had taken her she had seen the past in ruins –
plaster arabesques flaking away from spoiled ceilings, sumptuous
portières eaten up by mould, splendid rugs lying in tatters and rich
with rat droppings, magnificent canopies rotting over four-poster
beds, delicate chairs from which the gilt was peeling, elaborate doors
with intricate panelling sagging from their hinges, graceful windows
swinging in the October wind, their panes in fragments on the floor,
crystal chandeliers hanging askew; everywhere she followed Kevin
she saw nothing but what was mutilated past repair.

'Between the rain and the wind, the rats and the spiders there's not
too much to hope for, now is there?' said Kevin. 'She knows it, of
course. She's great plans for me to patch up the windows, rehang the
doors, mend some of the tables and most of the chairs, but there's
nothing I can do here with no proper tools, no putty, no plaster – not
even the odd screw or the odd nail – and she won't put her hand in
her pocket.'

'Just to get the place clean would be a month's work for three or
four people at it day and night,' said Gretchen.

'As it is I've plenty to do on the grounds,' Kevin said. 'And come
spring I'll be on my way. For the moment I'm glad enough of the
food and the lodging. Even a small job is scarce in the winter and
there's hundreds around here looking for work. But when the good

weather comes I'll be looking for wages. Now as to the chair –'

He led her along a passage into what must have been, in its time, a pretty writing room. There he pointed out a chair upholstered in green silk with a comfortable, well-stuffed seat and a heart-shaped back.

'It's sound,' he said. 'And if the height's right it might just do you nicely.'

He beat the dust out of it with his hands and wiped it off with the tail of his shirt.

'Sit in it,' he said.

'It's fine,' said Gretchen. 'It's really fine.'

'We'll take it along and try it,' said Kevin.

The chair was the right height for the table and Gretchen was about to thank Kevin when she was overcome by the giggles.

'Look at the place,' she said, in a burst of desperate merriment. 'One maroon bedspread, one electric blue table, one grass-green chair – if I go crazy in here will you send for a doctor?'

'You should be sending for a doctor yourself,' said Kevin. 'Mary told me about your arm. That's not funny, that isn't. For all you know you could be coming down with tetanus.'

'I thought about that,' said Gretchen. 'Perhaps I should try to reach a doctor this afternoon.'

'You'd be foolish not to ring one or another of them,' Kevin said.

By two o'clock Gretchen – who saw no point in summoning a doctor to the Hall when she could go to Dr Donovan, whom she already knew – was ready to start out for Ralston's Cove. She had given Kevin the money for the ointment for Solomon's ears; she had done her best to eat the lunch, which consisted of cold beef left over from the night before, something soft and grey which Mary assured her was a helping of mashed potatoes, and which tasted like wet paper napkins, something green and slimy which – if Mary were to be believed – was a purée of spinach, and something yellow and curdled which she took to be a custard of sorts. Miss Nellie and Seamus had gone to Port Ferris for the day.

'Once a month they go in after the coffee,' Mary had said. 'It's a miracle how they get home alive. Seamus never fails to put some damage on the car – through losing his patience with all the other drivers on the road.'

At two o'clock it was raining, but Gretchen was prepared for that. She set out in boots, a mackintosh, a wide-brimmed oilskin hat, and carrying a flashlight to see her way back to the Hall when darkness fell. All her money and her precious travellers' cheques were stuffed into the pockets of the mackintosh.

Climbing up the hill in Dufresne Village left her exhausted; at the top she paused for almost ten minutes, trying to catch her breath. Then she set out again – more briskly – and by four o'clock, when darkness was already beginning to enfold the town, she had found Dr Donovan's office, a little way along and across the street from the hotel.

Mrs Mullin led her into the waiting room.

'Dr Donovan's a great number of patients this afternoon,' said Mrs Mullin. 'You wouldn't consider seeing Dr Fir, I suppose?'

'No,' said Gretchen. 'I must see Dr Donovan.'

'You'll have a wait,' Mrs Mullin said.

'If that's so,' said Gretchen, 'perhaps I could do one errand and then come straight back.'

'Take your time,' said Mrs Mullin. 'There's seven or eight ahead of you.'

'Could you possibly tell me,' Gretchen said, 'where I could find a bucket? Just an ordinary bucket?'

The only bucket Gretchen could find was made of plastic in a stunning poster red. Thoroughly indoctrinated by Mary, she wondered if – did Miss Nellie ever catch her with so brazen a bucket in hand – she would be thrown out of the Hall lock, stock and barrel. Nevertheless she had had no choice of colour, and a pail, as she had learnt for herself – having, on several occasions been quite unable to work Charles Cutter and Sons' ancient mechanism – was an absolute necessity. In fact, that morning, she had been too nice to relieve her bowel knowing, as by then she did that, try as she might, she could not coax the lavatory to flush however she pulled, jerked or jiggled the chain. To her dismay the shop had refused to wrap the bucket and she quailed at the thought of smuggling it naked into the Hall and asked herself how – with any modesty – she could explain it to Dr Donovan when the time came for them to meet.

Back in Donovan's waiting room she sat on a low stool, – the only seat which was unoccupied, and gave herself up to a study of the Irish in the mother country. The first thing she noticed was that, like all practical folk, they had hung their overcoats on pegs – not meaning to be overheated indoors and risk a chill when, once again, they ventured out. But since all her funds were in her pockets, Gretchen kept her mackintosh on, rested the oilskin hat on her knees, and placed the bucket and the flashlight on the floor beside her.

Opposite, a weather-beaten, gargantuan woman sat with her feet

66

stoutly planted on the ground, her great legs wide apart, affording Gretchen, from her lowly vantage point, an unimpeded view of a dark triangle. Embarrassed, she cast her gaze higher. The woman was working with a crochet hook on what appeared to be a doily; her fingernails were broken and black at the rims, her sparse, grizzled hair was pulled back into a thin bun at the top of her head, and the stench which breathed from her made Gretchen uncomfortably nauseated. Shortly Mrs Mullin beckoned from the door, and the mammoth matron struggled to her feet and vanished. But the stench remained.

Two hours later Gretchen had concluded that not a single one of Dr Donovan's patients – that afternoon – had ever had a bath. The waiting-room was small and hot from the glow of an electric heater and although, one by one, patient after patient was called away by Mrs Mullin, the odour was constant and heavy as ever.

Gretchen had given her closest attention to feet and hands – not liking to stare boldly at the faces of her companions. The old men, three of them, were booted against the weather, as were two old women. But one young mother, beside herself with a fractious baby as well as a truculent toddler, and two girls were shod in thinnest patent leather, despite the rain. Not a fingernail, young or old, was clean; not a hand was cared for; not a shirt or a jacket, not a pullover or a sturdy, woollen frock was fresh. All three of the young women were chewing gum noisily; two of the old men coughed without let in harsh, dry spasms. One of the old women was idly reading a magazine, licking a finger each time she turned a page. The other, whose hat had tumbled awry, was napping; every so often a snore escaped her, at which she woke, nodded at her neighbours and fell asleep again.

It was half-past six before Gretchen was alone in the waiting room.

'Could I open a window?' she said to Mrs Mullin, when she passed the door.

'It wouldn't do any good,' said Mrs Mullin. 'The smell's penetrated into the wall-paper itself.'

Finally Gretchen found herself following Mrs Mullin down a narrow passage-way to a small office, with no window, which contained an examining table, two cabinets with glass doors, filled with medicines, two chairs for patients, and a desk behind which Dr Donovan was seated.

That he was shocked to see her Gretchen understood at once by a slightest but noticeable change in his expression – which was not welcoming.

'How did you get here?' he said, after a pause.

'I walked,' said Gretchen.

'From Dufresne Bay?' said Donovan. 'In this downpour?'

'I had a problem,' Gretchen said. 'I thought it might be urgent –'

She was still standing, the oilskin hat, the flashlight, and the bucket in her hands.

'What's the problem?' said Donovan.

'Could I show it to you?' said Gretchen.

'That's what I'm here for,' he said.

She put down her things, took off her mackintosh, her lilac cardigan, her white blouse, and began to unpin Mary's length of old sheeting bound round her left arm.

Donovan, plainly startled, rose instantly and gently undid the winding rag. Gretchen's gashes were deep and inflamed.

'Mother of God,' said Donovan. 'Did Seamus go at you with the carving knife?'

Fifteen minutes afterward – after Gretchen had described the spike in the mattress and assured him that she had regularly had tetanus boosters every two years – he had given her another booster, disinfected the wounds and bandaged them in a sterile dressing. All the while – except for his questions about the spike and the tetanus shots – he had said nothing. Gretchen dressed herself, put on the mackintosh and the oilskin hat, gripped the flashlight and the pail.

'Could I settle my bill with your office nurse?' she said.

'All my bills go out on Saint Valentine's Day,' said Donovan. 'Come along. I'll take you back to the Hall.'

'Oh, no,' said Gretchen. 'I can find the way. I've my flashlight on purpose, and going down the hill in Dufresne Village won't be a patch on climbing it.'

'I'll take you home,' he said. 'I'd like to see that mattress.'

'It's turned now,' said Gretchen. 'There's no more harm in it.'

'I'd like to see it all the same,' said Donovan.

With Ralston's Cove behind him and the car on the road to Dufresne Bay, Donovan glanced at the red pail in Gretchen's lap which she was embracing.

'Did Mike Healey ask you to pitch in at milking time?' said Donovan.

'Who's Mike Healey?' said Gretchen.

'He rents Miss Nellie's north pasture,' Donovan said.

'Are you indirectly referring to my bucket?' said Gretchen.

'I am,' he said.

'For pity's sake don't joke about it,' said Gretchen. 'And when we get to the Hall please distract Miss Nellie, if she's on the lookout for me, because I've got to get it up to my room before she has a glimpse of it.'

'It's not quite big enough to put out a fire at the Hall,' said Donovan.

'It's quite big enough for my purposes,' Gretchen said.

'You're thinking of drowning yourself?' said Donovan.

'Not yet,' said Gretchen.

Miss Nellie, who was known to have ears like a lynx, was at the front door by the time Donovan pulled up before the west tower.

'Is the girl with you?' she said. 'She's nowhere to be found and Mary tells me she missed her tea.'

'She's here beside me,' said Donovan.

'Well, come in out of the rain, both of you,' Miss Nellie said. 'You'll stay for dinner, of course,' she said to Donovan.

'I wouldn't dream –' said Donovan.

'Then don't,' said Miss Nellie. 'Come along, the two of you.'

In the darkness of the driveway Gretchen tore off her mackintosh and wrapped it round the bucket. Then, sedately, she followed Donovan and Miss Nellie into the entrance hall.

'I'll stay for dinner,' said Donovan, 'but I'll state my terms.'

'And what are your terms, pray?' said Miss Nellie.

'I should like your permission to examine Gretchen's bed, in your presence, naturally,' he said.

'Really,' said Miss Nellie, 'this is rather whimsical.'

'After which,' said Donovan, 'although I know your household runs by clockwork, I would hope that you would give Gretchen time to change her things as she's damp to the bone and still convalescent.'

'And why is she damp to the bone?' Miss Nellie said. 'Was she so foolish as to go out today – which one can only presume she did?'

'After which,' said Donovan, deaf to Miss Nellie, 'I would require a stiff whisky – Scotch, if you have it – for myself and for my patient before we go in to dinner.'

'All that can be arranged,' said Miss Nellie. 'I'll put it up to Mary. But first may we see to this matter of the bed?'

As soon as the three of them were collected in her room Gretchen stuffed the bucket, with the mackintosh around it, into the alcove and straightened up to face Donovan.

'Lend me a hand,' he said, pulling off the bedspread.

A moment later all the bedding was piled on the blue table and Donovan was turning the mattress. Under the glare of the overhead lamp the spike looked – to Gretchen – far more deadly than it had in the grey light of the morning.

'I have never seen such a thin',' said Miss Nellie, peering at it with extreme distaste. 'Not in all my life. I shall write to the manufacturers directly.'

'Before you do that,' said Donovan, 'it would be as well to make sure that the other side is sound.'

'Were you injured in the night?' said Miss Nellie to Gretchen. 'If so, I should report that, too, in my letter.'

'It was only a couple of scratches,' Gretchen said.

'You should have come to me at once,' said Miss Nellie.

'There was no need,' said Gretchen. 'Mary coped with everything.'

'If,' said Miss Nellie to Donovan, 'you're in any doubt about the other side of the mattress, she can sleep in the Chinese room tonight.'

Then she addressed herself to Gretchen.

'I'm very sorry indeed to think that anythin' disagreeable happened to you under my roof,' she said. 'However, one way or another, we'll make it up to you.

'And now,' she went on, 'I'll tell Mary to hold back dinner until nine o'clock. Nine o'clock *sharp*, you understand.'

When she had left the room Donovan pored long and hard over the piercing spike.

'I don't suppose that even Miss Nellie ever kept this mattress in the stables,' he said, and set to drubbing both sides of it until he was satisfied that one side was still sound.

Half an hour later the four of them were in the drawing-room, glasses in hand. Miss Nellie was drinking sherry, Seamus Irish whiskey, Donovan and Gretchen had each been offered Scotch. Gretchen disliked the taste, but just a drop or two rolling down her gullet warmed her and she had been, as Donovan had said, damp to the bone.

Four places were laid at the long dining-room table. Miss Nellie had Donovan on her right, Seamus on her left. Gretchen sat next to Seamus. No one made any conversation until Mary had tied a large and much-spotted bib around Seamus' neck. Then, together, Miss Nellie and Seamus made the most of Donovan, plying him with rumours of lots for sale, houses changing hands, quoting prices, crying extortion, while Donovan agreed that the McCreas were indeed selling and moving to County Kerry, or protested that he had not heard that Gerald O'Brien was getting rid of two meadows. Gretchen applied herself to the roast chicken, which had come away from the bone in long, dessicated splinters, and picked at a few chunks of grey matter which Miss Nellie had identified as braised celery. After tinned peaches they returned to the drawing-room,

70

where Gretchen avoided the armchair and Miss Nellie – for Donovan's enlightenment – described the misadventure of the evening before.

'I noticed the bruise on her forehead,' said Donovan, 'but as Gretchen didn't mention it, I assumed it was a personal matter.'

'It had nothin' to do with her,' said Miss Nellie. 'It was pure happen-chance.'

'To be sure,' Donovan said.

When they had had coffee Donovan rose to take his leave.

'If I may,' he said, 'I'll stop in tomorrow evening to have a look at my patient.'

'Tomorrow's Thursday,' said Miss Nellie. 'All the world knows you're away all day and never home from Port Ferris until Friday mornin'.'

'Every now and then I make an exception to a rule,' said Donovan. 'Particularly if it's one of my own.'

'Please don't come back early for my sake,' Gretchen said. 'I'll be all right. I promise.'

'I've reasons of my own for coming back early,' said Donovan and, after thanking Miss Nellie for his dinner, he left.

Over a generous night-cap he pondered on the 'reasons of his own'. In fact, he had planned to go to Dolly Marsh as usual, hoping that, in her company, he would remember himself as he had been before Gretchen stumbled into the hotel in Ralston's Cove, hoping that he could teach himself to take up his life again on the old terms – which had been so simple, so straightforward and, in the main, so satisfactory. But the sight of Gretchen, standing before him in his office, in the heart of his territory, standing in her mackintosh – her oilskin hat, her flashlight, her ridiculous bucket in her hands – had absolutely unmanned him. The longing which had risen up in him had been so powerful that he had hardly trusted his voice not to betray him or his arms not to seize her. And now, till her wounds were healed, he was, once again, committed to her.

'I've lost my bearings,' he said to himself. 'That's the long and the short of it.'

But it was not the long or the short of it; worse lay ahead of him.

'What am I to say to Dolly?' he said. 'After all these fourteen years what am I to say to her?'

And with that he found that he could not even remember what had once touched him in Dolly Marsh; he wished her and her bungalow and the very street in which she lived right off his map.

'Well,' said Mary, 'did you have a good night?'

'The rats do make a commotion, don't they?' said Gretchen.

'What did I tell you?' Mary said.

'May I bring the tray downstairs when I've finished my breakfast?' said Gretchen.

'Just you leave it on the bench in the corridor,' said Mary. 'Mind you don't leave it on the floor. I'd never get down so low.'

'But I could carry it to the kitchen,' Gretchen said.

'She'd give me the rough side of her tongue if she saw you with that tray in your hands,' said Mary. 'In this house I do the fetching, I do the carrying. She was brought up to eight or ten in help, you see. To do her justice she does the most part of the cooking. Do you fancy the fare in the Hall?'

'I haven't given it much thought,' said Gretchen, unwilling to meet Mary's inquisitive gaze.

'You may get used to it,' Mary said. 'Or then again, you may not. Meself, I'd be wasted to a shadow if it wasn't for me nice boiled eggs with me tea.'

Gretchen lingered over her breakfast feeling unaccountably tired. Her arm ached and, from time to time, she coughed.

After a cold bath she attacked the last two suitcases and when she had her books and papers in good order she felt a little more at home in the west tower, a little less overwhelmed by Edward VII in his heroic stance. She was not yet ready to go to work, but she was resolved to write to her mother before the day was over.

'She'll be worried about me if she doesn't get a letter soon,' Gretchen said to herself.

All morning long she had been aware of a great bustle in the tower: slow, heavy footsteps – Mary's – light, tapping footsteps – Miss Nellie's – up and down the stairs; Miss Nellie catechizing Mary, from one floor to another, in intermittent screeches like the cries of a peahen. When Mary rang the gong for lunch Gretchen came across Miss Nellie arranging a conglomeration of miscellaneous articles on the immense draw-table in the entrance hall.

'We're in our annual disarray,' said Miss Nellie. 'Gettin' set for the jumble sale on Saturday.'

Gretchen, who had no idea what a jumble sale was, had nothing to say to that. After lunch Seamus went straight upstairs while Mary called Miss Nellie to the telephone. Gretchen, whose curiosity was lively, stopped for a minute or so in the entrance hall of the west tower to look over Miss Nellie's hodge-podge of curious objects.

The wilting boa – which she picked up – instantly shed two or three large black feathers and she laid it down at once. An ornate brass inkstand, in pitiful need of polishing, held a square, glass inkwell with no cover; a bronze, beaded, lady's evening purse, missing a catch, yawned beside a coarse china mug cast in a horrible likeness of Winston Churchill; a chipped, cut-glass phial, for spirits of ammonia with a tarnished silver filigree stopper stood beside a reproduction, in a cracked, oval frame, of a child's head by Millais; a set of lace-bordered tea-napkins, crudely darned, lay on top of an ancient flowered quilt, whose grey stuffing was exposed along its edges; while five croquet mallets, a broken, wicker picnic hamper, a Meissen pitcher without a handle and a ruptured bellows completed the assortment at which Gretchen was still staring when Miss Nellie reappeared.

'All these things need mending, don't they?' said Gretchen.

'Doesn't matter a rap,' said Miss Nellie. 'They'll sell like hotcakes. Anythin' that comes from the Hall is snapped up immediately.'

'Do you mean they're to be sold?' Gretchen said.

'Naturally they're to be sold,' said Miss Nellie. 'At the jumble sale. Mary and I turn out the cupboards each autumn just for that. It's a labour of love but it's all in a good cause.'

'I see,' said Gretchen.

'This rain is maddenin',' Miss Nellie said. 'We must hope it holds off on Saturday. Not that anyone would dream of puttin' off the sale, rain or no rain. But people are pickier when they're wet. Last year it poured and the results were disappointin'.'

'Last year,' said Gretchen, 'was everything from the Hall sold?'

'That always goes without sayin',' said Miss Nellie.

It was the same afternoon that Gretchen searched the shattered mirror, over the chest-of-drawers, for a reflection of her face before she wrote to her mother. At five o'clock she went down to the drawing-room for tea, where she felt *de trop*, given that Miss Nellie was in ardent colloquy with the vicar about the jumble sale.

'I hope we can expect a fair turn-out,' said the vicar.

'I've already seen to that,' said Miss Nellie – leaving Gretchen to wonder about the nature of Miss Nellie's machinations, and Seamus to remark that Miss Nellie had been making a damned nuisance of herself as usual, and the vicar to asseverate that, without Miss Nellie, the parish would founder.

'Ben Daly would be glad to see the last of her,' said Seamus. ''Twas last week she was out ringing every doorbell up and down Dufresne Hill. When she got to his house the bell was out of order, so she threw pebbles from his garden at all his windows until the poor bugger came down barefoot with his face all lathered up and his razor in his hand. 'Tis a wonder he didn't cut her throat whilst he had

73

her on his doorstep and himself armed to the teeth.'

'We'll be seeing you on Saturday, of course,' said the vicar.

'You'll be seeing nothing of the sort,' said Seamus.

'We will both be there,' Miss Nellie said.

Gretchen would gladly have escaped as soon as she had had her tea and a slice of bread and honey. But mindful that Miss Nellie's provisions for the principal meal of the day left so much to be desired, she accepted Miss Nellie's offer of more tea, more bread, more honey – which, as Miss Nellie proudly announced, came from a neighbour's hives – before she slipped away. Upstairs she found Kevin sitting on the bench in the corridor outside her door.

'I've the ointment for Solomon,' said Kevin, in a low voice.

'Why, that's wonderful,' said Gretchen.

'Not so loud,' Kevin said. 'I'm not supposed to be in the west tower unless I've a job to do. If she was to catch me loafing around here I'd be kicked off the premises before you could say knife. I wasn't born to the purple, you see.'

'I'll whisper,' said Gretchen.

'What I was thinking,' said Kevin, 'was how much better I'd feel if you was to be there when I give the poor animal the first dose. That way you could tell me how to work the gadget. I've Solomon shut up in the west wing.'

'Let's go,' Gretchen said.

'Now then,' said Kevin, when he and Gretchen and Solomon were all together in what seemed to have been the morning-room of the west wing, 'I've cleaned off this bit of floor and Mary's lent me an old bed-cover. We could sit down on it and play with Solomon until he's relaxed entirely.'

Gretchen began by lovingly scratching Solomon's chest. He responded by closing his eyes in enraptured capitulation. Meanwhile Kevin had shown Gretchen the tube – with its nozzle.

'The trick,' said Gretchen, 'is to flap an ear back, lay it open – if you know what I mean – and very gently introduce the nozzle into the ear canal. If he'll hold still for that much you can give the tube a brisk squeeze and start again on the other ear.'

Solomon, bewitched by Gretchen's message, took no notice of Kevin; Kevin, unhurried, turned one ear up and over, dexterously inserted the nozzle, and squeezed the tube. Solomon opened his eyes in an instant's puzzlement but, shortly entranced again by Gretchen, peacefully submitted to Kevin, who doctored the other ear.

'It worked,' Gretchen said. 'If we keep at it maybe he'll get well.'

'There's eight tubes in the pack,' said Kevin. 'And they cost you a fortune. But we've lashings of ointment.'

'I ought to warn you,' Gretchen said, 'that we can't expect any improvement for quite a while. I remember, with Cyrus, after four weeks we none of us had seen any change at all. And then, just like that, during the fifth week his ears didn't smell any more and by the sixth week even the little ones in my family could play with his head and Cyrus didn't turn a hair. When six weeks were over the vet told us we could stop. He said we could always repeat the whole process, if necessary, but it never was necessary. He was cured.'

'Then, if you're game for it, that's what we'll do,' said Kevin. And this is as good a place as any. No one but myself puts a foot in here.

'Just the once she showed me over the wing, but when I let on that I couldn't make bricks without straw you could almost have heard her thinking about the pounds and the pence and she set me to work on the hinges of the kitchen door – which only needed a bit of oil.'

'The day after tomorrow we'll meet in the same place at the same time,' said Gretchen. And Kevin, with Solomon at his heels, led her back to the west tower.

At the very same moment, in Port Ferris, Donovan did not – in strict accordance with his inviolable custom – park his car round the corner from Dolly Marsh's house; he parked it directly in front of her door. When she came out to welcome him a strong odour of roast meat drifted out to the stoop.

'But Dolly,' he said, 'I told you on the telephone this morning that I couldn't stay for dinner, that I had to get back early to Ralston's Cove.'

'So I made it my business to see that dinner was ready the instant you came,' she said. 'I didn't like the thought of you driving those many miles in the dark on an empty stomach.'

'I can't stay to eat dinner,' said Donovan.

She took a step backward, leaving him still outside.

'Can't, or won't?' said Dolly.

'May I come in?' he said.

She made way, he crossed the threshold and shut the door behind him.

'It's not a question of 'can't' or 'won't',' said Donovan. 'The truth is – Dolly this is impossible to explain – that I don't want to stay for dinner. I don't know what's come over me –'

'You've found someone else to take my place,' she said.

'No one could take your place, Dolly,' said Donovan. 'We've been together too long, we know each other too well for that.'

'You're in love,' she said. 'It's written right across you.'

'In heaven's name,' said Donovan. 'I'm no schoolboy. I've fifty years on me.'

Softly, effortlessly, she began to cry. But, turned out in her best frock for him and proper to the last, she asked for no stay of execution.

'You'll go now, if you please,' she said.

Donovan turned, opened the door, stepped outside and closed the door behind him. Sick with shame, he started the car and drove off. All the long way to Ralston's Cove he loathed himself. Nevertheless there was no comfort he could hold out to Dolly. Much better than himself – who had been too craven to make a final accounting – she had understood that their affair was over. It was not until he had driven past his office, past the hotel, past the butcher's shop and the bakery, and rolled off the High Street onto the winding road to Dufresne Bay that the remembrance of her, dissolving in the tears she could not check, dispossessed in the little hallway where she always kept a bowl of fresh flowers for his arrival, began to blur and then to fade. By the time he had reached the top of Dufresne Hill he had recognised that he was free – free to belong to Gretchen. Just for a second or two he forgot that, if she thought of herself as free, it was, almost certainly, to belong to herself alone.

7

So little did Donovan like the look of Gretchen's arm when he had taken off the dressing and examined the wounds carefully that, after a brief telephone call – for which he promptly reimbursed Miss Nellie – he ordered Gretchen to get her coat.

'I'd like another opinion,' he said.

'But Mary's just brought the coffee,' said Miss Nellie. 'Surely the two of you can stay for a cup?'

Donovan declined for both of them, while Miss Nellie repeated her theme and Gretchen stood – in her mackintosh, since it was raining again – at the entrance to the drawing-room, feeling abashed. She was sure that Donovan must be tired after the day's work in Port Ferris and four hours on the road, there and back; yet here he was, at nine o'clock in the evening, taking on still another burden – herself. It was true that her arm was sore, but she had not expected it to keep her awake.

'It's very good of you to go to so much trouble for me,' she said, when they were in the car.'

'What you call 'trouble' is as much for my own sake as for yours,' said Donovan. 'I'm an internist. I don't enjoy surgical problems. I see them, I deal with them when I must, but if Harry Moore's willing to take a look at you – and he said he would – it will be a weight off my mind.'

'Is Harry Moore a surgeon?' she said.

'He is,' said Donovan. 'You'll be in good hands.'

'I was already in good hands,' said Gretchen.

'Then let's say you'll be in better,' Donovan said.

Harry Moore was in a smoking jacket; he had soft leather slippers on his feet and a pipe in his mouth.

'Eliza's glued to the telly,' he said. 'So why don't we go into the kitchen where there's a good light?

'Oh, yes,' he said, not more than five minutes later, 'the nodes in her axilla are considerably enlarged. We'd best bring up the heavy artillery.'

'If you'll tell me what you want,' said Donovan, 'I'll go by the hospital and pick it up.'

'The hospital?' said Gretchen.

'It's after hours,' Moore said. 'Frank MacMahon – the chemist – is closed.

'Mrs Sweeney's in charge tonight,' he said to Donovan. 'I'll just ring her and tell her what I want. While I'm at it I'll ask her to meet you in the dispensary. Leave the injured party here with me. I'll make some coffee.'

'Please, no,' said Gretchen. 'I don't want to be a public nuisance.'

'Do as you're told,' Donovan said.

'You can be a private nuisance,' said Harry Moore. 'For there'll be just the two of us – and the coffee pot.'

'So,' said Donovan, on his return, 'has she been disturbing the peace?'

'She's not a drop of Irish blood,' said Moore. 'Which is to say I couldn't get a word out of her. But she's a great gift for listening.

'What have you got *there*?' he said, goggling at Donovan. 'The *entire* dispensary?'

'Mrs Sweeney has no faith in your heavy artillery,' said Donovan. 'She gave me enough gauze bandage to dress the wounds from now to New Year's Day.'

'Oh,' Moore said, 'we should be out of the woods by Christmas.'

He poured a cup of coffee for Donovan, gave Gretchen a shot of antibiotic, and bound up her arm.

'One shot every twelve hours – or as close as you can make it – for

77

five days,' he said to Donovan. 'Then I'll come by and have a look at her.

'No, don't override me,' he said to Gretchen. 'I've never yet put foot inside the Hall. Now I've a grand excuse to storm Miss Nellie's stronghold.'

All night it rained. In the morning the darkness had lifted a little, the first early hours were punctuated by soft showers which, every so often, stopped as if to give the thick clouds a chance to come together once again, to close out the sky. Gretchen was still at her breakfast when Donovan arrived; as he approached her the carpet squelched under his tread.

'Did you sleep with both windows open to a torrent of rain?' he said.

'One pair of windows won't open,' said Gretchen. 'The other pair won't shut.'

'I'll give Miss Nellie a piece of my mind before I leave,' said Donovan. 'And I'll send Tommy Dooley round this afternoon to see to the windows that won't shut. As for the carpet –'

'I've learnt how to get to the work-table without wetting my feet,' Gretchen said.

'How do you manage that?' said Donovan.

'If I remember to do it,' said Gretchen, 'I climb over the bed.'

Donovan took her temperature and gave her a shot of Moore's antibiotic.

'You've just a trace of fever,' he said. '*Don't* get your feet wet and don't overdo.'

Gretchen, who had every intention of taking a bath – cold or hot – and of going up Dufresne Hill with the letter she had been at pains to write to her mother, merely nodded.

'If you take a bath,' said Donovan, who was mercifully ignorant of the fact that there was no hot water in the Hall, 'be careful not to wet the dressing.'

'I will,' said Gretchen. Then he was gone.

After she had shuddered through the third icy bath she had taken in the dark chill bathroom she set off for the post-mistress, having ascertained from Mary that she would find her in a sweet-shop half-way up the hill.

The shop was remarkably small and remarkably dim and dirty. Each little packet of sweets was as dusty as if it had been there, in its place, for decades. The post-mistress, an elderly woman of ample hips and ample bosom, with a plain, pleasant face, beamed on Gretchen.

'You'll be the young lady from the Hall,' she said.

'Miss Nellie was so generous as to take me in,' said Gretchen.

'She's good-hearted in her way,' said the post-mistress. 'Although I wouldn't cross her, if I was you.'

Picking up Gretchen's letter she weighed it with the greatest care, chose several stamps of different colours, licked each one, and stuck it, crooked, on the envelope.

'Next time you'd do better to write just the few lines,' she said. 'For this is so heavy it'll cost you dear.'

As Gretchen walked into the entrance hall of the Hall the huge clouds opened up again and rivers of water fell from them.

'Come into the kitchen,' said Miss Nellie. 'Do. We always have elevenses in there with Mary.'

The kitchen was warm and steamy; the tea was hot and strong.

'How's the arm today?' said Seamus – catching Gretchen by surprise with such a friendly question.

'It really doesn't bother me,' Gretchen said. 'But it's kind of you to ask about it.'

'We can't any of us forget about it,' said Seamus, on a plaintive and far more characteristic note. 'Not with Clement Donovan popping in and out of here like a jack-in-the-box.'

'He's sendin' Tommy Dooley round this afternoon to fix those windows in your bedroom,' said Miss Nellie, to Gretchen. 'I all but told him I wouldn't have Tommy Dooley in the house, but he was off before I could catch my breath.'

'Couldn't Kevin do something about them?' Gretchen said.

'Kevin?' said Seamus. 'Kevin Who? Who's Kevin?'

'Sure she must be thinking of Paddy McClure, come for the laundry yesterday,' said Mary.

'I know of no Kevin hereabouts,' Miss Nellie said, propping a slice of pound-cake against the saucer of Seamus' cup.

After Seamus had left the kitchen Miss Nellie turned to Gretchen.

'We don't mention Kevin to Mr Taylor-Dufresne,' she said. 'He has no use for young people. To be sure, if I'd thought the windows in your room were imperfectly fitted I'd have put Kevin onto them before you came.'

Gretchen was mystified. She knew – from Donovan – that Seamus walked part-way up Dufresne Hill to the pub every morning at about eleven-thirty and returned to the Hall in the nick of time for lunch. She knew – from Kevin – that he, Kevin, did most of his work on the grounds.

'But on his comings and goings Mr Taylor-Dufresne must have caught sight of Kevin working outside the Hall,' said Gretchen.

'He has nothin' against the odd-job man, off and on,' Miss Nellie said. 'But he'd be deeply displeased if he came to find out that Kevin boards and lodges here. He'd insist on references which, of course, the poor boy hasn't got – bein' only seventeen.'

'I'm very sorry to have put my foot in it,' said Gretchen.

'How was you to know?' said Mary.

Gretchen lingered over a second cup of tea. Miss Nellie was sociable and full of gossip, some of which Mary corroborated with gusto.

In the afternoon she was looking over certain of her notes for the first part of her thesis and her sketch for the preface when Miss Nellie, with a bearded man in tow, rapped at her door.

'This is Mr Dooley,' said Miss Nellie. 'Come to see about the windows. Particularly the ones that leak.'

Mr Dooley inspected the leaking French windows at his leisure.

'Sure both halves will have to be taken down and stored in a place that's dry and properly heated,' he said. 'When they've shrunk back to size they'll close nicely.'

'And in the meantime?' said Miss Nellie.

'That's not my problem,' said Mr Dooley.

'Your advice is every bit as useful as your father's before you,' Miss Nellie said.

'I'm that proud to be a chip off the old block,' said Mr Dooley.

'You'll send me an estimate, naturally,' said Miss Nellie.

'If there's one thing I've always deplored,' Mr Dooley said, 'it's a waste of time.'

'Then you will be so good as to leave,' said Miss Nellie.

'The same notion had taken me,' said Mr Dooley. 'Believe it or not.'

'Mary McDaid's waitin' just outside,' Miss Nellie said. 'She will show you to the door.'

'Never fear,' Mr Dooley said. 'I could find my way out of here in the blind dark.'

'It's not,' said Miss Nellie, to Gretchen, when Mr Dooley had left, 'as if the *whole* carpet were soakin'.'

'No indeed,' said Gretchen.

'Orderin' me to throw the house open to the elements,' Miss Nellie said. 'I'll have somethin' to say to Clement Donovan this evenin'.'

Once Miss Nellie herself had departed, Gretchen turned back to her manuscript. None of her notes spurred her to a word, a phrase, a sentence and, for a long time, she simply stared at the sodden carpet and listened to the rain – and to the television, two flights below.

Miss Nellie was on the watch for Donovan when he appeared in the drawing-room.

'I sent the girl upstairs to lie down when dinner was over,' she said. 'She looked peaked to me. I told her I'd send coffee up to both of you.'

Mary brought in a tray while Donovan was taking Gretchen's temperature.

'We'll drink the coffee before I give you the shot,' he said. 'It would be a shame to let it get cold.'

'The coffee's good here,' said Gretchen. 'So's the tea. So's the honey. So is the bread, as a matter of fact.'

'Miss Nellie thought you looked peaked this evening,' said Donovan. 'Do you feel peaked?'

'I'm a little worried,' Gretchen said. 'I must get down to work, but I don't get down to work. Tomorrow I'll try to pretend that I'm *not* here.'

'Is it as bad as that?' said Donovan.

'It would be better if I could close my door,' she said. 'Seamus looks at television all afternoon. She makes him stop at tea-time. Then he's at it again until dinner-time. After dinner they both watch it till they go to bed. And Miss Nellie never talks to Mary about the work she wants done. She just stands on the stairs and shrieks at her until Mary shouts something back from the kitchen or the laundry. I wonder if I'll ever be able to think above all that racket.'

Donovan rose and studied the door.

'It's good and solid,' he said. 'If it were shut I doubt you could hear the television. Even Miss Nellie's screams might be blunted if it were shut. And it's a simple repair. I'll find someone to do the job as soon as possible. Did Tommy Dooley see to the windows?'

'He said the pair that won't close would have to be dismounted and stored somewhere where it could dry out and shrink back to its original dimensions,' said Gretchen. 'Miss Nellie was not amused.'

'It was a foolish choice on my part,' said Donovan. 'I'd quite forgotten how much bad blood there was between the Dufresnes and the Dooleys. There's an old quarrel behind them – over an outstanding debt, I daresay – that goes back to Tommy's father's time.'

In that case why did Mr Dooley come at all?' said Gretchen.

'Probably just to get close enough to spit in Miss Nellie's eye,' said Donovan.

'There certainly wasn't much love lost here this afternoon,' Gretchen said.

Donovan finished his coffee, saw that Gretchen had finished hers, and stood over the bed to give her the shot.

'You took a bath this morning?' he said.

'I did,' said Gretchen.

'Did you keep the dressing dry?' said Donovan.

'Oh, yes,' she said. 'I was careful about that.'

'Do the ancient water-works function in the Hall?' said Donovan.

'You have got to be joking,' Gretchen said.

Shortly thereafter Donovan understood why she had needed the red bucket. He had also learnt that there was no hot water in the house.

'The bucket answers for the flush,' he said. 'So I won't touch on that. But the lack of hot water is another story all together. I've never lost a battle to Miss Nellie yet and we've had a number of run-ins.

'Be a little patient, because tomorrow's Saturday and I can't muster my legions until Monday. But on Monday – unless I lose this round to Miss Nellie – I'll see to the door, I'll see to the windows, I'll see to the immersion heater.'

'Turn that thing off,' said Donovan to Seamus, and pointed at the television set. 'I need to talk to both of you.

'Now then,' he said, 'Tommy Dooley was a mistake and I admit it. While it's true that those windows might shrink in a warm, dry atmosphere, they'd only swell up again once re-installed. They must be scraped down in order that they may be closed against the rain. You cannot expect the girl to live in an apartment which is continually flooded.'

'And who's to pay for your scraping?' said Seamus.

'I've not finished,' said Donovan. 'There's also the matter of the noise – the television going full-blast night and day. I told you she had a thesis to write, I told you she needed tranquil surroundings. On Monday I'll be here myself with Joe Fallon, who'll see to the latch on that bedroom door and you, Seamus, will remember you've a guest in your house and you'll keep the volume low when you watch your programmes.'

'I'm hard of hearing,' Seamus said. 'I've to keep the volume up if I'm to catch the voices.'

'You're deaf as a post when it suits you,' said Donovan. 'The rest of the time your ears are sharp enough.

'So far,' he went on, 'I've only mentioned trifles. Now let me remind you that for thirty-five pounds a week Gretchen has every right to expect a hot bath once a day.'

'Billy O'Connell's been here three times in three days,' said Miss Nellie.

'And he won't be back,' said Mary, coming into the drawing room. 'Not until you've met his bills for the past four years. He as good as told me so – last Thursday was it? Or last Friday?'

'He had my assurance that any arrears would be paid up as soon as we had hot water again,' said Miss Nellie.

'It wasn't your assurance he was after,' Mary said.

'You're on your way home, I presume,' said Miss Nellie.

'I was,' said Mary. 'But when I heard Dr Donovan on the warpath I thought I might just bring up the rear. Hardship in the summers I'm used to. But I won't be sticking my hands into freezing water throughout a winter. That I won't.'

'This is one bullet you'll have to bite, Miss Nellie,' Donovan said. 'Now I've an old patient in Port Ferris who owes me a favour or two. I could have him here on Monday to size up the situation. Whatever is wanted, he'd make you a far better price for it than any so-called bargain you could strike in Ralston's Cove.'

'You'd best take him up on the offer,' said Mary, looking Miss Nellie smack in the eye.

'What are you thinkin' of to speak to me so?' said Miss Nellie.

'Oh,' said Mary, with a broad wink at Donovan, 'I must have been after thinking of twenty-five years of aches and pains at the Hall and never a ha'penny piece changing hands.'

'Dr Donovan is a very old friend of the family,' Miss Nellie said.

'All the same he's responsible for that poor girl upstairs,' said Mary. 'Blue with the cold she is every morning, God love her. But clean as a whistle notwithstanding.'

'Of course,' said Donovan, 'I could come by tomorrow and take her away from here.'

'There never was any question of passin' the winter with no hot water,' Miss Nellie said. 'And since Billy O'Connell's let me down I'll see your man from Port Ferris on Monday.'

'Let me drive you home,' said Donovan, to Mary.

Mary lived with her father – who was in his nineties – next door to the pub on Dufresne Hill.

'That was no rearguard action,' said Donovan, pulling up in front of Mary's house. 'You were in the vanguard all the way up and over the top.'

'She can't do without me,' Mary said. 'And well she knows it. Ten years ago I handed in me notice. Next day we'd the new cooker in the kitchen I was angling for. Since then, whenever 'tis desperate at the Hall, I walk out on her. She comes round before I'm half-way home.'

'I don't suppose,' said Donovan, 'that you could bring a kettleful of hot water up to the third floor in the mornings – just until this difficulty's been overcome? If you could persuade my patient to take a warm sponge bath for the next few days, I'd be much easier in my mind.'

'Will I tell her it's doctor's orders?' said Mary.

'You'd have to do better than that,' Donovan said. 'Ever since she landed in Ireland she's disobeyed me at every turn.'

'Then I'll threaten to show the red bucket to her Ladyship,' said Mary.

'Blackmail is often effective,' said Donovan.

By ten o'clock Saturday morning Donovan had been and gone, Mary had prevailed upon Gretchen to forego a full body bath in favour of a warm sponge bath – just for the next few days – Gretchen herself had rediscovered certain of her own deep resources, had faced a blank and uninviting sheet of lined paper, had worked steadily, blocking out the preface to her thesis. The noise of the gong at twelve-thirty startled her.

'I forgot to warn you we'd be lunchin' early today,' said Miss Nellie. 'All three of us will be off to the jumble sale at two o'clock whilst you'll be mistress of the Hall until dinner-time.'

'Then you'll miss your tea,' said Gretchen.

'We'll be takin' tea at the sale,' Miss Nellie said. 'That's another way we have of raisin' money – chargin' for tea.'

Gretchen would have liked to ask what the jumble sale was raising money for, but she feared Miss Nellie might find the question an impertinence.

When lunch was over she went back up to her room, anxious to get back to work again. At ten minutes of two Miss Nellie, in a carmine cloak, carrying a large black umbrella, knocked at her door.

'Your tea's laid out in the kitchen,' she said. 'All you have to do is put the kettle on to boil. Don't bother to answer the telephone. Anyone wantin' me can call back later. If anybody comes to the door tell him the family's not at home.'

'Wouldn't it be safer to lock the door and take the key?' said Gretchen. 'All the way up here I might not hear an intruder.'

'The door at the Hall is never locked until the family retires for the night,' said Miss Nellie.

Gretchen concentrated on her work until four o'clock, glorying in the vast silence which enveloped her. Then, momentarily stumped for an adjective, a mischievous idea sprang into her head. That afternoon might be, she thought, the only time she would ever find herself alone in the Hall, the only opportunity she might ever have to explore the west tower's secret spaces. Even though she knew that she had no right to invade Miss Nellie's private dominions, she rose and crept out into the corridor. Opposite her own room was a door which she had never seen ajar. Nervous, if resolute, she opened it – on darkness, through which the glow of the lamps in the hallway at her back barely filtered. After a minute or two, her eyes growing used to the lack of light, she made out two pairs of French windows – like hers which overlooked Dufresne Bay. These obviously looked north, and soon she had opened one pair of them, opened the shutters which had closed out the last, late-afternoon glimmer, and saw herself in a room which was almost completely black – black and white striped wall-paper, black carpet, black curtains, black bedspreads on the high twin beds, and carved ebony furnishings throughout. This, she rapidly concluded, must be the Chinese room to which Miss Nellie had once referred.

In a black cabinet she gazed at a row of exquisite rice-patterned plates in finest porcelain, two small sang-de-boeuf vases, a large bowl boldly decorated in red and black. On the mantel-shelf were several figures – old men with long beards who, she supposed, represented the Chinese immortals, women who might have been goddesses – in beautifully sculptured wood. On the writing table was a fat, seated jade Buddha with a huge green belly. All at once she sneezed and, on the heels of the sneeze, she saw the motes drifting on the breeze which had rushed into the room when she had opened the windows. With the tip of a finger she touched the surface of the writing table and ruefully took account of the deep imprint she had left in the dust.

'Even this room isn't cared for,' she said to herself. 'Even here nothing's clean.'

Quickly she closed the shutters, closed the windows, left the room and closed the door. Then furtive, cautious, all too well aware that she was trespassing, she went down one flight of stairs – where she grasped the lay-out at once. The door at the end of the corridor led into the bathroom – as she had reason to know – and now she realised that the bathroom must be directly underneath the 'airing-cupboard', while the other two doors, toward the middle of the corridor, corresponded to the doors on the floor above. One of the doors was not quite shut and, diffidently, she pushed it open. Instantly she knew that she was looking into Seamus' and Miss Nellie's bedroom – which she now remembered was underneath her own.

There were the south windows, looking out over the bay. There was the fireplace on the west wall – surely it must be on account of the chimney which both fireplaces presumably shared that she could hear every word which Miss Nellie and Seamus exchanged in the mornings and at their bed-time. There on the north wall was another imposing chest of drawers and, on the east wall, a great bed – headboard and

85

footboard sprouting fearful beasts with cloven hooves and grinning, human heads.

Since it would have been unforgivably indelicate to cross the threshold, Gretchen simply glanced about her, noting that the bed was unmade, that on Seamus' side of it – the assumption was a certainty, given two overflowing ashtrays on the night-table, given that Miss Nellie did not smoke – there were little mountains of science fiction and cheap crime novels, in paperback rising from the floor whereas, on Miss Nellie's side, towering piles of newspapers made the bed almost inaccessible. Two chairs heaped with cast-off clothing flanked the fireplace – which was plainly in use, as hers was not. Suddenly she stepped away, closed the door with a sharp click, and was relieved to turn her back on so much disorder, so much ugliness.

Across the corridor the second door led into another bedroom, this one clearly below the black Chinese room upstairs. A pair of shutters was not fastened, hence there was just enough light to afford her a glimpse of the interior. It was done in pink, a colour Gretchen abhorred, and the curtains, the flounced bedspreads, the shag rug were all frail and faded, some of them ripped where the old seams had given way. There were no mysteries in the room to excite Gretchen's interest and she closed the door on it firmly. But before she left the second floor she walked down the corridor to see if there were another cubby-hole of a room like the little room upstairs which Mary had described as 'the back of beyond'. Sure enough there was a door and the door gave onto a small space crammed waist-high with what Gretchen took to be everything broken or discarded in the Hall during the last hundred years. Two stopped clocks, various pots without handles, cracked platters, innumerable articles of clothing, long since out of fashion, a clutch of rusting toys, three babies' bottles, and stacks of the all-too-familiar newspapers caught her eye and she noted that all the refuse was thickly shrouded in cobwebs.

One flight down and she was at the doorway to the drawing-room, which she had already studiously observed. One more flight and she was on the ground floor in the entrance hall – wide open to the rain which had begun to fall heavily. On her right, on the west wall, were two doors, one of which was not shut. It led to a square room lined with bookshelves. Gretchen – ever on the alert for something to read – approached the books and pulled out a leather-bound volume at random. Once dislodged, no longer supported by its neighbours, it fell apart in her hands, and she saw that the binding and the spine were so clotted with mould that, from the outside, it was impossible to distinguish its title or the name of its author. Pausing to look more

closely at its companions, she recognised that the whole library was claimed to rot. It was with some difficulty that she replaced the book which she had taken down and when she had done so the strip of leather protecting its spine now dangled by a merest thread, in pitiful testimony of the disturbance she had effected. Discouraged – and dismayed by her hands, which strongly smelt of mould – she walked out of the room remarking, in her passage, a monumental flat-topped desk littered with correspondence and a telephone fixed to the wall beside the door-jamb.

The second door was shut on a narrow, unventilated lavatory with a wash-basin – sporting a cake of soap but no soap dish – two pegs from which two soiled hand-towels were hanging, and a lavatory with a wooden seat and an overhead tank bearing Charles Cutter's impress. The two conveniences – the lavatory and the wash-basin – did much to explain why she had yet to compete with either Seamus or with Miss Nellie for the bathroom on the second floor.

She had already seen the kitchen, having taken tea and biscuits there with Miss Nellie and Seamus and Mary, but that morning she had not seen it in detail. Now at her leisure – and no longer feeling either guilty or apprehensive, since Miss Nellie had invited her to make tea for herself if she pleased – she scrutinised it closely. Saucepans, frying pans, roasting pans, cauldrons were crusted with the remains of thousands of meals – stewed, boiled, simmered, baked, or fried. Cups and saucers – no two matching – soup-plates, dinner plates, salad plates, butter plates, cake plates, bowls, tumblers, wine glasses, serving platters, forks, knives, spoons were – every one of them – greasy, and many of them were chipped, cracked, or bent. Grease ringed the shallow kitchen sink, a greasy dish rag lay on the wooden drain-board. A scarred table with six scarred chairs stood in the centre of the room, a door paned like a window opened out to the north, a door on her left opened on darkness.

Gretchen found a light switch, and presently she was wandering through a warren of small rooms, one for the laundry, where she saw a pair of set-tubs, a washing machine with a hose attached to a tap in the wall at one end of itself, the other end drooping over the opening of the machine – an arrangement which proclaimed that the washer was not automatic, a proclamation confirmed by two large wringers, with long handles to turn the rollers, stationed over a hole in the floor covered by a wire grill. From the laundry she passed through a room where she glanced at an ironing board and a sewing machine with treadles. Then, at the bottom of a small hallway, she came up against a venerable refrigerator, its motor exposed and poised on the top of the appliance. Off the hallway she had a glimpse of a woodshed and, returning to the kitchen by a narrow passage, she stopped to consider what was clearly a larder.

Suddenly she was swept by memories of home, of her mother's larder, of crocks and jars filled with cookies and doughnuts, of the great bread-bin, full of fresh-baked bread and rolls, or the large round tins where she had always been certain to find left-over layer-cakes or the remains of a pie, of the long shelf under the window with different kinds of cheese on cheese-boards and bowls of fruits in season. Miss Nellie's larder was all the more shocking after her wave of nostalgia for, in Miss Nellie's larder, on shelf after shelf, she saw enormous cardboard drums containing – if she were to believe. the labels – powdered vegetables, powdered potatoes, powdered soups, powdered custards, powdered pudding which required – again according to their labels – no more than the addition of milk or water or an ocasional egg, five to ten minutes of simmering or heating through and, presto!, the soups or the potatoes or the vegetables or the desserts were ready for the table. There was nothing fresh or homemade in the larder. Nothing at all.

Back in the kitchen she put the water on to boil. True to her word Miss Nellie had left the teapot, the tea caddy, a small pitcher of milk, two slices of bread, a jar of honey, and a cup and saucer out on a tray. Revolted by the kitchen, by the larder, depressed by the antique refrigerator, the laundry, the pressing room, Gretchen waited restlessly for the water to boil. When her tea was ready she made short work of it, anxious to leave the back rooms of the Hall behind her as soon as possible. It was while she was washing up the tea things that a new idea visited her and, when she had left the kitchen tidy, she turned on the lights in the passage-way which led to the dining-room and there she dwelt on painting after painting.

'I'm not half-witted,' she said to herself. 'And I'm sure I haven't lost my mind. But what could be the reason for all this chicanery?'

As she was slowly returning to the west tower she remembered her rendez-vous with Kevin on the third floor.

'What a fool I am,' she said, when she saw him sitting in the corridor. 'I made tea for myself and it never occurred to me to look for you to share it with me.'

'I'll make my own when we've done with Solomon,' he said. 'I know where Mary keeps everything.'

'It would have been much nicer if we'd had it together,' said Gretchen. 'But, to tell you the truth, I was in a hurry to get out of the kitchen. It turned me off.'

'Did it now?' said Kevin. 'Why was that?'

'It's filthy,' Gretchen said.

'Kitchens are all the same,' said Kevin.

With a start Gretchen remembered that Kevin – even though, from the first, she had looked on him as an ally – was himself Irish.

'Let's get on to Solomon,' she said, searching for common ground.

'We'll have to do him up here, if it's all the same to you,' said Kevin. 'For she's cut the power in the west wing. A needless extravagance she said it was and the electricity bills so high.'

'But what about you?' said Gretchen. 'She can't mean you to live there in the dark.'

'I'm to have candles,' Kevin said. 'And she lent me a torch. It would come in handy, I must say, if the batteries wasn't dead.'

Miss Nellie and Seamus and Mary returned from the jumble sale at about seven o'clock – by which time it was raining softly. Dinner was ready at eight. Donovan came by after dinner and again the next morning, after Gretchen's breakfast. When Donovan had departed Miss Nellie turned up in Gretchen's doorway. She was dressed in a dark blue suit with black facings on the collar and cuffs, conventional stockings, and low-heeled, dark blue shoes with buckles.

'Would you like to come to church with me this morning?' she said.

'It's very thoughtful of you to think of me,' said Gretchen, who was planning to attack her thesis immediately, 'but –'

'Then that's settled,' said Miss Nellie. 'We'll meet downstairs at a quarter to eleven.'

There might have been twenty people in the little church; all of them were elderly, most of them looked feeble. The walls, except where tall stained-glass windows interrupted them, were covered with long marble plaques, the large part of them inscribed – as Gretchen was to discover later on when, on a balmy spring afternoon she visited the church alone – with the annals of the Dufresnes, beginning with the arrival of the first Edward at the end of the sixteenth century.

The vicar's text was from I Corinthians, Chapter Thirteen. 'When I was a child, I spake as a child, I understood as a child, I thought as a child: but when I became a man, I put away childish things.' Gretchen stared at every face she could see and suddenly, irreverently, it occurred to her that the vicar was preaching in vain that, in all probability, not one of his faltering congregation had yet become a man – or a woman. And so little time was left for any of them to grow up.

'Will I be grown up before I die?' she asked herself, and thought of her mother. Then, although he was in no way connected to her mother, she thought of Dr Donovan. Both of them had certainly put away childish things. Possibly Miss Nellie – despite her eccentric housekeeping and her parsimonious ways – had grown up too. Seamus, of course, was an infant, but then Seamus was a Roman Catholic and Roman Catholics, Gretchen reflected, were not encouraged to be adults.

After the service a pale sun made a brief showing. Miss Nellie and all the others clustered round the vicar on the church steps. Gretchen drifted away from them and found that the church was set in the middle of a simple graveyard surrounded, on three sides, by meadows. Many of the graves were marked by slabs and Gretchen instantly decided to come back there, with her folder and her yellow pad, whenever the weather was fine. For there she could sit comfortably beside a slab and work, free of the hubbub in the Hall and, probably, unremarked by anyone. Just as she had arrived at the decision, a cloud passed over the sun, a few drops of rain began to fall, and the congregation dispersed rapidly.

'What did you think of the sermon?' said Miss Nellie, as they hastened toward the Hall.

'Saint Paul holds up well, doesn't he?' said Gretchen – a little vague because her eye was on the blue bird nestling in a mist of blue veiling on Miss Nellie's head. 'I've never seen such a pretty hat,' she said.

'It was my mother's,' said Miss Nellie. 'But it suited me, so I kept it.'

The evening brought Donovan. The following morning, Monday, brought Donovan again with a carpenter, who dismounted the French windows in Gretchen's room and planed the two sides which fitted into the door-frame. Back in position they came neatly together and could be securely locked against a strong wind or a driving rain. He also replaced the latch on the bedroom door, after which the door could be easily, and tightly, shut. Indeed, when he had finished, Gretchen could no longer hear the altercations between Miss Nellie and the man who, Gretchen supposed, must be Dr Donovan's electrician, the hero from Port Ferris who was to save the day. All the same Miss Nellie had been screeching like a parrot with colic.

'Tomorrow,' said Donovan, when he came by again to give Gretchen the evening's shot, 'you'll be able to have a hot bath by afternoon, God willing. For Miss Nellie's knuckled under – not without a courageous last-ditch stand in the boiler-room, or so Mary tells me.'

90

'I heard some of it,' said Gretchen.

'All the way up here?' he said.

'All the way up here,' said Gretchen. 'But when your carpenter man left – he was a god-send, by the way – I shut the door and since then I've hardly heard a sound. Just the faintest murmur of the television – not strong enough to bother me. So tomorrow will find me hard at work, I hope – with no more distractions.

'There won't be any more distractions – or hardships,' said Donovan. 'Mary and I have seen to that.'

Twenty-four hours later he had sworn off prophecies for the rest of his life, but that evening, on his way home, he was pleased with his efforts. Meanwhile Gretchen was in some perplexity. Everything he had done – or had caused to be done – had been for her comfort and her well-being. Before she fell asleep she taxed herself with questions. Why was he so solicitous about her? What difference did it make to him if the hue and cry in the Hall was insupportable, if she could or could not pretend to a hot bath? Could he imagine how guilty she felt when she thought of all the favours which she had more or less taken for granted?

Just the same the situation *had* been intolerable –

'That's what I'll tell him when I write to thank him,' she said, and was a little shocked to hear her voice so loud in the darkness.

8

On Tuesday, in the morning, Mary with the breakfast tray was followed by Donovan with his syringe, who was followed by Miss Nellie, once again attired in her church-going costume, in the dark-blue suit with the black facings – an indication, or so it seemed to Gretchen, that she was preparing for certain formalities in the course of the day.

'Would you be very much put out if I asked you to take a little picnic lunch here in your room at one o'clock?' said Miss Nellie. 'The vicar and Dr and Mrs Carroll and Mr and Mrs Chilcott are comin' to luncheon – Mrs Chilcott had been tottin' up the profits from the jumble sale and, in the beginnin', they were earmarked for the church roof. The Carrolls and the Chilcotts and I are hopin' to have it completely repaired, but there's been some squabblin' amongst the flock. The Thurlows would prefer to spend the proceeds scrapin' the lichen off the gravestones because the old inscriptions are illegible by now, and the Manders and their cohorts are worryin' about the organ. But the vicar is the linch-pin –'

Gretchen was able to make her contribution to Miss Nellie's project when Miss Nellie ran out of wind.

'I'd love to picnic up here,' she said. 'I can easily see that I'd be excess baggage at lunch.'

'That's most kind of you,' said Miss Nellie. 'Most kind. Shall we say that when you hear the gong you will simply pop down to the kitchen for your tray which will be ready for you to carry up here?'

Gretchen worked on her thesis, more and more deeply engaged with a paragraph which refused to take on a meaningful – or even an agreeable – shape. In the end, defeated, she tore up every line she had scribbled and acknowledged the necessity to change course.

'If I can't get at it from this angle,' she thought, 'I'll just have to try it from another.'

She had risen from her work-table, had stretched and flexed her cramped muscles when, from somewhere in the distance beyond the Hall there was a thunderous, reverberating crash. Shocked to think that so momentous a sound might possibly have originated in Dufresne Village, she stepped out onto her baclony. As she did so she heard the gong, portentously echoing, but since it was not herself who was summoned to the dining-room she remained on the balcony, peering west, her eyes searching the driveway of the Hall. At first there was nothing to see; then, just inside the gates which marked the access to the Dufresne properties, she saw – indistinctly – a cluster of moving objects. As the cluster proceeded toward the west tower she began to perceive individual forms and slowly, in horrified amazement, she recognised that the seething mass was, in fact, a drove of hogs, scuttling down the drive. When she had realised that the advance guard was lost to view directly beneath her balcony, that the drove was not continuing forward to the east tower, she suddenly understood, with a dreadful certainty that – since the front door was wide from early morning to late at night – the pigs must be literally breaching the west tower itself.

'None of this had anything to do with me,' she said to herself, as she turned back into the room. 'I'm deaf, I'm dumb, I'm blind, I'm working on my thesis. My thesis is all that matters –'

From somewhere in the depths of the tower she heard a scream, a scream which, undoubtedly, came from Mary. In an instant, her thesis forgotten, Gretchen was racing down the stairs. She had passed the drawing-room when she was summarily arrested by another scream. There and then she knew, without hesitation, that both cries had come from the kitchen. As soon as she reached the stair-landing below the drawing-room she saw the entrance hall bursting with the animals and she hastened down the last steps. Her back to the west wall, she inched her way to the kitchen door, shoved, jostled, all but trampled – yet mercifully ignored – by the surging beasts.

When she arrived at the kitchen at least twenty hogs were ravenously milling about – apparently excited by the dense odours of cooking with which the air was choked. They had already overturned the chairs and the table and, before she had moved from the doorway, they overturned the garbage bin. Grunting angrily they battled for the scraps and scrapings spilled out on the floor – amidst coffee grounds, tea leaves, chop bones, and cigarette butts. Yet it was not the internecine warfare over the garbage which gripped Gretchen in a spasm of terror but the hysteria with which Mary, hemmed in on all sides at the stove, was desperately lifting the soup cauldron, from which a furious cloud of steam was rising. Then, in a second, she had dumped its contents over the backs of the two pigs nearest to her.

Pandemonium ensued. The two scalded hogs, whose squeals might have been heard for miles beyond the Hall, beat a frenzied retreat, charging their way through the mindless horde, thrusting toward the kitchen door where, dazzled with pain, they dashed down the passage leading to the east tower and the dining-room. So much Gretchen had observed but, at the same time, she was aware that their demented departure had left – for a barest moment – a clearing. With all her strength she flung herself into the clearing, kicked and pummelled left and right as she struggled toward the stove, grasped Mary by an arm and – pulling and dragging her formidable bulk forward to the open door – miraculously reached the entrance hall.

There she and Mary were again engulfed in a vortex of swine but the hall was more spacious and less cluttered than the kitchen and, with a force she had never suspected she had, she succeeded in hauling Mary through, around, or past the wheeling pigs until they came to the foot of the staircase. Supporting most of Mary's weight she staggered up the stairs, leaving the marauders churning below. Finally she gained the drawing-room where, when she had pushed Mary down onto a chair, she released her hold and stood over her, gasping for breath.

It was a while before she noticed that Mary's high colour had been replaced by a dead pallor. Unnerved, she ran to the cupboards where she believed Miss Nellie kept her liquors and there, hidden away at the very back, she found what she had hoped to find – a bottle of cognac, almost full. The luncheon guests had left their empty sherry glasses on the little tables. Gretchen seized one of those, filled it with cognac, and held it to Mary's lips.

93

'Swallow this before you faint, Mary,' she said. 'Swallow it, for pity's sake.'

Mary drained the glass and leant her head against the chair. Her pallor was startling but the faint smile she turned on Gretchen was a wordless promise that – little by little – she would get herself in hand.

'There's nothing to be frightened of any more,' said Gretchen. 'They certainly won't try the stairs so you're perfectly safe here. Just rest. I'll leave you the glass and the bottle –'

She was determined to go back upstairs to her own room and her own world while her feet, out of step with her brain, started downstairs. Pausing on the landing above the entrance hall she was struck by the fact that the invaders had increased in number, that many of them were injured and bleeding freely, that some of them limped on three legs, and most of them were squealing pathetically, and that there was a gaggle of men and housewives and children on the threshold.

'This is the living end,' she said, aloud. 'How could I – how could anybody – do any serious work in this hell-hole? I won't be mixed up in any more of this. I won't –'

But angry and upset as she was, she could not quite forget Mary. Possibly it was unwise to leave her alone, possibly she ought to bring Miss Nellie up to the drawing-room.

Once more she made a way for herself through the band of hogs – an amazing feat when she thought back on it – and fled down the passageway to the dining-room. Miss Nellie and Seamus and their guests were still sitting at the table while the two crazed scalded hogs circled round and round the room with astonishing speed. For once Miss Nellie was clearly not mistress of a situation; she simply sat, pale, – but not so pale as Mary – in silent horror. Then both pigs abruptly began to roll on the floor, shrieking in anguish.

At that moment Seamus – conceivably supposing that the beasts were now *hors de combat* – rose from his chair. Simultaneously both pigs found their feet again and recommenced their lunatic circling. One of them collided with Seamus, who instantly measured his length on the carpet, after striking his head against a corner of the table in his fall. That galvanized Miss Nellie, who jumped up, scuttled across the room, and knelt by Seamus. Presently, lifting her eyes, she caught sight of Gretchen.

'He's hurt himself,' she said. 'Get me some ice at once.'

Gretchen, perfectly well aware that she could never navigate the narrow hall-way off the kitchen – where the refrigerator stood – unless the villagers had chased away the hogs, prayed that, at the very least, she could get to the upstairs bathroom whence she could bring

Miss Nellie some cold, wet cloths. When she had sped down the corridor to the west tower – all thought of Mary having escaped her mind – she was just in time to see a cocky boy standing close to the kitchen with a shot-gun in his hands – his back shielded by the door-frame.

'This should drive out the lot of them,' he said, and fired at the ceiling.

Upon the explosion the hogs in the entrance hall, barred from the front door by the crowd of shouting, gesticulating villagers, and barred from the kitchen – long since overflowing with their swarming brethren – trapped and panic-stricken, began to scamper up the stairs, tripping and falling over each other and shrieking defiance as they climbed.

It was then that Gretchen had a glimpse of Kevin leading five stocky farmers in caps and boots, each carrying a stout stick.

'Make way,' said Kevin to the crowd at the entrance and, as soon as there was no longer any barrier at the door, the farmers, clubbing the animals' back-sides and bawling at them, almost in unison, had cleared the hall.

'Now we'll shut that door,' said Kevin, 'and we'll go on to the kitchen.'

Gretchen, thinking that if the kitchen were evacuated she might, perhaps, be able to reach the refrigerator, followed in the farmers' wake. Two of them, prodding their way through a host of pigs, managed to get as far as the door opening out to the north and, after two or three minutes, while the other men beat, kicked and whacked the hogs, the kitchen, too, was clear.

'Kevin,' said Gretchen, 'there's quite a number of them upstairs.'

'Glory be to God,' said one of the farmers.

A little later she had reached the refrigerator, had found a small tray of minute ice-cubes – 'I wonder where her Ladyship keeps her microscope,' she had said – had wrapped them up in a tea-towel, and returned to the dining-room.

'Staunch the blood,' said Miss Nellie, and rose from her knees. 'I must telephone for help directly.'

'Let us try to keep calm,' said the vicar to the four guests – who had not left their places – while the scalded hogs careered wildly in one direction, then in another.

'Don't be upset, Mr Taylor-Dufresne,' said Gretchen, after she had pulled Seamus underneath the table to shelter him from the racing beasts. 'Your head is bleeding, but it looks to be nothing but a scalp wound.'

'I'm not upset,' said Seamus, in a strong voice. Whereat in angry – and in stronger – vein he said, 'Why doesn't someone get those damn pigs out of here?'

'Someone will be coming soon,' said Gretchen.

'I want Nellie,' said Seamus.

'She'll be here soon,' said Gretchen.

'She'll be here when it suits her,' said Seamus. 'Not a minute earlier, not a minute later.'

His colour was good, his breathing deep and even, his stare steady, his voice powerful, his words distinct.

'Call Nellie,' he said, very loudly indeed.

The visitors were still seated in their chairs and clutching the table for greater stability, in the event of a direct change. Gretchen was still pressing her cloth firmly against Seamus' wound. The two hogs were, momentarily, rolling on the floor again, both of them emitting squeals as piercing as a policeman's whistle – when Donovan, black bag in hand, walked into the dining-room with Miss Nellie leading the way. Gretchen ceded her place to Donovan, who went down on his knees to examine Seamus' injury.

'He'll never walk again,' said Miss Nellie, on a stiff, frozen note.

Even before she had time to be astounded by so bald a declaration, Gretchen caught the look exchanged between Seamus and Miss Nellie. In the electric darting of that look Gretchen understod that perfect comprehension had been instantly established between them. Seamus closed his eyes with the despairing air of a man who has seen death approaching, while Donovan glanced at Miss Nellie, and Gretchen, baffled, could almost have sworn that he was smiling.

'Noted,' said Donovan.

Hardly three minutes had gone by before two young men in white uniforms came into the dining-room. They were carrying a stretcher and had been preceded by Kevin and three booted farmers. The farmers still had their sticks and Kevin had found a broom somewhere.

'Afternoon, Miss Nellie,' said one of the farmers.

'Good afternoon, Mike,' said Miss Nellie.

'We've come to clear the way for the lads with the stretcher,' Mike said. 'Two of us'll go before and two of us'll go behind in such a way as Mr Taylor-Dufresne'll be safe as houses.'

'Are there still hogs on the loose in the west tower?' said Donovan.

'There's several on the first floor,' said Mike. 'Turned ugly.'

'After you've seen my husband into the ambulance,' Miss Nellie said, 'would you come back and help my guests to their cars and the vicar up the vicarage?'

'We will, of course,' said Mike.

Another of the farmers spoke up – most reasonably, it seemed to Gretchen.

'When we've done wouldn't it be only decent to put them two animals out of their misery?' he said, to Miss Nellie, and pointed to the pair of writhing hogs.

'No!' said Miss Nellie, and the one word she spat sounded like the crack of a pistol. '*Nothin'* is to be touched in the Hall. *Nothin'*. That is an order.'

'Very good, then. Very good,' said the farmer thus rebuked.

Two men slowly led the way down the long corridor. Behind them went the stretcher-bearers – with Seamus lying dead still on the stretcher. Kevin and the third farmer came after the stretcher-bearers, then Miss Nellie, leaning on Donovan's arm, while last – and quite alone – came Gretchen. When the procession reached the entrance hall the farmers, the stretcher-bearers and Kevin walked out of the west tower toward the ambulance.

'I want to speak to you,' said Miss Nellie, to Donovan.

'Go and tell Seamus to be of good cheer,' said Donovan. 'I'll meet you outside.'

The moment she had left the tower he turned to Gretchen.

'I'll take you out for dinner,' he said. 'I'll be here as close to seven-thirty as I can make it.'

Gretchen gave him a nod and steadied herself against the draw-table.

'Now I'll just go and have a word with the lads on the ambulance,' said Donovan. 'Rest if you can and expect me at half-past seven.'

Gretchen rested, in a manner of speaking, where she was, by the draw-table. Five stunned hogs lay at the foot of the staircase and there were sounds of a continuing struggle one flight up. Kevin and the three farmers who had defended Seamus on the stretcher returned. The farmers stepped over or between the prostrate beasts and took the stairs. Kevin stopped beside Gretchen.

'I never was much for pigs,' he said.

'How many of them are still up there?' said Gretchen.

'Only two or three, I'd say,' said Kevin. 'But they're mean now and when they're mean they're dangerous.'

'Oh, Kevin,' Gretchen said, '*Mary's* in the drawing-room.'

'No, she's not,' said Kevin. 'I myself took her upstairs and put her in the pink room. And I took care to close the door on her.'

'Thank goodness for that,' said Gretchen. 'Did you take up the bottle and the glass I left with her?'

'I call to mind a bottle,' he said. 'She wasn't about to let it go.'

'We really should search both floors above the drawing-room,' said Gretchen. 'Before these able-bodied men get away from us.'

'I'll do that,' said Kevin. 'You stay here where you're protected until I get back.'

He was hardly out of sight when Miss Nellie came into the entrance hall and cautiously shut the front door behind her. She made a *moue* of disgust when she saw the stupefied hogs at the bottom of the stairs.

' "What can't be helped must be endured",' she said. 'At least the ambulance and Clement Donovan in his car are well on their way to the hospital.'

The noises of heavy-booted feet and chairs and tables knocked every which way had been growing more and more ominous. At length all five of the farmers came down the stairs and removed their caps when they saw Miss Nellie.

'There's two of them up there clean off their heads,' said the one whom Miss Nellie had earlier addressed as Mike. 'Only that the room's so big we weren't killed entirely. As it was we'd space enough to dodge when they came at us. But you'll never get them out of there alive.

'Now if you was to lend me Mr Taylor-Dufresne's revolver and plenty of ammunition –'

'Hark,' said Miss Nellie. 'Here come the Gardaí.'

She vanished into the library, returned in a trice with a gun and a small box which she gave to Mike, while all of them listened to the sound of an automobile stopping on the drive. Instantly Miss Nellie opened the door to admit three men in uniform.

'Before we discuss this atrocity, Jack,' she said, to the first of them, 'would you go up one flight to my drawin'-room? Mike's armed. He'll do the necessary, but only with the three of you there to witness the slaughter.'

'Do you know,' said one of the farmers, 'we've forgotten the parson and your guests in the dining-room all together.'

'We must go to them at once,' Miss Nellie said.

As four farmers and Miss Nellie set off down the passage Gretchen heard a volley of shots overhead and saw Kevin coming down the stairs.

'That's done for the worst of them,' said Kevin. 'And there's none of them on the second floor or on the third.'

'There are two in the dining-room,' said Gretchen.

'It seems Miss Nellie's taken a fancy to those,' Kevin said.

Dr and Mrs Carroll, Mr and Mrs Chilcott, the vicar, the four farmers, and Miss Nellie came down the passage from the dining-room and arrived at the entrance hall where the law, having accomplished the mission in the drawing-room, was waiting with Mike. Even the presence of the police did not deflect Miss Nellie from lengthy apologies nor her aged guests from the commiseration which Miss Nellie's present circumstances required. It was the vicar who put an end to what promised to be an interminable social exchange.

'We mustn't keep you,' he said, to Miss Nellie. 'You've much to attend to.'

'But you must not hesitate to call on us at any hour,' said Mrs Chilcott.

'At *any* hour,' said Mrs Carroll. 'We forbid you to stand on ceremony.

Miss Nellie insisted on seeing them off. Three of the farmers dispersed the villagers gathered by the long wall which stood between the Hall and the sea, thus making a way for the Carrolls and the Chilcotts to reach their cars and drive slowly toward the gates, while the fourth farmer escorted the vicar, who was making his escape on foot. Those duties discharged, Miss Nellie returned to her post.

'Come along with me into the dinin'-room,' she said to the Gardaí, and to Mike. 'There are two more brutes to dispatch in there before we can get down to business.'

Left with Kevin, Gretchen turned to him.

'What happened?' she said. 'How did it happen?'

'Step outside and I'll show you,' said Kevin.

'Is every man, woman, and child from Dufresne Village here?' said Gretchen, as they walked down the driveway.

'Every one as has the use of his legs,' Kevin said. 'It's not a bad thing, if you come to consider it. For all the folk between here and the foot of Dufresne Hill should keep the hogs from the Hall – for the time being.'

Shots rang out as they went along.

'Miss Nellie will have ordered those two animals in the dining-room put out of their misery,' said Kevin.

At the foot of Dufresne Hill the sight which met Gretchen's eyes distressed her so that she clutched Kevin's arm fiercely enough to make him wince.

'Easy does it,' he said. 'If you can't stand to look at it I'll take you back to the Hall and all the way up to your room, where you could lie down if you'd a mind to.'

But Gretchen, who was wishing herself a thousand miles from Dufresne Bay, could not tear her eyes from the catastrophe at the foot of the hill, where injured hogs lay squealing piteously, where an enormous trailer truck lay overturned and the doors at the back, which should have been shut on its cargo – the pigs – were yawning.

'The way I see it,' said Kevin, 'he ran smack into the base of the monument and it tipped over.'

Only then did Gretchen remember the marble horse and the marble rider and, rounding the van with Kevin, she saw that the horse and rider had toppled off their pedestal and fallen on the cab, crushing it almost completely.

'Is the driver in there?' she said.

'He is,' said Kevin. 'A crane's been sent for to lift the statue away from the cab so someone can get at the poor man.'

'Is he alive?' said Gretchen.

'Oh, no,' Kevin said. 'You're looking at the last of him.'

'Let's get away from here,' said Gretchen.

But to go back to the Hall they had to walk around the van again.

'There's plenty of pigs left in there,' said Kevin. 'Too badly hurt to make a dash for it.'

'That's cruel,' said Gretchen.

'What beats me,' said Kevin, 'is how those heavy metal doors flew apart like that. Sure they could never have been properly bolted in the first place.'

'Do you think the brakes failed when the truck was coming down the hill?' Gretchen said.

'It's a possibility,' said Kevin. 'Myself, I think he was drunk from the time he took off this morning.'

'Why should you think a thing like that?' said Gretchen.

'Because if he'd been sober he'd have seen to it that those doors were bolted,' Kevin said. 'And then again, what was he doing in Dufresne Village when the road comes to a dead stop at the gates to the Hall?'

'Perhaps he had a girl in the village,' said Gretchen.

'He was never going courting with a load of hogs,' said Kevin. 'No, he started out from somewhere in the west for Port Ferris – that's where he must have been headed, that's where the slaughter-houses are. He'd have been on the main road running west to east. There's a branch off that four miles out of Dufresne Village and he'll have been so liquored up he'll have taken the branch road instead of continuing on the highway straight to Port Ferris.'

'He couldn't have been drunk first thing in the morning,' Gretchen said.

'When an Irishman wants a drink he doesn't look at his watch,' said Kevin.

It was mid-afternoon when Kevin and Gretchen returned to the Hall. By four o'clock Gretchen was in sole charge of Miss Nellie's kingdom. There had been some skirmishing between Miss Nellie and the Gardaí. Miss Nellie wanted nothing removed, righted or repaired until a police stenographer had listed the damages, room by room, corridor by corridor, stair by stair, and a police photographer had taken pictures throughout, with particular emphasis on the two dead hogs in the drawing-room, the two dead hogs in the dining-room, and the five hogs at the bottom of the staircase, which had also been shot. The Gardaí were willing to oblige Miss Nellie but not until after dark. The chief of them had telephoned to his superior at Ravensbrook to ask for instructions and had been advised that, for the protection of the inhabitants of Dufresne Village and *environs*, any hogs which were too mettlesome to be driven into an enclosed space, such as a barn or a store-house, must be put down before nightfall. Once night had fallen, such of the force in Ralston's Cove as could be spared was to come to the assistance of anyone who required it at the Hall. Miss Nellie, who had assumed that affairs at the Hall must take precedence over any other affairs wheresoever, was very much piqued.

'I never supposed you'd desert me, Jack, in an hour of need,' she said.

'We're not deserting you, Miss Nellie,' said Jack. 'We're just postponing the matter to take advantage of the light while it lasts. Sure with the help of all the lads hereabouts we should be able to round up the pigs very smartly.

'When may I expect you?' said Miss Nellie.

'We'll work outdoors till the light fails us all together,' said Jack. 'Then we'll have a break for tea to brace us a bit. Then we'll be here with a stenographer of sorts and a photographer – Ravensbrook's lining them up for us now.'

'I must go to the hospital,' Miss Nellie said. 'Mr Taylor-Dufresne has been very seriously injured. Very seriously indeed. When you come back someone will let you in – if I'm detained in Ralston's Cove. Can I rely on you to wait for me if I'm slightly delayed?'

'We'll all be here till cock-crow if necessary,' said Jack.

'Then you may go,' Miss Nellie said.

'Could I tag along and give you a hand?' said Kevin.

'You'd be welcome,' said Jack.

When the Gardaí and Kevin had gone, Miss Nellie went upstairs to pack a small valise with personal oddments for Seamus, and to fetch her coat, her hat and her hand-bag. Since she had told Gretchen to stay where she was, Gretchen waited.

101

'Would you be so good as to call Mary?' Miss Nellie said, as she came down the stairs.

'Mary's resting,' said Gretchen. 'She was faint after the tussle with the pigs in the kitchen.'

'Then I shall have to trust to you,' said Miss Nellie. 'In the middle drawer of my desk you'll find a large key. Brin' it here, would you?'

Gretchen went into Miss Nellie's library, opened the middle drawer of the desk, found the key and brought it to Miss Nellie.

'With this,' Miss Nellie said, 'you will lock the front door when I'm gone. Pocket the key – so that I can get in with my own when I return – and let no one in, if not Kevin or the Gardaí. Touch nothin'. Put nothin' to rights. Every crack, every chip must be photographed and verified by the law. You understand that *all* the evidence must be undisturbed until the work is done. There's tens of thousands of pounds worth of damage. I shall sue for every penny that's comin' to me.'

Then she smiled. Gretchen locked the door after she had left and reflected that she had not seen Miss Nellie smile before.

Standing by the door with the long key in her hand, Gretchen realised that she had no idea what to do with herself. She was worn and weary but far too agitated to rest.

'None of this is true,' she said to herself. 'None of it could have happened. And it's no use my thinking that it could only have happened in Ireland – even if I hate Ireland, which I probably do – because these events were impossible, are impossible, would be impossible *anywhere*. I won't believe in them. I won't. I can't. My sanity's at stake. And I'm still too young to be locked up raving.'

But all the while five dead hogs were lying at the foot of the staircase, not twenty feet from where she was standing.

'I must try to put my mind on something else,' she said.

Immediately she rememered that Dr Donovan was coming for her at seven-thirty. The remembrance comforted her; she shifted her weight and leaned against the front door, feeling a little less stiff than she had felt a moment earlier. None the less there were over three hours to kill before his arrival.

With the door closed on the entrance hall the only light which reached it came from the windows in Miss Nellie's library. Oppressed by the shadowy corners, the shadowed shapes of the paintings on the walls, the draw-table, the umbrella stand, Gretchen pressed the light switch. For a split second there was light and then, on the sound of a sharp report from the back of the tower, the light went out. On the same split second Gretchen smelt smoke.

As fast as she could she rushed to the kitchen, itself darkening in the gathering dusk, and saw plumes of smoke wreathing the oven door, red flames leaping behind the glass and, on the top of the stove, three saucepans – rocking with heat – boiled dry, their contents black and smoking.

Instinct warned her, even if it were possible, not to open the oven door, not to feed the encaged fire with the air it needed for its life. Making a thick wad of two tea-towels and the dish-cloth, to protect her hand, she managed to lift the saucepans off the stove and dump them into the kitchen sink. Actuated by terror, she regained Miss Nellie's library, found the telephone book for the area, and called the fire department in Ralston's Cove. And then, with the awful threat still confined to the kitchen, she stepped over the hogs at the foot of the stairs, climbed to her room, grabbed her winter coat, her purse, with all her money and her travellers' cheques, and rammed her notes and her burgeoning manuscript into a suitcase. It was not until she was on the ground floor that it occurred to her that she was no longer holding the key to the front door. Luck was with her, for she discovered it on the drain-board of the kitchen sink where, she supposed, she must have put it down as she prepared to deal with the saucepans. When she had unlocked the front door and hurried outside, hugging her purse and dragging her suitcase, she sat down on the sea wall and waited. Somewhere in the distance, not very far off, she could already hear the rising whine of a siren.

'That's it,' she said. 'Come along, fellows. Come along. Little Miss Goody Two-Shoes is expecting you –'

'You've a head on your shoulders,' said the man she took to be the chief of the brigade. 'Many another woman would have tried to douse that fire in the oven and the jig would have been up.'

'I was afraid the least draught would be my undoing,' said Gretchen.

'And so it might have been,' he said.

'But please don't leave me,' said Gretchen, 'until you've had a look at the fuse-box. There's a short circuit, I think – the fire could have caused that, I guess – but, as you see, everything in the Hall is so far out of date that I can't help wondering whether the wiring might not be overheated too. And that would be another hazard.'

By the help of his flashlight he and Gretchen found the fuse-panel – above the refrigerator.

'I wouldn't say there was more than ten or twenty violations there,' said the chief, coming down the ladder he had brought from the engine.

'What *can* be done?' said Gretchen, thinking of the return of Miss Nellie, of the police, and of all the damage to verify in total darkness.

'Tomorrow,' said the chief –

'Tomorrow won't do,' Gretchen said.

Hastily she sketched the disaster which had overtaken the Hall, she told him that the police were coming, along with a photographer and a stenographer.

'There *must* be light,' she said. 'There *must* be. And by now Miss Nellie's lost her faith in Billy O'Connell – if that's his name –'

'I'll see what I can do,' said the chief. 'If I could catch my brother-in-law –'

'Show me the telephone.'

'One last kindness,' said Gretchen. 'It's dark now. We're all right on account of your flashlight. On the other hand, when you go – unless I could get back upstairs and find my own flashlight – we'll be in a pickle here. But I think I remember two candelabra in the dining-room. If you could guide me down the passage I could find them and then, if you had a match, I could light the candles –'

They were a pair of three-branched candelabra; before the firemen left the Hall Gretchen had the light of six tall candles and Kevin had returned.

'I couldn't believe my ears when a young lad came along and told me he'd seen a fire engine heading here,' said Kevin. 'A bunch of us had walked up four hogs. We was way high up behind the church – where you can look down on the Hall – at the time he joined us. The light was failing, but when I made out that engine standing here, I legged it. I knew you was on your own, if you take me.'

Gretchen explained that she was under orders to admit no one except the police but that the fire-chief's brother-in-law was on the way to do what he could about the fuses or the wiring.

'So, Kevin,' she said, 'could you possibly keep watch over the Hall for an hour? I'm covered in blood and slime. More than anything in the world I want a bath and there's almost sure to be hot water in the boiler even if there's no more electricity for the time being. I'll give you three of the candles and the key. You could just sit in Miss Nellie's library until someone comes along.'

'I hope that someone turns out to be the electrician,' said Kevin. 'You take all the time you want. I'm not sorry to sit down.'

Gretchen turned on the hot tap over the bath-tub and, after she had waited for a minute or so, hot water – nearly at the boiling point –

issued forth. Reanimated by that, she gave herself up to an orgy of personal laundry and bathing. Her pale coral blouse, her deeper coral cardigan, even her white slip, were stained with blood; whether the blood had come from Seamus or the pigs was immaterial. Except for her tweed skirt, which required dry-cleaning, she washed all her clothing. Then she surrendered to the luxury of total immersion in the bath-tub in water which was not only hot but, for her purposes, abundant. She washed her hair, she washed her face, she washed her body and, when she had left the bathroom, while she was sitting on the edge of her bed, drying her hair by rubbing it hard with a towel, she felt strengthened and purified.

For Dr Donovan she put on a white woollen dress with long sleeves, a shawl collar and a broad, bright red belt – which she complemented by a pair of bright-red pumps with high, needle heels. Since the mirror over the chest of drawers was cracked she could only hope that she looked presentable enough for a restaurant, a public place.

The Hall was still in darkness and, high up in the west tower, she heard no sound. Then she remembered Mary, alone in the pink room, with no light. Holding the candelabra high and descending one flight of stairs very slowly – careful not to catch a high heel in one of the holes in the stair-carpet – she reached the second floor, where she knocked at the door to the pink room. When there was no reply she went in softly. Mary was lying on the bed and when Gretchen came near and touched her forehead she made no response. Worried, Gretchen shook her gently, but Mary slept on.

'Mary,' she said, 'wake up. Speak to me.'

Even her plea, pitched in urgency, failed to rouse Mary.

She moved a little aside and struck at something with one foot. Lowering her candles she saw it was the bottle of cognac she had found for Mary and, picking it up, she was in no doubt that it was empty.

Uncertainly she went back upstairs, sat down at her work-table, and asked herself whether she should summon Dr Donovan at once or whether she could afford to let Mary wait for his arrival. While she was still mulling the question over she heard a car driving up to the west tower. Immediately she stepped onto her balcony and called out.

'Who's there?' she said.

'Harry Moore,' said an answering voice below.

'Oh,' said Gretchen, 'I'll be *right* down.'

In the entrance hall she met Kevin.

'I heard you coming,' said Kevin. 'So I waited. For the electrician's

105

here – he's working at the back – and it's not the guards out there.'

'It's a doctor,' Gretchen said. 'Come to see about my arm.'

'Then you let him in,' said Kevin, and handed her the key.

Gretchen unlocked the dor, Harry Moore crossed the threshold, and Gretchen locked the door behind him.

'I'm so glad you've come,' said Gretchen. 'Not for my sake – I'm fine – but for someone else. Please, could you come upstairs?'

By the light of Gretchen's candles Moore saw the dead hogs at the foot of the staircase.

'What in God's name is going on here?' he said.

'Don't bother about those,' said Gretchen. 'We're getting used to them. It's just a little awkward getting past them to the stairs.'

'Their function, I presume, is purely decorative,' said Moore.

'Or possibly symbolic,' Gretchen said, and was startled to find herself so sharp and dry.

'They accurately reflect the *modus vivendi* on Dufresne Bay?' said Moore.

'All that would be in the eye of the beholder,' said Gretchen. 'They begin to look quite natural to me – right where they are. Here in the Hall.'

Moore followed her up two flights of stairs to the pink room. Gretchen motioned him forward and held her candles above the bed so that he could see Mary.

'I can't rouse her,' said Gretchen. 'I've tried but I can't. Somehow I don't think that kind of sleep is normal.'

Moore felt for Mary's pulse, lifted her closed eyelids, and turned to Gretchen.

'How long has she been like this?' he said.

'I don't know,' said Gretchen. 'At a guess, not more than four hours, not less than two. But perhaps you should take a look at this bottle.'

'Bottles like that are always more interesting when they're full,' said Moore.

'Four or five hours ago it was full,' Gretchen said. 'Or almost full, almost up to the neck. I know because I gave it to her.'

'Something had better be done about this,' said Moore. 'There's a telephone in the Hall, is there not?'

'It's downstairs,' said Gretchen. 'I'll show it to you.'

Kevin was sitting in Miss Nellie's library, his own three candles making a pleasant pool of light.

'Leave me one of the candelabra,' Moore said. 'You and the lad keep the other. Go back upstairs, don't disturb her in the least but if, by any chance, she should start to retch, turn her over instantly on her stomach and hold her head *away* down, over the edge of the bed. When I've done my business here I'll find my way back up to you.'

Twenty minutes went by very slowly. Gretchen and Moore waited in the pink room. Moore had sent Kevin back to the entrance hall. Mary had not stirred. Presently, for the third time that day, Gretchen heard a siren and, within moments, the same two young men in white who had come for Seamus came for Mary. Kevin had preceded them. He had shown them the hogs, the obstacles at the foot of the stairs.

'Four of us would be better than just the two,' said one of the stretcher-bearers. 'We'll be needing a good, firm grip – getting round those pigs.'

So it fell out that, when they had lifted Mary onto the stretcher, the two young men took the head of it, Kevin and Moore took the foot, while Gretchen went one step before them all to light the way. The footwork at the bottom of the staircase was a challenge to the bearers' balance, but the two young professionals managed it adroitly. Moore and Kevin were nimble enough. When Mary was in the ambulance, Moore held a short conversation with the man who was to ride in the back with her, as Kevin and Gretchen retreated to the Hall.

'And now,' said Moore, rejoining them, 'you come with me.'

'I can't,' said Gretchen. 'I can't leave Kevin all alone so soon.'

'Don't worry about me,' said Kevin. 'I've company out there in the back and I'll find something to eat in the fridge.'

'Besides,' Gretchen said, 'Dr Donovan's coming for me at seven-thirty.'

'No, he's not,' said Moore. 'After I'd laid on the ambulance I had a word with him. Your Mary's not up my alley but she's right up his. So he'll be going by the hospital and then he'll come straight to me to pick you up.'

'In that case I must get my coat and my purse and my flashlight,' said Gretchen. 'But how will I get in after dinner?'

'Take the key,' Kevin said. 'There's no need of keeping the door locked if I'm right here beside it.'

With Gretchen next to him Moore drove to the top of Dufresne Hill without making any conversation. Once on the level he glanced at her.

'Miss Nellie has a *penchant* for dead pigs?' he said.

'I don't know about a *penchant*,' said Gretchen. 'But she has a fair collection.'

'Tell me all about it,' said Moore.

Harry Moore – and afterward his wife, Eliza – had been so fascinated by Gretchen's account of the day's activities at the Hall that Donovan arrived before Moore had looked at Gretchen's arm. In no time he had whisked her up to a bedroom, ordered her out of her dress, cut off her bandages – which were exceedingly damp after her celebrations in Miss Nellie's bathroom – examined her calmly, and thoroughly, before declaring that, in his opinion, no more trouble was to be feared from that quarter.

'All the same,' he said, to Donovan, when he and Gretchen were downstairs again, 'she's a bit feverish to the touch.'

'I had a hot bath,' said Gretchen. 'It warmed me up.'

'Think of the day the poor girl's put in,' said Mrs Moore. 'Myself, I can't get over it. The nerve of that man, coming licketty-cut down Dufresne Hill in a great lorry –'

'He'll have been drunk as a lord,' Moore said.

'You don't *know* that,' said Gretchen. 'Kevin said the same thing when he showed me the wreck and I was furious. It seemed so unfair. How can a dead man defend himself?'

'What did Kevin say?' said Donovan.

'He went on about bolts not being properly shot,' Gretchen said.

'An observant lad,' said Donovan. 'I made a note of it too.'

'So the whole world's against the driver?' said Gretchen.

'She has a point,' Moore said. 'Not being Irish –'

'Would *everyone* in Ireland condemn him out of hand?' said Gretchen.

'Oh, everyone would,' said Mrs Moore. 'But don't you go losing any sleep over it. For the truth will be out after the post-mortem.'

'If it turns out he was sober,' said Donovan, 'I'd do well to go into early retirement.'

'You could leave the lass to Eliza and me,' Moore said. 'We'd keep an eye on her.'

'In the event you're not obliged to retire quite yet,' said Mrs Moore, 'why don't you bring her to dinner some night next week?'

'By next week the fellow who'll really be in want of aid and comfort will be Jim Farquahar,' said Donovan. 'Miss Nellie's with him now and she'll never let him go till he's promised her a king's ransom – which, of course, he can't do, under the circumstances.'

'Unless Gretchen's right,' Moore said.

Donovan lingered just long enough to thank Moore for prompt intervention in Mary's extremity.

'Everything's under control now,' he said. 'She's out of danger, although I daresay she'll wish she *had* died when she wakes up in the morning to discover herself on the ward.'

'Might she have *died*?' said Gretchen.

'If she'd begun to throw up and had aspirated her vomit, she might indeed,' said Donovan.

'So you understand,' Moore said, to Gretchen, 'you may have saved a life tonight.'

'He's not pulling your leg,' said Mrs Moore, seeing Gretchen doubtful. 'It's just his unfortunate manner.'

'She means it – about my manner,' said Moore. 'Do you know what her answer was when I asked her to marry me?'

'What was her answer?' Donovan said.

'She said, "Stop it Harry. I've never liked gallows humour",' said Moore.

'What else could I say,' said Mrs Moore. 'When Harry said, "I'd die for you, Eliza"?'

'So,' said Donovan, as he and Gretchen drove away, 'Eliza told me – while Harry was looking at your arm – that in the middle of the afternoon the Hall was on fire and you were all alone.'

'They don't live in Ralston's Cove, do they?' said Gretchen.

'Who?' Donovan said.

'The Moores,' said Gretchen.

'No indeed,' said Donovan. 'They live four miles to the north-west of Ralston's Cove. Harry has nothing but contempt for the town.'

'But he works there, doesn't he?' said Gretchen.

'Only on Thursdays,' said Donovan. 'The rest of the week he's in Port Ferris every working day. He's much too good for Ralston's Cove.

'But tell me more about yourself. You called the fire department?'

'To put out the fire,' said Gretchen.

'You're being very patient with me,' Donovan said.

He was almost sure she was sleeping as he drove through the night. But half an hour later, when he pulled up in the parking space beside the restaurant, she was out of the car in a flash.

'We're miles from anywhere, aren't we?' she said.

'We are,' said Donovan. 'But we're very close to an excellent dinner.'

The silence with which Gretchen countered that statement seemed, to Donovan, to hold a world of scepticism.

On entering, Gretchen saw a large room with a fireplace at both ends of it – in both fireplaces a welcome blaze – small tables, many of them in alcoves, elegantly set with brilliant white napery, three wine glasses at each place, a sweet bouquet of hot-house flowers at each

109

table, and no illumination save for candles on every table and sconces on the walls. A middle-aged man in a beautifully cut dinner jacket burst into a torrent of French as he recognised Donovan, to which Donovan replied with nearly the same fluency. Gretchen was swept on by both men. As if she were the heroine of a stranger's dream, she found herself in an alcove. The *maître d'hôtel* relieved her of her coat and ushered her to a banquette, where she sat down. More discussion ensued and, although Gretchen's French was limited to her grammar for beginners, she caught enough to know that dinner was under consideration. Presently the *maître d'hôtel* went away, but before she had said a word to Donovan, he was back with what looked to Gretchen like whisky – for Donovan – and a frosty glass full of ice-cubes and a clear liquid for herself.

'You didn't like the whisky Miss Nellie gave us the other evening, did you?' said Donovan.

'I didn't like the taste,' said Gretchen. 'But it made me warm.'

'This will make you warm too,' Donovan said. 'And it has no taste at all.'

For ten minutes they ate the *crudités* and sipped at the drinks. Slowly a gentle wave of well-being rippled over Gretchen. Donovan watched her sweetly yielding to the vodka.

'Better now?' he said.

'Much better,' said Gretchen. 'I hadn't realised how strung up I was. I was horrid, wasn't I?'

'Evidently you had reasons,' Donovan said. 'Eliza told me about the fire – so I'd already gathered that you'd saved an Irish monument from destruction, whilst I saw Mary with my own eyes. Quite possibly you did save her life.'

'Do you know,' said Gretchen – softly, loosely recollecting fragments of the day – 'when the chief of the fire brigade examined the fuse-panel he said he didn't think there were more than ten or twenty violations up there.'

'Why was he examining the fuse-panel?' said Donovan.

'Because,' Gretchen said, 'the fire in the electric oven blew the main fuse and I was afraid that if there were any defective wiring behind the panel it might be smouldering. Besides, it was almost dark.'

'Is it still dark in the Hall?' said Donovan.

'I hope not,' said Gretchen. 'I sort of pulled the fire chief's leg. I mean I convinced him that we were really in a crisis, so he called his brother-in-law – who had already arrived when I left.'

'If Joe Halloran was the man you took to be the chief of the brigade,' Donovan said, 'then I can tell you that his brother-in-law is the best electrician in the county. Miss Nellie won't be getting away with ten or twenty violations any longer.'

'There were so many things I wanted to ask you,' said Gretchen.

Just then a waiter brought a *boeuf bourguignonne* and a Château Mouton Rothschild.

'Oh, that was good,' Gretchen said. 'And the wine is unforgettable.'

'What did you want to ask me?' said Donovan.

'I don't remember,' said Gretchen. 'No, I do remember one thing. Why did Miss Nellie say – in that deadly tone of voice – that Seamus would never walk again? And why did Seamus close his eyes and play dead after she'd said it? And why did you say 'noted'? You understood her, didn't you.'

'Miss Nellie was in a sort of raptus,' Donovan said. 'She was looking ahead to the damages she meant to claim – she was calculating how many thousands of pounds might be coming to her if Seamus pretended to permanently incapacitated and adding all those thousands to the thousands she planned to list for everything the hogs had wrecked in the Hall.

'She was already building castles in Spain and so was Seamus – when he got her drift.'

'She must be entitled to damages,' said Gretchen. 'Lots and lots and lots of damages. The west tower's ruined. And the dining-room in the east tower's a mess.'

'I doubt she'll live to see a penny for any of it,' said Donovan.

'But why *not*?' Gretchen said.

'Because,' said Donovan, 'the kind of money Miss Nellie is fantasizing about can only be extracted from an insurance company. Small trucking firms haven't that kind of capital.'

'However insurance companies do,' said Gretchen.

'Precisely,' Donovan said. 'But insurance policies covering highway accidents are automatically void if the driver insured is drunk.'

'And you're sure he *was* drunk,' said Gretchen.

'It leapt to the eye,' said Donovan. 'In fact I telephoned Jim Farquahar to warn him that, in all probability, the insurance company wouldn't pay up, that she'd be reduced to litigation in court if she pressed for damages.'

'Who's Jim Farquahar?' Gretchen said.

'He's Miss Nellie's solicitor,' said Donovan. 'His father before him and his grandfather handled the Dufresne affairs. I don't envy the poor man the afternoon and evening he'll have spent with her.'

'But surely she was with Seamus at the hospital,' said Gretchen.

111

'She dropped in,' Donovan said. 'But her principal objective this afternoon was Farquahar. Seamus is fine, by the way. Six stitches closed up the scalp wound, the skull studies were negative. He'll be discharged – if his convalescence is smooth – after five days of observation.'

Gretchen was no longer listening to him. She was adrift on a drowsy tide of pleasure. 'I'll tell you something if you won't laugh at me,' she said.

'I never laugh,' said Donovan.

'Well,' said Gretchen, 'all those portraits in the long passage between the west tower and the east tower bothered me. It's true that I don't know anything about painting, but I did take a survey course in college and while it didn't teach me much about painters themselves, it taught me to use my eyes. And when Miss Nellie had the jumble sale – when I was all alone in the west tower – I went down the passage and I *really* looked at them, every single one. I know they represent nearly four hundred years of Dufresnes but, just the same, I could have sworn that they were all painted by the same hand.'

Donovan was thunderstruck. For him Gretchen was youth, grace, enchantment. When he was with her she seemed to him to be endowed with just those qualities; when he was away from her he enfolded her within them. But he had yet to reckon with Gretchen's intelligence, with her powers of perception; he had yet to acknowledge Gretchen's mind.

'Well, I'm damned,' he said, after a long pause.

'I'm sure you think what I've told you is preposterous,' said Gretchen.

'No,' said Donovan, 'I think it's almost certainly true.'

'You've noticed what I noticed?' Gretchen said.

'Not until it was suggested to me,' said Donovan.

'But maybe I'm not so far wrong?' said Gretchen.

'A long time ago,' Donovan said, 'in Miss Nellie's father's time, a man called Christie was a frequent visitor to the Hall. Although he insisted that he was merely an amateur, he had a professional eye for art. And he knew that Miss Nellie's father was a very competent Sunday painter. Over the years he came to supect that old Dufresne was secretly selling the genuine portraits in London – many of them were of great value – but not before he had copied each one and put it in the same frame which had belonged to the original. Mr Christie confided his suspicions to his son who, in turn, confided them to his son – who confided them to me.'

'What an extraordinary thing to do,' said Gretchen. 'Of course they were his, but –'

'Miss Nellie's father cared more for his thoroughbreds than for his wife, his daughter and his heirlooms all put together,' said Donovan. 'He was virtually bankrupt when he died but not a horse was sold nor a stable-hand discharged until after his death.'

'I'd hate to have been rich,' Gretchen said, 'only to come down in the world.'

After the *crêpes suzette* – which Gretchen said she had never tasted, whereat Donovan ordered them at once – and the coffee, their dinner was over. It was when they had left the restaurant, while they were walking to the car that Gretchen began to cough. The spasm lasted for more than two minutes and was so racking that Donovan put his arm around her waist to steady her. When she stopped coughing Donovan made no comment, but Gretchen was immediately on the defensive.

'I only do it at night,' she said. 'Or first thing in the morning.'

For quite a while they drove in silence until Donovan slowed before a fork in the road. His headlights caught an arrow, pointing right, and Gretchen read 'Dufresne Bay – 7'. All the same, Donovan kept to the left.'

'Aren't we going to the Hall?' said Gretchen.

'Not yet,' said Donovan.

'Where are we going?' she said.

'To Ralston's Cove,' said Donovan.

It was not until he had examined her in his office, listened to her chest, taken her temperature, not until they had stopped at the hospital – where a busy, bustling woman raided the dispensary for Donovan – that they started out for Dufresne Bay.

'What's the matter with me now?' said Gretchen.

'You would run before you could walk,' Donovan said.

'Somebody had to do something,' said Gretchen.

'That is quite beside the point,' said Donovan.

The Hall was a blaze of light. The front door was open. The Gardaí were present in the drawing-room where Miss Nellie was holding forth – presumably to the stenographer.

'Chippendale,' she said. 'With two ps.'

'Keep going,' said Donovan, and Gretchen and he climbed two more flights.

'Whatever is she doing at this hour of night?' said Gretchen.

'Listing the damages,' Donovan said. 'In front of reliable witnesses. Jim Farquahar's in there too.'

'How do you know?' said Gretchen.

'I reckognised his Citroën,' said Donovan. 'Take off your dress so I can give you a shot.

'Now,' he said, 'you have my permission to go downstairs – with the red bucket, if necessary – and brush your teeth. Then you are to get into bed and stay here. I'll tell Miss Nellie you're home safe.'

'Won't you even let me thank you for giving me such a happy evening?' said Gretchen.

'Don't interrupt,' said Donovan. 'I'll be by at eight o'clock tomorrow morning with your breakfast.'

'*What?*' Gretchen said.

'Unless, of course, you'd rather I sent it round by Dr Reilly,' said Donovan.

9

The next day was the beginning of an Indian summer for Donovan – a summer which was to last, without a break, for all of four weeks. Gretchen's blossoming bronchitis – a 'teaching case', as Donovan privately labelled it – was not, given the antibiotics at his disposition, alarming but, since it was slow to respond to treatment, it was menacing enough to command the regular attentions of any conscientious physician, whether or not he was in thrall to Gretchen. Donovan continued to remind himself that, where she was a source of light, he was no more than a dim, patriarchal shadow, and yet their relationship changed, by virtue of her malady. She was not his – nor had he the slightest hope that one day she might be his – but, by virtue of her malady, by virtue of the holocaust in the Hall, he was, quite unexpectedly, in a position to entertain the privilege of being hers – hers to rely on, hers to turn to, hers to wait for. Gradually he was almost certain to achieve a place in her life, a certain importance to which, earlier, he had not aspired. Minutes in the daytime, possibly whole hours in the evenings which he was about to share with her, lay before him and, if he did not look ahead to the time when she would no longer have any need of him, it was because he could not bear too much reality where Gretchen was concerned.

For a week he gave her a shot of an antibiotic in the mornings and at night; then, dissatisfied with his efforts – she was no sicker than she had been, but he knew that she had made no progress – he began to

114

give her an antibiotic from another group. A week later she was manifestly improving; he suspended the shots, but every evening for a fortnight he came by to check up on her – and to have a drink with her. It was during those four weeks of her illness that he slowly gained her confidence, that he persuaded her to give him a glimpse here and there of her background.

Not for an instant did he ignore the limits he himself had resolved to set upon their acquaintance. He would not, he could not, forget that the same fate which had brought the two of them together, on Gretchen's arrival in Ralston's Cove, would, shortly, insist on their independence of each other. It was unthinkable, it was shocking, that he should let himself imagine – even for a split second – that they might ever pair off in double harness. But surely no impropriety attached to the memory that Gretchen had flatly stated that she was different from any of her fellow-passengers on the airplane which had brought her across the Atlantic, thereby ensuring that, some hours afterward, she would finish up, literally, in his arms. Had he not carried her up the stairs in the hotel, had he not made every attempt to meet her on her own terms – were they the terms imposed by her influenza, were they the terms imposed by the necessity of a roof over her head when she was well enough to consider more or less permanent lodgings? Had he not earned a right of sorts to be fascinated by a slip of a girl who boldly presumed to a significant difference between herself and all the other travellers on the flight to Ireland? Might he not be excused if, now and then, he taxed her with the 'difference'?

Tax her he did, on various pretenses, until the bronchitis had yielded to his ministrations and there was no longer any pretext for him to visit her at the Hall. But by then he was undeniably close to her even though he had – with one or two trifling exceptions – maintained his professional stance. While Gretchen, when she had put him roughly in possession of her history, became free with him; like a guest divested of his overcoat at the door she was ready to enter into his world unencumbered, on a much less formal footing.

Gretchen was different from most of her contemporaries inasmuch as, in her family, the patterns of living, handed down through six generations, had been very little modified by changing times. Her great-great-great-grandfather had come from Germany to the New World in 1825 not as a footloose, improvident malcontent but as a young man of inherited means, a sensible imagination and an incontestable faith in a stern, yet a just and not implacable, God. A conviction that men and women had nothing but the tireless work of hands to render to the Creator still endured in Gretchen's father.

'My father is specifically Christian,' Gretchen had said. 'He believes that Christ *was* the son of God and that He redeems us every day if we're careful to bring Him the best we can do – whatever it may be.'

'Are you specifically Christian?' said Donovan.

'Not any more,' she said. 'When my mother thought I was old enough she gave me Emerson to read.'

Donovan, quick to Gretchen's moods, caught the accents of conclusion in her last words. Briefly she had been willing to touch on her ancestry, at random she had thrown in a remark about her father's religious bias, and then – by something in her tone of voice, by something in her manner – he had known himself dismissed, subtly warned against further trespass. Much as she had challenged him by declaring that she was 'different', much as he had hoped she would presently define the 'difference', it was patently inexpedient to press for anything more immediately. However, a little later, he was bold enough to try a long shot.

'Your great-great-great-grandfather must have been a forceful man if he left his sign on the five generations which came after him,' he had said.

'Why should you care about him?' said Gretchen. 'Or about his descendants?'

'I'm incorrigibly curious about unusual men,' said Donovan. 'I like to hear about their eccentricities.'

'My people weren't eccentric,' she said. 'They just persevered. They still do.'

'These days perseverance is an eccentricity,' said Donovan.

'I know,' said Gretchen. 'But we're used to it. And in my great-great-great-grandfather's time it was a standard thing.'

With that Donovan had had to be satisfied. He was learning that the race – where Gretchen was concerned – was not to the swift.

'Conceivably,' he had said to himself, 'it might just be to the guileful.'

On his next visit he had stooped to guile.

'It's not everyone,' he said, 'who can remember his great-great-great-grandfather.'

'You don't suppose for a moment that I remember mine?' said Gretchen. 'Or have you mistaken me for a reincarnated spirit?'

'Tell me more about what you don't remember,' Donovan said.

Whereupon, to his astonishment – and to his gratification – Gretchen obliged.

In 1825 the patriarch had invested his German legacy in four hundred acres of land in Pennsylvania. There he had maried a suitably hard-working and equally pious woman, there he had built a spacious house for his wife and their three sons. When the sons were grown and, consequently, the work of hands was trebled, they were prosperous enough to acquire adjacent tracts of property; the eldest son remained under his father's roof, each of his two brothers built a house for himself.

All this Donovan cautiously extracted, aware that Gretchen was by no means uninterested in, or uninvolved with, the details of her lineage. It was simply that she found them irrelevant to her relationship with him. But although she was not disposed to elaborate on any of the chapters in her chronicle, artful enquiry continued to elicit scraps of information which led Donovan through her past to her present.

Sons, and daughters, had been born to succeeding generations. Some of the sons had gone west, all of the daughters had married and left home. By 1920 Gretchen's grandfather – whose brother had been killed in the First World War – was the only survivor still living on the property in Pennsylvania. He had died before Gretchen was born, leaving Gretchen's father – who had married late, at thirty-seven – her uncle Matt and her uncle Luke. Her father had inherited the ancestral house, the uncles had moved into the two later houses, erected in the 1860s. Gretchen's widowed grandmother kept house for her uncle Matt, who had never married. Her uncle Luke, though he was married, had had no children.

'My father and my uncles were cut from the same old bolt,' Gretchen had said. 'The land's in their blood.'

It was the single coment she had volunteered and Donovan was grateful for it.

'There's strength in repetition,' he said.

'Then we must be strong,' said Gretchen. 'We're certainly repetitious.'

When Donovan had wished her a good night, left her room and shut her door, she gave a long sigh. She could not lie to him about her family; she could not pretend that they were polished or distinguished people. But Dr Donovan himself had such an air of distinction that she caught herself wishing that she had something *outré* – a statesman, an actor, a scientist, a musician – to offer him: an ancestor, a parent, a relative so extraordinary, so gifted that she could be excused at once if she referred to him with pride. However, she had no one of note to fall back on and she was afraid that her immense pride in her modest lineage could only provoke Dr Donovan to scorn.

Had she been able to make some fine, off-hand reference to some splendid appointment – 'While we were living in London when my father was the ambassador' – she might have chattered on indefinitely. But as things stood, if she were to show Dr Donovan her people as they really were, she would have to portray them in action – spreading manure on the fields, raking hay, shovelling ensilage, scrubbing the kitchen floor, hanging out the day's washing, scouring the roasting pan and, after any truthful portrayal, how could he, so urbane, so *soigné*, believe that she was deeply proud to be a daughter of the house?

'What it comes down to –' she said, aloud.

Yet what did it come down to, if not that she was a child of the soil who could not damn her parents with faint praise, to show how *mondaine* she could be, nor even hope to express how much she loved them – not in spite of what they were, but precisely because of what they were?

'If my family isn't good enough for him –' she said.

At that she caught herself up. Was it not possible that Dr Donovan might instantly recognise her people for what they were and respect each and every one of them for his or her honest labour? Was not Dr Donovan himself a man of independent spirit, of sensitive intuition, an amateur of the great and of the small?

'I'll just hope I'll never have to talk to him about me,' said Gretchen, getting out of bed, picking up her toothbrush and her toothpaste and the red bucket. 'Because things being what they are I'm pretty mixed up about me at the moment –'

'The last thing you said to me yesterday evening was that your family was repetitious,' said Donovan.

'Are you keeping a little black book of all my indiscretions?' said Gretchen.

'How repetitious?' Donovan said.

'My mother makes the Christmas cookies from my great-great-great-grandmother's recipe,' said Gretchen. 'My grandmother gave it to her when she came to our part of the world – after she and my father got engaged.'

'Surely you still travel by horse and buggy?' said Donovan.

'We have a lovely buggy,' Gretchen said. 'Every Hallowe'en my uncle Matt takes the little ones out in it. They call on all the near neighbours.'

'How long is it since *you've* gone for a buggy-ride?' said Donovan.

'Ages and ages,' said Gretchen. 'I grew up fast, you see. Would you like a look at my driver's licence?'

118

'So you haven't quite set your face against the world of today?' Donovan said.

'What do you mean by that?' said Gretchen. 'Speed?'

In mechanical and in scientific terms Gretchen's forbears had kept up with what was hailed as progress. Innovations, such as tractors or milking machines, had been added to their inventories if they had proved serviceable, new methods of cultivating or fertilising the soil had been adopted if they had been thought effective. But the ancient principles – industry, piety, courage and thrift – had filtered through to Gretchen's epoch largely unadulterated.

'Nobody on my father's side of the family – nobody who stayed put – ever saw the point of making alterations which weren't advantageous,' Gretchen had said. 'I suppose you might say that nobody was restless. Nobody's restless now, except for my sister Anna. And she's only restless because she's so clever.'

'Is your mother clever?' said Donovan.

'No,' said Gretchen. 'She's wise.'

Nothing which Gretchen had yet relinquished had had any private seal upon it, but what little she had told him had been enough to fix various impressions on Donovan. He had noticed that when she spoke of her father – when, more than once, she had used the phrase 'down through the years' – there was a faintest suggestion of impending decline, as if each generation were poised to descend a staircase. Her father himself would not reach the foot nor, possibly, would his offspring. But there might come a day when there would be no more sons to work the land, no more steps on that stair. Whereas, when she spoke of her mother, there were intimations of indefinite advancement, of generations to come indefinitely rising. Unlike Gretchen's father, Gretchen's mother was not, apparently, indissolubly attached to time or place; she lived to lift, to teach her children that, in the regions of the mind, there were no declensions, that ascent was limitless.

'My mother's family were school-teachers,' Gretchen had said. 'In all of them there was an inbred respect for learning. Or maybe reverence is a better word than respect. My mother herself taught school for two years before she married my father.'

Donovan had gathered that where, earlier, among her father's people, the emphasis had been on rearing young men, hardy and confident, sure to wrest a satisfactory yield from the earth, with her mother's arrival – through her mother's high resolve – the emphasis had shifted or, at least, been divided between the necessity for the development of practical skills in young bodies and the obligation both to stimulate and to discipline young intellects.

But just as he had perceived the glimmer of a luminescent spirit in the household, Gretchen transformed her mother into dominant flesh and blood by recounting her mother's initial triumph as a bride-to-be.

'My mother told my father she wouldn't marry him until he'd put another bathroom into the house, torn out the old boiler, and contrived a whole new system to supply continuous hot water night and day,' said Gretchen. 'No one in my father's family could imagine such a spree, but my mother wouldn't have him before it was done.

'Cleanliness and order,' she said, 'are first requirements to her.'

'They take precedence over the life of the mind?' said Donovan.

'In my mother's book,' said Gretchen, 'the external and the internal have to reflect each other.'

So far Donovan had come no closer to the heart of Gretchen. Only once, when she had burst into the impassioned account of the flight across the Atlantic, had he seen the flash of a vital force within her and that flash, he was convinced, had been ignited not nearly so much by an impulse toward confession as by the cryptic fire of her fever. The flaming self – of which, for a few moments, he had caught sight – continued to beguile and to puzzle him, but he doubted that – save in some unpredictable instant of poignant stress – she would ever reveal it again. There was a control, an innate reserve in Gretchen which Donovan could not help but recognise. She might seem to be on the edge of a deepening confidence, but on the edge she rested, at a set remove from anything touching either on revelation or indiscretion. However, even if she was unlikely to confide in him, he hoped, eventually, to discover more of her, to come across her – here and there – between the milestone of her childhood.

'How many brothers and sisters have you?' he had said.

'Four,' said Gretchen.

'Tell me about them,' said Donovan.

'I just did,' Gretchen said.

She was almost flirting with him; the mockery of her smile was entrancing but, once again, she had thwarted him.

Donovan had been interested in the history of Gretchen's father's family, and yet, although he had found it remarkable in its adherence to original attitudes, it was not until he had prevailed on her for various casual references to her mother that he could begin to infuse a wholeness into her 'difference'. Her father and her uncles, Matt and Luke, might or might not be out of date – depending upon the manners and morals of present-day farmers in Pennsylvania – but Gretchen's dedication to something other than anything which had animated her fellow passengers on the plane sprang, he supected, more importantly from her mother, who was 'wise'.

Up to that point it was clear that she had vouchsafed nothing which was central to herself; she had simply offered him certain evaporations from the yesterdays before her today, a drift of vapour from underlying springs to which she had – off-handedly – alluded. Laconic as she had been, she had allowed very little time for any condensation; very few drops had formed on the surfaces of Gretchen's abbreviated narratives. All the same she had told him something about her parents – and left him to draw such inferences as he pleased about herself. Donovan made do with his inferences for several days before risking another attack on her sources. When he moved again it was, curiously enough, Gretchen who gave him the opening.

'I had a long letter from my mother,' she said. 'So I'm all caught up with home.'

'Do you miss your family?' Donovan had said.

'Now and then,' said Gretchen. 'I wish you knew them. I wonder if you'd like them.'

Donovan had seen a rare opportunity and he had made the most of it.

Gretchen was the first-born. After Gretchen came Rufus, with four years between them, four years divided Rufus from Anna, four years divided Anna from David. There was an interval of six years between David and Little Will.

Rufus was not quick. Gretchen's mother had been infinitely patient, but exacting, with him until he had learnt to think for himself. Ultimately he had won a scholarship to Williams where, in June, he had had his B.A. Yet higher education or no, Rufus meant to follow in his father's footsteps; like his father, the land was in his blood. For the next two years Rufus would be going to an agricultural college to learn, if it were possible, certain techniques of farming which his father and his uncles had never known.

Anna, at seventeen, was, as Gretchen had already remarked, clever. Ideas came to her too easily. Her mother was afraid that, unless Anna appreciated the necessity for intellectual drudgery, she would never be anything but scatterbrained and shallow.

David, at thirteen, was, according to Gretchen, bound to be an astronomer.

'He's not quite in this world,' she had said. 'He wouldn't talk for a long time. And then one night he was looking out of his window up at the stars and he said, "what are they doing there?". That's still what David means to find out. He has charts of the heavens all over the walls of his room.'

Little Will was only seven and spoiled. Even Gretchen's mother had a soft spot for Little Will.

Gretchen spoke of Rufus on an intonation of tenderness, her intonation when she spoke of Anna was humorous and slightly rueful. Of David she spoke with delight, of Little Will with indulgence. For her mother, very much the presiding presence, she appeared to have an abiding respect. Gretchen's mother had even succeeded in training a pitifully retarded girl called Sally to do all the ironing and most of the house-cleaning.

'Only my mother could have taught Sally to do anything,' said Gretchen. 'In the beginning she was a hopeless case. Now she's indispensable. She's simple, poor girl, but she's happy with us. When my mother's pleased with her she's ecstatic.'

'Is your mother so hard to please?' said Donovan.

'Praise from my mother is hard to come by,' Gretchen said. 'But it's worth winning.'

Even Donovan, rarely at a loss for a last word, could hardly refute that. He was coming to understand that her family was, in Gretchen's view, made up of splendid men, women, and children, but could they, he asked himself, be, in fact, so exceptional? Yet as soon as he put the question he began to wonder if they might not be indeed exceptional, that if they were good enough for Gretchen, if she was proud of them, might they not, in their everyday lives, live up to her proud conception of them? Might not Gretchen owe her own quality to the people whence she came?

'Are *you* lost in thought or have *I* just lost you?' said Gretchen.

'I must be homeward bound,' Donovan said.

Over his nightcap he reviewed Gretchen's comments, that evening, on her family. She had been so outgoing that he had come away well rewarded. He could place her, finally, in a group of people, each of whom she had endowed with a flicker of personality. He knew where and what she came from, he knew with whom she had lived. On a next occasion, if the occasion seemed ripe, he expected to discover the patterns of life in Gretchen's household. For, until then, in spite of all she had told him, she herself had scarcely entered on the scene. Now, he thought, she had given him enough so that he might net her in the family's daily round, provided he could prompt her to enlarge

122

on that. Soon he made another tentative advance.

'These days,' he said, 'would you say a country childhood was an advantage or a handicap?'

'I think of mine as privileged,' said Gretchen, and before the evening was over Donovan was an astounded man.

Gretchen's family had no next-door neighbours and the school, in Knightstown, was twelve miles away. Gretchen's mother considered that what the school had to offer was insufficient to the shaping of well-rounded minds. Hence, after the children had done their homework – often with their mother's help or under her supervision – after the early supper which directly followed the evening's milking, as soon as they were old enough they were made to read for an hour before bedtime. Each child began with Howard Pyle, went on to Stevenson, then to *Robinson Crusoe*, then to *Gulliver's Travels*, and proceeded to Dickens, Hawthorne, Melville, George Eliot.

'My mother's dowry was her grandfather's library – which was fairly extensive,' Gretchen had said. 'But if an important author was missing she made small economies and bought him for us out of her savings.'

The supreme literature, however, lay in the Bible. Although the family did not go to church – both Gretchen's parents agreed that the preacher in Knightstown was a tiresome and pretentious man – on Sunday mornings Gretchen's mother read from the Old Testament, urging the children to associate the problems which Abraham and Moses and all the other heroic figures had faced with the problems of the present as they knew it or could imagine it for themselves. Gretchen's father read from the New Testament, urging the children to contemplate such Christian values as were imperishable. At the end of each reading Gretchen's mother and, after her, Gretchen's father, spurred the children to discuss, or even to argue against, what they had just heard.

'Neither of them ever demanded that we swallow a reading whole,' said Gretchen. 'But they expected us to give the Bible very serious consideration.'

'Did you enjoy those Sunday mornings?' said Donovan.

'They were good,' she said. 'Because my father and my mother were together, and together they gave the most they had to give to us.'

During the winters, in addition to the reading prescribed before bedtime, a part of Saturday mornings and a part of Sunday afternoons were set aside for books, Gretchen's mother reading aloud to the little ones. During the summers the children were taught to milk, pitch hay, feed and water the livestock – instructed by their father and their uncles.

'Besides, in the summers,' said Gretchen, 'Rufus and I learned German. Anna and David are doing that now.'

'Did your *mother* teach you German?' said Donovan.

'No,' Gretchen said. 'She's rusty.'

It appeared that her mother's aunt Emma, who had spent her life teaching German, had been for some years in retirement. Gretchen's mother, knowing her aunt to be hard up when she had to get by on her pension, had arranged for her to come to Pennsylvania and board, for a modest sum, with Gretchen's uncle Luke and his wife Jean. The old lady kept her hand in by giving her great-nieces and nephews lessons in what was their own ancestral language.

'She gets on like a house on fire with my father's family,' said Gretchen. 'Sometimes, for a fling, she goes to call on my grandmother. My uncle Matt bought her a television set last winter.'

'Is that the only television set in the family?' said Donovan.

'The only one,' Gretchen said. 'Uncle Luke and Aunt Jean don't like television. Uncle Luke says it gives him a headache, and my mother thinks it's just for people who can't read or write.'

Donovan was speechless, thinking of the antennae on the roof of every Irish hut, whether or not the household went barefoot, whether or not there was running water in the house.

'Didn't you, doesn't Anna or Rufus or David feel somewhat divorced from your own times?' he said.

'I don't believe so,' said Gretchen. 'We're all in touch with reality. Reality is making both ends meet, you know. And a working farm is no ivory tower.'

'What about friends of your own ages?' Donovan said. 'What about the little frivolities?'

Gretchen explained that they had made friends at school. But she reminded him that Knightstown – where the school, where sundry little frivolities were to be found – was twelve miles away from where they lived.

'My people aren't long on little frivolities,' said Gretchen. 'But it wouldn't be right to suppose that we don't have any fun. We have ice-skating in the winter, swimming and picnics in the summer. Hallowe'en, Thanksgiving, Christmas, Easter, and the Fourth of July are great holidays in our house.'

She left Donovan to digest that for a moment or so and then, suddenly, she laughed at him.

'We were *all* innoculated against whooping cough and all those other things,' she said.

124

'And against the culture of the twentieth century as well?' said Donovan.

'Some of it is noxious,' said Gretchen.

'When did you find out that?' Donovan said. 'When you went to college?'

'Perhaps so,' said Gretchen.

'Were you shocked by the great unknown?' said Donovan.

'By some aspects of it,' she said. 'But I was awfully busy in college. You have to remember that I only got there because I won a scholarship. All along I knew I'd need very high grades to get a grant for post-graduate studies. So I *had* to work hard.'

'And when you went home on vacation you had to follow the plough?' said Donovan.

'I had to do my share,' said Gretchen.

'What are you going to do when you grow up?' Donovan said, keeping a straight face.

'Do you really think I'm still in pigtails?' said Gretchen.

Donovan himself was not sure whether Gretchen ought to be still in pigtails. She had been in Ireland for five weeks before she had reached that point in her disclosures which had provoked his bantering questions and her equally bantering, interrogative responses. She had denied that she was out of touch with reality; she had said that a working farm was no ivory tower, that reality was making both ends meet. And that, Donovan thought, was an adult truth – a truth at which children in pigtails could not yet arrive. Moreover Gretchen's dignity, although it sometimes resembled the natural dignity of a very young child, also bespoke maturity; it was the mark of a responsible woman.

But if she was in touch with the reality of making both ends meet she was, he was certain, far out of touch with the vulgarity which was the common currency of the day and age – as represented in virtually every offering of the ubiquitous television set. Doubtless, through the disciplines forced on her, she was practically and academically knowledgeable but, in her sovereign isolation from the present tense – as it was constantly expressed in every crowded city on the face of the earth, as it was regularly experienced in buses, in subway trains, in airplanes, as it was repeatedly exhibited on television – she was extraordinarily innocent, extraordinarily vulnerable.

Five weeks after her arrival Donovan would have come to her in a suit of armour, his sword gleaming like a bolt of lightning – if through such a measure he might have protected her from the monstrosity of the contemporary world. For, by that time, he had

125

conceded that she was, indeed, 'different'; more, the difference had come to seem to him rare and precious, worth defending, worth celebrating. On the other hand he saw, only too clearly, that no one but Gretchen herself could defend her own essence; the most he could do for her was to try to teach her to be continually on her guard – if she allowed him to teach her anything.

'For what am I that she should be mindful of me?' he said to himself.

In fact he had ceased to struggle against her influence. He was helplessly in love with her; he knew that, on one pretext or another, he would often seek her out. So long as she never suspected his feeling for her no harm could home to her. The risk, if there were one, was his own. But now that he had lost his heart to her, what else had he left to lose?

So much undemanding submission, however, was not his style; that much he understood. Somehow, some time a wrong note might be struck, the sounding board might crack. More and more frequently he asked himself how long it would be before Gretchen began to hear that his instrument was off pitch and then began to see through the oddments of his disguise, to perceive the man behind the stethoscope or the black bag. If that happened would she still suffer him gladly or would she retreat at his coming? Uneasily he promised himself again and again that the risk, if there was one, was entirely his own.

' "Sufficient unto the day",' he said to himself, but the words did not brace him as he had hoped they would.

The first morning after the great *débacle* Gretchen's alarm clock woke her at a quarter to eight. Lazily she stared at the dial and wondered why the alarm had woken her so early. Then she remembered the besiegement, the pigs and, simultaneously, she remembered that she had only fifteen minutes before Donovan's arrival. Whereupon she was out of bed in a bound, not wishing him to find her mussed in sleep and unresponsive. When he did draw up to the Hall the door was still closed and he thought that, possibly, the bell would not be answered at such an hour. As it was he waited less than a minute before Miss Nellie, in a black kimono emblazoned with prodigious gold and ruby-red butterflies, let him in.

'Gretchen's not well,' he said. 'I've brought her breakfast.'

'And a good thin' too,' said Miss Nellie. 'The kitchen's demolished. Last night I arranged to take my own breakfast at the vicarage.'

Gretchen was sitting up in bed, with Solomon at the foot, when

Donovan reached the top of the west tower.

'You've company, I see,' he said.

'Poor Solomon,' said Gretchen. 'When you left last night he crawled out from under the bed. I suppose yesterday was just too much for him.'

Donovan set his basket down on Gretchen's work-table and unpacked bread, butter, honey, a plate, a butter knife, a cup and saucer, a spoon, a large thermos, and a clean napkin. He had also brought a tray which he neatly made up.

'Is all that for me?' said Gretchen. 'I think I'm going to cry.'

'It's not polite to cry before you've tasted my offerings,' said Donovan.

'It would be even more discourteous afterward,' said Gretchen, and submitted to an examination and a shot.

'Be brave,' Donovan said. 'Eat my breakfast, take a bath – *if* the water's hot – get back in bed and work with your pad propped up against your knees.'

He was gone before Gretchen had had time to pour a cup of coffee. Still holding the flask upright, she frowned as she puzzled over him. For a little while she tried to invent a circumstance – *any* circumstance – which might have brought Dr Jackson from Knightsgown with her mother's breakfast in a basket and shortly abandoned the effort.

'If Uncle Matt's old sow could fly,' she said to herself, 'it wouldn't be so remarkable as the merest notion of Dr Jackson's arriving in my mother's bedroom at eight o'clock in the morning with her coffee in a basket. What possessed Dr Donovan to be so kind to me? Is it because he's Irish? Was I, am I, on the verge of underestimating a whole island full of good-hearted people?

'Possible he's mad,' she said. 'Insane. Out of his mind.

'But he can't be mad. He's a doctor. Flocks of patients rely on him. They go to him when they get sick and he cures them. If he really were mad they'd be dying like flies.

'Or perhaps,' she said, 'he thinks I'm too left-footed to get my own breakfast – if Mary's still in the hospital. Perhaps he doesn't believe Miss Nellie would take care of me. Personally, I don't think Miss Nellie *would* take care of me.

'Or,' she went on, 'maybe before he left last night he saw the kitchen. Maybe he knew that nobody could make anything in there until Miss Nellie gets a new stove. Maybe he brought *her* breakfast. Maybe he brought *Kevin's* breakfast.

'Or maybe,' she concluded, '*I'm* mad. Maybe I'm making a mountain out of a molehill. Maybe Dr Donovan's just being neighbourly and I'm just a foreigner who doesn't understand what it is to be Irish – or to be compassionate.'

She revelled in her breakfast. Donovan's bread, his honey, his coffee were as good as Miss Nellie's and there was so much of everything that she could share her feast with Kevin, who had knocked at her door after Donovan's departure.

'I wouldn't have thought to bother you,' said Kevin, when he had eaten, 'but, as I told you, I'd been looking high and low for Solomon and, at the last, I said to myself he might be here with you.'

'Bring him back in the afternoon,' said Gretchen, 'and we'll do his ears. It's his day, today.'

Donovan was at the Hall at one o'clock with her lunch.

'My housekeeper and I have thrashed this out,' he said. 'I can't bring you a hot meal for, between Ralston's Cove and the Hall, it would be cold on delivery. But I can bring you hot soup and hot coffee at lunch-time and at dinner-time. I've laid in a good stock of thermos bottles.'

'On account of me?' said Gretchen.

'On account of you,' said Donovan. 'You must understand that, before this morning, I was never heavily into catering.'

'I *am* a nuisance,' Gretchen said. 'An awful nuisance.'

'So you are,' said Donovan.

'But before I took my bath,' she said, 'I washed up the breakfast things in Miss Nellie's bathroom.'

'You needn't have bothered,' said Donovan.

'It was the least I could do,' Gretchen said. 'I worry about Miss Nellie. Who's looking after her?'

'The rector and Jim Farquahar are seeing to it that she's fed at intervals,' said Donovan.

'And what about Mary?' said Gretchen.

'I've had a talk with Mary,' Donovan said. 'For the nonce she'll stay in hospital – not because she's not fit to leave but because she's not fit to put the Hall to rights. Mary's not strong, for all she's bulky.'

'Putting the Hall to rights would be a labour for Hercules,' said Gretchen. 'Are those five hogs still at the bottom of the stairs?'

'They are,' said Donovan. 'But don't fret about them. Eat, sleep and work on your manuscript. You did your stint yesterday.'

Gretchen lunched on split pea soup, cold chicken, potato salad, an apple, a piece of fruitcake and coffee. To her surprise Kevin came by at two o'clock.

'I just stopped in to warn you there'll be an uproar in this place this afternoon,' he said. 'It seems the parson had a little chat with

Father Murphy, Father Murphy had a little chat with Danny O'Toole and some of the other fellows round about, and the upshot of the whole thing is that half of Dufresne Village and three or four of the farmers in the vicinity will be invading the Hall in a few minutes. The men will get rid of the pigs and take on the worst of the heavy lifting. The women will be doing the cleaning.'

'They won't get much done in a single afternoon,' said Gretchen. 'There's pigs' blood, pigs' urine, pigs' droppings everywhere. All of the carpets will have to be sent out and cleaned and practically all the furniture in the kitchen and in the drawing-room is broken.'

'Father Murphy's got things in hand,' said Kevin. 'His gang – all of the women, at any rate – are to stay on the job till the end of the week when, with the help of God, it'll be over. Old man Garrigan – at the top of the hill – he's to mend the chairs and tables. He was a joiner in his time, so they say. Danny O'Toole's brother Frank will bring the carpets along to Cork in the morning. Danny himself will get the chairs and the tables up to Garrigan.'

'Has Miss Nellie agreed to pay for all of that?' Gretchen said.

'There's the beauty of the business,' said Kevin. 'I'm told that Father Murphy's promised indulgences to anyone who takes part in the operation. So, as you can imagine, everyone's willing and able. Of course Miss Nellie will have to pay for cleaning the rugs and she'll have to buy a new cooker or there'll be no more meals in the Hall. As for myself, I've had a stroke of luck.'

'What's happened?' said Gretchen.

'Mrs O'Toole's desperate for firewood,' Kevin said. 'It seems her husband never gets round to it – although they've a grand electric saw. So I'm to see to the firewood and in return I get three meals a day and a good dinner for Solomon. Neither the poor beast nor I will starve before the end of the week, if all goes well.'

'We'd better do Solomon now,' said Gretchen. 'If the house fills up with strangers he might go into a flat spin.'

As Kevin had warned, it was bedlam in the Hall for several days. Even with the door closed tight Gretchen could hear men cursing – presumably as they hoisted heavy or ungainly objects and bore them away or shifted others so that their wives could run their mops or brushes right back to the baseboards – women bawling jokes or snatches of gossip at each other while they scrubbed and scoured. But at the top of the west tower she felt secure and cosseted. With Seamus off the premises Kevin was able to come and go as he pleased, bringing her news of the struggles below her fastness. Miss Nellie – by no means unaware that, if the Hall was not a burnt-out shell, she had Gretchen to thank for the fact that it was still, in essence, what it had always been – poked her head around Gretchen's door in the mornings, gave her a glance, a nod, and left her with a sharp comment on the foul weather. And three times a day Donovan brought his basket to her bedside.

'I wouldn't feel so much like a millstone,' said Gretchen, to Donovan, 'if you just brought me an apple a day. But when I said as much to Kevin he said you *had* to feed me. He said the kitchen's clean now. That *can't* be true, but we'll let it go. However, Mr Garrigan hasn't yet finished with the table and the chairs and, apparently, Miss Nellie has yet to provide for a new stove.'

'Unfortunately I can't bring you an apple,' said Donovan. ' "An apple a day keeps the doctor away" and you need a doctor.'

'I don't much like apples, to tell you the truth,' Gretchen said. 'But whatever you bring me is always delicious.'

'My housekeeper will be glad to hear it,' said Donovan. 'She racks her brain over cold concoctions.'

For Donovan, even for Kevin, Gretchen strove to be cheerful but, for the first time in her life she was deeply, and inexpressibly, depressed. Sooner or later, she promised herself, she would get down to sustained hard work on her thesis. Sooner or later she hoped she would be proud of it. But once it was finished she could not imagine what she was to do with the rest of her life. Up to the moment every step on her way had been marked out for her; never, so far as she could remember, had she made a choice between one field of endeavour or another, never had she been able to tell herself that she had chosen – or would, one day, be free to choose – a life for herself, a life of her own. Her thesis was important to her; she hoped to distinguish herself when she was better, when she came to write it. Unquestionably she would give her best to the thesis but then –

Irish writers had been her passion since she had first read *The Playboy of the Western World*, when she was sixteen. But many and finer scholars than herself had examined, were examining, the best – and, possibly, the worst – of Irish writings. Could she make new studies – the one more brilliant than the last – and, even if she could, where was the money to come from for such a self-indulgence?

'I'll have to get a teaching post by hook or by crook,' she said to herself. 'And when I do I'll just have to grin and bear it. I'll have to learn to fit into an academic world no matter how restricted it is, no matter if I hate it, no matter if I'm an old fossil by the time I'm thirty.'

Between the cough and the fever and the uncertainty of the future she was often in danger of feeling sorry for herself. But Donovan's arrival invariably banished her fretful humours. He not only kept her nourished, he supplied sundry comforts which made her illness far easier to tolerate. On the first day after the great *fiasco* with the pigs he took into account that Gretchen's overcoat was partly covering her, as she sat in bed, and he remarked on it.

'Have you no place to put that?' he said.

'I could hang it up in the alcove,' said Gretchen, 'but Miss Nellie's wire hangers are too flimsy to bear its weight.'

'Then I'll bring you a proper coat hanger,' said Donovan.

'No, don't,' Gretchen said. 'The coat helps to keep me warm.'

That evening he brought her dinner, an old eiderdown and a sturdy hanger.

'Will I ever be able to do anything for you?' said Gretchen.

'I'll let you know,' he said.

Just as he was leaving he stopped in the doorway.

'If you read after dark,' he said, 'you've to get out of bed and cross the room to put out the overhead light before you sleep?'

'What else can I do?' said Gretchen.

'At that, it's a very poor light for reading or working in bed. Now if there were to be a socket at the back of one of those two night-tables –' he said.

With an effort he pulled the little commode on Gretchen's left hand forward and peered behind it.

The next morning, in addition to her breakfast, he brought a small table-lamp, just right for a bedside.

'With this you should write a better thesis,' he said.

Gretchen was both touched and delighted; at the same time she was apprehensive about the day which lengthened ahead of her.

'On Thursdays you always go to Port Ferris, don't you?' she said.

'In general I do,' said Donovan. 'But I'm not going to Port Ferris today. To date not one of my patients has died of malnutrition.'

'Meaning me?' said Gretchen.

'Meaning you,' Donovan said.

'But there must be people in Cork who'll miss you terribly if you don't go,' said Gretchen.

'Next week they'll appreciate me all the more,' said Donovan. 'Have you enough to read?'

'For a little while longer,' she said.

When he arrived with her lunch he was carrying a bag of books: A.P. Herbert's *The Water Gypsies, Two Years in the Forbidden City* by the Princess Der Ling, the collected short stories of Somerset Maugham, Rosamond Lehmann's *Dusty Answer* and Laclos' *Les Liaisons Dangereuses* in translation.

131

'There are plenty more where those came from,' said Donovan.

'I won't do any work for ten days at least,' said Gretchen.

'They're not meant to muzzle the Muse,' Donovan said. 'They're simply for moments of leisure – or repentance.'

'Of what should I repent?' said Gretchen.

'Possibly of the error in judgment which brought you to Ralston's Cove and *environs*,' said Donovan.

On Friday evening he came by with her dinner earlier than usual and caught her in her dressing-gown and her bedroom slippers, sitting on the floor and crooning to Solomon while Kevin worked on the dog's ears. The three of them were so deeply committed to their ritual that Donovan went unnoticed; from the doorsill he regarded the operation with an increasing respect for Gretchen – calm, unruffled, in absolute mastery of Solomon – and acknowledged Kevin's delicacy and skill. When they had finished he stepped forward and inquired about their ministrations.

Gretchen explained that the preparations they were using was designed to cure mastitis in cattle. Donovan looked over the list of the ingredients in the ointment, as printed on the label of the tube.

'You might just be onto a good thing,' he said. 'Which of you decided the dog needed treatment?'

'There was no decision,' said Gretchen. 'We both knew we needed help.'

'And which of you prescribed the ointment?' said Donovan.

'She did,' Kevin said. 'I wouldn't have had the wit.'

Late that night Donovan's thoughts were, as always, gently revolving around Gretchen. But the tenderness he had felt as he had watched the three of them – the dog so quiet and trusting, Gretchen so serious and compassionate, Kevin so serious and dedicated – had, momentarily, altered his vision of Gretchen. He had seen her, not as an elusive yet beckoning nymph, but as a grave and earnest child, one with Kevin in her concentration on alleviating the dog's affliction. For an instant he reflected on the pleasure he would have derived if, at the end of the day's work, he could have come home to the boy and the girl and the dog, each of them so simple and artless – at least for so long as they were together. Feeling tired and elderly he dwelt on Gretchen, and on Kevin, as if they had been the children he had never had, the children he might have loved – and been allowed to love. But soon Kevin and the dog had slipped from his mind; only Gretchen – the child in the woman, the woman in the child – remained to haunt him and to remind him that, whenever he thought of her, it was not as his daughter but as a mysterious, magnetic force which, however powerfully it attracted him, he must – given his fifty years – at all costs evade. And then, as each day he did, he told himself severely that she must not suspect him of any sentiment not entirely consonant with his purely professional obligations.

By Monday morning Mary was back at her old stand, Miss Nellie had gallantly paid for a new stove, the kitchen had been scrubbed down, the kitchen chairs and table had been repaired, Seamus was to be discharged from the hospital that afternoon, and life in the Hall had resumed, for the most part, its former aspect. However, the six days of adversity had bound Donovan more closely to Gretchen; for Gretchen, he was certain, was beginning to look on him as one with the rest of the furniture of her life, even if she was still punctilious about expressing her gratitude for the least of his attentions.

Every evening he had silently smoked his pipe while she ate the dinner he had set in front of her. When she came to her coffee they had made conversation – he probing as tactfully as he could for her particulars and reaping occasional, slim rewards, she begging him for the anecdotes touching the lives and the idiosyncrasies of a number of the citizens of the county, which he could recount so easily and enliven with the wry, running commentary which came so naturally to him. As of the Wednesday following the upheaval in the Hall until the Sunday night which marked the end of the disordered week, he himself had hastily lunched and dined on sandwiches – much to his housekeeper's disapproval. But making time for Gretchen was his first concern and several of his patients had found him restless, intolerant of a wealth of clinical detail, or of the unremitting complaints and expositions to which he had used to listen with such sympathetic interest.

As of Mary's return to a kitchen in working order there was no longer any necessity for Donovan to provide Gretchen's meals. Gretchen, unhappy to put too much strain on Miss Nellie's meagre domestic resources, asked to be permitted to take her lunch and her dinner in the dining-room, but Mary would not hear of it.

'I'll fetch and carry for you morning, noon, and night,' she said, to Gretchen – in Donovan's presence. 'Who was it saved me from those wild beasts in me kitchen if not yourself? She never gave a thought to me though I was screaming me lungs out, and sure I'd have been trampled underfoot if you hadn't sailed to me rescue.

'When Dr Donovan says you can go downstairs for your lunch and your dinner, well and good. Until that time you'll stick tight up here whilst I take care of you. What's more, I'll bring you me nice eggs –

poached or boiled or scrambled – for your dinner, instead of them powdered concoctions she dotes on. Even Solomon won't touch them; so, I ask you, why should you?'

Once Mary was in charge Donovan revised his program for the evenings. He took to coming by at seven o'clock – well before the dinner hour at the Hall – with whisky and soda water for himself, vodka for Gretchen, and a bucket of ice so that she could drink it chilled. Although Gretchen was still a long way from taking him wholly into her confidence she let herself float on the vodka, she accepted him gratefully and if, for a while, she maintained her reserve when he inquired too closely into her affairs, she did not disguise her enjoyment of his company.

Twelve days after the day of the pigs Gretchen asked, and received, Donovan's permission to work sitting up at the table, wearing her winter coat and wrapped, below the waist, in a blanket. Within a week he had caught her still sitting at the table when he came in with his whisky, his soda water, his vodka and his pailful of ice. All her attention was focussed on a typewritten sheet which she was reading over; she was not aware of his arrival. To her left a small saucepan, filled with water, had been set down on a straw mat beside a perforated spoon. Those objects in themselves, so far from their usual environment, were curious enough; far more curious was the fact that, in each hand, Gretchen was holding an egg.

'Are you engaged in some sort of fertility rite?' Donovan said.

Gretchen turned, glanced at him, glanced at her eggs, and shook her head. Carefully she put the eggs into the saucepan, threw her coat and her extra blanket over the foot of the bed, and clambered into it.

'Don't you make fun of my eggs,' said Gretchen. 'Specially not in front of Mary.'

'I can take an egg as seriously as the next man,' said Donovan.

'Here comes Mary,' Gretchen said. 'Now, please, make no scornful reference to fertility rites or whatever.'

Mary greeted Donovan affectionately and made a bee-line for the saucepan.

'Had you enough rag?' she said.

'I had plenty,' said Gretchen.

'Well, I'll be back with the eggs freshly boiled when you've had your dinner and your coffee,' said Mary. 'Meantime you keep your hands under the covers – except when you need them to eat your meal.

'If you'd ever seen her fingernails when I brought up her lunch,' she said, to Donovan. 'Let me tell you I was that thankful when she suggested the eggs –'

'Dr Donovan's in the dark,' said Gretchen.

'I'll leave you to get him out of it,' Mary said.

'My hands got so cold,' said Gretchen, to Donovan, 'that my fingers were almost too stiff to hold my pen and much too stiff to type out what I'd written in longhand. And then I thought that if I could hold on to something warm every so often – like an egg, like a hard-boiled egg –'

'When the eggs are boiling hot, too hot to hold, she wraps them in a bit of rag and takes them in her hands for a few minutes,' said Mary. 'Then she puts them back in the saucepan and, of course, when she needs them again, they've cooled off to the point where she can handle them without the rags. It's a grand invention, wouldn't you think?'

'I would,' Donovan said.

'For say what you like, It's not healthy up here,' said Mary. 'The carpet'll never be dry till the month of June at the earliest. She could perish of the cold when the winter comes.'

'Take it away,' said Gretchen, the next morning. 'It's very kind of you but I can't afford it.'

'I'm just after telling him you'd make a desperate fuss,' said Mary.

'Just set it down by the hearth,' she said to the man tottering under his burden. 'And tell her what Dr Donovan told you.'

'Dr Donovan said for you not to worry,' said the intruder. 'He said his housekeeper would be glad of it for the back of the house when you've no need of it any more. Now I'll bring up the cylinder and you'll be warm as toast in ten minutes.'

'It's too much,' said Gretchen, to Mary. 'I can't be indebted to Dr Donovan for every breath I take. I can't let him do all this for me.'

''Tis a fine thing indeed,' said Mary. 'And it runs on gas so herself can't be at you for wasting her precious electricity.'

'But you don't understand –' said Gretchen.

'There's no arguing with Dr Donovan,' Mary said. 'He's taken it into his head that he wants you snug and cosy –'

'There we go,' said the man. 'Now I'll show you ladies how to light it –'

'And if we've any complaints?' said Mary.

'Here's my name and there's my number,' the man said, handing Mary a crumpled card. 'Call me if ever you're so inclined. This day week I'll be by with a new cylinder. Seven days – if you run the fire continuously – is about what you'll get out of this one.'

With that he was gone.

'Oh, Mary,' said Gretchen, 'I wish he hadn't done it. How am I ever to repay him?'

'There's a lot of folk in Ralston's Cove ought to be asking themselves the same question,' said Mary. 'But don't be taking it out on yourself. All he wants is a smile and a welcome when he stops in this evening.'

Gretchen could have given Donovan much more than a smile and a welcome, had she been able to yield to her own impulsive promptings. As it was, she kept a tight rein on herself whenever they were together since, from the very beginning, she had been in awe of him. His patrician good looks were not lost on her; they had led her to suppose that almost any woman would be his for the taking if he indicated the smallest proclivity for an *affair de coeur*, and she had often asked herself why he wasted, and kept on wasting, so many hours of his hard-earned leisure on her. Face to face with him, daunted by his lofty bearing, disconcerted by the wit which never made him more accessible and often tended to put him further off than ever, and instinctively aware of his capacity for harsh disapproval, if it was called for, she felt raw and inconsequential. Yet raw or inconsequential though he might take her to be, not once had he failed to lend her comfort and reassurance.

Many times she had planned to redress the balance slightly, to insist on a bill for his services, partly to re-establish her independence and partly to challenge his supreme authority. But too many weeks had gone by, he had bestowed and she had accepted too many favours, it was too late to pretend that all his thoughtfulness, his generosity had a price and could be paid for. Yet for all he had given, for all she had received, she could not imagine that he was drawn to her – as a man may be drawn to a woman. She could only assume that he was pledged to relieve distress, she could only regret that, effectively, he must find her beneath his notice. Thus, when he asked about her family, when he expressed an interest in her own so uneventful life, she shielded herself against the strength of his presence, sure that his interest must be perfunctory, certain that whatever she vouchsafed would leave him cold. Nevertheless each day she waited for his steps on the stairs as if she could rely on him to take her seriously, and each time he made ready to go she longed to say, 'Don't desert me yet, it's much too soon.' If anyone had suggested to her that he was living for his visits to the Hall she would have recoiled in disbelief. For – so she was convinced – it was her cough and her fever which held him to her; once she was well she would lose him as naturally, as inevitably, as she had claimed him when she was stricken.

And yet, occasionally, she wondered if he might not be somewhat ashamed of himself for having so airily installed her in the Hall –

where the plumbing failed to function, where the wind and the rain swept in through every crack in many a door or a window, where the sharp weather left her with fingers too chilled and numb to hold a pen, where there was no escape from the ear-splitting television or the even more ear-splitting squabbles between Mary and Miss Nellie, where a host of pigs could occupy the premises for most of a whole afternoon, bringing filth and chaos wherever they trotted or charged –

'Is it conceivable,' she said to herself, 'that he feels guilty whenever he thinks of me here in all this foul disorder, that he's trying to make things easier for me partly he thinks of himself as responsible for everything I've had to put up with in this tricked-up slum? Or does he simply see me as one more of his lame ducks? He must have scores of them. Perhaps I'm just another variation on lame-duckery. Very likely that's it. Very likely when I'm sound of wind and limb he'll write me off. He'll celebrate my recovery by making love to a famous beauty or a Bulgarian spy or a duke's daughter –

'What difference does it make?' she said. 'I've just *got* to get well. I've just got to *work* –'

One evening, eased by vodka, a little slack, a little frivolous she had mentioned, *en passant*, that she was lonely without a mirror.

'Ever since I came to Ireland,' she said, 'I've never been able to brush my hair in front of a mirror. In fact, I've forgotten what I look like.'

'The one over the chest of drawers is certainly useless,' said Donovan. 'But surely there's a mirror in the bathroom.'

'There is,' said Gretchen. 'But it's at one end of the room, over the wash-basin, and the light bulb's at the other. I can see myself in the half-dark but I'm not quite sure it's my own face looking back at me. I wish I knew how Seamus pretends to shave in there.'

'He only pretends to shave on Saturdays,' Donovan said. 'And not every Saturday at that.'

'One can understand it,' said Gretchen.

The next evening he brought her a small article loosely wrapped in tissue paper.

'It's just to remind you,' said Donovan, 'what a delicious morsel you are – as Harry Moore would say.'

Gretchen, suspicious of sarcasm, unprepared for a tribute, pulled off the tissue paper and saw a delicate hand-mirror, the back and the handle charmingly decorated with seed pearls. She could not know that it had been his mother's, nor could she know that it was all he had left of his mother, but she understood at once that it was something rare and meaningful.

'Perhaps after all,' she said to her herself, when Donovan had gone, 'he's a little bit fond of me.'

It was her first tentative acknowledgment that Dr Donovan's interest in her might not be wholly expressed in gas heaters or injections of antibiotics, and no sooner had she made it than she took herself to task for such temerity. But when she turned out the bedside lamp and settled herself for sleep she was ridiculously happy. In the morning she gazed at herself in Donovan's glas and wondered how he could have imagined that she deserved so exquisite a souvenir.

Four weeks from the day that the pigs had overrun the Hall Mary brought Gretchen her tea, as she had every day since she had taken up her rounds again, and Gretchen noticed that the tray was set for two.

'Her Ladyship's coming to have her tea with you,' said Mary. 'Seamus is plagued with the tooth-ache, so he's off to Ralston's Cove and the dentist.'

Miss Nellie, who had recently exchanged her habitual rose-pink and mauve outfit, in its unholy alliance with her green stockings and her scarlet slippers, for a yellow and violet combination, underpinned by Prussian blue stockings and the same scarlet slippers, exerted herself to please, and Gretchen found her delightful. Indeed she talked to Gretchen as if they were old friend, on intimate terms, and Gretchen felt favoured.

The first topic under review was the state of the Hall. The carpets had been cleaned at Cork and returned; they were to be laid on the following day. Many of the little tables from the drawing-room were still in Mr Garrigan's hands, but the chairs, in a hit-or-miss fashion, had been mended. As for compensation –

'I've quite lost my respect for Jim Farquahar,' Miss Nellie said. 'He has none of his grandfather's vigour. And none of his father's, if it comes to that. You may doubt my word, but I assure you that he's tried to dissuade me from pressin' for damages. To be sure the lorry-driver was all but embalmed in liquor, or so they say, which means that the insurance company can decline to respond for what those unspeakable animals did in here. But there's a large firm behind that lorry, they've dozens of lorries on the roads and I shall brin' suit against them to the value of their entire holdin's. Moreover I'll win, even if I give over the rest of my life to litigatin'.'

Gretchen, primed for the worst, expecting Miss Nellie to continue in that vein until her indigantion was drained away, and she assumed that Miss Nellie's indignation was boundless. But after pouring a second cup of tea Miss Nellie abruptly changed the subject.

'You were in luck when you came across Clement Donovan,' she said. 'He's the best there is in all of the county. Why he's not practisin' in Dublin is somethin' I cannot fathom. After the sorry childhood he spent in this part of the world one might have thought he'd have shaken off the dust of Ralston's Cove the very minute he'd escaped to the university.'

'What went wrong with his childhood?' said Gretchen.

'His mother walked out on him – and on his father – when he was hardly more than a baby,' said Miss Nellie. 'She was French. I never knew her myself but I've been told she was lovely-lookin'. No one blamed her over-much – poor Donovan's father was a dipsomaniac even by Irish standards – but there was quite a little feelin' that she should have taken the child with her, back to France, or wherever she went.'

Miss Nellie's answer to her question was so unexpected that Gretchen's eyes were stung by sudden tears. All at once she longed to comfort Dr Donovan – the man, Donovan, who had, once upon a time, been only a little boy. Before she could think of anything to say, Miss Nellie was off again on her own.

'After it was plain that the child's mother had cleared out for good,' said Miss Nellie, 'Jim Farquahar's grandfather – he was an old man then – wrote to Donovan's grandfather who was makin' a fortune in Australia. He pointed out that the boy's father was absolutely unfit to brin' him up – there was a good deal of correspondence between the two of them – and it was arranged that his great-aunt should take him in.'

'So he was more or less an orphan,' Gretchen said, and prayed that her voice was steady.

'He was,' said Miss Nellie. 'His great-aunt was a Miss Donovan, his grandfather's sister, and she was none too pleased to have the child billetted on her. Adeline Donovan was the busiest woman you ever saw, servin' on every committee from here to Port Ferris, pokin' into the private affairs of all her neighbours, preachin' reform and temperance, raisin' money for good causes east, west, north and south. In short she'd no time to spare for a little boy; she found him a frightful nuisance, and there's no doubt she let him know it.

'Just about the time that Clement Donovan went off to the university in Dublin his grandfather came home. He'd made a killin' in Australia and before he died he meant to put every nose in Ralston's Cove out of joint. So he built himself a great mansion in the town – for show, if you understand me – as he took no account of anyone close by. The only man in Ralston's Cove to cross his threshold was Jim Farquahar's father.'

139

'Didn't he even open his door to his grandson?' said Gretchen.

'Not in the beginnin',' Miss Nellie said. 'He hadn't the least affection for his grandson. He'd paid all his expenses while he was livin' with his great-aunt and he went right on payin' for him in Dublin. But at first – so Jim Farquahar told me years ago when he'd had one over the eight – he left all his money to build a new school and a monstrous big library in Ralston's Cove. However young Donovan had made a splendid record for himself away from home and had made a fine start here when he came back. Once his grandfather was convinced that he was nothin' like his drunken father – who did, verily, die in a gutter – he changed his will. He left everythin' he had to his grandchild, and none too soon either. Within a month of drawin' it up he was in his grave.'

'Dr Donovan must have been rich after that,' said Gretchen.

'He was indeed,' Miss Nellie said. 'Yet the queer thin' is that Clement Donovan's never appeared to have any use for money – although Jim Farquahar believes that he's probably the richest man in the county. All the same he keeps to himself, lives in his grandfather's house with only one woman to help out. He does love to sail and he has a boat. And once in a while he takes a vacation on the Continent. But he works harder than any other doctor in Ralston's Cove – or any doctor around here – quite as if he had a wife and ten or twelve children to support.'

'Has he never married?' said Gretchen, and hung on Miss Nellie's reply as though the reply were of the greatest importance to her.

'He married about twenty years ago,' Miss Nellie said. 'But evidently it didn't work out. His wife had a baby that died and afterward she left him. Four or five years later she came home and inside of a week she was dead.'

'So he's really never had anyone for long at the very centre of his life?' said Gretchen, coming as near as she dared to the heart of the matter.

'No one,' said Miss Nellie. 'Clement Donovan's a law unto himself and responsible to nobody but himself. However nothin's too much for him where a sick man or a sick woman or a sick child's concerned.'

'Will I take the tea-tray?' said Mary, marching in. 'That's if you've finished with it, of course.'

'Yes, take it,' Miss Nellie said. 'I've been talking too much. I got carried away.'

'I was following every word,' said Gretchen.

'He's a fascinatin' man, Dr Donovan,' said Miss Nellie.

That same evening Donovan pronounced Gretchen well enough to

140

do without a physician in residence.

'So if I'm lonely,' said Gretchen, 'I'll have to break a leg to see you again?'

'I'm used to dropping in at the Hall,' Donovan said. 'Seamus has a trick knee which slips from time to time and a number of minor vexations. It relieves Miss Nellie when someone else happens in who can field Seamus if he's feeling abused and overlooked.'

'Is Seamus interested in anything but Seamus?' said Gretchen.

'He's interested in steeple-chasing and why not?' said Donovan. 'After all, while he was in England, two of the horses he trained were placed in the Grand National. But Miss Nellie's not interested in horse-flesh, so Seamus can only talk himself out in the pub.'

'Whenever I've seen them together,' Gretchen said, 'it's been Miss Nellie who made the conversation.'

'Seamus has the gift of the gab too,' said Donovan. 'But not after he's been drinking hard. And between what he knocks back at the pub before lunch and here at the Hall before dinner, he's apt to be particularly tearful at meal-times.'

They had come to an end of sorts, and both of them knew it.

'I've a housecall to make this evening,' said Donovan, rising.

'Then you must go at once,' Gretchen said.

He put on his coat, picked up his black bag, as Gretchen waited for him to take his leave. Instead, much to her surprise – and much to his own – he walked back to her.

'Shall we celebrate your recovery by going out for a good dinner on Thursday?' he said.

'That would be lovely,' said Gretchen, hoping she sounded willing but not uncommonly eager.

'In that case I won't bother to say good-bye,' he said.

'What will you say?' said Gretchen, keeping him beside her for just a moment longer.

'*A bientôt*,' said Donovan.

10

There was no question that the food at the Hall verged on the inedible, no question that Gretchen – industrious as she had become, ever since she had been able to sleep through a whole night without coughing – had a right to a good meal at least once a week. For Donovan both assertions were irrefutable; he rehearsed them each Thursday when, in the late afternoon, he drove straight from Port

141

Ferris to the Hall at the end of the day's work.

'But I thought you spent every Thursday night in Port Ferris,' Gretchen had said. 'Miss Nellie told me you did.'

'Miss Nellie was right,' he had replied. 'But I was finding it increasingly difficult to get up early enough on Friday mornings to have time for breakfast before I went on to the hospital in Ralston's Cove or got started on housecalls.'

Thus on Thursday evenings Donovan took Gretchen to the Cygne d'Or and neither of them had the smallest suspicion of how the other felt about the arrangement. Donovan believed that if Gretchen had been anywhere else – had not been isolated in the west tower – flocks of admirers would have cut him out in short order. Gretchen believed that Donovan was kind to her much as she was kind to Solomon, simply because, as she had done with Solomon, he had thought her in need of attention. For both of them the dinner at the Cygne d'Or was the highpoint of the week; Gretchen was so forthright as to admit it.

'You can't imagine how I look forward to Thursdays,' she said.

Donovan was more cautious.

'A break now and then from Miss Nellie's instant fare probably does you no harm,' he said.

On the first Thursday he had remarked on her self-confessed passion for Irish men of letters.

'I'm not going to talk about it,' said Gretchen. 'Every time we're together we talk about me. We never talk about you.'

'I left it to Miss Nellie to give me a clean bill of health,' said Donovan.

'It wasn't so much a clean bill of health as a certificate of merit,' Gretchen said, hoping she could coax Donovan to round out Miss Nellie's cast of characters – French mother, alcoholic father, ungenerous aunt, runaway wife – while Donovan merely asked her if she had read *The Crock of Gold*.

Frequently Donovan stopped in at the Hall, ostensibly to give Miss Nellie a little fillip and boost Seamus' sagging morale by lingering over a cup of coffee with the two of them. Earlier it had been true that he had regarded his visits to Dufresne Bay as errands of duty and mercy and if, later, he came because he was starved for a glimpse of Gretchen, between one Thursday and the next, only Miss Nellie was perceptive enough to divine that, since Gretchen's arrival, Donovan was a differently motivated man.

Sometimes he came too late for a sight of her. On those evenings Miss Nellie invariably offered to call her while Donovan invariably insisted that it was not Gretchen but herself and Seamus whom he had come to see. Whereupon Miss Nellie tempered his disappointment by making Gretchen the subject of their conversation.

On one occasion she launched forth on Gretchen's clothing.

'She's been very well brought up, that girl,' said Miss Nellie. 'She's nothin' like the young people one runs into everywhere these days. Do you know she'd been here six weeks before she asked me if she could come to lunch in blue jeans? I told her that of course she could. At the same time she faithfully promised that she'd dress for dinner, and she always does. I'm not talkin' about evenin' frocks, you understand. Her frocks are very simple – and very becomin'. What I'm referrin' to is the effort she makes to look presentable at dinner-time.'

As it happened Donovan was especially fetched by Gretchen's clothes. He was bored and disgusted by the jeans and T-shirts he met every day and proud to have Gretchen on his arm when they entered the Cygne d'Or. The next Thursday he repeated Miss Nellie's remarks as they sat over cocktails.

Gretchen remained for so long without speaking that Donovan wondered if she had simply not bothered to listen to him.

At length she said, 'I never expected a compliment from Miss Nellie.'

'She's not much given to panegyrics,' said Donovan.

Toward the beginning of December Donovan waited until they were at their coffee to give Gretchen a warning.

'You won't like what I'm about to say,' he said. 'You've never taken my advice unless it suited you but what I have to tell you tonight is so grave that you must listen to me. Some fourteen or fifteen months ago a girl of nineteen was raped and mutilated near Limerick. Since then six others have met with the same fate. From our point of view, from the point of view of Ralston's Cove, each affair was reprehensible but not very close to home. However some of us noticed that the psychopath – the Gardaí think one man is responsible for every crime – was working in a jagged line running south and slightly west of Limerick. Last night there was another victim. An old poacher came across her late this afternoon just on the fringe of the woods behind Harry Moore's east meadow. I heard about it because I chanced by the Gardaí – for quite a different reason – at about seven o'clock this evening.'

'Weren't you in Port Ferris today?' said Gretchen.

'Yes, but I was back in Ralston's Cove by seven,' said Donovan. 'Brian Touhey was on duty at the post and he told me what he knew about it, which is what I've told you. Now I'll come to the point. The victims had six things in common. They were all raped, they were all mutilated, they were all killed, they were all young, each of them was alone – forasmuch as has been ascertained from their parents, their relatives, and their friends – and each of them was attacked in a lonely place after dark. By this time I know you well enough to be quite sure that if there came a clear, moonlit hour after dinner at the Hall you might easily take it into your head, on the spur or the moment, to get away from the television, from Seamus and Miss Nellie – and go for a little stroll. You're a high-spirited, courageous, independent person, no doubt you discovered the hill above the graveyard which looks down on Dufresne Bay when you went to church with Miss Nellie. It would be like you to strike out all by yourself after nightfall – I often did the same thing when I was more or less your age and fed up with Ralston's Cove. Don't do it. Don't leave the Hall when it's dark unless you've a man beside you. Don't take any risk at all until this killer is under lock and key.'

'And when might that be?' said Gretchen. 'Have the police anything to go on but the *modus operandi*?'

'They have,' said Donovan. 'Brian Touhey was guilty of an indiscretion when he told me about the murder here – but he's been my patient ever since I first set up shop in Ralston's Cove. The Gardaí have found pubic hairs on three of the young women which match, and one clear thumb-print on the metal clasp of a large hand-bag lying beside one of the bodies.'

'How did Mr Touhey know all that?' Gretchen said. 'Was Ralston's Cove expecting this murder?'

'Apparently the whole area was alerted after the last one,' said Donovan. 'The Gardaí thought there was a good possibility the man would keep on heading south.'

'From what you've been saying,' said Gretchen, 'it seems to me there's a good possibility he'll keep on moving – period. West now, perhaps, since he can't go much further south. Still, after what you've told me, wild horses wouldn't get me out after dark – even if there are times when I'm afraid I'll blow my mind, bottled up in the Hall.'

In fact Gretchen was no longer in danger of blowing her mind in the Hall. During her first six weeks in Ireland she had been so ill, in the hotel, and later so distracted by Miss Nellie's foibles and by Seamus' moods and by her surroundings in the west tower and, later still, so discouraged by the bronchitis which had kept her cloistered in her room that her manuscript had come to seem a lifeless thing. But although very few of her early efforts at the long blue table between the French windows would stand as she had written them, through her protracted labours the dissertation had quickened once again. Soon her writers were more real to her than Miss Nellie or Mary or Seamus. They clamoured for recognition and Gretchen recognised them. It was hard for her to disregard them for an hour once a week in order to write a letter to her mother. They had become part of her thoughts at breakfast, of her last reflections before she slept. Only when she was with Donovan could she put them aside and that, inevitably, with a little wrench, a nagging sense of being, herself, somehow displaced, out of her own province. Donovan had observed that until she was established across from him at their sheltered table, until she had begun to drink her vodka, she was distant, she was elsewhere.

'Is the thesis with you late and soon?' he said.

'It's filling up all my empty spaces,' said Gretchen. 'I haven't much room left for extra luggage.

'But,' she said, with sudden animation, 'I was forgetting something cheerful. Solomon's ears are cured. Kevin and I decided yesterday that he didn't need any more medication. So, you see, I've always had a little room for extra baggage. And *please*, the next time you call on Miss Nellie and Seamus, play with Solomon's head. Then you can tell me if we're right, Kevin and I.'

'Has Miss Nellie remarked on a change?' said Donovan.

'In a way,' said Gretchen. 'I heard her tell Seamus she wasn't going to take him back to the vet in Ralston's Cove for a while because his ears didn't seem to be bothering him.

'Vets in cattle country are all alike,' she said. 'They don't know anything about cats and dogs. Our vet in Knightstown's slightly different from most of the others. He breeds setters so he has to be on the *qui-vive* for rickets and worms and distemper and canker and things. But he knows absolutely nothing about cats. When our Siamese was dying he wouldn't even come, though my father can get him any time for a first-calf heifer in labour.'

'You're a true-blue country girl, aren't you,' said Donovan.

'I'm certainly no city slicker,' she said. 'To be truthful I did fall in love with New York – I went there for every Easter vacation while I was an undergraduate – but maybe that's because I was with Aaron so, of course, I wasn't frightened or lonely.'

'Who is Aaron?' said Donovan – and dreaded the answer, if she supplied one.

'Aaron is someone I met at the beginning of my freshman year at college,' said Gretchen. 'We lived together for all the four years until we graduated – over the week-ends and during some of the holidays, that is to say.'

145

'And will you be going back to him?' Donovan said. 'When you leave Ireland?'

'No,' said Gretchen. 'When Aaron marries – if Aaron's ever ready to get married – he'll be looking for a domestic slave.'

'And when you're ready to marry?' Donovan said. 'What will you be looking for?'

'I don't know,' said Gretchen. 'Somebody strong, probably. Somebody stronger than me.'

Although Donovan felt as if his jacket concealed a knife-wound in his chest, he could not let Aaron leave Gretchen's stage. He had – if possible – to come straight up against him.

'Were you faithful to your Aaron for all of the four years?' he said.

'Of course,' said Gretchen. 'We were right for each other as long as we were doing the same things.

'Besides,' she said, 'it was Aaron who taught me to look at pictures, Aaron who made me take the survey course in art in college, Aaron who made me listen to music. His parents had brought him up to the arts – they collected paintings, they went to concerts. They were rich, you see, and influential. I wouldn't have missed the years with Aaron for anything. Sometimes I think I learned as much from him as I did from the university.'

In spite of the agony, Donovan craved more salt in his wound. If he was to suffer – and a desert of suffering stretched before him – he would suffer at the hands of a rival made of bone and sinew, not through the agency of a ghost of his own invention. He would study Gretchen's Aaron at close range, as though he were seeing him fixed in a photograph – did Gretchen comply.

But Gretchen did not comply. Instinctively she understood that what Donovan really wanted was to learn how she herself had felt, or still felt, about Aaron and, in the same instant, she understood that she had not the subtlety to explain that, while she would love Aaron until the day she died, it was the friend, but no longer the lover, to whom she would unquestionably be faithful.

'I couldn't make Aaron interesting to you,' she said, when Donovan pressed for details of Aaron's preferences in painters and musicians. 'He's in the past tense, don't you understand?'

'He was very important to you,' said Donovan.

'So he was,' said Gretchen, and diplomatically refrained from announcing that he was still important to her. 'But the affair's all over,' she said. 'Now he's got his life. I've got mine.'

She broke off as the maître d'hôtel approached, followed by the waiter who was bringing their dinner.

'This fish is delicious,' she said.

146

'Isn't it?' said Donovan, and made a stab at the sole for which he had no appetite.

It had never crossed his mind that Gretchen might have belonged to any man. She was, to him, so separate, so proud to walk alone. The knowledge that she had been able to surrender a part of herself to anybody stirred him to sensations which he had never before associated with her. All at once he wanted the evening to end, he wanted to walk by himself along the black shores of the night-struck sea until he had put such a distance between himself and Gretchen that there could be no turning back.

'You're not hungry,' said Gretchen. 'You're tired, aren't you?'

'I am,' said Donovan. 'I was up till all hours with a patient last night.'

'Then let's go now,' Gretchen said.

'We'll go when we've had coffee,' said Donovan, and lapsed into a silence which – except for the necessary exchanges with the waiter and the maître d'hôtel – remained unbroken for the rest of the evening.

'Thank you for everything,' said Gretchen, when Donovan had brought her back to the Hall.

'It was my pleasure,' he said.

From his bedroom Donovan heard the long-case clock strike midnight. Then one o'clock, two o'clock, and still there was no sleep for him. At three o'clock he went down to the library for a long drink of whisky.

Gretchen had a friend whose parents were cultivated people, a friend who had been kind to her, who had introduced her to painting, to music, to a great city, a friend who had been constant for four years, a friend who had helped to shape her mind and instruct her body.

It took a while before the whisky washed over Donovan. When it did it flooded him with a gross physical desire for Gretchen. He had longed to protect her chastity but –

There was nothing to protect. Now there was nothing to prevent him from making love to her. Where was the woman who would ever have refused him if he had wanted her? He was powerful, he was personable, he was potent –

'God, what a dirty old man I am,' he said, and struggled to forget that Gretchen had had a young lover who had filled her life for four whole years, who had taught her the meaning of desire and, probably, the ecstasy of fulfilment –

'I must go to bed,' he said, and poured another glass of whisky.

'Nothing is changed,' he said to himself, during the next four or five days.

But the knowledge that Gretchen had used her lovely body, which he had yearned to defend, as a currency of sorts tortured him. It had brought her what he could never offer her – the *entrée* into a high and wealthy society and the fidelity of a champion who had, very likely, shared a springtime of delight with her. She was not a sleeping beauty over whom he, Donovan, had been, accidentally, elected to keep watch. To be sure, she was radiant, to be sure she was far from home, but she was no longer sleeping, she was wide awake and, thanks to her Aaron, she was undoubtedly capable of keeping watch over herself – and undoubtedly aware of her value in the market-place. Yet, however much he tried to see her with the hard eye of disillusion, however much he stripped her of the innocence in which he had so ingenuously encapsulated her, for however much he told himself that she was, like all the rising generation, profligate and promiscuous, he only desired her all the more, knowing her versed in the ways of men with women.

'I'm too old for her,' he said to himself in the mornings.

'She's too young for me,' he said to himself in the afternoons.

'This has got to stop,' he said, when he came home and sat down to a drink in the evenings. 'I must stay away from her.'

'She's all my happiness,' he said, after his dinner, idling over a night-cap.

On a Tuesday, five days after the dinner with Donovan at the Cygne d'Or, Mary brought Gretchen's tea up to her room in the west tower.

'Herself's in Ralston's Cove,' said Mary. 'And Seamus is worse than no company at all. So I thought you'd rather take your tea by yourself.'

When Gretchen had finished the last of the bread and honey she went downstairs to the bathroom. Coming out of it she could hear Miss Nellie's pattering feet below and, since she had the red bucket in hand, she was about to race upstairs when she heard Miss Nellie, on the ground floor, shout for Mary with such piercing insistence that she stopped for a moment.

'What is it you're wanting?' said Mary, matching Miss Nellie decibel for decibel, presumably emerging from the kitchen or the laundry.

'Clement Donovan is either dead or dyin',' said Miss Nellie.

'By all the blessèd saints,' Mary said. 'What happened to him so?'

'He was in an accident on the highroad to Port Ferris,' said Miss Nellie. 'I wouldn't be surprised if he'd been called out for an emergency in McBride's Landing. Poor old Mrs Wainwright was in a very bad way the last time I heard of her.'

'Is he in hospital then?' said Mary.

'I don't know any more than what I've told you,' Miss Nellie said. 'I had it from the girl at Flood's. As it happened, I thought my right front tyre was low, so I drove into the garage to have it seen to. But there was no one at Flood's to look at the tyre. The girl told me Arthur Flood had gone home for the day and young Willie and that new boy they've taken on had gone off to tow Dr Donovan's car back to Ralston's Cove.

'I asked her what was amiss with Dr Donovan's car and she came out with the story. Dead or dyin' she said he was and that was all she could tell me.'

Some time later Gretchen took the tea-tray down to the kitchen.

'I don't want any dinner tonight, Mary,' she said. 'I don't feel well. I'm going to bed now and see if I can sleep.'

Clearly Mary had been crying, but Gretchen affected not to notice her tear-streaked face.

'At the least I could bring you up a cup of hot broth,' said Mary.

'I don't want any broth,' said Gretchen. 'Please let me sleep.'

As soon as she was back upstairs she shut her door and turned off the cruel overhead lamp. In a few seconds her eyes had adjusted to the evening dark and she saw that the room was filled with moonlight. For over two hours she sat on the edge of the bed, waiting for the end of the night, the beginning of another day – waiting. Finally, feeling insufferably constricted, she put on her winter coat, went out onto the balcony, and stood quite still, looking down at the moonlit bay. After a while she heard a car nearing the Hall, a car which stopped at the entrance to the west tower. Instantly Miss Nellie's cry rang out.

'Who is it?' Miss Nellie said.

'Am I too late for coffee?' came the answer.

The voice was Donovan's. It carried up to Gretchen, high above.

'Is it really you?' said Miss Nellie. 'I was told you were dead. Dead or dyin'.'

'Good news travels fast,' said Donovan.

'Come in. Come in,' Miss Nellie said. 'The wind's bitter at this time of year.'

'That girl at Flood upset me dreadfully,' said Miss Nellie. 'She must be half-witted to have spun me a yarn like that. But what possessed her to tell me such a frightful thin'?'

'She was mixed up,' said Donovan. 'It was Reilly's car the lads at Flood's had gone to tow in to Ralston's Cove.'

'Is Dr Reilly dead, in that case?' Miss Nellie said.

'Not a bit,' said Donovan. 'He'd been to Port Ferris – as you know he always goes to Port Ferris on Tuesdays – but he had only a handful of patients to see today so he quit early and started for home. About ten miles from Ralston's Cove – on the blind curve just past Fletcher's Bridge – some madman was trying to overtake a lorry. He couldn't make it because Reilly's car was coming straight at him from the opposite direction. Poor Reilly – in order to avoid a head-on collision – swung off the road and wound up in a ditch. The motorist who had been some way behind him for several miles stopped at Casey's Tavern, walked back, found Reilly unhurt and raging. Between the two of them they were unable to budge Reilly's car. Naturally the other fellow gave Reilly a lift to Flood's. And there's the tale in a nutshell.'

'Have you yourself seen Dr Reilly?' said Miss Nellie.

'I have,' Donovan said. 'He came by the office toward five o'clock cursing like a sailor in the brig.'

'He was lucky, all the same,' said Seamus.

'You try telling him that,' said Donovan.

'Well, we've spent a most disagreeable evenin',' Miss Nellie said. 'I daresay Mary's still snifflin'.'

'Does Gretchen know about my death?' said Donovan.

'We didn't tell her,' said Miss Nellie. 'She told Mary she was off her feed and wouldn't have any dinner. We thought it best not to disturb her.'

'Might I go and check up on her?' said Donovan.

'By all means,' Miss Nellie said.

Donovan climbed the stairs, rapped at Gretchen's door, waited a little, and opened the door softly. The room was dark, but by the light from the corridor he could see that a pair of the French windows was open to the frosty night. Very slowly he crossed the doorsill. As he did so Gretchen turned in from the balcony and, with the moonlight at her back, Donovan saw her framed between the windows. There she stood – still, rigid, making no motion, giving him no sign. Only fifteen feet separated them but, in her marble attitude, Gretchen was unapproachable.

'Shall I stay or go?' said Donovan, after many seconds had passed in the wan stillness which kept him apart from her.

'They said you were dead,' said Gretchen, not moving, stiff, speaking as if she spoke to a phantom.

150

Donovan went toward her and took both her hands in his. They were so cold that he was shocked by them.

'Come nearer,' said Donovan. 'Let me close the windows.'

He shut the windows, but he could not shut out the moonlight which lay around her like a spell.

'They said you were dead,' she said again, in the same hard, flat voice.

Donovan dropped her hands, walked away from her, and closed the door leading out to the corridor, cutting them off from the babble of the television set below and from the yellow lamps in the hallway. Then, stepping through the moonlight, he went back to her.

'Gretchen,' he said, 'I'm going to make love to you. Here. Now.'

'Do you want me to belong to you?' said Gretchen.

'You already belong to me,' Donovan said.

At five o'clock the next morning, after having driven slowly through the night – often, by his own choosing, over rutted lanes or stony cart-tracks crossing meadowlands – Donovan had reached the westernmost coast of County Kerry. Three times, as a young man, and once, only two years past, he had sailed from Dufresne Bay around the south-west of Ireland and put in, at the end of his voyage, a bare fifty yards from where he had pulled up and left the car. It was still dark as midnight, the unseen Atlantic crashed and thundered, the sky was studded with frozen stars. His back to a rock, his hands thrust deep into the pockets of his overcoat, Donovan listened to the sea and, in his dreaming, lay with Gretchen. In that cold, sleeping world even his love for her was at rest; in fact, in his triumphant solitude, only the measureless ocean lived to hurl its huge force at the unresisting shore. All else, even the day-break, was wrapped away, sealed off from his uninterrupted vigil.

'There will never be anything to say,' he said to himself. 'Now she knows everything I've never said, everything I could never have told her. She knows it all.'

He was not tired, he was not restless, he was not impatient. He was alone with the sea and his love lay at peace within him. Sooner or later he would go back to her, when he was ready. There was no hurry. He had wholly expressed the inexpressible and she had understood. It was the most that he had ever done, the most that he would ever do. Meanwhile the sea was running strong against the soundless night and he was there, by himself, and unsuspected in the lengthening hour.

'Well, you're a sight for sore eyes,' said Mrs Coogan, the moment she had opened the door to him.

151

'Have you a bed for me just for one night?' said Donovan.

'Sure you can have Tommy's,' she said. 'I made it up fresh yesterday, seeing he's gone to County Mayo where his girl's after finding herself a job.

'But what in the name of God are you doing here before sun-up?'

'When I saw the smoke from your chimney I knew you were awake,' said Donovan.

'I've put the coffee on already,' said Mrs Coogan. 'But tell me now – you never put out in a boat on this heavy sea?'

'No,' he said, 'I came by car. I wanted a sight of this part of the world.'

'Wait till Dad sees who's here,' said Mrs Coogan. 'He was that blue, last evening, when there was only just the two of us and Tommy off on his own.'

Later, when the sun had risen, in a sky full of clouds, on a sea responding in a roar to a ferocious wind, Donovan telephoned his office and his housekeeper.

'I'll be off-duty until Friday morning,' he said, to Mrs Mullin, and charged her to entrust five of his patients, and any unforeseen illness among his faithful, to Dr Fir until his return. Then he informed his housekeeper that he expected to be home late Thursday night.

Despite the lack of sleep, despite the cold, he spent the morning ambling along the shore. After lunch he took the car and followed the coast as closely as he could, almost to County Limerick, stopping wherever it pleased him till the clouds converged in a drenching rain.

'You'll be dropping on your feet,' said Mrs Coogan, when supper was over. 'What with driving all last night and roaming about all the day long –'

He was dropping on his feet, but before he slept – in the bed newly made for Tommy – he listened to the rain, to the immense rhythms of the sea, and thought that, when spring came, he would take Gretchen out in his boat and the breeze would catch in the sail, catch in her hair, and there would be no need for either of them to say a word on the breast of the oceana.

11

Alone during the watches of the night, after Donovan had made love to her, Gretchen lay in the timeless regions of exhaustion. Until she had heard Miss Nellie announce that Donovan was dead or dying she had been unaware that she had been slowly transposing him to the core of her existence. When she had believed him irrevocably lost to her she had been swiftly overmastered by the stunning discovery that he was vital to her. For so long as she had sat, motionless, in the room, her mind, at odds with the silence of absolute destitution, had been busy with a strange tabulation of its own, an arithmetic, as it were, of bereavement. One by one it had reckoned up her mother, her father, her brothers, her sister, Aaron himself and, in an awful summary, it had concluded that she could, in the face of irreversible accident, have sustained the loss of any or all of those persons and fought against despair. At last, when she had gone out onto the balcony, she had understood that she had no desire to survive without Donovan, that without him no other love would ever touch her.

Then she had heard his voice and, after the first extremity of relief, she had remembered that Donovan could have no inkling that she loved him – up to the twilit hour of Miss Nellie's arrival she had had hardly an inkling of it herself – nor was it possible for her to believe that he could or might love her. What was she to Donovan but a brief interruption, a feeble irrelevance, a clumsy, homeless child whom he had been so altruistic as to befriend? The freezing wind had only seemed to confirm that she could never hope to reach him, move him and, when she had turned in, when she had seen him beyond the moon-blanched waste in which she stood, she knew that whatever she might say – if she were able to say a word – would be meaningless to herself and to him as well.

Then he was making love to her and the self which had been her own gave one last shudder before it died, while a new self was born into his possession, flowing into his body like a stream losing its essence in a vast river. When he was gone she could not bring herself to understand that he had left her. Was she not now part of him, impossible to dislodge, impossible to expel, to leave behind?

Before morning, recollections began to thread in and out of the thoughts which had started up in her loneliness. She reflected on her own body, the body which had been so useful to her, the body which had learnt so easily to swim, to dive, to ice-skate, to hold itself in perfect balance against Aaron's drive and thrust, the graceful, competent servant of her design, always at her command, subordinate to no one else. Her body, her pupil which, in Donovan's arms, had come into another life, into an ascendancy to which Donovan had lifted it, high and higher still, beyond a summons, beyond her control.

'But does he care for me?' she said to herself. 'Or was it just that I was there?'

For a moment she almost hated him for having transformed her into

153

one single, living impulse, dedicated to himself alone, for having effected such a supreme transformation without a promise, without a word of love. And then, too tired for a question with no answer, far too tired for sublime remembrance, she slept.

For the next two days, Wednesday and Thursday, she was unable to work. On Wednesday she sat piously over her manuscript but her inner clock had stopped while Donovan made love to her. All her waking hours slipped away from her and, when she was once again in bed, ready for sleep, she was still too languid to accuse herself of a prodigal waste of time. On Thursday she was no longer languid; she floundered in waves of panic. Over and over she asked herself if he would come for her as usual that evening or if – given that she had surrendered herself to him as though her body could answer for her soul – he had found her too easy with her favours, too loose for his liking. Nevertheless, despite her misgivings, she dressed to please him, she was prepared for his arrival fully half an hour before she had the slightest reason to expect him.

'Perhaps I'm a trifle early,' he said, when he came.

'I thought you might be,' she said. 'I don't know why.'

Neither of them leant to conversation, but their silence was a thing shared, they were alone together which – at their cocktails, at their *gigot d'agneau* – was all either of them demanded of the evening until they had had their coffee.

'Will you come home with me for a night-cap?' said Donovan.

'I will if you want me to,' Gretchen said.

As soon as his front door had closed them off from the world outside, Donovan took her in his arms.

'Do you really want something to drink?' he said.

'No,' said Gretchen.

'I'll call Miss Nellie,' said Donovan. 'I'll tell her I've taken you to Port Ferris for dinner and ask her not to lock up when she goes to bed. You can do it when I take you back to her.'

It was nearly dawn when he drove her to the Hall. As they swept through the night Donovan, in a glow of well-being, felt suddenly magnanimous – and quite sure that he could afford a little magnanimity. He had looked on Gretchen's Aaron as a rival and all the while he had been no more to Gretchen than an agreeable memory.

'Do you and your friend Aaron write to each other?' he said – to show, as much to himself as to Gretchen, that the young man no longer posed any threat to the present, that his place was in the past, just as Gretchen had said.

'Neither of us is any good at letters,' said Gretchen. 'I don't suppose he misses me. I don't miss him – although I often have a queer feeling on Saturdays and Sundays. Maybe, unconsciously, I still look ahead to the week-end.'

'Even in darkest Ireland,' said Donovan, 'people look ahead to week-ends. On Saturday evening I'll come for you at seven o'clock. And I'll get Miss Nellie to give you a key of your own.'

No plans were ever proposed and agreed upon by the two of them, but from then on they dined together on Thursdays at the Cygne d'Or and on Saturdays at a quiet, luxurious hotel – with an exceptionally good restaurant – recently opened by a hard-working Dutch couple. On Sunday afternoons Donovan drove Gretchen, rain or shine, along the country lanes or down to the small harbours of the county before bringing her home with him to a cold supper for two, left by his housekeeper. On each of those evenings, after they had eaten, they made love in Donovan's bed until Donovan, never quite heedless of the passing hours, remarked that it was time for him to drive her back to the Hall. On Christmas Day he took her to the Moores for Christmas dinner. On New Year's Eve they drank champagne.

'I must say it's considerate of your patients not to call you out after dark,' said Gretchen.

'There's no consideration involved,' Donovan said. 'All of my patients are simply instructed to call Dr Fir in case of an emergency after six o'clock on Saturday evenings and all day Sundays. He's still a stripling; a little leg work, now and then, won't hurt him.'

'Nobody bothers you on Thursdays either,' said Gretchen.

'On Thursday evenings,' said Donovan, 'I've always been officially in Port Ferris. Reilly covers for me. I cover for him on Tuesdays.'

Neither Gretchen nor Donovan could – since they had shared such nights together – imagine life without the other, but neither of them could profess the truth. Donovan was increasingly aware that twenty-five years divided them; he had promised himself that he would not, whatever the primal urge, bring the pressure of his love to bear on Gretchen. He would wait – he did wait – for Gretchen to tell him that she belonged to him, that no one else could ever dispossess him. From the first evening that he had made love to her he had known that she was absolutely his own. He had been so sure of it

155

that, Aaron notwithstanding, he felt that no one but himself had ever wholly claimed her, that until he had taken her she had been truly inviolate. But he had yet to be certain that Gretchen herself was aware that she had made a conclusive choice and, until she could articulate that much, he was surely obliged to leave her free – free to be uncommitted, free to wake up and fall out of love with him because he was too old for her. Every time he looked at her across a table, every time he held her naked in the dark, he prayed that she would find the words to tell him that she could not live without him, and every time he prayed in vain.

Meanwhile Gretchen was waiting for Donovan to make a signal commitment. She was too young to believe – every day, all day long – that Donovan's love was all-abiding, while she could much too readily imagine him brilliantly seductive and brilliantly seduced by brilliant women, far more beautiful, far more experienced, far more voluptuous than herself. The awful images tortured her when she was away from him. Only when she lay beside him did she understand that he was indeed in love with her, only on those occasions did she all but hold her breath as she waited for the words that would have made him hers forever. But for so long as Donovan was unready or unwilling to tell her that he loved her, that he wanted her close to him always, she was both too shy and too proud to speak of love to him. So they went, politely in parallel, uneasy when they were apart, formal even in their passion when they were together.

One high, cloudless morning Gretchen was disinclined to consider Irish writers at the very beginning of a new day. Ever since she had started to work in earnest on her thesis she had discovered that there were times when it was useless to be impatient with herself, times when it was best to leave her manuscript alone, to search for other occupations. That morning – cold, still, and bright – seemed to be calling her out of the Hall and, after an hour or so of indecision, she wound a scarf around her throat, buttoned up her winter coat and put on boots and woollen mittens. At the bottom of the stairs she met Miss Nellie in the entrance hall.

'Goin' out for a stroll?' said Miss Nellie.

'I thought I might climb the hill behind the church,' said Gretchen. 'I'd like to see what Dufresne Bay looks like from way up there.'

'To get to the foot of the hill you'll have to go by the vicarage,' Miss Nellie said. 'There's nothin' wrong with that if one is in company, but it can be risky if one is alone.'

'Risky?' said Gretchen.

'There's an elemental in the vicar's hedge,' said Miss Nellie. 'Known to be spiteful or threatenin' or, at least, very disagreeable. You must repeat the Lord's prayer out loud for so long as it takes you to pass the hedge. otherwise there's no tellin' what might happen to you.'

'Thanks for the warning,' said Gretchen, wondering if Miss Nellie had taken leave of her senses overnight.

When she came abreast of the gates at the end of the drive she paused to study the pair of great, wind-twisted oaks – which guarded the gate-posts – whose branches seemed, for an instant, to be alive and writhing upward to the sky. Immediately she remembered the fairy-tales illustrated by Arthur Rackham in what had been her maternal grandmother's favourite book for children.

For several minutes she lingered between the trees asking herself if it were possible that the Irish essentially belonged to Arthur Rackham's world of myth and magic, taxing herself with a want of imagination whenever, lately, she fell to considering Ireland and the Irish and found them easier to dismiss than to welcome or to analyse.

Eventually she turned and began on the slight ascent which led toward the churchyard. Soon, on her left, she came to the long hedge which shielded the vicarage from the road and, in spite of her common sense, her healthy scepticism, she recited aloud the Lord's prayer over and over until the hedge was at her back. After another turn, to her right, she went up the stone steps leading to the cemetery and halted mid-way to listen to a sweet melody drifting over the graves. For a little she waited before she started up once more. At the top of the steps she saw an old man standing by a headstone, his flute lifted to the morning. When he caught sight of her he interrupted his song and lowered his instrument.

''Tis mad I am,' he said. 'I'm known to be mad.'

'You play beautifully,' said Gretchen.

'Ten years and gone I lost my wife,' he said. 'There's them as thinks I should have forgotten her entirely, long ago. But I can't forget her and the first sunny day of each month I play the chunes she used to love right here, where she's buried. They'll never lay me to rest beside her, for I'm a Catholic, you see, whilst she was of Anglican persuasion. Nevertheless, for so long as I'm left on the face of this earth I can pipe to her. But what are you doing in this place – young and living for romance, as I've no doubt you are?'

'I was hoping to go up the hill beyond the church,' said Gretchen.

'You've fine weather for an excursion,' said the old man. 'At the back of the church you'll find a gate. Climb over that and follow the

157

path straight on to the summit of the rise.'

Even when she had reached the summit Gretchen could still hear his flute, faint in the distance, and she stopped on her peak listening to his lovely music floating up from the graveyard below. From the pinnacle she could see Ireland's pastures, Ireland's woodlands, Ireland's stony shores yielding to a quiet sea, turned silver in the timeless, noon-tide light and, for some while, she dwelt on the vision, in her mind's eye, of the whole emerald island lapped and defended by the all-powerful, all-encircling Atlantic. In a moment of magical suspension between the gentle earth and the translucent sky even Yeats' darkening flood was still, and the flute-song was the only sound to reach her ears. Enchanted, she gazed at the beauty of the land, the majesty of the ocean disclosed to her alien eyes, and asked herself if she could have shared such things with Donovan before she remembered that all of what lay around her was part of himself. Only when her feet were aching with the cold and she felt her fingers growing numb did she admit that she could not spend the day on a crest of the Irish world as it was that morning. Then slowly, reluctantly, she went down the footpath, climbed over the gate behind the church and started on her way, as softly as possible – not to disturb the stream of music flowing across the churchyard. But the man standing over his wife's grave came to the end of his melodies and, when he turned, he saw her at once.

'We should both be off,' he said, 'before we're quite changed to marble.'

Together they walked down the stone steps and, at the bottom of them, he said: 'Now you'll do as I say. You carry my flute in one hand and give me the other to hold in my left hand. Meantime, with my right, I'll be showing my crucifix before the two of us and with that we'll be safe from harm. Make no conversation whatsoever but concentrate on the blessèd saints whilst we're passing the hedge yonder.'

Gretchen grasped the flute, grasped the old man's left hand as, with his right, he raised his crucifix so that he and she could see it going, as it were, before them.

'Now I'll trouble you for my flute,' he said, when they had gone the length of the hedge and he had put his little cross into his pocket. 'So here we are, safely out in the open once again. I'll just see you to your gates.'

'How did you know I was staying in the Hall?' said Gretchen.

''Tis known to one and all,' he said. 'And a very good morning to you. A very good morning indeed.'

For a little space of time she stood where she was watching his figure dwindle the further he went up Dufresne Hill. Then, glancing at the Arthur Rackham oaks Gretchen believed that she was ready to ascribe any amount of myth and magic to the Irish and to their island. For, high above the churchyard, she had experienced a sense of extraordinary release which sprang, she understood, from the countryside she saw in the embrace of the ocean and the flute-songs threading their way in and out of her delight. As she began to walk toward the Hall she was convinced that her passionately negative assessment of Ireland and of all things Irish must have been false. In fact, it had been a wonderful morning and she meant to store it up and tell everything she could remember of it to Donovan. It was rare that she talked to him about herself but if she did he listened –

When she had arrived in her own room at the Hall and had taken off her coat, her scarf, her boots, and her mittens, Donovan was still uppermost in her thoughts.

'Perhaps,' she said to herself, 'I've finally seen and heard *his* Ireland. Certainly what I saw was beautiful, what I heard was bewitching – and surely singular. I could never have heard it or seen it anywhere else and there's no doubt but what it was real. Where I'll find the words to describe what happened to me up there, entranced by every single thing, near or far, I can't imagine but I hope I'll be able to tell him how it felt to discover his birthright, to say that I began to understand his country and his countrymen when I stopped before those ancient trees at the gates, when I prayed – and almost believed in my prayer – while I was passing the hedge around the vicarage, when I came across that gallant old man and listened to his flute –'

At that Mary beat the gong for lunch.

Too uplifted to notice what she was trying to eat, inedible though it was, scarcely aware of Miss Nellie nattering at Seamus, or of Seamus' sobbing, Gretchen clung to her recollections of the churchyard and of the hill behind it. Doubtful about the rancid custard which Mary had put before her, she hesitated, spoon in hand, over the shallow bowl on her table.

'You'll not get me to touch this mess with a barge-pole,' said Seamus.

'I won't have any of that,' said Miss Nellie. 'You'll eat what's given you.'

Seamus bowed his head over his bowl of custard and effortlessly vomited the lunch he had just eaten. Gretchen shot out of her chair, left the dining-room, took the corridor in long strides, rapidly climbed the stairs and sat down on her bed.

'I take it back,' she said, loudly enough to be easily overheard. 'This morning I must have been hallucinating. The real Ireland out there? My foot. *This* is the real Ireland. *This* rat-hole is Irish reality. *That* disgusting old brute downstairs is every inch an Irishman. So much for Yeats, so much for Joyce, so much for their parlour tricks. I was right all along. The whole island is nothing but a cess-pool –'

''Tis that,' said Mary, marching in. 'Get that good stout coat of yours and we'll go up to Ben Daly on the hill. This is no fit place for you and if her Ladyship thinks *I'm* about to clean up after that drunken wretch she's got another think coming –'

Ben Daly made coffee for Gretchen and provided a glass of ale apiece for Mary and himself. Encouraged by his audience, he reeled out a stream of anecdotes and, within a few minutes, Gretchen was in fits of laughter.

'Ben's a treat, isn't he?' said Mary, two hours later as they ambled back to the Hall.

'I don't know what I'd have done without either of you this afternoon,' said Gretchen. 'I was just beside myself –'

'Didn't I hear you at it?' Mary said. 'But don't you go telling Dr Donovan about Seamus at lunch today. He's enough troubles on his shoulders without worrying himself over the old bugger.'

'Sometimes it seems to me that he has his ear to the ground to catch the goings on at Dufresne Bay,' said Gretchen.

'Does he, indeed?' said Mary.

Donovan did. Often he required a report from the Hall. He had come to realise that, although it was true that Miss Nellie seldom disturbed Gretchen at her work, the uneven tenor of the days in the west tower of the meal-times in the east tower, was, in itself, unsettling. On Wednesdays Gretchen was virtually a participant in the weekly tragedies precipitated by the delivery of the clean household linens from the commercial laundry. Mary was willing to do Seamus' shirts and socks – a negligible labour, since they were so infrequently changed – and the nylon sheets and pillowcases on the double bed in the master chamber, which needed no ironing. But table linens, bathroom linens, sheets and pillowcases from Gretchen's bed were sent to Port Ferris. Not a week went by without a disaster which Miss Nellie, busily unpacking and sorting in the airing-cupboard next door to Gretchen, relayed to Mary, washing up the luncheon dishes in the kitchen, in a volley of shrieks which, almost infallibly, provoked Mary to take the stairs and examine a

160

scorched napkin, a ripped sheet, a stained pillowcase, or confirm that a bathtowel was missing. According to Gretchen, Miss Nellie never failed to wring at least an hour of wrathful lamentation from the derelictions in Port Ferris. ,

'The worst that can happen, from my point of view,' Gretchen said, 'happens when the laundry sends back something that doesn't belong to the Hall. Then they're both in overdrive, declaring it cheap, hideous, positively useless, and speculating as to whose it is. That can go on, embroidered with any small talk which may occur to either of them, until tea-time. Meanwhile I'm fuming. I can't think, I can't even type up a little fair copy with all that caterwauling going on just beyond me.'

Lunch was often a trial.

'Miss Nellie gets a lot of letters – really a lot for someone as old as she is,' Gretchen said once.

'Her father's father had eight sons and daughters,' said Donovan. 'If I'm not mistaken, all of them – bar the first-born – fetched up in England. At all events she has hosts of cousins – several contemporaries left, the rest at various removes – and she keeps in touch with every one of them.'

'Well,' said Gretchen, 'the postman comes by at about eleven and by lunch-time she knows the prices of everything in England by the pound – lamb, beef, fish, butter, sugar, fruit, vegetables – and she shouts the figures at Seamus. I used to bring a book to the dining-room, but in the middle of the day I don't do it any more. No one could read with all that hullabaloo.'

'Can you read at dinner?' said Donovan.

'That more or less depends on Seamus,' Gretchen said. 'He's never hungry at dinner-time and he starts to sob when Mary brings in the soup. Sometimes he shuts up after a good tongue-lashing – Miss Nellie's incisive – but sometimes he's still sobbing when we get to the dessert. Then Mary mops up his tears with his bib, while Miss Nellie tells him he's *disgustin'*, and I feel sort of beached up nowhere.'

Donovan was distressed by Gretchen's recitals. He suspected her of understatement – to spare him anxiety for herself. It worried him to think that between Miss Nellie and Seamus she could count on so little peace of mind. But he was greatly amused by her account of the early mornings.

'At about eight o'clock they really fight,' she said. 'I can hear every creak of the bedsprings. I know precisely when Miss Nellie has gotten out of bed. Then, as best I can reconstruct it, she goes to the bathroom for five or ten minutes. When she comes back she begins to put her clothes on. Seamus says, "Mother of God, woman, cover

161

your old blue legs", and she says, "There was a time when you couldn't wait to get between them", and he says, "There was never a time I couldn't wait. In those days I'd plenty of fancy distractions. No, 'twas yourself, way-laying me at every turn –"

'And then they're off and at it,' said Gretchen. 'Miss Nellie reminds him she could have made a far better match and he gets back at her by telling her there wasn't a prick big enough for her in all the British Isles –

'Why are you laughing?' she said, to Donovan. 'It's a ghastly business.'

'It's not,' said Donovan. 'It may be shocking to overhear, but they're both having the time of their lives, believe me.'

Now and then, during the month of January, Gretchen, having saved up various *pièces de résistance*, amused him at Miss Nellie's or at Seamus' expense.

'When you've finished your thesis,' said Donovan, 'you can write a book entitled "My Life at the Hall".'

'If it were my life, or any part of it, I might do just that,' said Gretchen. 'But it's not my life. It's theirs. And I don't understand anything about either of them. The only thing they see eye to eye on is money.'

'That's rare in a marriage,' Donovan said.

'Neither of them could countenance the most minute extravagance,' said Gretchen. 'Except for Seamus' whiskey. Maybe they both think its medicinal. Mary says he runs through a bottle a day and Miss Nellie doesn't turn a hair.'

'I'd prescribe whiskey for Seamus myself,' said Donovan. 'He has murder in his heart when he's sober.'

One Thursday evening, when he came to call for her, Gretchen stumbled as they walked toward his car.

'I'm sorry,' she said. 'I'm still shaking all over.'

'What's happened to make you shake all over?' said Donovan.

'I'll tell you that when we get to the restaurant,' said Gretchen. 'I can't tell you while we're driving. I'm off the internal combustion engine for the time being.'

At the Cygne d'Or she asked for a second vodka, which was so unlike her that Donovan – although he ordered it at once – scowled at her.

'I really need it,' she said. 'On my word of honour. I'll explain in a minute or two.'

When the new glass, brimful, was in her hand, she sighed.

'You know,' said Gretchen, 'that sometimes I go to Ralston's Cove with Miss Nellie – if I'm out of soap of Kleenex or tooth-paste. It's always nerve-racking because I know she's quite capable of forgetting me after her errand's done. Once I walked almost half-way to Dufresne Bay before she remembered that she'd left me at McMahon's. When she did remember me she was already at the Hall. But at least she was conscientious enough to set out again and she picked me up, plodding my way home. Anyway, I went in to town with her today for the usual things. She had a lot of shopping to do and it was six o'clock before she was ready to call it a day. I was waiting for her in the car. She backed out of the parking lot – everything seemed perfectly fine – but then she couldn't get the car into first – or even into second. I offered to try but she wouldn't let me.

' "We'll just have to put a good face on it," she said. "Flood's is closed by now so there's no help for us."

'You won't believe me,' said Gretchen. 'However, I swear we drove straight through Ralston's Cove, turned onto the road for Dufresne Bay, and kept going for seven miles at a great clip, took Dufresne Hill – I will say she braked often on the descent – and fetched up at the entrance to the west tower – all that, the *whole distance*, in reverse. Now are you still wondering why I needed a double vodka.'

'Sweet Jesus,' said Donovan.

'That's about everything you could say,' said Gretchen. 'Though I might remind you – in case the full horror hasn't got to you yet – that she made it in the pitch dark.'

As soon as they were alone together in his house Donovan held her in his arms as if he could never let her go.

'Next time you want soap or toothpaste,' he said, 'you'll go in to Ralston's Cove with me on a Saturday afternoon.'

'I couldn't even change my dress for you tonight, when I got back to the Hall,' said Gretchen. 'I was too shattered.'

'I know. I know,' he said.

Early in February, on a Tuesday, Gretchen was astonished to find Donovan at her door just before tea-time.

'There's trouble here,' he said. 'Miss Nellie's eldest son, Edward, died this afternoon in Dublin.'

'Oh, how dreadful,' said Gretchen. 'How did he die?'

'He died of a coronary,' said Donovan.

'Surely I ought to leave,' said Gretchen. 'She'll want her house to herself.'

'That was the first thing I thought of when I heard the news,' Donovan said.

'How did you hear the news?' said Gretchen.

'Edward's doctor's a good friend of mine,' said Donovan. 'He rang me a little while ago. Randall had already called Miss Nellie.

'I got here as quick as I could, precisely to tell her that I'd find some other place for you. But she'd have none of it.

' "The child is to stay where she is," she said. "I'll make shift one way or another."

'So I told her I'd take you away with me now in order that she and Seamus could have tea and dinner *en famille*. She agreed to that but she begged me to come back with you in time for after-dinner coffee.'

'How is she?' Gretchen said. 'Is she terribly shocked?'

'She's shocked,' said Donovna. 'Seamus is too. But neither of them gave a row of pins for Edward. If it had been Randall Seamus would have collapsed, if it had been Quentin Miss Nellie's heart would be breaking. As it is, it's knocked the breath out of both of them but there won't be any weeping and wailing over Edward.

'Now could you bring a book to Ralston's Cove and read in my office? There are three patients waiting whom I must see and then we could be off and away.'

'Give me five minutes to change my clothes,' said Gretchen, 'and I'm all yours.'

'Whatever happens,' Donovan said, when they had arrived at the Cygne d'Or, 'it won't be a tragedy at the Hall. A nasty little comedy may be in the making as soon as Miss Nellie is *au fait* with the details of Edward's death.'

'She *couldn't* find anything to laugh at in the death of her eldest child,' said Gretchen. 'Besides, Miss Nellie never laughs.'

'No, she doesn't,' said Donovan. 'But she has a knack for turning things inside out. When she learns that Edward had his first attack while he was copulating with his mistress and died four days later in her arms she'll want vengeance – and she'll get it, if I know Miss Nellie.'

'Is she such a prude?' Gretchen said.

'She takes a dim view of impropriety,' said Donovan. 'Amazingly dim, when one thinks of her salad days.'

'You've lost me,' said Gretchen. 'I can't follow you, probably because the only Miss Nellie I see is the clockwork Miss Nellie and I know nothing at all about Edward.'

Donovan, who knew a good deal about Edward's irregular life and times and had had the facts concerning his death from the physician in Dublin, proceeded to enlighten Gretchen.

Edward had married one Beatrice Nolan, some thirty years earlier,

Miss Nellie had disapproved of the match because Beatrice was a Catholic, whereas very few Dufresnes – and no first-born sons – had ever stooped so low. All the same, if the marriage had been a painfully erratic affair, Miss Nellie had conceded – over two or three decades – that Edward was largely at fault. Beatrice had continued to love him, had been a loyal wife to him and a self-less mother to his two children, while Edward had spent the better parts of his days and the best parts of his nights gallivanting with other women. Most of his antics had come to Beatrice's ears sooner or later and her lavish supply of ready tears had been an ample source of irritation to Edward, who was a heartless, good-looking bounder.

'It would appear that his last mistress was unusually smitten with him,' said Donovan. 'I have it from Dublin that she went to the hospital in the ambulance with him, posing as his wife – that although she was not allowed near him for so long as he was thought to be in critical condition, she never left the hospital. Then – since he was considered to have made a remarkably rapid recovery – he was transferred to a private room. From that room he telephoned Randall. Randall got in touch with Edward's own doctor and with Beatrice. They arrived at the sick-room post-haste, only to find the mistress in a chair at the bedside holding hands with the patient.

'That was too much for Beatrice. She fled. Edward's doctor – my friend – went over the findings on admission and over the history of the convalescence and was persuaded that, with adequate medication, there was a fair outlook for Edward. He told as much to Randall. Randall decided not to distress his mother and his father with the news of Edward's illness since Dr McLaughlin was cautiously optimistic about the future. Wherewith, to everyone's surprise, Edward had another coronary. The only person present at his final, conscious instant was his mistress. When Miss Nellie gets wind of that the fat will be in the fire.'

'Will she get wind of it?' said Gretchen.

'Randall will see to that,' Donovan said. 'He's a born mischief-maker. And if Randall doesn't Mad Monica – who loves a good laugh – will.'

'Just who is Mad Monica?' said Gretchen.

'She's a woman of abundant common sense,' said Donovan.

The Nolan sisters, Beatrice and Monica, came of unlettered peasant stock but their father, a shrewd, hard-driving man – never at any time too nice about the letter of the law – who had started out as a small contractor, had made money hand over fist. So much money that when his daughters were in their teens he was able to install his family in Dublin, in a handsome Georgian house. Neither of the girls lacked for *beaux*, but where Beatrice was only pretty – which gave many people to predict that if she succeeded in finding a husband it would, very probably, be on account of her father's wealth – Monica was so beautiful that half the eligible young men in the city were violently in love with her. Monica amused herself at house-parties. She rode, she swam, she danced, she flirted, until one morning, without a word to her parents – or to foolish Beatrice, already married, already pregnant, already miserable – she disappeared. True, Monica left a note saying that she was leaving of her own free will, that no one was to worry about her, but two years went by without another line from her. And then one day she turned up – in a nun's habit. From then on she had been known as Mad Monica.

'For,' said Donovan, 'there was no one in Dublin who could believe that unless she was demonstrably insane Monica Nolan could ever have taken the veil. But she did and the life seems to suit her. No doubt you'll make her acquaintance before the week is out.'

'Will she be coming to Dufresne Bay?' said Gretchen.

'I assume she will,' Donovan said. 'Edward will be buried beside his ancestors – Miss Nellie will insist on that – and Beatrice will be obliged to come but not, I suspect, without Monica to protect her from the heathen.'

'Edward didn't turn Catholic when he married?' said Gretchen.

'No,' said Donovan, 'he dug in when Beatrice tried to make him change his faith. Apparently it made no difference to old man Nolan. Marriage to a Dufresne was such a social step-up for a Nolan that Beatrice's father winked at formalities.'

'I'm too primitive myself to understand much about formalities,' said Gretchen. 'But didn't Seamus want his children brought up as Catholics?'

'Oh, he wanted it,' said Donovan, 'but Miss Nellie put her foot down. She's never thought of the children as Taylors. They're Dufresnes to her and they belong to the Church of Ireland. When Seamus is in his cups he cries for their souls in hell. Miss Nellie just shrugs.'

'Yet she seems to me a religious person,' said Gretchen. 'She's well up on the Bible and she goes to church with real eagerness.'

'She *is* religious,' Donovan said. 'But she takes it for granted that there's a special place in heaven for every Dufresne – something very likely reminiscent of the Hall – properly staffed.'

They returned to the Hall in good time for coffee. Gretchen would have gone directly to her room but Miss Nellie stopped her.

'When I asked Clement Donovan to come by after dinner,' she said, 'it was understood that I was invitin' both of you.'

166

Seamus was weeping in the wing chair.

'He's been enjoyin' himself all evenin',' said Miss Nellie. 'But Hugo and Magda had been splendid. Quite splendid. Between the three of us we've made the most satisfactory arrangements.'

'What have you arranged?' said Donovan.

'Everythin',' said Miss Nellie. 'Beatrice and Monica will be sleepin' in the pink room – it's close to the bathroom. Randall and Constance will be in the Chinese room. Hugo and Magda will put Quentin and Rhoda up in the east win', along with young Edward and Martin. Their wives won't be comin' – young Edward's wife broke her ankle last week and Martin's wife's in London, visitin' relatives. None of Randall's brood and none of Quentin's will be comin' either, neither will any of Edward's grandchildren. That would be puttin' too much of a strain on Hugo and Magda – and, as you know, the west win' is gone to rack and ruin.'

'What about Catherine?' said Donovan.

'God bless my soul,' Miss Nellie said, 'I'd forgotten about Catherine. She's comin', of course, and goin' into the east win' with the rest of them. Everyone will be arrivin' Friday afternoon. We'll all be dinin' at home as usual – Danny O'Toole's wife will be here and Mike Healey's too to lend a helpin' hand to Mary. Mary and Jane O'Toole will do the breakfasts for all of us in the west tower, Hugo's staff will answer for the others in the east win'. After the service – at eleven o'clock Saturday mornin' – Hugo and Magda will be givin' a luncheon for the whole crowd. On Saturday afternoon the pack of them will be goin' back to Dublin.'

'Have you been in touch with Randall and Quentin?' said Donovan.

'Oh, yes,' Miss Nellie said. 'Randall's takin' care of the body and the coffin and the hearse, thin's like that – he'll be bringin' Beatrice and Monica. Beatrice has gone all to pieces, Quentin says.'

'That's natural,' said Donovan.

'Myself,' said Miss Nellie, 'I think there's somethin' fishy in Denmark. What it is I don't know, but I'll get it out of Randall when he phones tomorrow night or, if not, I'll get it out of Monica when she comes.'

'Nellie's got a suspicious mind,' said Seamus, blowing his nose.

'So I have,' Miss Nellie said, 'when I'm not permitted to speak to my own grandsons after their father's death. I asked particularly to speak to young Edward, but Quentin said he was too upset to come to the telephone. Then I asked to speak to Martin, but Quentin said he was with Beatrice. There was somethin' positively *unnatural* about Quentin's voice – he didn't sound like one brother grievin' for another. He was keepin' somethin' from me, was Quentin, and

167

makin' dead sure it was kept from me by not lettin' me speak to either of the boys.'

'Have you seen the rector?' said Donovan.

'I sent for him at tea-time,' said Miss Nellie. 'We went over the prayers and the hymns together. He's a comfortin' man. He'll be goin' after Mike Healey and Danny O'Toole first thin' in the mornin' about diggin' the grave. He said we should take advantage of the dry weather while it lasts and quite right too.'

'Well,' Donovan said, 'I must be going. I'll take Gretchen off your hands in the evenings. And all day Saturday. Could Mary give her a sandwich at lunch-time for three days?'

'For the next three days,' said Miss Nellie, 'it'll be business as usual at the Hall.'

By the late afternoon on Friday the clan had gathered. Gretchen kept to her room until she heard Donovan's car slowly approaching the west tower. Then, as quickly as she could, she tip-toed down the stairs, past the drawing-room, filled with strangers, and met him in the entrance hall.

'All those people in the Hall – which are home to them, obviously – make me feel like a visitor from another planet,' said Gretchen.

'At this time tomorrow it will be over and done with,' Donovan said.

They lingered over their dinner, Donovan took the road back to Dufresne Bay at an unusually moderate speed.

'It's almost eleven o'clock,' he said. 'If we're lucky everyone will have gone to bed when we get there.'

But luck was not with Donovan, nor with Gretchen. Miss Nellie heard them coming in and, refusing to take no for an answer, led them into the drawing-room, introducing them all around. Everyone made much of Donovan. Gretchen sat on the edge of a chair, feeling out of place but, curious as ever, she studied the company.

Randall was a dapper man, a sharp dresser. Gretchen, who had never been in a casino, imagined him at once as a croupier in an elegant gambling house, done in red velvet and flaunting huge chandeliers. The black mourning band on his sleeve was like a badge of evil, a pledge to the powers of darkness. His wife, across the room, talking to Hugo and Magda, was an artful platinum blonde and, although she was dressed in black, her make-up was flamboyant, incongruous in an assembly of the newly bereaved. Quentin, with a shy, troubled face, was staring into a glass of whiskey as if it were a crystal ball, while his wife, a thin, nervous woman, whose black hung loosely over her shoulders like an outsize hand-me-down, sat beside him, one bony hand on his knee. Edward's sons – flabby young

168

Edward and heavy Martin, with a thick neck – moved awkwardly in and around the group, silently refilling glasses, each of them a little unsteady on his feet, while a glance at the tea-table, presently serving as a bar, revealed half a dozen bottles of Irish whiskey, at least two of them empty. Catherine, grimly well-tailored, in dark grey, sat straight-backed by Seamus, talking to him *sotto voce*, although Seamus was patently not listening, although, in fact, he was calling out for more whiskey.

Hugo Dufresne was a magnificent figure of a man, somewhat over six feet tall, with a rich mane of white hair dropping almost to his shoulders, impeccably attired in a dinner jacket, evening trousers with strips of grosgrain running down the sides, black silk socks and black pumps. His wife, Magda, was in black satin, reaching to the floor but slit, on the left side, from her high-heeled satin slippers nearly to her hip. Her shiny black hair was shingled to her head. Her fingernails were as long as a raven's beak and lacquered vermilion. She was smoking a cigarette in a slim, black holder of eye-catching length and using it like a conductor's baton to underscore her every comment. Mad Monica, stout and genial, in a rumpled habit, was intently drinking, throwing her head back with each swallow. Of the widow, Beatrice, there was no sign.

When everyone but Catherine, who was – as Gretchen later learnt – the head-mistress of a girls' school in Wicklow, had made the most of Donovan, Catherine rose.

'I have something to say to Clement Donovan – and to all of you,' she said.

'Well, get it off your chest,' said Seamus. 'There's no stopping you, at any rate.'

'I make no bones about the fact that I am very much vexed with Randal and with Quentin,' Catherine said. 'Beatrice doesn't count, as she's been plainly *non compos mentis* since Tuesday. But Randall and Quentin have let the family down and I look to Dr Donovan to bear me out in this.'

'Catherine, must you take all night over whatever it is?' said Miss Nellie, who was herself in black, even to black shoes and stockings.

'After Edward died,' said Catherine, 'I had a long talk with Henry McLaughlin. He told me that on the day before Edward's death he himself had examined Edward most scrupulously and had come across what was undoubtedly a lump in Edward's abdomen. When I heard that I demanded a post-mortem examination, but Randall and Quentin shouted me down.

'However Edward's not buried yet and I put it to you, Dr Donovan, is it not of supreme importance to us, the survivors, to know if there's cancer looming over the Dufresnes?'

All eyes were fixed on Donovan, but before he could say a word Mad Monica, too, rose to her feet, waving her glass and chuckling.

'Ah, Catherine, how you do run on,' she said. 'A lump in Edward's abdomen? Sure, 'twas nothing but the neck of the bottle.'

Seamus burst into a great guffaw and Donovan turned aside to hide his grin.

On Saturday morning thunder had been rumbling in the west since break of day. Some time after ten-thirty Gretchen went out onto her balcony whence she could catch sight of Donovan's car as soon as Donovan came for her. Standing there she watched the little procession leaving the Hall on foot for the church and saw, for the first time, the corpulent widow, veiled in black, supported on either side by Quentin and Mad Monica. Just ahead of the mourners rolled the hearse – very slow and not, from Gretchen's elevated vantage point, unlike a snail – which had brought the remains of Edward Taylor-Dufresne from Dublin.

'The orchestration for Edward's reunion with his ancestors is a touch ominous,' said Donovan when, a quarter of an hour later, he and Gretchen set off together and thunder swelled again in the distance.

'I hope it won't rain quite yet,' Gretchen said. 'It would be hard on the family to get soaked at the interment.'

'No doubt the rector will see to it that Miss Nellie shelters under his umbrella,' said Donovan.

'Where will we shelter?' said Gretchen.

'At the Dutch hotel,' Donovan said. 'Harry and Eliza Moore are joining us there for lunch. When lunch is over, if we're not in for a deluge, I'll take you to Port Ferris, just to show you that Ralston's Cove isn't the whole of Ireland.'

Gretchen was disappointed in Port Ferris.

'It might have been a charming city,' she said, 'if only there weren't such ugly buildings on both sides of the river.'

'Shall we go to a film?' said Donovan. 'Afterward, since my housekeeper never expects us on a Saturday, we could buy some sandwiches – there's a good pub around the corner – bring them home and eat them in front of my fire.'

'It's donkey's years since I've been to the movies,' Gretchen said.

During the small hours of Sunday morning Donovan woke Gretchen. She had fallen asleep with his arms around her; he himself had dozed.

'It's all over now,' Donovan said, as he drove her to the Hall. 'Miss Nellie and Seamus will be quite by themselves and the younger generations will be in Dublin, snug in their beds, where they belong.'

At noon he was back at the Hall, calling for Gretchen. Miss Nellie ensnared them at the door.

'I want you both here this evenin' for after-dinner coffee,' said Miss Nellie, looking worn and choleric. 'A matter has come to my attention which must be seen to immediately. If Magda is able to make the necessary arrangements by telephone this afternoon, I shall be leavin' for Dublin tomorrow.'

'Just for the day?' said Donovan.

'I'm not anticipatin' a lengthy sojourn,' Miss Nellie said. 'But I shall stop there until wrong is put right. Unfortunately the affair doesn't rest entirely with myself.'

'She's wise to Edward's fatal fling,' said Donovan, to Gretchen, when they were alone in the car. 'I wonder what the devil she's up to. Even Miss Nellie can't be planning to burn Edward's mistress at the stake.'

At nine o'clock they returned, as bidden, to the Hall, where Miss Nellie and Seamus, Hugo and Magda were having coffee in the drawing-room. Magda was wearing a sheath of silver lamé with a red satin rose at the waist, Hugo was in a dinner jacket, Miss Nellie was still in black, and Seamus, who had reverted to his woollen shirt and his shabby corduroy trousers, had fairly recently shaved, presumably for the funeral service.

'We're layin' out our programme,' said Miss Nellie, to Donovan. 'Although Magda's afraid that Mme Kirova may have some trouble gettin' through to Edward –'

'When people have just passed over they're apt to be hard to pin down,' said Magda, explaining the difficulty to Donovan. 'A number of them rebel at finding themselves discarnate. They won't associate with other spirits – not even with the spirits who were close to them on the earth plane – who might help them to re-establish contact with their loved ones here. Then again, at a first *séance* – and this one will be a first for both Nellie and Edward, not to mention Beatrice – Hugo and I have known Mme Kirova to fail occasionally. When that happens she requires two or three days' rest before she feels strong enough to hold another sitting.'

'Is that so?' said Donovan.

'You're determined,' he said, to Miss Nellie, 'to reach Edward?'

'Naturally she's determined to reach Edward,' said Hugo. 'Why wouldn't she be?'

'Hugo and I are quite in agreement with Nellie on that score,' said Magda. 'We simply aren't sure that the time is ripe.'

171

'Beatrice won't stand for it,' Seamus said. 'It's sacrilege, that's what it is.'

'Beatrice will be dragooned,' said Miss Nellie. 'Hugo and I will see to that.

'No, Beatrice is not the problem, lily-livered as she is. Yet after all, it's only Beatrice we're thinkin' of – Hugo and Magda and I. The humiliation was indescribable –'

'Of course,' said Magda, to Donovan, 'you might be forgiven if you were somewhat mystified by all this. That is to say if you weren't acquainted with the circumstances of Edward's final indiscretion –'

'I've gathered that Beatrice was displaced by Edward's current mistress in the few days before the end,' Donovan said. 'But what could Edward do about that now? He's six feet under.'

'Mme Kirova will get in touch with him,' said Magda. 'If not directly then through her guide. We can bank on that. The only question is how soon will she be able to do so.'

'When she's in touch with him,' said Miss Nellie, 'Edward will apologise to Beatrice. She'll be instructed to make certain that he does.'

'What's your opinion?' Hugo said, abruptly turning to Gretchen.

'I can't imagine interfering with the dead,' said Gretchen. 'Even if it were possible.'

'The child's too young for the fine points,' said Magda.

'I'm with the girl,' said Seamus. 'The dead should be left to rest in peace.'

'There'll be no peace for Edward on the other side,' Miss Nellie said. 'Not until he's expressed a decent contrition.

'Mind you, I hold no brief for Beatrice. No sooner was young Edward born than she began to let herself go. Shockin' dowdy and unkempt she was not two years after she was married, and eatin' chocolates, puttin' on weight without a glance in the looking glass. If Edward had a rovin' eye she brought it on herself. But at the last Edward went too far – pushin' his whore over and above his lawful wedded wife for all the world to see.'

'Magda will give you a sleeping draught tonight,' said Hugo, to Miss Nellie. 'Tomorrow will see us in Dublin.'

'Will you be going with them?' said Donovan, to Seamus.

'I will not,' Seamus said. 'I won't be a party to Nellie's shenanigans. 'Tis blasphemy she's after getting into her head.'

'Well,' said Donovan, to the others, 'I wish you all a safe journey, I hope you'll soon be safely back. Before I leave I'll see Gretchen up the stairs and then I'll be on my way.'

At the top of the west tower Gretchen stared at Donovan.

'I'm so startled, so disgusted I can't speak,' she said.

'In the morning, after you've had your breakfast,' said Donovan, 'pack a suitcase with whatever you need for a few days. Meanwhile I'll be looking for someone to take you in. You cannot stay alone at night with Seamus in the Hall. That's flat.'

12

For over a week Gretchen stayed with Harry and Eliza Moore – a week which, when she looked back on it, seemed to have been a well of silence. Not a voice was ever raised, not a stair ever creaked, not a door ever slammed. Harry left, with the dawn, for Port Ferris. Eliza, at the top of the house was busy all day with illustrations she was doing for a children's book. A placid woman, called Maureen, came in early each morning, saw to the household chores, served cold meat, cheese, and salad to Gretchen and Eliza at lunch-time, and went off when she had washed up after tea and left the evening meal ready for the oven. Gretchen was able to write at the desk in the library which Harry was too pressed to use except on an occasional Sunday, a place was laid at the dinner table for Donovan who came by at the end of every day.

In private Gretchen told Donovan how much she had admired Eliza' small pastels, each of which was to accompany a fairy-tale.

'I wish you could see them,' she said, to him. 'Each one is as delicate as a snowflake.'

'You've had a great compliment,' said Donovan. 'Eliza won't even show her work to Harry. Harry himself has no idea of what she's been doing until the book's in hard covers.'

In public Gretchen made a *gaffe* when Harry remarked – on the third evening of her visit – that she seemed quite happy in the Moore *ménage*.

'I'm awfully happy being with you,' said Gretchen. 'It's not a bit like being in Ireland.'

Although she bowed her head in shame instantly, mortified by her involuntary discourtesy to her hosts – and to Donovan – both the Moores were chortling the moment the words were out of her mouth.

'I'd no right to be so rude,' she said. 'After all, what do I know about the real Ireland? Nothing but Ralston's Cove and –'

'Ralston's Cove is the real Ireland in miniature,' said Harry. 'Slipshod, sleazy, down-at-the-heel and out-at-the-elbows, full of the

173

glib, mendacious, torpid remnants of humankind –'

'Why,' Gretchen said, too astonished to be tactful, 'you've stolen the best part of my vocabulary.'

'I've never heard you exercise it,' said Donovan.

'It would be extremely ungracious if I did,' she said. 'After all, it's your country –'

'Is there any singular aspect of the Irish which strikes you particularly?' said Eliza.

'Nobody walks tall,' said Gretchen. 'Not even the young people. I look at them specially when I go to town with Miss Nellie. I watched them when I went to Port Ferris with Dr Donovan. Most of them slouch and shamble as if they had nowhere to go and were in no hurry to get there.'

'Most of them haven't anywhere to go,' said Eliza. 'And hardly any of them are in any hurry. Why Harry and I didn't clear out of here whilst we were young enough to have a choice I will never understand.'

'Of course Dublin must be completely different,' Gretchen said.

'What makes you think that Dublin's completely different?' said Donovan.

'I've seen it,' said Gretchen. 'I mean in the college library there were two portfolios filled with the most beautiful water-colours of Dublin. Only privileged students were allowed to see them and only the librarian was allowed to handle them, to turn them over. I'd never imagined such exquisite houses, I couldn't get St. Stephen's Green or Merrion Square or North St. George's Street, Pembroke Street, Harcourt Street, Henrietta Street out of my head if I tried.'

'When were the water-colours done?' Donovan said.

'About a hundred years ago, I think,' said Gretchen.

'I see,' he said.

'What do you see?' said Gretchen.

'If you answer that,' said Eliza, to Donovan, 'I'll cry. Fifty years ago I was born in Merrion Square.

'You're not meant to understand what this conversation's about,' Harry said, to Gretchen.

'I should never have started it,' said Gretchen. 'I'm only a stranger here.'

'On your next holiday you should take the lass to Venice,' said Harry, to Donovan. 'She's on the look-out for something memorable.'

'For the time being,' Donovan said, 'I can only take her as far as the Cygne d'Or.'

'Well, that's not Ireland,' said Eliza. 'That's pure escape.'

Harry poured more coffee for all hands and stopped when he came to Gretchen.

'Does everybody walk tall in America?' he said.

'That's a pretty sweeping question,' said Gretchen. 'All I can tell you is that people are proud where I come from, they carry themselves straight. And when I went to college I found that students and faculty alike were – almost all of them – purposeful. They *strode*. New Yorkers very nearly *run*, as if there isn't a minute to lose.'

'You'll be homesick in the Hall,' said Harry.

'I couldn't be homesick there,' Gretchen said. 'Absolutely nothing in the Hall so much as reminds me of home.'

'Ruth without a tear amid the alien corn?' said Harry.

'Ruth close to tears before the *instant* corn,' said Donovan. 'Neither you nor Eliza has ever had a meal at the Hall.'

'To be sure it's not fair to judge a whole nation by Seamus and Miss Nellie,' Gretchen said.

'They'd be far out of context anywhere else but here,' said Donovan, at which a peal of sudden laughter broke from Gretchen.

'Really they ought to be stuffed and mounted when they die,' she said.

The next day was a Thursday. Donovan, over Eliza's protests, took Gretchen to the Cygne d'Or for dinner.

'I daresay,' said Harry, seeing them to the *porte-cochère*, 'that a glimpse of Gretchen buoys up M. Vergnol's morale.'

'It's Dr Donovan he waits for,' Gretchen said. 'He greets him like a long-lost brother.'

'The fact is,' said Donovan, as he and Gretchen were driving to the restaurant, 'I'm greatly relieved that you're contented at the Moores.'

'*I'm* the one who's relieved, to put it mildly,' said Gretchen. 'I would have been frightened to have been alone with Seamus in the Hall. You see, on Monday morning, about half an hour before Miss Nellie went off to Dublin, they had an ugly skirmish. It was nothing at all like their usual mock battles. No, on Monday the hostilities were brutal.'

'What was the bone of contention?' said Donovan.

'The bone of contention was the *séance* Magda had laid on,' Gretchen said.

Seamus, it appeared, had been so powerfully opposed to summoning Edward from his eternal rest that he accused Miss Nellie of treachery to her eldest child and infidelity to her much-vaunted Church.

175

'You'll live to regret this day,' Seamus had said.

'He was in a passion,' said Gretchen. 'But Miss Nellie – who was ice-cold – was worse. She told Seamus that, in two or three days he'd be on his knees, begging for her return.'

'I'm puttin' a spoke in your wheel, Seamus Taylor,' she had said. 'Before the week's out you'll be fit for nothin' but the rubbish heap – which is where you've belonged for forty years.'

When Miss Nellie had gone Mary had tried – and failed – to soothe Seamus.

'I'll see the Hall burnt to cinders for her home-coming,' Seamus had said.

'They seem to have got down to bed-rock,' said Donovan. 'Have you ever heard anything like that before?'

'I have not,' Gretchen said. 'You told me that they never enjoyed anything so much as their daily duel. But I don't think either of them enjoyed the contest on Monday morning.'

'What do you suppose Miss Nellie meant by 'putting a spoke' in Seamus' wheel?' said Donovan.

'I had a feeling she'd already seen to it that Seamus was to have an exceptionally unpleasant time without her,' said Gretchen. 'When she comes back –'

'– they'll kiss and make up,' Donovan said.

'Will they?' said Gretchen. 'I hope you're right but –'

'They can't do without each other,' said Donovan.

'I'm sure that Seamus couldn't do without Miss Nellie. However, I suspect that, in the long run, Miss Nellie could do very nicely without Seamus,' Gretchen said.

By four o'clock on the following afternoon Donovan had seen six patients and was both surprised and disquieted to find that the seventh was none other than Mary McDaid.

'What's the trouble?' he said, immediately certain that a crisis was in the making.

'There's no trouble with me,' said Mary. 'But I'm not staying in the Hall until herself gets back. I cadged a lift from Ben Daly all the way here to warn you that Seamus has taken leave of his senses all together. Sure, he's smashed half the furniture with his bare hands and half the crockery by hurling it at me. And maybe worse is yet to come.'

'What's got into him?' said Donovan.

'It's what *not* got into him,' Mary said. 'Listen, till I tell you what she did before she set out for Dublin. First thing in the morning – likely whilst he was still in his pyjamas and having a pee – she went through his trousers and pinched all his cash. Later, a good while after breakfast, she marched into the pub on the hill and told Dan O'Malley that if he gave Seamus anything to drink 'twould be on the house, since she wouldn't pay for so much as half a pint from that day forward. Then she crossed the road, knocked up Ben and told him she'd not be responsible for any loans to Seamus and, if that wasn't enough, she must have made Mr and Mrs Hugo stop the car here, in Ralston's Cove – along their way to Port Ferris and on to Dublin – where she told the off-licence to give Seamus nothing on credit and then she rushed to the bank and drew out every farthing from the account she shares with Seamus.'

'It takes some believing,' said Donovan. 'You're right about that. I never thought Miss Nellie would go so far as to deprive Seamus of his liquor. She's known for years that's asking for disaster.'

'Things weren't too bad on Monday and Tuesday for he still had the odd bottle in the house,' said Mary. 'All the same he was wild when O'Malley refused him the usual on Monday morning and again on Tuesday. On Wednesday he drove up to the off-licence here, where he had no comfort, so he went straight to the bank, only to find there wasn't as much as five pence left in the kitty. On the way home he pulled up on the hill and tried to touch Ben, but Ben wasn't having any of that –'

'Hold on,' said Donovan. 'How do you know what you've been telling me?'

'Seamus told me she'd been through his wallet,' Mary said. 'I got the rest out of Ben – you've to remember that Miss Nellie'd been round to him – who told me that Don O'Malley'd been spreading the news to all of his customers. Ben got the bit about the off-licence and the bank in Ralston's Cove from Seamus himself.'

'It's against the law for an off-licence to give over a bottle on credit,' said Donovan.

'They may have bent it a bit for Seamus now and then,' said Mary. 'Just to get him off the premises.'

'It's possible,' said Donovan. 'I don't think it's probable.'

'Anyway,' Mary said, 'Wednesday forenoon Seamus was dry as a bone and raving. That's when he started smashing up the furniture. There was no halting him and no cajoling him. I stood by for a while but I wasn't putting me hand in me pocket for him, seeing as it's four months and over since I've had a penny of me wages. Then who should come along but Danny O'Toole wanting to borrow me wire-shears, for his own wanted sharpening.

' "Well," says Danny, when he'd seen what Seamus was up to in the drawing-room, "sure he'll have the place destroyed if nobody gives him a drop to drink.'

'So Danny goes home, comes back, and fixes him up with a bottle. Seamus was good as gold for what was left of the day. Oh, he was as sullen and disobliging as you could hope to find him, still there was no more of a rumpus. But by yesterday morning Danny's bottle was empty and no sooner did I get into me kitchen than he came charging in after me. That's the moment he started pitching the cups and saucers at me head. There I was ducking and dodging whilst he was dancing with rage – like a grasshopper on a griddle he was – until he missed his footing and fell right over a chair. I ran for me life, I can tell you. Now I'd no intention of putting foot in the Hall until her Ladyship was back from Dublin. But it happened the parson came knocking at me door this morning just as I was having me elevenses. It seems he went calling on herself – not knowing she was away – and after he'd spoken with Seamus for a minute or so he hot-footed it to me. To hear him tell it Seamus has the drawing-room wrecked entirely and the whole place is in worse shape than ever 'twas when we had them pigs in there. I didn't doubt that, not for a second, but then the parson told me something I couldn't fancy at all. For somehow or other it seems that Seamus has tumbled to Kevin. Not that the parson knew there was anything to hide about Kevin. What he had to say came out natural. But even he himself fell to wondering when Seamus told him that Kevin had been living in the west wing since September – as if 'twas something marvellous. Deathly quiet, he was, the parson said, when he mentioned that.

' "Comes from Limerick, does he?" says Seamus, to the parson.

' "Well," says the parson, "I don't know where he comes from but he's a nice lad. Everyone hereabouts has a good word to say for him."

' "Do they, so?" says Seamus, and all the while he's smiling and smiling. "I had it from his own lips he was born and bred in Limerick."

' "I fear the man is quite, quite mad," says the parson to me. "The destruction he's caused is indescribable. And his smile was most peculiar. Most peculiar indeed. Would you think of putting the matter up to Dr Donovan? For Miss Nellie will be fearfully distressed when she sees the havoc he's wrought in there and who can tell if more is not to follow?"

'So that's me story,' Mary said. 'And sick with worry over Kevin I am, although what Seamus could do to him I can't say, of course. Unless he's thinking to lay his hand on that gun. Still and all, if I had you by me side I'd go, only the once, to the hall and take Kevin away with me before the poor boy comes to any harm.'

'Is Ben Daly waiting outside for you?' said Donovan.

'He is, God love him,' said Mary.

'Then go home with him,' Donovan said. 'And bolt your door. When I've finished here I'll come along to Dufresne Bay with some whiskey for Seamus and I'll bring Kevin back to my house until this blows over.'

It was nearing seven o'clock – and the darkness had brought rain on its coming – when Donovan reached the gates of the Hall. Just inside, on the driveway, he saw Mary – in a thick overcoat, with a shawl over her head – caught in his lights. He braked at once. Mary yanked at the passenger's door, eased herself into the seat beside him, and gave herself up to convulsive sobs which sounded, to Donovan, like blasts from a great bellows.'

'What's upset you so?' he said. 'Take your time, go slow, but tell me.'

Mary gasped for a lungful of air, little by little the blasts abated.

'Whilst I was in Ralston's Cove with you,' she said, 'the guards came for Kevin.'

'The Gardaí took Kevin away?' said Donovan. 'In pity's name what for?'

'Seamus sent for them,' said Mary. 'When they got here he told them Kevin was the man all Ireland was looking for, the man who raped and killed all them innocent girls. Dufresne Hill was talking of nothing else when I got back from your office.'

'It doesn't seem possible,' Donovan said.

'Ben Daly was just coasting along to me door when I spied Mike Healey and Danny O'Toole going into the pub together,' said Mary. ' "That's queer," I says. "Neither the one nor t'other's the drinking sort. Not at this hour of day with the milking ahead of them." '

'Ben went into the pub after the two of them. Presently the three of them comes out. By that time I'm standing on the pavement.

' "You tell her, Mike," says Ben to Mike Healey.'

'And Mike confirmed the fact?' said Donovan.

'Mike was mending fence where his pasture touches on the meadow north of the east wing,' said Mary. 'Danny O'Toole and Kevin were giving him a helping hand with the work when up comes Seamus with the guards behind him. One of them was Jack Ross.

' "There's your killer," says Seamus, pointing at Kevin. "There's the murderer of that girl who was hacked to pieces in Limerick and of all the others who came afterwards." '

'Danny O'Toole did his best to quash Seamus – Kevin had done a few jobs, off and on, for his wife, and both the O'Tooles are fond of the boy – but Seamus would have it that Kevin was the guilty party. In the end Jack put the lad in the car and drove away with him.'

'I'm not surprised you're miserable,' Donovan said, starting the car and letting it roll slowly up to the west tower. 'Cry your eyes out and wait for me while I go upstairs with my bottle for Seamus. When I come down I'll drive you home. Then I'll go and see what can be done for Kevin.'

He found Seamus in the drawing-room, which looked as if a hurricane had torn a path directly through it. Tables and chairs, – arms and struts half-disjointed, had been overturned or flung in all directions. Seamus was stuffing the fire with the legs from one or two of them.

'I heard you were dry,' said Donovan. 'So I brought something to wet your whistle.'

Seamus straightened up, seized Donovan's bottle, unscrewed the cap with his teeth, and swallowed half the contents before he looked Donovan in the eye.

'Nellie's not home,' he said.

'I know that,' said Donovan.

'I'm the boss here,' said Seamus, glancing around at his handiwork.

'So I see,' said Donovan. 'Shall we go for a ride? You could bring the bottle.'

'Why should I go for a ride?' Seamus said.

'The Gardaí want you to stop in and sign some papers,' said Donovan. 'I understand you put them onto a good thing.'

'That I did,' said Seamus.

'Then come along,' said Donovan.

'Half a tick,' Seamus said.

He opened his fly and urinated carefully all over the chintz armchair by the fireplace.

'I shit on Nellie's side of the bed,' he said. 'I piss wherever the spirit moves me.'

'That's telling 'em,' said Donovan.

'So it is,' said Seamus. 'You're not a bad sort, you know.'

'When you're ready –' Donovan said.

Gloating, and holding fast to the bottle, Seamus went down the stairs. Donovan helped him into the back of the car. Not a word came from Mary, whom Donovan let off on Dufresne Hill. By the time he reached the hospital Seamus was singing.

'I've a large package to pick up here,' Donovan said. 'Would you help me to put it in the boot?'

'If you like,' said Seamus.

He lurched out of the car, grasped Donovan's arm, and doddered into the emergency admitting room, where an orderly, with considerable assistance from Donovan, got him into a straight-jacket. Donovan left orders with Mrs Sweeney while the orderly held onto Seamus. Then he drove to the centre of Ralston's Cove where he could see that there was still a light in Jim Farquahar's office window.

'I was just on my way home,' said Farquahar.

'Spare me a few minutes,' said Donovan. 'I'm in a quandary.'

'My fee for a quandary's exorbitant,' Farquahar said. 'Particularly on an empty stomach.'

'May I use the telephone?' said Donovan.

'He didn't explain,' said Harry Moore. 'He simply said to go ahead without him and to put something aside – for himself and, possibly, for Jim Farquahar – in the event that they turned up between nine o'clock and ten.'

'It's lucky I've a roast,' said Eliza.

'Somehow I doubt we'll be seeing either of them this evening,' Moore said.

Donovan and Farquahar went together to the Gardaí.

'We've come about the boy you picked up in Dufresne Bay this afternoon,' said Jim Farquahar.

'I don't know what to do with him and that's the truth and nothing but,' said Jack Ross. 'Sure, when that van tipped over he walked up ten or fifteen loose pigs with us, and a more helpful lad I couldn't have hoped to find.

'Now if it had been Miss Nellie to send for us I'd be a bit puzzled by the errand; all the same I'd see my duty plain. But Seamus Taylor's word against the likes of Danny O'Toole and Mike Healey is hard to swallow – leastways for me.'

'Have you charged the boy yet?' Farquahar said.

'I have not,' said Ross. 'I've taken his photograph and his fingerprints and pulled a few hairs from his crotch just in the event they match the trace evidence Limerick's holding. And I've locked him up and sent Brian Touhey round to the pub for sandwiches and a pint. But like it or not, I'm bound to call Ravensbrook, I am. Though I'm minded to wait till the boy's had something to stick to his ribs.'

'Could we see him for a moment?' said Donovan. 'We'd like him to know we're behind him, that nobody believes there's anything to connect him with the crimes.'

'Comes with me,' Ross said. 'If it wasn't out of order I'd tell him myself that the sooner he's released the better pleased I'll be.'

181

Harry Moore was sitting down to Eliza's roast, and Gretchen's gravy, when the telephone rang again.

'Harry, in God's name meet me at emergency admitting,' said Donovan. 'I've an ambulance on the way for a boy who's cut both his wrists and his jugular and there's no one but the nursing staff in the hospital at this time of night.'

'Must you go?' said Eliza, to Harry.

'I must,' said Harry, pulling on his coat. 'Don't wait up for me. And don't wait up for Clement Donovan either. I'll be needing him in the operating room.'

'Perhaps I can teach Gretchen to play Russian Bank,' Eliza said.

'Go home,' said Harry Moore. 'I'll stand the watch.'

'You go home,' Donovan said. 'He's my patient.'

'He was your patient,' said Moore. 'He's been mine ever since he was wheeled into the operating theatre. Truth to tell you I was sure we'd lose him on the table.'

'How do you rate his chances now?' Donovan said.

'Only fair,' said Moore. 'But he's young.'

Both men fell silent. Kevin lay as still as stone. A machine beside his bed recorded his heart-beats which trailed across a screen. Harry Moore kept his eyes on the moving chart. Donovan thought about Gretchen.

He would have to tell her the truth and he knew in his bones that she would interpret the calamity as a purely Irish phenomenon and she would see Seamus Taylor as the living embodiment of everything that was specifically Irish and native to Ireland alone.

'Gretchen isn't going to like this,' said Harry Moore, suddenly.

'What can I say to her?' said Donovan. 'If I tell her that Seamus is off his head she'll believe I'm urging a plea for diminished responsibility. If I concede that Seamus is evil – which he is – she'll take evil as a synonym for Irish.'

'She wouldn't be far off at that,' Moore said. 'On the whole we're a self-serving tribe, squabbling amongst ourselves in our gutters. But if I were you I'd bring Seamus into very sharp focus. It would probably be easier for her to confine her hatred to one iniquitous individual. She's too fine-tuned to hold an entire nation in contempt.

'What time is it, by the way? My watch has gone back on me.'

'It'll be well past midnight,' said Donovan, putting his hand into his pocket. 'It's one seventeen exactly.'

'If you could see yourself –' said Moore.

Briefly Donovan surveyed his sleeves, his trousers.

'The lad had a quantity of blood in him,' he said.

'His vital signs are improving,' said Harry Moore. 'What time is it now?'

'It lacks five minutes to four,' Donovan said.

'What would you say to calling in that young fellow Fir?' said Moore. 'If we could leave Kevin with a doctor standing by we could both get a couple of hours' sleep.'

It was raining when they walked into the hospital parking lot.

'This has been a night to remember,' Harry Moore said. 'I haven't seen a wound in the jugular since I was a medical student.'

'Before you go off to work,' said Donovan, 'tell Eliza to hide the papers from Gretchen. Danny O'Toole's wife, Jane, has a brother who's a journalist in Port Ferris. If Kevin does nothing else with his life he'll make the headlines today.

'Sooner or later you'll be round yourself to see the lass?' said Moore.

'I will,' Donovan said.

'Was Harry conscious when he left for Port Ferris this morning?' said Donovan.

'He was conscious enough to wake me just to tell me to hide the newspaper from Gretchen,' said Eliza. 'Doctor's orders – meaning yours.'

'You will have a cup of coffee, won't you?'

'With pleasure,' Donovan said. 'Has Gretchen had breakfast?'

'She hasn't had coffee yet,' said Eliza. 'She's gone for a wrap. It *is* cold today. Maureen's a nice fire going in Harry's library for her when she gets down to work.

'Ah, her she is.'

'Good heavens,' Gretchen said, smiling at Donovan. 'Are you off duty so early?'

'I wish I were,' said Donovan. 'This is a duty call. I'm here to tell you about Kevin.'

'What's happened to Kevin?' said Gretchen, on a new note, high and cutting.

'Last night Harry saved his life,' Donovan said. 'Or, at least, from what I've just seen at the hospital, it seems to me he'll survive. Drink your coffee and I'll explain.

'I don't want coffee,' said Gretchen. 'I want to know about Kevin.'

'Would you like me to leave you alone with Gretchen?' Eliza said, to Donovan.

'I would not,' said Donovan. 'I'll be banking on you to support her all day long.'

He stood on his refusal to say another word until the three of them had had their coffee. Eliza made light conversation, pronouncing Gretchen a most promising beginner at Russian Bank.

'I needed that,' said Donovan, when his cup was empty. 'Now, please, both of you listen to me and hold your peace till I'm done. I'll try to tell you everything I know about his matter. But first, perhaps, I should explain Kevin to you, Eliza –'

'Gretchen's talked to us about him,' Eliza said. 'She told us about the spaniel at Dufresne Bay and his diseased ears. And Harry remembered him. He met him that evening after the fire at the Hall.'

'Good enough,' said Donovan. 'Then here's the tale with no frills. It probably began two or three days ago when – who knows how – Seamus found out that Kevin had been living in the west wing since September and had also found out – almost certainly from Kevin himself – that the boy had been born in Limerick.'

With that he told them how Miss Nellie had left Seamus with no funds, about Seamus' behaviour when he had nothing left to drink, about the rector's call on Mary and what the rector had had to say about Seamus. Gretchen and Eliza listened in silence, but the strain of deepening anxiety told on Gretchen.

'In such a state of mind did Seamus try to kill Kevin?' she said, interrupting Donovan in spite of his injunction.

'He did worse,' said Donovan, and recounted the particulars of Kevin's arrest, went on to tell of his own arrival – with Jim Farquahar – at the police station, and when he had described the injuries which Kevin had inflicted on himself, alone in a cell, Gretchen hid her face in her hands and lowered her head.

'I thought prisoners were invariably stripped of the means to do themselves bodily harm before they were put in a cell,' said Eliza.

'Indeed I fear things will go very hard on Jack Ross for that omission,' Donovan said. 'It was, of course, the measure of Jack's lack of faith in Seamus' accusation. In his heart he was sure there was no evidence against Kevin, sure that in the normal course of events he'd shortly have been released. But there's no denying that he locked the boy up with a pen-knife on him.'

'Will an attempted suicide prejudice public opinion against the lad?' said Eliza. 'Might it come to seem a tacit admission of guilt?'

'That's what's worrying me and worrying Jim Farquahar,' said Donovan. 'Kevin's already under twenty-four-hour surveillance in spite of the fact he's too weak to lift an eyelid.'

With which he rose and put his hands on Gretchen's shoulders.

'Have patience,' he said. 'I hope things can be put to rights in the near future, but Rome wasn't built in a day.'

'I'm going to be sick,' said Gretchen, and darted upstairs.

'All this is not about to endear the Irish to the poor girl,' said Eliza.

'Don't let her see the papers,' said Donovan. 'As of this morning Kevin's been tried and convicted in the press.'

'Oh, dear God,' Eliza said, 'Maureen does the housework with her radio turned down low. I'll tell her to shut it off for the next few days. And we won't watch the telly. Not until somebody gets to the bottom of what must be a cruel misunderstanding. What does Jim Farquahar think of the affair?'

'Jim's reasonably sanguine,' said Donovan. 'He says that if Kevin is not responsible for the killings there won't be any evidence on which to build a case against him. With no evidence the law can't bring the lad to trial. When I asked him if attempted suicide might be made to count as evidence of a guilty conscience he said that, theoretically, it couldn't possibly stand up in court. But he did admit that it might seriously prejudice a Roman Catholic jury. He advised me to pin my hopes on another murder, now that Kevin's under constant observation.'

'Is Jim on the boy's side?' said Eliza.

'He's against Seamus Taylor and has been ever since their first meeting,' Donovan said. 'He'll waive legal fees for Kevin – because he's so outraged by Seamus' conduct – and if he has to brief a barrister I'll tell him to brief the best in Ireland and I'll pay counsel.'

'You're for Kevin all the way, aren't you?' said Eliza.

'Once,' said Donovan, 'I watched him and Gretchen ministering to the spaniel at the Hall. I had a fantasy that they were my own children. He's a taking lad.

'I must go. Try giving Gretchen some neat vodka. And don't press her to eat.'

'I'll give her all the vodka she wants,' said Eliza. 'And I'll tell her that you and Jim have promised to provide Kevin with legal representation – the best there is – if he needs it.'

'You might also mention Harry's part in this sorry business,' Donovan said. 'Simply to remind her that there are good men here and there in Ireland, for however much the Irish may disgust her. It's no overstatement to tell her that, without Harry, Kevin would have died last night.'

'Don't be so solicitous about me,' said Gretchen, to Donovan and to Harry Moore, that evening. 'It's true that I was bowled over this morning when I heard what Seamus had done. I did cry for Kevin

185

and Mrs Moore had to comfort me. But by this afternoon I realised that I'd been crying as much because I was angry as because I was heart-broken. The more I think about Seamus the angrier I grow. I couldn't cry any more if I wanted to. So I'm very sorry – I'm ashamed of myself – to have made such a fuss.'

'What did I tell you?' said Harry Moore, to Donovan.

'You told me to go heavy on Seamus for Gretchen's sake,' Donovan said.

'I don't understand,' said Gretchen.

'Did you know that Seamus' father killed a man?' said Donovan.

'He did?' said Moore. 'Who told you that?'

'Jim Farquahar's father told me years and years ago,' Donovan said. 'Seamus isn't one of us, you know. His mother was born in Kerry. Her name was Taylor. What Seamus' father's name was I don't know. But Seamus grew up – speaking Irish – on one of the Blasket Islands. After his father had bludgeoned a man to death his mother came back to the mainland, bringing Seamus with her. When Seamus came of age he took his mother's name.'

'Does that mean that blood will tell?' said Eliza.

'Seamus is a man of the soil, not of the *parquet*,' said Donovan.

'Where are the Blasket Islands?' said Gretchen.

'Off the coast of Kerry. Off Dingle Bay,' Moore said. 'Irish is still spoken there. Or was, when Seamus was a boy.'

'Seamus was bellowing in Gaelic when I stopped by to see him after breakfast,' said Donovan.

'Won't it be a bit dodgy holding him in hospital until his wife gets back?' said Harry Moore. 'You've no grounds for detaining him against his will, have you?'

'*I've* no grounds at all,' Donovan said. 'But the law's taken an interest in Seamus.'

'The law?' said Gretchen.

'The law,' said Donovan. 'Between one thing and another Jim Farquahar and I have had a busy day.

'Jim doesn't keep office hours on Saturdays, but Miss Nellie's Mary McDaid ran him to earth at home. She'd already guessed – and rightly – that I must have put Seamus in hospital and she'd recognised that my position was a little delicate, to say the least. So she announced to Jim that she was on her way to the Gardaí to lodge a complaint against Seamus – for assault and battery. She explained to Jim that, if Seamus were at liberty, she herself might be at considerably personal risk. Jim, mindful that a noxious stain on Seamus' character would be very good news for Kevin, coaxed a full account of Seamus' recent misdemeanours out of her. Just as he was plying her with tea and buns I rang him to say that Kevin's condition looked pretty stable to me. Whereupon I was invited to join forces with himself and Mary.'

'What did Jim want with you?' said Eliza.'

'Collaboration,' Donovan said.

'Did he get it?' said Moore.

'He got it,' said Donovan. 'We went to the police – he and Mary and I. Jim told them that he had been retained by Mary and saw to it that the complaint was duly lodged. Then I, in my professional capacity, gave it as my opinion that Seamus was a public menace in his present plight. I confirmed Mary's statement about the wanton destruction of property at the Hall and declared that I had put Seamus in hospital last night because I considered that he was potentially too dangerous to be at large. I went on to say that I couldn't be responsible for him indefinitely unless I had the law's permission to keep him under restraint. At Mary's suggestion it was arranged that the police should investigate the damage at the Hall and interrogate Danny O'Toole – who had seen Seamus at his most manic.'

'You be exhausted,' said Eliza. 'Harry is. I can see that. But Kevin's mending, is he?'

'Oh, yes, he's mending,' Moore said. 'I saw him just before I came home.

'I couldn't go so far as to tell him that things were looking up,' he said, to Donovan, 'because I didn't know anything about what you've told us here. But if Seamus Taylor's word can be invalidated I should suppose that, from Kevin's point of view, they are.'

'The trace evidence in Limerick doesn't match up with Kevin,' said Donovan. 'Jim got that much out of Brian Touhey this afternoon.'

'Then the police will have to Kevin free,' said Gretchen.

'It might want a little more pressure,' said Harry Moore. 'A psychiatrist's affidavit that Seamus is not quite right in the head.'

'Sad to say,' Donovan said, 'Jack Ross resigned from the force this morning. I ran into him in town and he told me he'd resigned before he could be demoted. But his father has a going concern in Clare, a dry-goods business, and Jack says he presumes he can learn to tell the difference between a bolt of silk and a bolt of tweed in the fulness of time.'

'Another victim for Seamus,' said Harry Moore.

'You're worn out,' said Eliza, and turned to Gretchen.

'It's time for Harry to get some sleep,' she said. 'The front door key's in the latch. Give Dr Donovan a night-cap and lock the door after him when he leaves.'

'While Harry and I were keeping watch over Kevin last night,' said Donovan, to Gretchen, 'we talked a little about you. Harry said that he and Eliza would be delighted to keep you here for as long as you like, right up to the day you finish the thesis, if it suits you.'

'Mrs Moore said the same thing to me at tea-time,' said Gretchen. 'But I couldn't accept so much from either of them. It's extraordinarily kind of both of them but I've already said no thank you.'

'When Miss Nellie comes home she'll see to it that Seamus is released in her custody,' Donovan said. 'You'd have to put up with him at tea-time, at meal-times, you'd have to put up with the television day in, day out. Could you face that all over again, knowing, as now you know, what Seamus can do when he's vicious?'

Gretchen had spent most of the day asking herself that very question. She had been almost sure that Eliza Moore would offer to keep her, but if she chose to stay with the Moores it would mean the end of the nights with Donovan. At the Hall she was her own mistress. She could come and go as she pleased. However, she was convinced that, were she Harry Moore's guest, Donovan would feel compelled to a circumspection which was quite unnecessary when she was at Dufresne Bay. Had she but known it, the same nice consideration had been tormenting Donovan; he had called up all his strength to tell her that she had a choice at lodgings.

'At the Hall I'm free,' said Gretchen.

It was the closest she could come to telling Donovan that she loved him, and she spoke very low.

'What did you say?' said Donovan who, although he had heard her perfectly, wanted more than a circumlocution.

Gretchen looked up at him. There was no tenderness in his face; there never was, unless he was alone with her and – even if the Moores had gone to bed – neither of them felt alone with the other under Harry Moore's roof, sitting by Harry's fire.

'I said that here I couldn't pay my way,' Gretchen said. 'I'd be under a tremendous obligation to both Mr and Mrs Moore.'

'So, Seamus or no, you'd prefer the Hall?' said Donovan.

'Yes, I would,' Gretchen said. 'In spite of Seamus.'

'Make me the night-cap Eliza promised,' said Donovan, dazzled by a shining relief.

'What it comes down to is that Ben Daly and Jane O'Toole would work shoulder to shoulder with you?' said Donovan, to Mary.

It was the following day, a Sunday, and he and Mary were looking over the ravages in the drawing-room at the Hall.

'They would indeed,' said Mary.

'You wouldn't be so foolish as to try to put things straight all by yourself?' Donovan said.

'I couldn't,' said Mary. 'I'm past that, at my age. But Ben and I went through the whole place yesterday afternoon and then we went through the west wing. There's a few tables and chairs in there that might just serve in here and, seeing as it's Sunday, Mike Healey and Danny O'Toole have agreed to come by after lunch and put all these broken things in the old stables – nothing in this room could ever be mended. Anything that's upholstered would have to be re-covered, for what Seamus couldn't do with his hands he did with his bladder. Anyway, if this room were clear, I could get the carpet up for the cleaners – Paddy McClure would take it to Port Ferris for me – and perhaps Port Ferris could get the smell out of it. There's only one thing that's worrying me.'

'And that is?' said Donovan.

'Her bedroom,' Mary said. 'Seamus emptied his bowels on her side of the bed – several times, I'd say. There isn't a thing anybody could do about the mattress any more. It should be burned, it should. Now there's two single beds in the west wing with decent mattresses which the rats haven't got to as yet. Would she have me hide, do you think, if Danny and Mike was to move the big bed into the stables with everything else that's ruined and move them two beds from the west wing into her own room?'

'You'd do better to air out one of the spare rooms and make it ready for her return,' said Donovan. 'She might rather a new mattress for her own bedstead than the two smaller beds from the west wing.'

'Will I leave her room as it is and lock the door on it?' said Mary.

'I would,' Donovan said. 'Seeing is believing. It wouldn't hurt if she herself were made aware of what she achieved when she left Seamus dry.'

'Then that's what I'll do,' said Mary. 'I'll prepare the pink room for herself.

'As to that poor girl, what I'm thinking is that between Jane and Ben and me the worst should be over by Tuesday evening. Wednesday Ben could take me into Ralston's Cove for new supplies and the child could come back on Wednesday afternoon. I'd sleep in the Chinese room across the hall from her until her Ladyship elects to come home. That's if Seamus Taylor's right out of circulation, of course.'

'I'll answer for Seamus,' said Donovan.

'Then we'll leave it at that,' Mary said.

13

'I'm sorry to be so late,' said Donovan.

'Fix yourself something to drink,' said Eliza. 'I'm holding dinner back for Harry.'

'Is he not home yet?' Donovan said.

'He hadn't but crossed the threshold when the telephone rang and off he went again,' said Eliza.

'Have you seen Kevin?' said Gretchen.

'Not an hour ago,' said Donovan. 'He's growing stronger with ever day that goes by. And I have more news for you.'

'For me?' Gretchen said.

'Hugo and Magda are back from Dublin,' said Donovan. 'Magda called me just before I left the office to invite you and me to dinner tomorrow evening. I told her I'd put it up to you. Let me say that I hope you're disposed to accept.'

'Are you as curious as I am about the east tower?' said Gretchen.

'Probably not,' Donovan said. 'But I'm late tonight because I dropped in on Mary to see if she was bearing up. She insisted on a short visit to the west tower so we went down to Dufresne Bay. Between herself and her helping hands the worst of the work is done – except in Miss Nellie's bedroom, which I advised her to leave untouched. But she's tired. I thought if you were to dine in the east tower tomorrow evening and to dine with me on Thursday evening it would give her a chance to catch her breath.'

'I'd love to see what the other half of the Hall is like,' said Gretchen.

'Harry and I will miss you sorely when you go,' said Eliza.

'Not as much as I'll miss both of you,' Gretchen said.

'When Miss Nellie sees what Seamus has done will she forgive and forget?' said Eliza, to Donovan.

'A long time ago,' Gretchen said, 'Dr Donovan told me that, come what might, Seamus and Miss Nellie would always kiss and make up.'

'I begin to wonder about that now,' said Donovan. 'What she did to Seamus cut very deep. Since I've been keeping him in liquor he's open about that. He weeps the whole day long. But what he's done to Miss Nellie may cut deeper still. Did I tell you he'd slashed every portrait in the long passage?'

'Oh, no!' said Gretchen.

'Effectively Miss Nellie hasn't an ancestor left to her name,' Donovan said.

Donovan and Gretchen were greeted on their arrival at Hugo Dufresne's portion of the Hall by his chauffeur and were surprised not to be admitted to the east tower but to be ushered into the east wing. Hugo, in a crimson velvet smoking jacket, came forward to welcome them.

'Magda's just stopped meditating,' he said. 'She's been making up for lost time. Neither of us could meditate in Dublin, what with Nellie talking sixty to the dozen night and day.

'Leave your coats down here. We'll wait for Magda – she's dressing – in the drawing-room.'

The stern elegance of the entrance hall, the thick stair-carpet, the magnificent portières in the drawing-room and the richly polished furniture, the sparkling mirrors left Gretchen nearly speechless.

'I couldn't have imagined anything like this,' she said. 'I'm accustomed to the west tower and I've been through the west wing –'

'Tragic,' said Hugo. 'Absolutely tragic. Nellie's utterly irresponsible. By now it would cost thousands of pounds to restore the place as it should be restored. As it is, it's shocking. Simply shocking. And our housekeeper has told us that there were outright acts of vandalism in the west tower while we were away.'

'Seamus went on the rampage,' said Donovan.

'We do not receive Seamus,' said Hugo. 'We never have. Nor do we associate with Nellie amongst her ruins. Until two weeks ago we hadn't even stepped inside the west tower for forty years. It was understood that, if she wanted anything from either of us, she could come to the east tower – alone.

'Naturally, when she lost her eldest son we made an exception to one of our unwritten laws. We felt constrained to stand by her at such a time.'

'Naturally,' Donovan said.

Hugo bent his attention on Gretchen.

'If,' he said, 'you're familiar with the west wing would you like to see more of its counterpart? Magda may not be down for ten or fifteen minutes.'

'She can't wait,' said Donovan, who had been quick to notice Gretchen's sudden air of expectancy.

'This wing,' Hugo said, 'antedates Nellie's wing. Except in here – where Magda and I decided to put the emphasis on comfort – all the rooms are almost as they were in the seventeenth century. We *have* added bathrooms, but as unostentiously as possible, we've also been

191

obliged to replace curtains, bedspreads, linens and, as you must have been aware, we've laid on central heating and electric lighting. What we've been at pains not to disturb is the character of the wing.'

Trotting after Hugo through one severe and stately room after another Gretchen found herself a little breathless before so much austere splendour, and far too shy to make any comment. Donovan, usually so sparing with a word of praise, could not refrain from complimenting Hugo on the solemn grandeur which he and Magda had so carefully protected.

'Has Miss Nellie seen this?' he said, to Hugo.

'As a child,' said Hugo, 'she was in and out of both wings, both towers, all the time. But since her return from exile in Leicestershire she has only visited us – occasionally – in the east tower.'

Slowly, stopping here and there to admire a bench, a chest, a painting, they regained the drawing-room, where they found Magda, in black sequins, brooding over the glass in her hand.

'Here you are, my darlings,' Magda said, rising to give Gretchen a peck on the forehead and kissing Donovan on both cheeks. 'How terribly, terribly thirsty you must be. Are they terribly thirsty, Hugo?'

'I'm thirsty,' said Hugo.

They had champagne cocktails and caviar on thin rounds of toast.

'Hugo and I are worn to the bone,' Magda said. 'Right to the bone.'

'Is your mission accomplished?' said Donovan.

'My dear, if you only knew,' said Magda –

Nine days earlier, on a Monday, they had gone to Dublin. From Tuesday – the day after their arrival in the city – through Friday Mme Kirova had given them daily sittings. A reluctant and tearful Beatrice, a wrathful and determined Miss Nellie had been instructed that no one was to move a muscle or make a sound while the medium was in trance.

'We told them that *any* disturbance might be frightfully dangerous to Mme Kirova,' said Magda.

'Both of us hammered on that point,' said Hugo. 'We believed we had driven it home.'

During the first three *séances* Mme Kirova had invoked her guide, a Mexican juggler, who had done his best to discover the newly discarnate Edward.

'In vain. In vain,' said Magda.

'He got on to Teddy Roosevelt and Mme de Staël,' said Hugo.

'But neither of them was of the slightest interest to Beatrice,' Magda said.

'Nellie found Mme de Staël most offensive,' said Hugo.

'So did I,' Donovan said. 'When I was boning up on Napoleon.'

At the last sitting the medium had tried to reach Edward directly.

'She was in deep trance,' said Magda. 'Nellie was stiff as a ramrod, Beatrice was bundled up and quaking, as always –'

'– when all of a sudden,' said Hugo, 'Mme Kirova's voice – which we hadn't heard for some time – turned into a rough, baritone shout.

' "Tell the meddlesome bitch to leave me alone," said the voice –'

'At that,' Magda said, 'Beatrice bounded out of her chair.

' "That's him," she shrieked. "That's my Edward,' she shrieked again –'

'– positively *shrieked*,' said Hugo –

'– and Mme Kirova went into shock,' said Magda.

'It was appalling,' Hugo said. 'Perfectly appalling.'

'The maid hurried in when she heard Beatrice,' said Magda. 'All the same there was nothing for it but to call a doctor.'

On the following day, Saturday, Mme Kirova still kept to her bed. However one of her *protégées* – a young sensitive named Blanche – agreed to give them a sitting.

'But without Beatrice,' Magda said. 'We couldn't have trusted Beatrice ever again. It was out of the question.'

'Blanche got in touch with one of Edward's cronies,' said Hugo –

'– and would you believe it,' said Magda, 'he told us that Edward couldn't be interrupted because he was playing stud poker.'

'Edward was playing stud poker with Bach or Shakespeare or Albert Einstein?' said Donovan.

'You don't understand how many levels there are on the other side,' Hugo said. 'Edward couldn't have been in select company, given what he was on the earth plane.

'Dr Donovan was only being playful,' said Magda.

'How did Miss Nellie take to the poker?' said Donovan.

'She was struck dumb, for a wonder,' Hugo said. 'All day Sunday she had hardly a word to say for herself. On Monday we took her to Dr Adelson, who's very good at automatic writing. He gave her an appointment for the next day, yesterday –'

'– but Hugo and I had shot our bolt,' said Magda.

'Our bolt was definitely shot,' said Hugo.

'We came home and left Nellie to fend for herself,' Magda said.

'It was four o'clock yesterday afternoon when we got back,' said Hugo.

'Beatrice is a coarse woman,' said Magda.

'Distinctly coarse,' Hugo said.

'Dinner is served,' said a manservant, from the entrance to the drawing-room.

193

Never before had Gretchen sat down to six courses and two wines. Half-way through the meal she was restless; the cutlery which still flanked her place was a promise of much more food to come and she was no longer hungry. Moreover the conversation bored her. Magda and Hugo – the one supporting the other – dwelt in great detail on their flat in London, on the house they had had in the Bois de Boulogne, on the villa they could not bear to part with in the south of France.

'We tend to roam,' Magda said. 'But lately we spend more and more time here. So many of our old friends have died, don't you know, and so many of our new friends are hardly more than acquaintances.'

'Are you happy in Dufresne Bay?' said Hugo, to Gretchen.

'It must be very pretty in the spring and summer,' said Gretchen, surprised in secret reverie,· hastily inventing an appropriate answer for Hugo.

'So you are not happy in the west tower,' he said. 'How much do you know of Ireland?'

'Almost nothing,' said Gretchen, unreeling another automatic response. 'I've set my heart on going to Dublin one day.'

'Hugo will take you to Dublin in less than three weeks' time,' said Magda.

All at once Gretchen was the centre of attention. Embarrassed, she waited for Donovan to come to her rescue, but Donovan said nothing.

'I go to Dublin twice a year,' said Hugo. 'In March and in September I consult my astrologer before making any alterations in my investment portfolio. I shall be leaving in the motor on a Monday and returning on a Wednesday. On the Tuesday morning I shall be busy over my chart, but on Tuesday afternoon and on Tuesday evening I should be enchanted to show you the city.'

'He knows it like a stoat,' said Magda. 'You couldn't do better.'

'I'm sure I couldn't,' said Gretchen, helplessly encircled by her hosts and thoroughly alarmed by the prospect of spending three days with Hugo.

'Then I shall look forward to a delightful excursion,' Hugo said.

After dinner Magda rose and took Gretchen's arm.

'You and Dr Donovan are to have your coffee here,' she said, to Hugo. 'Gretchen and I will be served in the tower.'

'Such a charming little frock,' said Magda. 'Did you make it yourself?'

'My grandmother helped me,' said Gretchen.

'Too sweet,' Magda said. 'Now aren't we comfy?'

'It's a lovely place,' said Gretchen, overpowered by warmth, luxury, and a profusion of roses and lilies of the valley. 'Where do all the flowers come from?'

'From our florist in Port Ferris,' Magda said. 'As of the first of May through to the end of November we can depend on the garden, but in the dead of winter we're reduced to importing whatever we need.'

Half an hour later she showed Gretchen the other rooms in the tower. At the top of the stairs she led Gretchen into a room that, except for two prayer rugs on the floor, was completely bare.

'We meditate in here,' said Magda. 'Sometimes we meditate together, sometimes we meditate separately. Meditation greatly enriches our lives.'

'I knew a girl in college who used to meditate,' said Gretchen. 'We thought it was because she came from California.'

'One has to be totally mature before one can meditate,' Magda said. 'Shall we join our gentlemen?'

On their way to the east wing Magda said: 'We never entertain in the tower. And we never use the wing unless we have guests.'

Gretchen expected Magda to take the staircase to the drawing-room but Magda went forward on the ground floor, passing the dining-room, whose double doors were shut, and leading Gretchen into a spacious ball-room.

'You've had coffee?' said Hugo, coming toward them.

'We've had coffee and *crème de menthe* and a few girlish giggles,' said Magda. 'Now we're ready for a ball.'

'In the east wing,' Hugo said, to Donovan, 'we invariably dance a little after dinner. This evening we rather fancy a Charleston. What do you say to that?'

'It's late,' said Donovan. 'I must be up early in the morning.'

Neither Hugo nor Magda appeared to have heard him. Magda put a record on the gramophone and presently she and Hugo were doing the Charleston with notable skill. When the music ended Donovan expressed his thanks for the dinner, Gretchen followed suit.

'Do stay a moment longer,' said Magda, while Hugo turned the record over.

'We really must go,' said Donovan.

Magda drifted into Hugo's arms, then waved a good-bye at both of them. Directly after that swift valedictory gesture she and Hugo were caught up again in the intricacies of their steps, while Gretchen and Donovan went away.

'Their faces are awfully queer,' said Gretchen, as soon as the front door to the east wing was closed behind herself and Donovan. 'What makes them look so inhuman?'

'Every two or three years they go to Paris for cosmetic surgery,' said Donovan. 'Hugo was born with the century, which makes him seventy-nine. Magda's almost as old as he is.

'Get into the car and we'll stop at the west tower.'

Mary had left the stair-light on for Gretchen. Donovan came in carrying her suitcase and her typewriter – which had not yet been unloaded since they had arrived at Dufresne Bay from Harry Moore's house. They walked softly up to the top of the tower so as not to wake Mary in the Chinese room across the hall-way.

'Tomorrow's Thursday,' said Donovan, just above a whisper.

'Will you come for me at seven-thirty?' said Gretchen, whispering herself.

'Are you sure you wouldn't prefer to spend the evening meditating?' Donovan said.

'There's been another murder,' said Donovan, as he and Gretchen were driving toward the Cygne d'Or. 'Near Kenmare. Jim Farquahar has already demanded Kevin's unconditional release.'

'Will he get it?' said Gretchen.

'Eventually,' Donovan said. 'The Gardaí are still struggling to put a good face on Kevin's arrest. But, according to Jim, the press is now after them in full cry. The blunder will be exposed for what it was tomorrow morning on all the front pages in Ireland.'

'What a relief. But what a muddle,' said Gretchen. 'I was about to say that the police deserve every syllable of criticism they receive. Yet when I think of that man, Jack Ross, with his career all botched up, I don't see how justice can ever be done – unless Seamus were to be drawn and quartered on the steps of the post-office in Ralston's Cove.'

'Miss Nellie may see to Seamus in her own way,' said Donovan. 'How does it feel to be living in the Hall as it is at present?'

'This afternoon I tried to put myself in Miss Nellie's shoes,' Gretchen said. 'I asked myself if the shock would leave her bloody but unbowed or just numb.'

'She may be numb when she sees the entrance hall and the drawing-room,' said Donovan. 'But when she sees the bedroom she'll be flaming.'

'Are you sorry for her?' said Gretchen. ·

'Oddly enough I am,' Donovan said. 'Even if she brought disaster on herself. I can't forget the lifetime of courage and patience she's expended on Seamus and the slim pickings she's had in return.'

'Both of us should be drummed out of town,' said Gretchen. We've considered Kevin, considered Seamus, considered Miss Nellie, but has either one of us stopped to consider the latest victim of this maniac?'

'We've been all together preoccupied by a victim much closer to home,' said Donovan.

'Nevertheless Kevin isn't dead,' said Gretchen. 'He's not going to die.'

They rarely talked after they had made love, but that night, still clasping Donovan, Gretchen was moved to speak.

'You understood why I wanted to leave the Moores and go back to the Hall, didn't you?' she said.

'No,' said Donovan. 'I only understood why *I* wanted you to leave the Moores and go back to the Hall.'

'It comes to the same thing, doesn't it?' said Gretchen.

'Not at all,' Donovan said.

'You're splitting hairs,' said Gretchen.

'And what are you doing?' said Donovan.

'I'm not doing anything,' Gretchen said. 'I'm just a lady in waiting.'

'For whom are you waiting?' said Donovan.

'You,' said Gretchen, and fell asleep almost immediately.

'The top of the morning to you,' said Mary, bearing Gretchen's breakfast tray.

'What sort of morning is it?' said Gretchen, who was still half-asleep after the long night with Donovan.

'At that, maybe I'd best inspect it,' Mary said. 'Seeing as it might be the last I'll ever see.'

'Is Seamus on the loose?' said Gretchen, abruptly wide-awake and apprehensive.

'If he was you and me wouldn't be lollygagging here together,' said Mary. 'We'd be haring off and away.'

'So it's Miss Nellie who's arriving,' Gretchen said.

'You've hit the nail right on the head,' said Mary. 'Arthur Flood's just after ringing me. She'd called him from Dublin to send a car to Port Ferris and pick her up at the airport. And she told him to let me know she'd be here in good time for tea.'

'We'd better get a message to Dr Donovan,' said Gretchen.

'Put it on my bill,' said Miss Nellie.

197

'I was told it was cash,' said the driver.

'It's never been cash and it never will be,' Miss Nellie said. 'Take my luggage inside, if you please.'

All that had drifted up to Gretchen, whose windows were open to a breeze trailing a flash of spring. Swiftly she went to the head of the stairs, ready to stick up for Mary, if Mary needed a champion.

'Are you moving in or moving out then?' said the driver, from the bottom of the stairs.

There was no rejoinder. Warily Gretchen started on the steep descent. From the drawing-room landing she could see Miss Nellie, standing in the vacant entrance hall, gripping her hand-bag and her furled umbrella. Then Miss Nellie looked up at her.

'Where are my thin's?' she said.

'You mean the furniture that used to be here?' said Gretchen.

'Just that,' said Miss Nellie.

'Mary dealt with it,' Gretchen said. 'She did everything she could.'

'Where's Mary?' said Miss Nellie.

'Mary's in the kitchen, I think,' said Gretchen. 'Perhaps she didn't hear the car.'

'I'm here,' said Mary, rounding the kitchen door. 'As for your things,' she said, to Miss Nellie, 'some parts of them are in the old stables, some parts of them was tossed on the fire.'

'What fire?' said Miss Nellie. 'Was there a fire in the Hall?'

'Night and day,' said Mary. 'Until Dr Donovan took himself away. A week ago Thursday – yesterday – that was.'

'Dr Donovan took Mr Taylor-Dufresne away?' Miss Nellie said.

'That he did,' said Mary. 'And just in the nick of time, I'd say. The roof on this old place might have been next on his list for all anyone knows.'

Gretchen took the stairs down to the ground floor.

'May I take your suitcases up for you?' she said, to Miss Nellie.

'Kevin can do that much,' said Miss Nellie.

'Kevin's not here any more,' said Gretchen.

'The kettle's on,' said Mary. 'Will we all have a nice cup of tea in the kitchen?'

'I'm accustomed to my tea in my drawin'-room,' Miss Nellie said.

Holding her head high she walked up one flight. Gretchen followed with two small suitcases. Mary, on lagging feet, came last. Stiffly Miss Nellie marched in to the drawing-room. Nothing was left of the original furnishings but Seamus' wing chair and the television set. Even the curtains were gone and the frail gilt chairs, the two delicate round tables from the west wing stood on the bare floor-boards, lost in the enormous, empty space.

'Possibly I would be more comfortable upstairs,' said Miss Nellie.

Rapidly Gretchen and Mary preceded her up the next flight. Mary opened the door to the pink room, Gretchen brought the suitcases inside.

'This is not my room,' Miss Nellie said.

Mary fished a key out of her pocket and opened Miss Nellie's bedroom door on the huge, unmade bed, covered with excrement, on a stench that turned Gretchen's stomach.

'Close the door,' said Miss Nellie. 'The pink room will have to do.'

'Will you have your tea in here?' said Mary. 'Or will you join us in the kitchen?'

'Have I seen the worst?' Miss Nellie said.

'No, you have not,' said Mary.

'I should like to see everything,' said Miss Nellie.

'Later,' said Gretchen. 'After some tea.'

'Now,' said Miss Nellie.

Once again they took the stairs down to the most piteous objects of Seamus' brutality. Mary slipped into the kitchen, Gretchen led Miss Nellie along the passage between the west and east towers. Miss Nellie glanced at the first portraits which Seamus had slashed and halted.

'Are all the others the same?' she said.

'I'm afraid they are,' said Gretchen.'

Miss Nellie broke away from her, retraced her steps, and went into the kitchen.

'Where is Mr Taylor-Dufresne?' she said.

'Sure, the guards have him in custody. For over a week now,' said Mary. 'But 'tis Dr Donovan who saved the day for him by keeping him in the hospital.'

'Dr Donovan's coming to see you after dinner,' said Gretchen, coming on her wake.

'Be so good as to brin' my tea to me in the pink-room,' Miss Nellie said.

'She's waiting for you on the second floor,' said Mary. 'Tell her I'm just on me way up with coffee for the two of you.'

'Is she rallying her forces?' said Donovan.

'So far I haven't heard a bleat out of her,' Mary said. ''Tis the calm before the storm, that's what 'tis.'

The next morning the storm had yet to break. Miss Nellie ordered Mary to remove her clothing and every single one of her personal articles, right to her hat-pins, from the bedroom she had shared with

Seamus or forty years, and distribute everything in the *armoire* or in the chest-of-drawers in the pink room.

'Sure, 'tis impossible,' said Mary. 'The chest-of-drawers and that armoyer in the room is full to bursting.'

'Find some place for all those clothes,' said Miss Nellie. 'They belonged to my great-aunt Letitia. Many of them might do for the jumble sale in the autumn.'

''Twill take me a day or so,' Mary said. 'What with the meals and the washing-up besides –'

'When were you ever quick?' said Miss Nellie.

That evening, Saturday, Donovan came for Gretchen at seven o'clock. He found her waiting for him by the sea wall.

'How's it going?' he said.

'Miss Nellie's slowly establishing herself between the pink room and the library,' said Gretchen. 'Mary's been moving all her effects out of her own bedroom and across the hallway. On the surface we're cool and collected, but Mary and I suspect a ground-swell underneath the surface which may be deadly.'

'She was gradually freezing into a glacial wrath last night,' said Donovan. 'I couldn't strike a spark from her – not even when I flatly reminded her that, if she'd left Seamus in funds, Mary could have managed to keep him on an even keel until she came home.'

'Then what did you find to talk about?' Gretchen said.

'She asked me if I knew why Kevin had gone away,' said Donovan. 'I asked her if she hadn't seen a newspaper in Dublin. She said she'd been too busy to bother with the papers. So I told her what Seamus had done to Kevin and what Kevin had done to himself.'

'What did she say about that?' said Gretchen.

'She thanked me for coming by,' Donovan said. 'And saw me down to the door.'

'No questions about Seamus himself?' said Gretchen.

'Not a one,' said Donovan.

After lunch on Monday Miss Nellie closeted herself with Mary in the library. Late in the afternoon she drove to Ralston's Cove and Mary made tea for herself and Gretchen.

'Wait till I tell you what she's got planned for the poor old bugger,' said Mary.

Miss Nellie had gone to Ralston's Cove to see Jim Farquahar and find out if Seamus could be released in her custody. If he could, then he was to come home to the Hall and spend one week in solitary confinement in the very bedroom he had defiled, to live for seven

200

days and seven nights with his own, still rotting excrement. Three meals a day would be brought up to the second floor, every morning he would be given a bottle of whiskey. If he held out on that regimen for a week he would be transferred to Kevin's room in the west wing until such time as Miss Nellie could find a crew of men and women to disinfect the bedroom, burn the mattress, remove the bedstead, and replace them with a bed and a mattress – if there were a suitable bed and mattress – from the west wing.

When the bedroom was again fit for human occupancy he was to move back into it provided that he bathed, shaved, made a complete change of clothing, and behaved like a gentleman. There were to be no more tears – for any reason whatsoever – no more television in the afternoons.

'And,' said Mary, 'for the crowning touch *she's* to chose the programmes they'll look at after dinner. There's to be no more soccer, no more boxing, no more horse races for Seamus ever again.'

'Miss Nellie's going to stay in the pink room indefinitely?' said Gretchen.

'She is,' Mary said. 'For just so long as Seamus Taylor's above ground.'

The storm which Mary had predicted broke that evening in the dining-room. She had just brought in the coffee for Miss Nellie and Gretchen. Ever since her return Miss Nellie had ignored the drawing-room. Not even a fire to off-set the all-pervasive chill had been lit on the hearth.

'So,' said Miss Nellie, fixing Mary in a glassy stare, *'you're* at the bottom of this business. *You* went to the Gardaí and lodged a complaint against Mr Taylor-Dufresne.'

'I'll not deny it,' said Mary.

'You must withdraw the complaint,' Miss Nellie said. "Immediately. Tomorrow morning at the latest. I'm orderin' you to do as I say.'

'I don't take orders,' said Mary. 'I just might look kindly on a request –'

'Don't favour me with your impertinence,' said Miss Nellie. 'You will go to the Gardaí with Mr Farquahar –'

A beaming smile like sunshine in August irradiated Mary's face.

'I'm beginning to see the light,' she said. 'You can't do without me. Even Mr James Farquahar can't do without me. At that, I'd be willing to pay a call on Mr Farquahar at me own convenience. Mr Farquahar's a kindred soul.'

'How dare you be so insolent?' said Miss Nellie.

'I've a rare courage this evening,' said Mary.

Gretchen swallowed the last of her coffee, picked up her book, and took to her heels.

'You're gettin' much too big for your breeches,' Miss Nellie said, to Mary, as Gretchen left the room.

At five o'clock the next afternoon Mary summoned Gretchen to the kitchen for tea.

'Missed me this morning, I'll be bound,' she said.

'I certainly did,' said Gretchen. 'Where were you?'

'Up to Ralston's Cove,' said Mary. 'I was over two hours with Mr Farquahar.'

'And where's Miss Nellie now?' said Gretchen.

'She's gone to the parson's for her tea,' Mary said. 'Told me off good and proper before she left.'

'What for?' said Gretchen.

'For telling her how Mr Farquahar says I can't withdrew me complaint against Seamus,' said Mary. 'She wants him home she does. She's looking forward to the torments she's inventing for the old sot. But wanting and getting's two different things entirely.'

In the morning, in Ralston's Cove, Mary had given Jim Farquahar the gist of Miss Nellie's tirade at the dinner table.

'Now I'd not go to the guards alone,' Mary had said, to him. 'I'd go with you and no one else. But I'll not withdraw me complaint until her Ladyship gives me me back wages – almost five months she's owing me – and gives me six months pay in advance. And then I'd be asking a day off during the week – every week – something I've never had in fifty years at the Hall. That's what I came to say and since I've said it I'll wish you a good morning –'

'Not so fast,' Jim Farquahar had said.

For some minutes he had sat, stroking his beard, and looking out of his soot-stained window.

'You've been very concise,' he had remarked. 'You'd make an admirable showing in a witness box. But let me make one thing clear at the outset.

'In this business I will not be acting in the interest of either Mr or Mrs Ţaylor-Dufresne. *You* are my client. Hence, before we proceed to any other affair which may be troubling you, I must assure you that it is not possible for you to withdraw your complaint against Seamus Taylor. The matter no longer rests with the Gardaí but with the public prosecutor. After the charge has been examined it will be up to a court of law to determine whether or not your complaint was justified. The police will be called and can only re-inforce your position – after all, they investigated the damages at the Hall and heard Danny O'Toole's testimony as to Seamus' state of mind on the preceding day. What is more, consider the mortification they've endured since the murder near Kenmare and the collapse of every rudiment of a case against the lad, Kevin, a case constructed solely on Seamus Taylor's baseless allegations. No, the Gardaí will be your allies and it will be my pleasure to see that you have vigorous and persuasive legal representation once the proceedings are under weigh. But all that is in the offing. In the meantime, would you care for my assistance in presenting your claims to your employer? And ultimately – no doubt – to the law? If so, we might draw up a few figures – your basic monthly wage, which may easily be below the lawful minimum, the amount owing, the anticipated payment to ensure good faith, the compensation for no time off and no holidays in fifty years, very likely long overdue contributions for social security, health insurance and, if you wish, all legal expenses incurred in bringing these abuses to the attention of the appropriate authorities, plus any legal expenses incurred in prosecuting your case against Seamus Taylor.'

'So that's how I spent me morning,' said Mary, agreeably conscious of having been notably faithful to Jim Farquahar's diction.

'Your head must be reeling,' Gretchen said.

'No one ever said a truer word,' said Mary. 'Mr Farquahar made up such a colume of figures as you never saw – fifty years and not a single day off and never a vacation, just you think of that. The long and the short of it was that he sent out for sandwiches for the two of us. When everything was ship-shape I went to Flood's. 'Twas Arthur Flood himself to come to Dufresne Hill for me at ten o'clock and Arthur to drive me home. You won't find a better man in Ralston's Cove than Arthur Flood. So I took the occasion to tell him that if he was to stop by Mr Farquahar's office with all the back bills she's owing him he might see some action.'

'In the meanwhile,' said Gretchen, 'what's going to happen to Seamus?'

'How should I know?' said Mary. 'For the moment he's far better off where he is than in that stinking hole upstairs. As for meself, I'll be giving her a month's notice starting tomorrow unless she settles up with Mr Farquahar and gives me me due.'

Matters came to a head that evening. Just as Gretchen and Miss Nellie were finishing the apple tart which had come from Ralston's Cove they heard footsteps along the passage and, shortly, Donovan walked in upon them.

'Will I bring coffee for three in here?' said Mary.

'I'll take my coffee in my room and leave you with Dr Donovan,' said Gretchen, to Miss Nellie.

'That will be quite unnecessary,' said Miss Nellie. 'I do not suppose for an instant that Dr Donovan has anythin' of a privileged nature to say to me.'

'I've come about Seamus,' said Donovan. 'I can't keep him in hospital any longer, I'm sorry to say.'

'Is he makin' a nuisance of himself?' said Miss Nellie.

'No more than usual,' Donovan said. 'But – as Jim Farquahar, who's on the board of directors, would be happy to explain to you – it's against hospital policy to keep patients who are either chronically or terminally ill except for a very few days. The hospital – as its charter affirms – was founded for the care of such of the ailing as can be presumed to respond positively to suitable treatment. Beds are in demand and, in a word, Seamus has outstayed his welcome.'

'Then he must come home,' said Miss Nellie. 'It's as simple as that.'

'Unfortunately it's hardly simple,' said Donovan. 'The Gardaí were compassionate enough to let me keep him in detention – upon my assurance that I would be responsible for his movements – but in the morning it will be my duty to surrender Seamus to the police. I cannot hand him over to you. Doubtless you can arrange for bail, pending a hearing in court. That, however, is a matter of personal choice. Myself, I have no choice, which is what I came to tell you.'

'Why did you come to me at all?' Miss Nellie said. 'Why didn't you present the problem in good time to Jim Farquahar?'

'I've just come from Jim Farquahar,' said Donovan.

'Well?' said Miss Nellie.

'I think you would be wise to get in touch with him yourself,' Donovan said.

'I shall ring him straightaway,' said Miss Nellie.

Donovan and Gretchen could hear her tripping down the passage. Then Donovan glanced over his shoulder.

'What are you doing there?' he said.

'Oh,' said Mary, ''twas too much for me back to keep me ear to the keyhole, as you might say.'

'Mary, come all the way into the room,' said Gretchen. 'Please. Please tell Dr Donovan what you told me about Miss Nellie's plan to lock Seamus up for a week with his own filth still in his bedroom.'

'I'll have to make it short and sweet,' Mary said. 'I wouldn't want her pouncing on me for talking out of turn.'

She made it short but hardly sweet.

'If that ever comes to pass,' said Donovan, 'you leg it up to Ben Daly. He has a telephone and Miss Nellie can't overhear you if you ring from his house. Call Mrs Mullin and tell her to find me wherever I am and send me instantly to the Hall.'

'The both of you may as well have some more coffee,' said Mary. 'There's plenty left in the pot.'

'I've got to talk to you,' Gretchen said, to Donovan, when Mary had left the room.

'Get your key as quick as you can,' said Donovan. 'Then ask Mary to tell Miss Nellie I've taken you out for a while.'

Gretchen took off her shoes and flashed almost soundlessly down the long passage. As she came close to the library – whose door was ajar – she could hear Miss Nellie shrieking into the telephone. As fast as possible she went upstairs, found her key, and came down, still holding her shoes in her hand. Donovan was waiting for her in the entrance hall. Not a murmur was to be heard from the library, but Donovan put his finger to his lips when he caught sight of her and gestured at the library door. Gretchen glided into the kitchen to leave Donovan's message with Mary.

'So the ship's sinking,' said Mary, with a wide, conspiratorial smile. 'A pair of rats, that's what you are, you and Dr Donovan.'

14

Never before had Gretchen seen Donovan furtive. But furtive was the word for him as he edged her out into the darkness and guided her to his car, parked by the west tower.

'I'll make a fine noise starting up the engine,' he said. 'But we'll stop when we get to the gates. Then we'll creep back, like thieves in the night, and pray that our luck holds as far as the east tower.'

'But of course you're not intruding,' said Magda. 'Don't be ridiculous. We're enchanted to see you both.'

'Cognac? Grand Marnier?' said Hugo.

'Cognac would do me nicely,' Donovan said. 'Gretchen might be happier with a Grand Marnier.'

'So be it,' said Magda. 'We were expecting you. We had a sort of sixth sense that things were going from bad to worse in the west tower.'

'That's why I'm here,' said Donovan. 'And that's why I've brought

Gretchen. Not five minutes ago she told me in a whisper that she had to speak to me. Under the circumstances – she's living on the slope of a volcano, as close as she is to Miss Nellie and to Mary McDaid – I thought it would probably be more fitting if she spoke to you directly.'

'Don't be modest,' said Hugo, to Gretchen. 'Speak your piece.'

'Her piece might be out of context,' Donovan said, 'unless I'd already given you a little chapter and verse.'

'Nellie must be in real trouble if you've come to the east tower as a last resort,' said Magda, to Donovan.

'She's in real trouble,' said Donovan. 'Much more trouble than she could possibly suspect –

'Let me preface my story by saying that Jim Farquahar – who's writing out the chapters and the verses – is, and always has been, one of my very good friends. Much of what I know I've known in confidence for several weeks. But Arthur Flood came to see me in my office this afternoon and from Arthur I discovered that the cat was out of the bag. Then I called on Jim after hours and he confirmed the worst.'

For as much as forty years – so ran Donovan's history – Jim Farquahar's father and later Jim himself had taken care of Miss Nellie's affairs. Not a single bill for services rendered – and a great many services had been rendered – had ever been met. Then came the incursion of the pigs and the subsequent damages in the west tower and in the dining-room of the east tower. Miss Nellie had required Jim to be present while, for over four hours, the police, with a photographer and a stenographer, had inspected, photographed, listed, and described every table, chair, lamp, carpet, bit of bric-à-brac or other which had been impaired. Miss Nellie had had a vision of a fortune falling into her hands as a result of the cataclysm.

When Jim had told her that such insurance as might have covered the driver, the lorry itself, its freight, and any injuries to persons or property which might have been incurred, was automatically void since the driver was found to have been under the influence of alcohol, Miss Nellie had waved all that aside and instructed Jim to bring suit against the company which owned the van. He had done his best to persuade her that a lawsuit would surely be protracted and costly, that a favourable outcome could not be guaranteed. Miss Nellie would have none of it.

'So patronising was her air, so offensive her manner,' said Donovan, 'that, as Jim put it to me, the worm turned. In that moment Miss Nellie lost the best friend she had in this county. Jim compiled some sixty odd sheets of figures, comprising the substance of every bill rendered over nearly two generations of Dufresnes and added up the total outstanding. Then he told Miss Nellie that unless she was prepared to initial every page, sign the last page with two witnesses present to attest to her signature, and leave him with a promissory note for the full amount he would refuse to represent her in the matter of the pigs. Miss Nellie, high and mighty on her chariot in the clouds, merely asked him if, after she'd signed whatever papers he needed, they could get down to business. Jim had assured her that they could. With that she initialled each page, signed the last, Jim saw to it that her signature was duly witnessed and, at the end, she signed the promissory note. The note falls due on Monday, five days from today.

'This morning Mary McDaid went to Jim, and between them they drew up a list of earnings, holidays, various compensations – most of them withheld – and Mary later advised Arthur Flood to strike while the iron was hot. As of this evening Jim is ready to act for Arthur, for Billy O'Connell, for Ryan's, where Miss Nellie gets most of her groceries, for George Haskell, from whom she gets all her meat, and for the chemist, Frank McMahon – as soon as all of them have their documentation in order. When I saw Jim this evening I asked him if Miss Nellie could meet all those demands. He reminded me that she owns the Morrison house at Wykham Bay and over three hundred acres behind it – which might easily be sold off in quarter-acre lots – two cottages and a good deal of acreage near King's Cross, several meadows to the north-west of the Hall, a strong-box in the bank full of the Dufresne jewels, and then – obviously – she owns the west tower and the west wing. There's no doubt that Jim means to press for payment for himself, for Mary, for Arthur Flood, for Billy O'Connell, for Ryan's, for Haskell, and for McMahon. Moreover he's not going to lift a finger for Seamus. Nor will he represent Miss Nellie in the affair of the pigs until she pays him every penny she owes and gives him something substantial on account before he goes ahead with a lawsuit.'

'Frightful,' said Hugo. 'Absolutely frightful. This calls for more cognac.'

'I was hoping,' said Donovan, holding out his glass to Hugo, 'that you could convince her that these things won't go away. Not even for Nellie Dufresne. If there's a short in the wiring Billy O'Connell won't come, if she goes in to Ralston's Cove for household supplies or medications she'll have to pay cash at Ryan's, at Haskell's, at McMahon's. Arthur Flood won't jump to her bidding any more, and without Jim to smooth my way I don't think I can get Seamus Taylor into a nursing home, pending a hearing. So unless Miss Nellie doesn't care if he goes to gaol, she'll have to raise bail for him, and if she can stand bail who's to represent her before a magistrates court and gain Seamus' liberty for the time being?'

'Nellie never listens to Hugo,' said Magda, 'unless he tells her something she wants to hear.'

'What was it,' Hugo said, to Gretchen, 'that you wanted to tell Dr Donovan?'

'I wanted to tell him about Mary's visit to Mr Farquahar,' said Gretchen. 'Evidently he knows about that.

'But did you know,' she said, looking at Donovan, 'that tomorrow she's planning to give Miss Nellie a month's notice, that she'll leave if Miss Nellie doesn't meet her claims?'

'No, I didn't know that,' said Donovan. 'I'm not sure how long Miss Nellie would survive if Mary were to leave her.'

'And I'll tell you one other thing,' said Gretchen. 'When I ran upstairs to get my key Miss Nellie was talking – or, rather, screaming – on the telephone to Mr Farquahar. I heard her tell him that he wasn't the only solicitor in the county.'

'No solicitor in the length and breadth of Ireland would do battle for Nellie against Jim Farquahar,' said Hugo. 'Myself I wouldn't give her the time of day if it meant crossing Jim.'

'We could ask her to lunch tomorrow,' Magda said. 'After lunch you and she could be tête-à-tête.'

'Somehow she'll have to understand that the jig's up,' said Donovan.

'I'll do what I can,' said Hugo. 'Although I'd prefer to talk to Jim before I talk to Nellie.'

'Jim himself suggested a meeting between the two of you,' Donovan said. 'He's too good a lawyer to want to get involved in litigation. He's hoping that Miss Nellie will see reason and settle out of court. But he means to get everything that's coming to him and all the others he's representing.'

'He'd love to see Seamus Taylor go to gaol,' said Magda.

'So would Gretchen,' said Donovan. 'Every time she thinks of Kevin.'

At ten o'clock the next morning Gretchen was making corrections on the most recent pages of her manuscript when she was interrupted by a rapping at her door.

'Why, Mrs Dufresne,' she said, 'you *have* surprised me.'

Magda, superbly turned out in a charcoal-grey woollen dress and a poncho of silver-fox, came into the room and settled herself lightly, like a moth in winter fur, on the edge of Gretchen's bed.

'This is no place for you today,' she said. 'I've come to bear you off with me. Are you working in longhand?'

'Yes, as a matter of fact I am,' said Gretchen.

'Then give me your pad and your notes,' said Magda. 'Get your coat – it'll be cold on the way to the east tower – and bring your purse and your key. Don't worry about Mary McDaid,' she added, as they went down the stairs. 'I've already told her you'll be lunching with me.'

Sitting at Hugo's desk Gretchen did her best to concentrate on her thesis, but Magda had disturbed her train of thought and her mind kept faltering over the task in hand. Close on to one o'clock Magda took her across the hall to the morning-room in the east tower and gave her a glass of sherry.

'We'll be alone at table,' said Magda. 'Hugo's lunching with Jim Farquahar.'

'Why did you want me out of the west tower?' said Gretchen.

'It was Hugo's idea,' Magda said. 'After breakfast he made the appointment with Jim and then he walked over to the west tower to ask Nellie if she'd dine with us. If you remember, last evening he said he'd prefer to talk to Jim before interfering with Nellie.

'At all events Nellie was just starting her car when he got there. He asked her where she was going and she said she had shopping to do in Ralston's Cove. Hugo almost warned her not to go to Ralston's Cove – ever again – when it occurred to him that if she found out for herself that she had no more credit at Ryan's and couldn't get any meat from George Haskell unless she forked over cash that might make any suggestion coming from him much more plausible. So he let her go. But he was afraid she'd throw a tantrum after she got back to Dufresne Bay – which is why he wanted you here, not there.'

'Does Miss Nellie throw tantrums?' said Gretchen.

'She was famous for them as a child, or so I'm told,' Magda said.

'Tired, my love?' said Magda, to Hugo, at tea-time.

'Extravagantly tired,' said Hugo.

'Where have you been, all day long?' Magda said.

'Well,' said Hugo, 'I went by the police to find out what might be done about Seamus, then I had a protracted lunch with Jim Farquahar. He insisted that Nellie must mortgage the Morrison house and the Morrison land immediately, in order to meet his promissory note next week. I didn't like the notion of Nellie paying God only knows how much interest on a bridging loan while she waited for a buyer, or buyers. I asked him to hold off until I could see

209

whether Ray Connors would be interested in the Morrison property.'

'Is Ray still speculating in real estate?' said Magda.

'I think so,' Hugo said. 'I haven't been around to him yet. But he seemed anxious to see me tomorrow when I spoke to him on the telephone.'

'Ray must be older than God's mother,' said Magda. 'Did you spend all afternoon arguing with Jim?'

'I spent most of it in his company,' said Hugo. 'Along with Clement Donovan.'

'With Dr Donovan?' said Gretchen.

'I stood bail for Seamus,' said Hugo. 'But I needed Jim's help before the magistrate and Donovan's expert opinion to keep Seamus out of gaol and get him into a nursing home where he can be treated like the lunatic he is and permitted liquor in moderation.'

'Is Nellie coming here for dinner?' Magda said.

'That I don't know,' said Hugo. 'I wanted my tea before I tackled Nellie.'

'I think it was awfully nice of you to raise bail for Seamus,' said Gretchen. 'Will you get your money back?'

'Almost certainly,' Hugo said. 'Security's tight where Seamus is going.'

After tea Gretchen went back to the west tower with Hugo.

'It's terribly quiet in here,' she said. 'Shall I see if Mary's in the kitchen?'

'Would you?' said Hugo.

'Sure, Dr Donovan's been and gone and taken herself away,' Mary said.

'Mr Dufresne waiting in the hall,' said Gretchen. 'Come with me and tell him about Miss Nellie.'

'There's not that much I can say,' said Mary, to Hugo. 'We made out a shopping list early, she and me, the two of us. Then she drove up to Ralston's Cove. Not an hour later she was back, empty-handed. One way or another she'd had a desperate shock, I'd say. I helped her up the stairs to the pink room. She lay down on the bed. When lunch was ready I rang the gong but she never came. So I dragged me old bones up the stairs again to look at her. She hadn't stirred an eyelash and her face was something fearful. Grey it was. What could I do, I ask you, but ring Dr Donovan?'

'And when Dr Donovan arrived he took her away?' said Hugo.

'That he did,' Mary said. 'He told me to throw a few of her things – like her toothbrush – together. When me bag was full of this, that, and the other – she's fussy over certain articles, she is – the both of them was already in Dr Donovan's car.'

'What time was this?' said Hugo. ,

'Half two,' said Mary. 'Give or take a minute here, a minute there.'

'Now if you've no other plans,' she said, to Gretchen, 'I'll make a dash for it and pick up one or two things of me own. Then I could make you a little supper – we've plenty of eggs, God be praised – and tonight I could sleep in the Chinese room.'

It was Hugo's turn to speak to Gretchen.

'Magda and I would be very pleased to give you dinner and put you up,' he said. 'But perhaps you'd be more comfortable with all your paraphernalia here. And if Mary's willing to spend the night with you, you'd be quite safe.'

'I'll stay with Mary,' said Gretchen. 'But thank you very much.'

'When Dr Donovan calls – as surely he will,' said Hugo, 'would you tell him to give me a ring, if it's not asking too much?'

'Certainly,' said Gretchen.

'Miss Nellie's in auricular fibrillation,' said Donovan, when he telephoned. 'Do you know what that is?'

'My father fibrillates from time to time,' said Gretchen.

'I hope to get her under control shortly,' Donovan said. 'But I believe it would be as well to keep her in hospital for a couple of days even if she stops fibrillating in the next hour or so. Is Mary staying the night with you?'

'Oh, yes,' said Gretchen. 'Everything's fine here.'

'I'll be by for you at seven-thirty tomorrow evening,' said Donovan. 'I must go to Port Feris in the morning but Reilly will keep an eye on Miss Nellie for me. If anything bothers you in the next twenty-fours hours, anything at all, go straight to the east tower.'

'Mr Dufresne wants you to call him,' Gretchen said. 'He's anxious about Miss Nellie.'

'I've just talked to him,' said Donovan. 'If I can get out of Port Ferris early I'll be meeting him at the hospital at half-past five.'

'Mary would like to say a word to you,' said Gretchen.

'I've only just the one problem,' Mary said, shouting into the telephone. 'Apart from coffee and tea, which I have in plenty, there's nothing left in the house but eggs and cockroach powder.'

'Get Ben Daly to take you up to Ralston's Cove in the morning,' said Donovan. 'Go directly to my office. I'll leave you some money with Mrs Mullin.'

It was nearly eight-thirty when Donovan arrived at the Hall the next evening.

'You're much too tired to take me out to dinner,' said Gretchen.

'One look at you would wring tears from a hanging judge. You ought to go home and go to bed right away.'

'There's nothing wrong with me that a couple of drinks won't cure,' said Donovan. 'And a little gentle company. Get into the car and let's go.'

'Well,' said Gretchen, after Donovan had swallowed the first whisky, 'what's the score?'

'I've stopped keeping score,' said Donovan. 'I will say that Hugo Dufresne has been a god-send. In all these years I never had any opinion, one way or another, of Magda and Hugo. They were just a pair of well-heeled, meaningless eccentrics to me. I was quite wrong.'

'They were very good to me yesterday,' Gretchen said.

'Hugo's been busy,' said Donovan. 'Yesterday, over lunch, he got Jim Farquahar cooled off to such a point that they could work things out together. By yesterday afternoon they were almost in partnership. Did Hugo tell you that he'd gone bail for Seamus?'

'Yes, he did,' said Gretchen. 'It was kind of him, since he can't bear Seamus and I suspect Miss Nellie irritates him thoroughly.'

'So do I,' Donovan said. 'But that's all by the way. Early this morning Hugo went to the bank and made the manager, Bill Rowan, give him a fair idea of what a quarter-acre lot near Wykham Bay and a large house facing the bay with eight bedrooms, two baths, servants' quarters, and what-not would be worth. He explained to Rowan that the house stood on three hundred acres of land, that he presumed virtually all of the land could be sold off in very small lots, since the bay's very attractive to summer visitors. He also explained to Rowan that he expected to offer the property to Ray Connors, who's been speculating in real estate for most of his life. When he had hard figures from the bank he collected Connors and went over the Morrison estate inch by inch, as it were. Then, instead of asking Connors to make a bid, Hugo gave him his asking price. He, Hugo told me this evening that it took him two argumentative hours and half a bottle of the best Irish whiskey to soften up Connors, but in the end he agreed to pay what Hugo had been insisting on from the beginning. His next move was to take Connors to Jim Farquahar to prove to Jim that Connors was ready to make a *bona fide* offer in writing – tomorrow, if Jim wishes – for the Morrison house and land. Connors asked for ten days to raise a deposit and was willing to sign a legal document promising the balance directly title was cleared on the property. Then Jim got off his high horse and said that if Miss Nellie were persuaded to accept the offer he would let his promissory note run on for a few days over the due date.

'I came for you as late as I did this evening because – since Miss Nellie's not fibrillating any longer – I let Hugo have a crack at her, in my presence. Miss Nellie's drained. There's no fight left in her. She had an appalling experience in Ralston's Cove yesterday morning. Gregory Ryan threw her out of his shop while half the town looked on.'

'The poor woman,' said Gretchen.

'She deserved what she got,' said Donovan, 'but that's neither here nor there.

'The upshot of the whole business is that she's agreed to let Jim Farquahar draw up a power of attorney for Hugo, under the terms of which he will be authorised, by Miss Nellie, to settle every single one of her debts, even if it means liquidating more of her holdings in land – which Hugo says, and Jim concurs, will probably not be necessary if Connors does indeed buy the Morrison property at Hugo's price. It's extremely valuable in today's market.

'And now,' said Donovan, just managing a smile for Gretchen, 'if it won't displease you, I'll have another double Scotch.'

When their coffee was served, Donovan, who had been half-asleep during dinner, roused himself with a start.

'You were almost right,' he said, to Gretchen. 'I was almost too tired to eat. And you've been a good girl all evening. Not once have you pestered me about Kevin.'

'I hadn't forgotten Kevin,' said Gretchen. 'I know you told me that I couldn't see him till he'd recovered his strength and spirit. But I can't understand what harm it would do him to know that lots of people – like me and Mary and probably Danny O'Toole and maybe Mike Healey – are thinking about him and wishing him well.'

'All in good time,' said Donovan.

On Friday evening he had coffee in the Hall with Gretchen, while Mary – who mistrusted coffee – looked on.

'I've come to tell you that I'll be away all day tomorrow and possibly all day Sunday,' Donovan said. 'I may have found a place in County Kerry for Kevin, a place where he might be able to convalesce and later, if he wishes, to learn a trade. I'll be driving over to Kerry now and in the morning I'll see how the land lies. If all goes well I'll drive back tomorrow afternoon, getting home late at night. Then I'll start out again with Kevin on Sunday morning.'

For a moment Gretchen was woebegone, thinking of a whole week-end without Donovan, but Mary was all agog at once. Donovan told them about his friendship with Mr and Mrs Coogan.

'I was with them for one night a few weeks ago,' he said. 'They were blue without their only son, Tommy, who'd gone to Mayo because his girl had found a job there. For no reason that I can put my finger on I had a hunch that Tommy might decide to stay in Mayo. If he did, I knew it would be a body blow to his father, who's a boat-builder and had been training Tommy to follow in his footsteps.

'So, to make a long story short, I called Mrs Coogan and she wept when she spoke to me and confirmed that Tommy did, in fact, want to strike out for himself in Mayo. Which being the case, the Coogans might come to look with favour on Kevin if, when he's strong enough, he makes an eager apprentice. However I must tell them that Kevin is the lad who was mistakenly taken off by the Gardaí after Seamus' false accusation and that he's gradually getting better after trying to make away with himself in his first despair. They'll have to be warned that Kevin has a past – through no fault of his own – which made headlines throughout southern Ireland.

'As for Miss Nellie,' Donovan said, 'I'll be keeping her under observation for a while longer.'

'You'll never believe the news,' said Mary, to Gretchen, on Monday at lunch-time. 'Mrs Hugo's to take her ladyship to the south of France for three weeks and Seamus is to stay in that place where Dr Donovan put him till well after herself gets back. For Mr Farquahar says the judge – whoever he may be – has too much on his calendar to do anything about Seamus for a month or more.

'Now won't it be lovely, you and me having the west tower all to ourselves and no one underfoot at all, at all?'

'It'll be wonderful,' said Gretchen. 'But how did you find out all this?'

'Mr Hugo stopped in – toward eleven o'clock it was – to tell me the news. What's more, to hear Mr Hugo tell it, I'll be rolling in money by the end of the week.'

'Oh, I *am* happy for you,' said Gretchen.

'I was that worried about me old age,' Mary said. 'For I'm sixty-nine if I'm a day, I'll have you know, and what was I to do when I couldn't carry on like this for the rest of me life? But to hear Mr Hugo tell it, I could retire next week and buy meself some decent clothes. I could even go to Lourdes, if the fancy took me, which it might. I've always wanted to go to Lourdes, me back being what it is. However I couldn't just up and leave her Ladyship high and dry, now could I? All the same, sooner or later she'll have to find someone to take me place.'

Gretchen saw nothing of Donovan until the next Thursday.

'What's the stink?' said Donovan, when Gretchen came out of the west tower to meet him.

'Danny O'Toole's burning that dreadful mattress from the bedroom Seamus and Miss Nellie shared,' said Gretchen. 'Yesterday Hugo ordered the whole room disinfected and Mary got a crowd of neighbours over to help out. Now there are two beds from the west wing where the big bed Seamus fouled used to be and Mary says the mattresses are in fair shape.'

'Why didn't Danny get on with the burning before this?' Donovan said.

'Yesterday it rained,' said Gretchen.

'So it did,' said Donovan. 'Have you been able to work at all?'

'I really and truly have,' Gretchen said. 'Yesterday was a little wild but when Mary's alone she's quiet and considerate and, although it's a horrid thing to say, I don't miss Miss Nellie in the least. While Seamus –'

'Forget about Seamus for the time being,' said Donovan. 'He's lucky to be where he is.'

'Hugo comes by every morning to find out if I'm all right,' said Gretchen. 'It's kind of him, isn't it?'

'Hugo seemed to be as solid as a rock,' Donovan said. 'I'd badly underestimated him. He and Jim Farquahar are hard at it, preparing to reimburse Miss Nellie's creditors – once Jim's made certain that their books aren't cooked. I met him on the street this evening and he told me some dozen more have jumped on the band-wagon with nearly half a century of bad debts to lay on the line.'

'Will you, will I, ever forget all these horrors?' said Gretchen.

'Would it help if I told you that Kevin's happy as a clam with the Coogans and the Coogans swear he'll shape up to be a master-builder?' said Donovan.

'That would help a lot,' Gretchen said.

'At first,' said Donovan, 'Harry Moore was worried about how much damage Kevin had sustained in his right hand. He nicked a tendon when he cut his right wrist. But Kevin told me on the telephone that he was getting along despite some loss of function.'

'When we get to the Cygne d'Or let's drink to Kevin,' said Gretchen.

'When we get to the Cygne d'Or let's pretend it's spring,' Donovan said. 'In the month of May we'll go sailing, you and I.'

15

Only three hours after Donovan had brought Gretchen back to the Hall Mary came upstairs with her breakfast tray, half an hour earlier than usual.

'It was now or never,' said Mary, finding Gretchen baffled in the mists of sleep.

'Are you beforehand or am I behind?' said Gretchen, picking up her alarm clock and studying its face.

'Sure, the clock's not at fault,' Mary said. ''Tis only that her Ladyship's on her way home. She's to have her things packed by ten o'clock when Mrs Hugo's coming to fetch her.'

Donovan had kept Miss Nellie in hospital for nine days. She had stopped fibrillating soon after admission, but he had judged her too exhausted to return to the Hall only to face the vast emptiness of the drawing-room, the terrible reminders of Seamus' fury every time she passed the gaping portraits in the long passage, the lonely nights in a bedroom which had never been her own. However, he had been more than willing to discharge her as soon as Magda was ready to embark on the journey to the south of France.

'I'd better not take a bath until Miss Nellie's been and gone,' Gretchen said, to Mary. 'She has so much in the bathroom she may want to take with her on the trip.'

'Just keep to yourself,' said Mary. 'I'll be up to tell you when the coast is clear.'

'So you're deserting me tomorrow,' said Donovan, to Gretchen, on Sunday afternoon.

'You won't miss me on a Monday or a Tuesday or a Wednesday,' said Gretchen. 'Except when the world comes to an end we never see each other on those days.'

'When Magda first proposed the jaunt I was somewhat uneasy about it,' Donovan said. 'I thought *you* might be uneasy in three days with Hugo. But now that I've seen him in quite a different light I'm glad you're going.'

'Until I've seen Dublin I can't be sure I really am in Ireland,' said Gretchen.

'You may not fall head over heels in love with the place,' said Donovan.

'I mean to fall head over heels in love with the place,' Gretchen said. 'I'm already in love with it. I've been in love with it for a long time.'

It was a very subdued Gretchen who waited for Donovan on Thursday evening, twenty-four hours after her return from Dublin.

'Why didn't you tell me not to go?' she said.

'You wouldn't have listened to me,' said Donovan.

'Why didn't Harry or Eliza Moore warn me?' said Gretchen.

'They tried,' Donovan said. 'By indirection. But you had the bit between your teeth.'

'Well, I've seen Dublin now,' said Gretchen. 'Hugo took me to all the streets I'd remembered from the water-colours I saw in the college library. And to a lot of others. He told me that my heart would break and it did. So many – *so* many – of those lovely houses gone and in their places the worst of new urban architecture. And the wreckers' balls waiting for the houses still to be demolished. And such a number of the houses still standing turned into slums – rat and rot infested tenements. I couldn't sleep when I went to bed on Tuesday night.'

'Where did you put up?' Donovan said.

'At a ridiculously pretentious hotel,' said Gretchen. 'I wanted to pay my way but Hugo wouldn't let me pay for anything. I'm sure the place was terribly expensive but it was dirty and dreary and the food was horrid.'

'Did Hugo take you to any of Dublin's pubs?' said Donovan.

'On Monday night we did what he called a "pub crawl",' Gretchen said. 'He told me that before the war the pubs we passed were famous for the conversations of gifted and distinguished men. But the pubs I saw with Hugo were either shrill with American hard rock or ringing with deafening television programmes. Hugo and I didn't stop in any of them. We just raced on.'

'And you never came across the ghosts of Joyce or Synge or Yeats or Lady Gregory?' said Donovan.

'Don't tease me,' said Gretchen. 'I'm miserable enough as it is.'

'You look as if you'd been left out all night in the rain,' Donovan said.

'That's the way I feel,' said Gretchen. 'Before I came to Ireland a girl called Rebecca told me to leave Dublin alone. She said it was nothing but a third-rate tourist trap. At the time I thought she was insensitive. Now I wish I'd paid attention to every word she said.'

'You had to see for yourself,' said Donovan.

'I know,' said Gretchen. 'And everything I saw was worse than the last thing I'd seen.

'On Tuesday morning Hugo had an appointment. He gave me a

217

little map and he said that Grafton Street was where I'd find the best shops in the city. I walked the whole length of it and back. Not even Knightstown can boast of anything as tacky as Grafton Street.

'There isn't any Ireland, is there?' she said. 'It was all in my head, wasn't it?'

'The Ireland in your head was real toward the end of the last century and continued through to the establishment of the Irish Free State in the early twenties of this century,' said Donovan.

'I wonder if it was real even then,' said Gretchen. 'I wonder if the Ireland I looked forward to didn't depend for its very existence on the English. On English standards, English style, English habits of mind, English elegance –'

From the Cygne d'Or Donovan telephoned to Harry Moore. After their dinner he took Gretchen to have coffee with the Moores.

'So,' said Harry, opening the door to them, 'the lass has been to Dublin.'

'One look at her was enough to tell you that?' said Donovan.

'You and Eliza and I,' Harry said, to Gretchen, 'will form a little league for the suppression of the Irish in Ireland. We'll put an end to the myths of the Emerald Isle and its inhabitants.'

'Am I to have no part in your league?' said Donovan. 'Am I to be one of the first suppressed?'

'One of the first,' said Eliza, giving him a hug in passing. 'Let's all have a farewell coffee on the strength of it.'

'Hold your horses,' Harry said. 'I want to know right away if anyone walks tall in Dublin.'

'Everyone I saw was pretty sloppy,' said Gretchen. 'But I wasn't really looking at people. I was looking at houses that weren't there.'

'Why did you let her go?' said Harry, to Donovan.

'I couldn't have stopped her,' Donovan said. 'She wanted a taste of the Pierian spring. Now she's had it.'

'And it doesn't agree with her?' said Harry.

'No, it doesn't agree with me,' Gretchen said.

'Wake up, light of my life,' said Donovan. 'It's almost four o'clock and I must take you back to the Hall.'

On the way to Dufresne Bay he turned for an instant to look at her.

'How much of your thesis is finished?' he said.

'The preface and the first half are set,' said Gretchen. 'I'm in the middle of the battle with the second half just now. To tell you the truth, I'm beginning to wonder if I've bitten off more than I can chew.'

'Would you lend me the preface and the first half?' said Donovan. 'I'd be very careful of the manuscript and I'd bring it along to you on Saturday before we go out to dinner.'

'Why should you want to read it?' Gretchen said. 'It's your territory I'm invading. You don't need me to lend you a map.'

'It's your map I'd like to see,' said Donovan.

'Your own map must be better than mine,' said Gretchen. 'You know Irish writings by the yard. You grew up with them.'

'Then lead me back to fond memories,' Donovan said.

On Saturday evening he brought the manuscript with him when he came to the Hall for Gretchen. Alone, on Friday evening, he had read as much of her thesis as was completed and had conceded the last word to Gretchen. She *had*, he thought, bitten off more than she could chew. But when he had laid the last sheet aside he had a sense that he had lost something infinitely precious. His Gretchen was plucky – he remembered that, newly come to Dufresne Bay, she had walked all the way to Ralston's Cove when her arm had been injured. His Gretchen was competent and self-confident – he remembered how effectively she had dealt with each crisis when the hogs had invaded the Hall. His Gretchen was born for friendship wherever she came to rest – he thought of Eileen, of Mary McDaid, of Kevin, of Harry and Eliza Moore, of Magda and Hugo. His Gretchen was made for him – for his eyes, for his arms, for his bed. But it was not his Gretchen who had written the work which lay beside him. That Gretchen might elude him always. That Gretchen might reserve her best gifts for the world of letters, might – in other studies – develop a fine, analytical faculty and then –

Then he might join her, he might celebrate her, but had she a pad of paper and a pencil she might, whenever she chose, escape him instantly, like a sea-gull on the wing, making for the horizon, soon lost to sight.

'I wasn't quite sure of you this evening,' said Gretchen. 'I was afraid you might have been stunned by my *magnum opus*.'

'I'm hard to stun,' said Donovan.

'But you did read it?' she said.

'I read it,' said Donovan. 'If you persist in your scrutiny of writings which interest you, one day you might make your mark in literary circles. But long before that you'd have outsoared me.'

'I couldn't outsoar you,' Gretchen said. 'Unless you wanted me to go.'

It was the moment he had been waiting for. Given another couple of seconds he would have told her that he loved her, that he could never let her go, and waited for her to promise that she would never leave him. However, no couple of seconds was granted to him.

'You've a great evening for an outing,' said Mary McDaid, coming toward them from the kitchen. ''Tis a spring wind blowing in now.'

On Sunday evening they dined in the east wing with Hugo.

'I'll be leaving in the morning,' Hugo said, after he had supplied Gretchen with vodka, Donovan with whisky, and himself with gin and tonic. 'Magda telephoned on Thursday to say that she could *not* endure another moment alone with Nellie. But she went on to say that Nellie was as taut as a fiddle-string, as yet in no shape to take up her burden in the west tower.'

'I had lunch with Jim Farquahar yesterday,' said Donovan. 'He told me that you and he had spent Friday evening clearing the decks for your departure.'

'Just so,' said Hugo. 'Jim has – most nobly – taken it upon himself to ascertain whether or not each creditor's claims on Nellie are valid. But he can't authorise the bank to cover any of her debts because, of the two of us, I'm the one with her power of attorney.'

'I gather that Ray Connors will raise the cash for the Morrison property,' Donovan said.

'Connors asked for ten days to give us a large deposit,' said Hugo. 'In writing he promised us the rest as soon as title was cleared. But, in fact, on the Monday after I first saw him, he was ready with the deposit. If I'd realised how eager he was to get his hands on that estate I'd have asked for twice the price I quoted.

'I have the funds in a special checking account. Jim was satisfied about six claims and I authorised payment of those when title was cleared and the balance due deposited in the account. Early in the week I'd already authorised a partial settlement for Jim – the rest to follow when the account was credited by Connors' final payment – and a full and immediate settlement for Mary McDaid – who's been walking on air since Friday afternoon, when I gave her her cheque.'

'How long will you be staying in France?' said Gretchen.

'On the long distance Magda and I agreed on six weeks as of tomorrow,' Hugo said. 'Magda says she thinks she can hold out that long if we're together and take turns fielding Nellie. In six weeks Jim may have had time to examine all the other outstanding accounts.'

'And Seamus?' said Gretchen.

'Jim had the hearing fixed within about seven weeks from now,' said Hugo. 'We'll all be back from France by then. In the meanwhile Seamus will remain in the mad house.'

'How many creditors is Jim dealing with?' said Donovan.

'I don't know,' said Hugo. 'They keep turning up from under stones. One of the Dufresne bills which has never been met is for two saddles and three bridles. The saddler's grandson – who looks to be in his fifties – presented it in person. Then our Mr Garrigan, at the top of Dufresne Hill, has bills from Nellie's father's time for cabinet work done in the west wing, plus the bills for repairs – after Nellie had all those pigs to luncheon.'

'Six weeks,' Gretchen said, almost to herself. 'Mary and I can eat real food for six whole weeks.'

'Has anyone told you how Nellie comes by that dehydrated rubbish?' said Hugo, to Gretchen.

'No, no one,' said Gretchen.

'Ten or twelve years ago,' Hugo said, 'she discovered a wholesaler somewhere between Ralston's Cove and Port Ferris. He provided that junk for hotels or *pensions* only. Nellie persuaded him that she was the *directrice* of a small hotel in the area and since that dreadful day nearly every comestible in her dining-room is powdered. She says she saves a fortune on every meal she serves, and she will have it that she sets an excellent table.'

Donovan noticed, with some amusement, that Gretchen was very much at home with Hugo, and that the avuncular role which Hugo had assumed for her suited him to a T. At the dinner table he made light of her disappointment in Dublin and remarked that he wished he could take her with him to the south of France and show her the Mediterranean – which, he assured her, had yet to be taken over by Irishmen.

'You were very good to me in Dublin,' said Gretchen. 'Several times you must have wanted to smack me for my miserable airs.'

'I found them most becoming,' said Hugo. 'Over the last twenty or thirty years I've been increasingly depressed – and incensed – by what's happened and what has yet to happen in Dublin and, at the end of each trip, I've been increasingly thankful for the comfort and security of the Hall – or, rather, of the east tower and the east wing.'

'Why wasn't the Hall burnt in the Troubles?' said Gretchen.

'We were probably saved by my uncle Edward's trainer,' Hugo said. 'Denis McCarthy was a man who got along with the whole world. No one hereabouts would have done him an injury. Harm to the Hall was indirectly harm to McCarthy, who depended for his livelihood on the Dufresnes. But not many people were as lucky as we were. Malcolm Chilcott's father's house was burnt to the ground. To this day the Chilcotts live in what used to be the gate-house. And

Geoffrey Carroll's grandfather was inadvertently shot by the Black and Tans. Not much later that house went up in flames too.'

'Were you here when all of that was going on?' said Donovan.

'Some of the time,' said Hugo. 'Some of the time I was in London with my mother. My father sent her away when he saw danger encroaching everywhere.'

Just as Donovan and Gretchen were making to leave Donovan paused in the entry.

'By the way,' he said, 'did Miss Nellie get any letters from Edward during the last of her stay in Dublin?'

Hugo burst out laughing.

'Nellie is quite beside herself,' he said. 'I have it from Magda. Nellie saw Dr Adelson three times. Twice she drew a blank. But on the third try Adelson's paper ran to two pages of invective. Magda told me on the telephone that she'd never imagined its like. And Nellie positively identifies the writing as Edward's hand.

'Edward was a rotter. We should never have tried to put Nellie in touch with him. It seemed expedient at the moment, although Magda thought it was too soon to reach him. All the same we *did* reach him –

'Like father, like son.'

'Will Miss Nellie put that construction on it?' said Gretchen.

'By now she'll have made the connection,' said Hugo. 'Even Nellie understands that she could never have made a gentleman of Seamus.'

16

March, in Gretchen's view, had neither come in like a lion nor did it go out like a lamb. But every so often a day had brought intimations of spring – clear in the early morning and gently drifting to its close on the approach of twilight. In April there were mornings misted over and luminous afternoons of pure sunshine. On such afternoons Gretchen worked in the churchyard, herself seated on the soft-green grass, a stone slab her writing table. Sometimes, if she was incautious, a breeze would frisk over her manuscript and make off with an odd-dozen pages, which would send her chasing her papers, fluttering between the graves.

One Saturday afternoon Donovan came to the Hall at a little before five o'clock.

'Sure, if you want her this early,' said Mary, 'you'll be obliged to go after her in the cemetery.'

Gretchen was so rapt in her scribbling that she knew nothing of Donovan's coming until his shadow fell over her shoulder.

'It can't be seven o'clock,' she said.

'No, it can't,' said Donovan. 'But I've wangled an invitation from Professor Ryle – for years he was head of the English Department at the University in Dublin. He's long since retired now – he has a small house not a mile from here – and he said he'd be delighted to have us for tea. You could talk Joyce to him to your heart's content.'

'I couldn't talk Joyce to anybody,' said Gretchen. 'First, I'm only a beginner in classical mythology. Second, I've never read Freud. And, third, nobody could discover Joyce in Dublin any more.'

'Well,' Donovan said, 'if, when we get there, you're stranded, you can always fall back on the weather.'

The old man was so brittle that Gretchen instinctively lowered her voice when she spoke to him, as though the least aural disturbance might blow him to dust. Donovan said very little, but Dr Ryle had been brisk in welcome and, quite soon, he and Gretchen were talking about Louis MacNeice and Seamus Heaney.

'You've done me a world of good by bringing her here,' said Dr Ryle, to Donovan, as he and Gretchen rose to go. 'There's nothing so bracing as a young mind. Will you bring her again?'

'With the greatest pleasure,' said Donovan.

Thereafter Dr Ryle expected them each Saturday for tea, and whether they talked about Sheridan or Oscar Wilde, O'Casey or Beckett, Gretchen was quick on the uptake and the professor charmed to find a foreigner so well-read in the writers he could quote by heart.

'Do you talk writing to Dr Donovan?' he said.

'Hardly ever,' said Gretchen. 'I'm bashful when I'm with Dr Donovan.'

'I always thought he had a natural literary streak in him,' said Dr Ryle. 'Indeed, I asked myself if it might not be a loss to letters when he went into medicine.'

'I wish the two of you wouldn't talk about me in my presence,' Donovan said. 'It makes *me* bashful.'

'Impossible,' said the professor, and saw them out still smiling to himself.

'A glad, confident morning to you, then,' said Mary.

'Where in the world did you get that?' said Gretchen.

''Tis what her Ladyship's father used to say every time he sat down to his breakfast,' Mary said. 'What it means I couldn't judge.'

'It's our last glad, confident morning,' said Gretchen.

'Are you telling me?' Mary said.

May had come in, bright and bold. The rhododendrons along the drive to the Hall had begun to blossom. Small craft with the wind in their sails went racing across Dufresne Bay. Gretchen had exchanged her winter clothing for light summer dresses. But, although she and Mary would have conceded that God was probably in his heaven, all was no longer quite right in their world.

'What time do you expect her?' said Gretchen.

'In time for tea, chances are,' said Mary.

'I hope she'll be pleased to see that the Hall is still standing,' said Gretchen.

'She'll find something to fault, never fear,' Mary said.

'How's it going?' said Donovan, three days later.

'There are to be some replacements,' said Gretchen. 'Hugo took her up to Port Ferris for a ware-house sale yesterday of the furniture of a family called Driscoll. She was in a good humour when she came back. She'd bought a sofa and some over-stuffed chairs and a tea-table and curtains for the drawing-room, and some straight chairs and a chest for the entrance hall.'

'The Driscolls had beautiful things,' Donovan said. 'Whatever Miss Nellie's bought could scarcely help but be an improvement on all the old flotsam and jetsam in the drawing-room.'

'But it's not that everything's coming up roses,' said Gretchen.

'Is there a spanner in the works?' said Donovan.

'Seamus may see it that way,' Gretchen said. 'She's moved his wing chair and the television set down to the dining-room. He's not to put foot in the drawing-room ever again. What's more, he's to eat at my table and I'm to take my meals at the long table with Miss Nellie. So between the separate bedrooms and the separate tables and the separate television sets – she's about to rent one for herself, in the drawing-room – Seamus will find himself a rank outsider, if the law assigns him to her custody.'

'What does Mary make of that?' said Donovan.

'Mary says she means to drive him to the grave,' said Gretchen.

'She might just be right,' Donovan said. 'Deprived of his *amour propre* I can't think what Seamus will have left to live for.'

'He'll have to find his feet if he expects to find his bottle,' said Miss Nellie. 'And before long he'll be wantin' the bottle.'

'Please let me call Dr Donovan,' said Gretchen.

'Not on *my* telephone,' Miss Nellie said.

'I know it's midnight,' said Gretchen. 'But please could you come? Seamus fell on the stairs on his way up to bed and Miss Nellie has every intention of letting him lie where he's fallen.'

'Let me speak to Miss Nellie,' said Donovan.

'I can't,' said Gretchen. 'I'm not calling from the Hall. She wouldn't let me use the telephone for Seamus. So I'm calling from Mr Daly's house, right next to the post-mistress' shop. Mr Daly says to tell you that he'll help if there's lifting to be done.'

'The top of the evening to you,' said Ben Daly, who had put on a mackintosh over his pyjamas.

'I'm sorry you've been put out this way,' said Donovan.

'Think nothing of it,' said Ben.

'What's Miss Nellie doing now?' said Donovan, to Gretchen.

'She's in the pink room with the door shut,' said Gretchen.

'Were you there when Seamus fell?' Donovan said.

'I was on my way down to brush my teeth when I heard him fall,' said Gretchen. 'So I knocked on Miss Nellie's door to tell her what had happened and she told me to leave him where he was. Seamus being Seamus I'd have liked to have done just that – but I couldn't.'

'I had to pass him on the stairs when I decided to ask Mr Daly if I could use his telephone. The whole left side of his face is – is fallen in. I don't know how to describe it. I wondered if he'd had a stroke.'

'Sure, in the mornings he can't make it to the pub any more,' said Ben. 'His legs won't carry him up the hill and, in any event, he hasn't the wind.'

At the end of the week Donovan invited himself to lunch at the east tower.

'I'm always the bearer of bad tidings when I come here,' he said. 'Unfortunately I'm not *persona grata* to Miss Nellie at the moment, which means that I can't talk the problem out with her.'

'*You're persona non grata to Nellie?*' said Magda.

'On my own hook I sent for an ambulance for Seamus on Tuesday night,' said Donovan. 'Miss Nellie was locked into the pink room and refused to open the door to me.'

'Is it possible that we're back to Seamus *again*?' Hugo said.

'He's had a cerebral haemorrhage,' said Donovan. 'His whole left side, including his face, is involved and he's incontinent of bowel and bladder. The hospital won't keep him past Monday. Thus Miss Nellie must make up her mind whether to bring him back to the Hall –

225

where he'll need nursing care – or whether to find a bed for him in one of the nursing homes for incurable patients between here and Port Ferris. Since she won't receive me I've come to you. As you're perfectly aware I have no authority whatsoever in this matter.'

'Bloody hell,' said Hugo. 'I suppose I shall have to go and reason with her myself.'

'If I may,' Donovan said, 'I'll stop by at tea-time just to find out what instructions I'm to give the hospital on Monday morning.'

Shortly before five o'clock he left Gretchen with Professor Ryle and went back to the east tower. At six o'clock he had picked up Gretchen and was driving toward the Dutch hotel where, every Saturday evening, they dined.

'You're so angry you're stiff as a poker,' said Gretchen.

'I may be on the verge on a sympathetic cerebral haemorrhage,' said Donovan. 'Hugo tells me that Miss Nellie has agreed to bring Seamus home *provided* I recall Kevin from wherever she presumes I'm keeping him and send him back to the Hall. For, as she sweetly explained to Hugo, Kevin could look after Seamus very well indeed and – at the Hall – he'd be quite happy to work for his bed and board in *lieu* of wages.'

'I hope you broke her neck,' Gretchen said.

'The hospital will keep him if he's evidently making progress,' said Jim Farquahar, on Monday.

'He's made remarkable progress,' said Donovan. 'If he goes on at this rate within ten or twelve days he might be able to walk, with a stick.'

Miss Nellie had a bed moved to the entrance hall so that Seamus would never again be compelled to take the stairs. Within a week Seamus was in it.

'You must see to it that he moves about,' said Donovan, to Miss Nellie. 'If he doesn't, he'll get bed-sores.'

'Ben Daly will come round twice a day to help him dress in the mornings and undress in the evenings,' said Miss Nellie.

'Be good to him,' Donovan said. 'You won't have him much longer, you know.'

A trickle of tears made bright furrows in Miss Nellie's withered face.

17

On the first Saturday afternoon in June Donovan took Gretchen out in his boat. Although she had never been sailing before, she learnt to hold the sheet and to duck when Donovan shouted 'Coming about'.

'I think this is the happiest day of my life,' she said, and gave him the sheet to hold while she dived over the side and into the ocean.

'Glorious,' said Gretchen, when Donovan had pulled her aboard again.

'It's not often that I have a mermaid to crew for me,' said Donovan.

'If I were a mermaid,' Gretchen said, 'I'd put a spell on you. I'd keep you in my grotto forever. But I'm not a mermaid. Shall I tell you who I really am?'

'Who are you?' said Donovan.

'I'm someone who had a piece of work to do,' said Gretchen. 'Now my work is done. Yesterday, after tea, I finished my thesis. All I have left to do is to type out eleven pages of fair copy. And when that's over what's to keep me in Ireland?'

Donovan looked beyond her to the open sea. 'Only myself,' he said, to the wind and water.

'Why have you turned away from me?' said Gretchen.

'Because,' said Donovan, 'I have no words to help me.' Slowly he turned back to her, his eyes met hers. 'I can't face a life without you,' he said. 'You know that.'

'All these weeks, these months, I've been waiting for a sign,' said Gretchen.

'Do you understand how old I am?' said Donovan.

'Quite old enough to tell me if you love me,' Gretchen said.

'I love you,' said Donovan. 'You're my joy, my comfort, my enchantment.'

An ecstatic thrill of triumph flashed through Gretchen.

'I couldn't have borne it if you'd let me go,' she said, very softly.

'I could never let you go,' Donovan said.

In Donovan's house, on Sunday evening – over a cold chicken and Chablis – they came down to practical matters.

'Once you've put the last eleven pages of the manuscript in fair copy you'll be restless at the Hall with nothing to do,' Donovan said.

'Could you bear a few idle days before you go home – as a special favour to me?'

'Why should I go home?' said Gretchen. 'Last night you told me we could be married right away. All I need to do – when those last pages are in fair copy – is to put the manuscript in the mail and address it to my professor at the university.'

'I've thought better of it,' said Donovan. 'You must go home – if not for your own sake then for mine. You must tell your family that you're to be married. They deserved that much after all their faith in you.'

'I suppose I'd feel better myself if there were no loose ends,' Gretchen said. 'And I'd hate to hurt my mother.'

'We'll go out to dinner every night of the coming week,' said Donovan. 'Except for Thursday. On Thursday morning I shall have to fly to London. I'll be back here at about noon on Friday. And I want you here next week-end for a reason which I can't explain quite yet. However, before I go to London, I'll book your flights for the next week – Port Ferris to Dublin, Dublin to Shannon, and Shannon to New York. I'll also book you into a hotel for a night in New York so that you can break the long journey to Pennsylvania.'

'A week in America would give me plenty of time to do everything,' said Gretchen, who had been ruminating.

'I'll get you an open return,' said Donovan. 'With that your professor might have a chance to read the manuscript and, if he finds that any revisions are in order, you could review his sugestions with him before bringing the thesis back to Ireland for finishing touches. But I hope he won't be fussy because, as soon as we're married, I'll take you to Italy for four or five months. I've never had a decent vacation since I first hung out my shingle in Ralston's Cove.'

Gretchen said 'Oh', and then no more.

'A pleasant atmosphere,' said Donovan.

'It's one of the more comfortable clubs in London,' Robert Christie said. 'And the food is excellent. It's still a trifle early for lunch. What wil you have to drink? Whisky? Gin?'

'At mid-day a dry sherry and my pipe would suit me best,' said Donovan.

'What are you doing here?' said Christie. 'What do you want with me?'

'I've come about the house,' Donovan said. 'Do you remember that six months ago, after your father died, we lunched together and you told me that you would, almost certainly, put the house on the market?'

'Have you found me a prospective buyer?' said Christie.

'I have,' said Donovan. 'But I've come to London because I wanted to sit down with you alone, without going through Jim Farquahar. You see I'm particularly anxious to know – if you do sell the house – what you will do with the contents.'

'There's the rub,' Christie said. 'I've been dilatory about putting the house on the open market since I can't think what to do with the furniture, the books, the paintings, the *objets d'art*, the crystal, the china, the silver, the linens. Everything in the house is beautiful, everything breathes of my father and mother, and of my grandparents before them, everything in the house *belongs* to it. I don't want anything out of it – bar the portrait of my mother – since my house in Devonshire suits me, suits Ellen right to the ground. But where, on the one hand, I can't bear to strip the house, on the other hand I can't bear the thought of putting it up for sale as is. It seems a profanity of sorts to let a stranger move in and dispossess my ghosts – just by his presence, if by nothing else.'

'I thought as much,' said Donovan. 'I never knew your grandparents but I was devoted to your mother and to your father, as you know. Do you think their shades would be safe with me?'

'*You* want the house?' said Christie. 'Just as it *is*?'

'That would be my condition,' Donovan said.

'It's yours,' said Christie. 'You can have it for a song. And I can go to my grave knowing that I protected my forbears – up to the hilt – from the barbarian.'

'What about Mrs Trask?' said Donovan. 'Would it be too much to hope that she'd come with the house? And Tony and Mario as well?'

'They'll all be overjoyed to stay on,' Christie said. 'They're all your patients, aren't they?'

'They are,' said Donovan. 'Tony and Mario have never paid me. In exchange for professional services they keep an eye on my grandfather's garden – out of hours, as it were.'

'Speaking of his garden,' said Christie, 'would you like to let the purchase ride until you get his house off your hands? I assume you don't want two houses and, so far as I'm concerned, you could move into mine tomorrow and pay me once the big house in Ralston's Cove is sold.'

'That's extremely kind of you,' Donovan said. 'However, yesterday, when I talked to Jim about the possibility of selling it, he advised me to dangle it before the municipal authorities for a while. It's much too large for the average buyer but it's so centrally located in the town that it might be ideal – after remodelling – for office spaces. Reilly and I, for example, would jump at the chance of a *suite* of rooms on the ground floor looking out, at the back, over a scrap of green and two flower-beds. Our office is pitiful. Yet it's the best we can do and has been for twenty-five years.

'My grandfather's house aside, perhaps we might get on with lunch. I should go to see my financial adviser here, in the City, and warn him that I'll be invading capital shortly.'

'Are you flying home tomorrow?' Christie said. 'Because, if you are, I'll come with you. I must instruct Mrs Trask to dispose of all personal things – clothing, eyeglasses, medicines, and such. But since I don't think it's fair to ask her to face all those heart-breaking reminders alone I'll have to play my part. So perhaps we might dine together this evening.'

'Done,' said Donovan. 'You'll be *my* guest at dinner. By the way, I should tell you that Jim will have my power of attorney in this affair. I'll direct my man in the City to take his marching orders from Jim and to see to the first payment whenever Jim has seen to the paper-work and to the second when title is cleared. Myself, I'm going to the Continent within a couple of weeks for at least four months.'

'God knows, from everything I've heard from Jim, you're more than entitled to a proper vacation,' said Christie. 'Incidentally, there's one room in the house you may never have seen. It's just off the main entrance on the south wall, and the door is usually shut. It's known as the gun-room and it's overflowing with fire-arms, fishing gear, riding boots and such. It's very large and square and it has a fireplace. Cleared out it would make a magnificent library – and I don't suppose you mean to leave your books in Ralston's Cove. What's more, quite by chance – I don't remember how the subject came up but it did, after my father's funeral – Jim told me he had a first-rate cabinet maker in Port Ferris. Perhaps he could do book-shelves for you while you're abroad.'

'I was wondering what to do with my books,' Donovan said. 'I'd hate to part company with them. They've been my friends for so long.'

'Your housekeeper has been your friend for a long time too, hasn't she?' said Christie. 'Won't she be unhappy to be turned out to pasture?'

'For the last ten years she's been dreaming of the day she'd be pensioned off,' said Donovan. 'Every year I promise to look for a replacement but I never get around to it.'

'You'll be in luck with Mrs Trask,' Christie said. 'She's only thirty three. She'll probably out-last you.'

'You look like the cat who swallowed the canary,' said Gretchen, on

Friday evening. 'I've never seen you so self-satisfied.'

'There's always a first time,' said Donovan.

He had, he thought, every reason to be pleased with himself. The truth was that he knew the Christie house intimately, having taken care of Robert Christie's mother and father for years, having gently ushered them out of the world when, the one after the other, they had begun to fail. Their ghosts would smile on him and on his Gretchen as they settled in to what was, for him, the loveliest house he had ever known. In his mind's eye he could see Gretchen working in Mrs Christie's morning-room, on the first floor, with windows looking south to the sea and west over the Christie gardens.

'Is the canary so indigestible that you can't talk to me tonight?' said Gretchen.

'I'm fresh from an extraordinary stroke of luck in London,' Donovan said. 'I'll tell you about it in good time.

'Before I forget them, here are your tickets for Wednesday of next week – I'll drive you to the airport in Port Ferris – and the confirmation of a room in the St. Regis hotel for one night.'

'Can we go sailing tomorrow?' said Gretchen.

'No,' said Donovan. 'Both Reilly and I are looking forward to fewer working hours and more time off. We aren't either of us getting any younger and, for some months, we've had our eyes on a promising young fellow in Port Ferris who, we've been hoping, might come into the practice with us – and with Dr Fir, of course. Reilly sewed him up on Thursday and he's to start work on Monday.

'Tomorrow afternoon he's coming to look at a cottage for sale some way out of Ralston's Cove. Reilly and I will help him out with the purchase – he can begin to pay us back when he's established here. But both of us want to have a look at the cottage, too, just to be sure that no one is buying a pig in a poke.

'All the same you and I will go to tea with Dr Ryle. Last week he was disappointed when I told him we wouldn't be coming, and it's only right that you should say good-bye to him before you go back to the States.'

'Do you think Miss Nellie would mind if I left most of my things at the Hall?' Gretchen said. 'One small suitcase for the trip is all I need.'

'Pack everything,' said Donovan. 'You can leave whatever you like with me. I don't want you beholden to Miss Nellie for so much as a pair of shoe-laces.'

'I ought to say good-bye to Mr and Mrs Moore,' said Gretchen.

'So you ought,' Donovan said. 'I'll invite us there for dinner on Monday evening.'

231

'In New York I'll have to look for something special to bring back to Mary,' said Gretchen. 'Is there anything you'd like me to bring back to you?'

'You know what I want you to bring back to me,' said Donovan.

'Just myself?' said Gretchen. 'Only me?'

'Just yourself,' Donovan said. 'Only you.'

Sunday was cool and clear, with such a spanking breeze that Gretchen had tied her hair into a pony-tail to keep it from blowing every which way.

'We've never taken this road before, have we?' she said.

'I've been saving it for an afternoon like this,' said Donovan.

Driving due west he came to a fork in the road and kept to the left. Ahead of them a narrow lane curved steeply as it wove over the crests of hills, flattened out as it cut across pastures or through wooded groves, only to rise again on its approach to yet another hill.

'How far have we come?' said Gretchen.

'We're about fifteen miles from Dufresne Bay,' said Donovan. 'And about twenty from Ralston's Cove. Pretty soon we'll be at the top of the world.'

Some time afterward he turned sharply left again.

'Now,' he said, 'we're on the driveway to the Christie place.'

'Look at the rhododendrons,' said Gretchen. 'I've never seen rhododendrons with such delicate flowers. Beside these Miss Nellie's are obscene.'

'The rhododendrons are only the beginning,' said Donovan.

Presently the driveway bent to the right and described a semi-circle before it brought them to the entrance of the house itself. Pulled off onto a gravelled clearing Donovan saw the Ford Escort which Robert Christie had rented at the airport. Gretchen was out of the car almost before he had shut off the ignition.

'Let's climb up the cliff for a moment,' he said. 'Then you can explore the gardens to your heart's delight.'

Together they followed a path winding slightly upward and suddenly they could see a vast sweep of a white-capped Atlantic in the west while, a long way down and directly below them, they could see the roof-tops of a fishing village and the blue waters of a small harbour.

'Now turn around,' said Donovan.

As soon as Gretchen obeyed she saw great stretches of flowering shrubs on every hand beneath her and ancient oaks standing guard in the distance.

'Shall we descend to ground level?' Donovan said. 'There we can walk through the gardens.'

An hour later an enraptured Gretchen paused for breath.

'I've never seen anything as beautiful as this in all my life,' she said. 'Surely the peonies must really have come from China, and I never knew that roses could be so long and proud and lovely and all the garden walks flanked by all those deutzias and azaleas and hibiscus – oh, I can't remember all the marvellous things we've seen. May I go back to the rock garden again?'

Without waiting for Donovan's reply she sped away. Donovan, who had always been especially fond of the jasmine which cloaked the south wall of the house, turned to look at it more closely. As he did so he heard a window opening and, looking up, he saw Christie leaning out above him.

'There was more to this business than I'd expected,' said Christie. 'Mrs Trask and I have been hard at it since Friday afternoon.'

'I'm still marvelling at the gardens,' said Donovan.

'Take all the time you like,' Christie said. 'I'll be here for another four hours at the least.'

After a few minutes Donovan caught sight of Gretchen again.

'Come with me,' he said. 'We'll go look over the house together.'

'You mean go inside?' said Gretchen. 'Oh please, no. We mustn't spoil this wonderful afternoon. Hugo told me all about the house. He said it was the biggest fake in all of Ireland. He went on and on and *on* about the first Mr and Mrs Christie – how they brought Italians artisans from Italy, men of every trade and craft to build the house, and then filled it with nothing but Italian things. He talked about it endlessly. He told me everything. He said he couldn't understand why they'd had to graft such a thing onto Ireland when they could have bought a villa in Italy just as well.

'So couldn't we forget the house? I want to go up the path once more, where I can see clear to paradise –'

Donovan let her go. As she had talked a terrible vision had assailed him. He had seen her in the house – while the winter's rain drummed on the roof and beat against the windows – his prisoner, thirty miles from anywhere, with no friends of her own choosing, no new experiences to shape into other writings, bored and lonely, with nothing to wait for but his return in the evenings, no challenge to look forward to, no more adventures just around a corner, thousands of barren days and sleepless nights looming ahead of her, her talent lifeless, her spirit crushed, his Gretchen, alone and desolate, in silent rebellion against a house whose very perfections might still the murmurings of a young soul –

'It's magnificent up there,' she said, when she had dashed back to him. 'But if you really want to see the house –'

'That was just a whim,' said Donovan. 'We'll go back to civilisation now.'

'Why are we going to the Hall?' said Gretchen, when she recognised the top of Dufresne Hill.

'Because I'm an old man,' said Donovan. 'And very tired this evening.'

'Will you come for me at dinner-time tomorrow?' said Gretchen.

'No,' Donovan said. 'Not tomorrow.'

Leaving Gretchen speechless by the sea wall Donovan turned the car around and began all over again to drive toward the Christie house. He set out with the intention of telling Robert Christie that he had changed his mind, that he was no longer interested in the property. But as he started along the driveway, as the house and grounds came into view, he could see Gretchen everywhere. He understood that he could ask for no more than to spend the rest of his life in the very places where he had seen her so joyous, where he had loved her more than ever. In his old age, he thought, he could sit anywhere he chose in the gardens and feel her presence next to him.

Before he could ring the bell the front door opened and Robert Christie made him welcome.

'Mrs Trask thought you'd driven off a while ago,' said Christie. 'I knew she must have been mistaken.'

'Could I take one quick look at the gun-room and have one quick word with Mrs Trask?' said Donovan.

From the Christie house he had telephoned Ralston's Cove and persuaded Jim Farquahar to share the cold supper which his housekeeper would already have prepared for himself and Gretchen.

'How soon can you get the power of attorney ready and valid?' said Donovan.

'There you're in luck,' said Farquahar. 'Ralph Crosby's coming to my office at ten o'clock in the morning. I'll ring him and ask him to bring his seals – I can have the instrument drawn up before his arrival – and, if you get to me on time, he can authenticate your signature at once and you can be off.'

'It's good of you to take this on for me,' Donovan said. 'You're sure that seeing to the book-shelves in the gun-room isn't too much of a leg-pull?'

'I'm sure,' said Farquahar. 'It gives me a perfect to talk Christie into selling me his father's fly-rods.'

234

When Farquahar had gone, Donovan went up to his library. Before the dawn he had finished a whole bottle of whisky and his anguish had not in the least abated.

Too stunned to make any sense of Donovan's *volte-face*, Gretchen crept away from the Hall. The only thing she felt sure of was a hard determination not to come face to face with Miss Nellie until she could regain some measure of composure. Her only sanctuary was the churchyard, and it was not till she was all but hidden between the headstones that she gave herself up to despair. It was a despair she could not alleviate since, try as she would, she could not imagine why Donovan had cast her off. After hours of sheltering beside the graves of one John Drew and his wife, Bridget – both of whom had died more than seventy years earlier – the despair gave place to rage. Rage brought her to her feet before she was entrapped in darkness. Rage spurred her on, down the little hill, through the gates, along the drive, into the Hall, and up to her own room. She could not hope to sleep but she could – so she thought – devise a plan, an excuse to meet Donovan head-on and make him talk to her. By the time the night was over she had made a decision. She would wait out the morning but, in the afternoon, she would go to his office and confront him on his own ground. She would storm his defences and then expose the suffering he had inflicted on her and cry out for the love he had, so abruptly, withdrawn, the love she was certain that he felt for her, the love she could not live without.

In the morning she went back to the churchyard. By the position of the sun in the sky she believed she would be able to tell when it was time for lunch – a lunch she would try to eat to give her the strength to walk all the way to Ralston's Cove in the heat of the day.

Having timed her return by the sun she walked back to the west tower. A car she did not recognise was parked by the entrance. She was about to move around it when a stout, middle-aged man, carrying a black bag, stepped outside. Inevitably she said good morning.

'Good morning,' he said.

'Are you a doctor?' said Gretchen, alarmed – for no reason – by the sight of the black bag.

'I'm Dr Reilly,' he said.

'Dr Reilly?' said Gretchen. 'But I thought Dr Donovan took care of Mr and Mrs Taylor-Dufresne.'

'He does,' said Dr Reilly. 'But I'm pinch-hitting for him. Mr Taylor-Dufresne slipped his right knee a little while ago. I've just put it right.'

'Dr Donovan couldn't come?' said Gretchen.

'Dr Donovan's gone to France,' Dr Reilly said. 'He left about an hour ago. He won't be back until some time in the autumn.'

With Miss Nellie's help Gretchen arranged for Arthur Flood to come to the Hall for her at two o'clock.

'I want to go to the bank in Ralston's Cove,' she said. 'And then stop for a moment at Dr Donovan's office before coming back here.'

In the bank a clerk helped her to decipher the figures on the tickets which represented the price of the flights.

'But surely that's ridiculously expensive,' said Gretchen.

'You're booked into first class from Shannon to New York,' said the clerk.

For an instant Gretchen thought of exchanging the first-class ticket for tourist-class accommodations. But then she realised that Donovan had paid the full price for a first-class seat and she meant to reimburse him for every penny he had put out for her. When she had signed a number of travellers' cheques she asked the young man to give her the exact amount for the tickets in one pile and any cash left over in another. When that was done she asked for an envelope.

'You're Mrs Mullin, aren't you?' said Gretchen.

'I am,' said Mrs Mullin.

'Would you be so kind as to deposit this to Dr Donovan's account at the bank?' Gretchen said, giving her the envelope. 'I hoped to catch him before he left but I understand from Dr Reilly that I'm too late. Perhaps you could make a memorandum for Dr Donovan simply saying that the sum deposited to his account represents payment in full of airlines tickets to New York.'

On Tuesday, in a glittering fury, she packed her suitcases with care and patience, neatly folding and fitting her belongings so that, when next she unpacked, she would see no trace of the storm which was ravaging her soul.

'When I get home,' she said to herself, 'I'll teach myself to hate him and I will rejoice to think that one fine day he'll find himself crippled and scorned.

'I could kill him,' she said. 'But that would be too good for him. Too good. Too quick. I hope he lives to be as old as Methuselah, ignored and forgotten for centuries. The moment I get off this God-forsaken island I'll be free. The moment I walk into my own dooryard I'll forget him forever –'

At six o'clock on Wednesday morning Gretchen, with her five suitcases and her typewriter, was on the road to Port Ferris with Arthur Flood.

'I daresay you'll be happy to be on your way home,' said Mr Flood.

'There are people who love me where I'm going,' Gretchen said.

Epilogue

'In all my life I'd never seen anything so sumptuous and fashionable as the lobby of the St. Regis hotel,' said Gretchen. 'I just lost my nerve. That's the only way I can explain how I came to barge in on you –'

'My dear child,' said Mrs Isaacs, 'you're not barging in. 'You're always welcome –'

'The porter who took my luggage must have thought I was crazy,' Gretchen said. 'I never even got as far as the reception desk. I told him to take me to a telephone, I called you, you said I could come, so I gave the man three dollars and told him to put me in a taxi –'

'You missed Aaron by only a few hours,' said Helen Isaacs. 'He's landed a client who wants him to do a house in Connecticut. It's his very first job all on his own since he graduated from architectural school. So he came to lunch, left me with a mountain of laundry, and pinched five of Ephraim's shirts and several pairs of socks –'

'He has the makings of a wonderful architect,' said Gretchen.

'But not of a wonderful husband,' Mrs Isaacs said. 'There, although it goes against the grain, I have to agree with you –'

When Gretchen had had milk and cookies, unpacked a few overnight things, taken a bath and changed her clothes, Ephraim Isaacs had come to cocktails with his wife.

'Great day in the morning,' said Isaacs, when Gretchen appeared in the doorway. 'Did you cross the Atlantic on a raft?'

'She's obviously exhausted,' said Mrs. Isaacs. 'I want to fatten her up before she goes home to her mother.'

'Lately I can't sleep,' said Gretchen. 'I've lost the knack.'

'Helen will see to that,' Isaacs said. 'She has some sleeping pills that could carry you right over to Judgment Day.'

The next morning Gretchen had breakfast with Mrs Isaacs. Ephraim Isaacs had already gone to work.

'Gretchen,' said Mrs Isaacs, 'my memory's not what it used to be

237

but, in my recollection, you went to Ireland to write something. What was it?'

'It was my thesis,' said Gretchen. 'I wrote it there.'

'What's it about?' Helen Isaacs said.

'It's a study of Irish writers in two parts,' said Gretchen. 'The first part is called "The Written Word" and deals with prose. The second part I've called "The Spoken Word" and that deals with Irish theatre.'

'Yes,' said Mrs Isaacs, 'I remember now that you did talk to us a little about just that. What are your plans for the future? Have you a job lined up already?'

'I wish I had,' Gretchen said. 'If I were lucky enough to find a teaching post –'

'Stop right there,' said Mrs Isaacs. 'If you could stay with us for just a few days Ephraim might have a job for you. But you'd have to give him time to read the second half of your thesis.'

'I don't know anything about television,' said Gretchen.

'Ephraim's been directing plays for television for twenty years,' Helen Isaacs said. 'If I'm right, if you *have* something to offer him, you'd learn the ropes soon enough.'

Over the week-end Isaacs read Gretchen's thesis.

'Every once in a while Helen has a brain-wave,' he said, mixing cocktails at seven o'clock in the evening. 'Would you like to work with me?'

'What could I do for you?' said Gretchen.

Just at that moment the doorbell rang.

'We're expecting a couple of people for Sunday night supper,' said Isaacs. 'Get Helen to explain the situation to you in the morning.'

'Ephraim talked to me about the second part of your thesis before we went to bed,' Mrs Isaacs said, to Gretchen, over a second cup of coffee. 'Just by chance your study of the Irish theatre dovetails with a dream he's had for a long time.'

It appeared that, for several years, Ephraim Isaacs had been hoping to present, each season, a series of plays linked together by a common thread. It had already occurred to him that he could hardly do better than to devote the first season to Irish playwrights.

'And then you turned up,' Helen Isaacs said. 'When Ephraim had read your manuscript he saw that, in the second half, you had linked playwright to playwright, and theme to theme. Now this coming winter, although he knew he'd be directing plays long since scheduled, he was also longing to be laying the ground work for the year to follow. And, on reading your piece, he found plenty of groundwork already laid. So he has a simple proposal to put to you. Would you come to him as his special advisory assistant on or about September fifteenth? He couldn't go at it much earlier because he's given me his word of honour – which he's been breaking every since we got married – that he'll take me to Europe for an extended tour this summer. But to come back to you – he'll make sure you get a good salary and you and he will examine the possibilities together – what you'll produce – if you get the backing – in what order you'll present the plays, whether or not they should be prefaced by a short, introductory commentary on the playwright's life and circumstances –'

Ephraim Isaacs came home in the mid-afternoon.

'Everything's all wound up,' he said, to Mrs Isaacs. 'So you can start packing. We'll be off in three days.

'Incidentally, did you talk to Gretchen about coming to work with me?'

'I did,' said Helen Isaacs.

Isaacs turned to Gretchen.

'By September of this year I'll have my work cut out for me, tackling the plays we're presenting this season,' he said. 'However, I could still make time around the edges for lengthy confabulations. Undoubtedly I'll have to send you to Dublin now and then – don't worry about the money, you'll have an expense account –'

'It seems,' he said, 'that I've forgotten to ask you if you'd like to collaborate on this business –'

'If you really think you can teach me to be useful,' said Gretchen –

'That's no problem,' Isaacs said. 'While Helen and I are away, cudgel your brains a little. Ever since I read your thesis I've been asking myself if, perhaps, we could wring two Irish seasons out of this first project. What would you say to taking your playwrights for a start – the Irish writers who stayed home and, in the following years, lead off with Sheridan, then Wilde, then Shaw – the renegades –'

'Ephraim's beginning to lean on you already,' said Helen Isaacs, to Gretchen. 'But, seriously, once you get the hang of things in the studio, you could make a behind-the-scenes life for yourself in television, if you liked the challenge –'

For what was left of June and then, during July, August, and part of September, Gretchen drove herself from dawn until late in the evening. Often she was up before her father or her uncles, making the barn ready for the morning milking. She worked all day with the men in the fields, helped with the evening's milking, helped her mother clear up after supper, read aloud to Little Will. If it rained which, occasionally, it did, she took down the curtains in the parlour or in the kitchen, washed them, ironed them, and hung them up again. But no matter how long or hard she worked she could not get back into her childhood. Never, not even for an instant, had she any sense of being home at last. Perversely it was *Ireland* that she missed, Ireland, the country where she had finally grown up, Ireland, the scene of her coming into full maturity. What was worse, all the anger against Donovan – the anger which had sustained her through her leave-taking, through her visit to Aaron's parents, through the welcome which all of her family had lavished on her – had slowly frozen. Week after week, month after month, she had lived with her anguish, with her longing for Donovan. She found relief only when she considered putting an end to herself – since she could not imagine where she could find the strength to face a lifetime of unremitting despair.

'You'll kill yourself, my darling, if you go on like this,' said her mother.

'Will I?' she said.

'I don't want you loading ensilage this morning,' said her father. 'I want you to rest.'

'I can't rest,' she said.

'You've changed,' said Anna.

'I know,' she said.

If anything could have helped her it should have been the collaboration between herself and Ephraim Isaacs. He was a vigorous, sensitive, exciting man and, when he had taken her measure, he thrust enormous responsibilities onto her young shoulders. Throughout the first season, when the Irish plays were yet to be selected, scheduled, studied, cast, or rehearsed, he sent her twice to Dublin, with introductions to the foremost men, the most gifted players in the Irish theatre. Such people she approached with various *précis* of Isaacs' visions of specific plays or playwrights, or periods, and made shrewd notes on their reactions or their suggestions. She was wined and dined and taken to the theatre and all the while she was fencing with Ireland's most brilliant master of stagecraft and learning more than she could hope to remember.

When she had first come to New York to work for Ephraim Isaacs she had had what Mrs Isaacs referred to as 'beginners' luck'. Isaacs' secretary – the same Rebecca who had advised her to go to Ralston's Cove – had grown tired of commuting from Long Island to

Manhattan every day and had found a ramshackle apartment which was too big for her. Hence she was looking for someone with whom she could share it and, after a searching conversation, she decided to share it with Gretchen.

'It's a good omen,' said Mrs Isaacs. 'You'll be within ten minutes' walk of the studio.'

Nor did Gretchen lack for pleasant company. Rebecca had scores of friends, many of whom were connected with the theatre. She and Gretchen kept open house – provided each guest brought a contribution to the fare – each week-end. Gretchen did her best to be light-hearted, but she accepted no invitations to dinner à deux. Everywhere she turned Donovan's shadow lay over her.

The next summer she took only four weeks' vacation – and, figuratively speaking, followed the plough again – since Ephraim Isaacs' plans for two whole seaons of Irish plays, especially redesigned or slightly restructured for television, were already taking on the realities of works in progress. Irish actors and actresses had already been engaged, many of them for several rôles, for several different productions. In October Isaacs opened the series with *Juno and the Paycock* and the season was under way. It was immediately a *succés fou*. Ephraim Isaacs was triumphant, Helen Isaacs was jubilant. Gretchen recognised that she had answered for a considerable part of the project, but what was uppermost in her mind was the recollection of her misery, throughout both trips to Dublin, at finding herself geographically so close to Donovan, in the heart of his country, feeling him everywhere and remembering, every time, that she had no right, no access to him. And then, one Sunday, late in November, Mrs Isaacs took a hand in her afairs.

'Gretchen,' she said, 'how much do you weigh?'

'I don't know,' said Gretchen. 'About a hundred and twenty five pounds, at a guess.'

'Come into my bathroom,' said Mrs Isaacs. 'There's a balance scale in there.'

'We have the whole afternoon and evening,' Helen Isaacs said. 'Ephraim won't be back from London until tomorrow.'

'I really must go back to work,' said Gretchen. 'I'm behind with things Mr Isaacs needs. To be perfectly truthful, he could use two of me.'

'You thought you weighed a hundred and twenty five pounds,' said Mrs Isaacs. 'On my scale you weighed ninety-six – right after lunch. A thirty-pound weight loss is no joke. Tell me, Gretchen, are you ill, or are you desolate even in the midst of Ephraim's uproar?'

241

'How could I be desolate when I have such a fascinating job?' Gretchen said. 'Half of New York City would change places with me in a flash.'

'You're off at a tangent,' said Helen Isaacs. 'If you think back you'll remember that you came to us before you went to Ireland to write your thesis. You were joyful then. What happened to you in Ireland that's led you to so much suffering?'

There was a quietness which Gretchen had always felt in Mrs Isaacs' presence.

'It's a long story,' said Gretchen. 'I've never spoken to anyone about Ireland.'

'We have all the time in the world,' Mrs Isaacs said.

All at once Gretchen realised that Helen Isaacs was offering her release at last from the silence in which she had been living for almost a year and a half, the silence in whose darkness she could not sleep, in whose brilliance she could not eat, from whose iron hold – were she to reach out – she could touch no one.

'I'll tell you how it was,' said Gretchen.

Then slowly, truthfully, she began to tell Mrs Isaacs everything she could remember about the Irish sojourn. Now and again she was interrupted by a penetrating question and, when she understood that she had caught Mrs Isaacs' imagination and had her sympathy, she found herself talking with no reserve whatever.

She told her about the flight across the Atlantic, the illness which had crept over her, the trip on the bus from Port Ferris to Ralston's Cove, her loss of consciousness in the lobby of the hotel, the squalor of the hotel itself, and Donovan's ministrations while she kept to her bed. She told her about the Hall, about Mary McDaid, Miss Nellie and Seamus, Kevin and Solomon, she branched out to Harry and Eliza Moore, to Hugo and Magda. She described the wicked spring in her mattress, the incursion of the hogs, the weeks when she was laid up with bronchitis, Edward's death, Miss Nellie and her mediums, Seamus' lunacy, Kevin's dire misfortunes, her trip to Dublin, and always, central to almost every topic she broached, was Donovan.

Mrs Isaacs stopped her when she spoke about the first time that Donovan had made love to her – on the same night that she had through him dead – to ask if she had ever told Donovan about Aaron and whether, if she had, Donovan had made love to her before or after he knew that she was not inexperienced in the matter of sex. She clearly remembered the dinner at the Cygne d'Or, when she had spoken of Aaron, she remembered that it was on the following Tuesday, at tea-time, that she had believed Donovan had died and that, much later, on the same Tuesday, he had made love to her for the first time.

Then, clasping her hands so tightly that the knuckles went white, she told Mrs Isaacs about the afternoon in the Christie gardens, the sudden change in Donovan's manner and then – leaving her no message – his almost immediate departure for France. After she had revealed her agony she looked to Helen Isaacs for a comment – any comment – certain all the while that nothing she might say could alter her despair.

'Let's draw the curtains and light the fire,' said Mrs Isaacs. 'It's blowing up for a nasty evening out there.

'And now,' she said, 'let's come back to your chronicle. Admittedly *I* wasn't there in Ireland and I don't know your Dr Donovan, but I have a very strong feeling that he didn't leave you because he loved you too little but because he loved you too much. You were, by your own account, so happy in the gardens of the Christie house and, by your own account, so was he. Nevertheless you didn't want to go into the house.'

'Does that excuse, does that explain his cruelty?' said Gretchen.

'Just ride this one out with me,' Mrs Isaacs said. 'Shall we suppose that, for some reason or other, the owner of the property didn't want to live in Ireland. Suppose he meant to put the house and the grounds on the market. Suppose Dr Donovan had asked him for a first refusal – pending the moment that he could show you the house and ask you if you thought you could live happily there.'

All of what faint colour she had ebbed from Gretchen's face.

'And I wouldn't go inside?' she said, in a merest whisper.

'Isn't it conceivable that he suddenly saw – putting himself in your place – the house as a cage?' said Mrs Isaacs. 'Gilded, to be sure but, by its nature, designed to keep you in while years went by. Isn't it possible that, in such a moment, he felt he had to let you go, to leave you free – free to work, free to travel, free for new interests, new studies, other writings? You say he'd read half of your thesis. He may well have asked himself, there and then, how you could write anything more if you were shut off from the world where there were happenings, where there was grist to your mill. He may very well have concluded that you had a right to a wealth of experience, a wealth of challenge.'

'But he couldn't understand that I loved him?' said Gretchen.

'Throughout your saga,' Helen Isaacs said, 'you made it abundantly clear that Ireland did, indeed, disgust you. That may also have weighed with him. But let us imagine that Dr Donovan were to ask you to come back to him. Would you go, even if it meant living in his country?'

243

'I'd live in a sewer for him,' said Gretchen.

'Before the misunderstanding in the enchanted gardens did you ever stop to consider the risk to yourself if, in fact, you and Dr Donovan *were* married?' said Mrs Isaacs. 'Did you ever face the prospect of losing him – simply through such a disparity between his age and yours – twenty, forty years ahead of your own dying?'

'I faced the risk,' said Gretchen. 'And I faced it down.'

'It's true,' Mrs Isaacs said, 'that every once in a blue moon a marriage does seem to have been made in heaven and your case may be one of those rare happen-chances. Moreover you lived with Aaron for nearly four years, and although you were happy in the relationship he didn't move you as Dr Donovan has done. It just might be that this Donovan is the only man you will ever know who is capable of touching you so deeply.

'From this moment forward I think you should analyse the situation as objectively as you can, because I believe that if you were to aproach Dr Donovan directly, to describe to him frankly your sufferings without him, he might well take you back – convinced at last that he really is necessary to you.'

'How could I approach him?' said Gretchen. 'I may be wretched, I *am* wretched, but I'm not on my hands and knees. I won't crawl back to him. My pride is all I have left to sustain me.'

'Your pride won't keep you warm on a cold night,' Helen Isaacs said. 'When are you going home for the Christmas holidays?'

'I don't think Mr Isaacs expects me to take any time off for Christmas,' said Gretchen.

'Well,' said Mrs Isaacs, 'I'm not so sure that sitting around and brooding for any length of time is indicated in your condition. But you must take two weeks off – say between December fifteenth and the New Year – to rest and, above all, to eat. I'd like to telephone your mother – if you'll allow me – and tell her to treat you as an invalid, pro tem.'

By the time Gretchen had left Ireland and disembarked in New York, Donovan was in the south of France, in a little villa on a hillside overlooking the Mediterranean.

'A lucky break for you,' said the real estate agent.

'How does it happen not to be let for the summer?' said Donovan.

'It was let,' the real estate agent said. 'By a gentleman who's taken it every summer for the past ten years. But he died in Paris a week ago.'

Donovan laid in a good supply of whisky and rented a boat for the season. Every morning he had coffee and a *brioche* at a café close to the shore, bought a packet of sandwiches, a half bottle of red wine, and put out in his boat. Every day, except when it rained – which it did infrequently – he was on the sea, he never put in until it was almost dark. In the evenings he shortly became a regular client of a small restaurant, he had his own table and his own napkin in a napkin-ring. When he had eaten he went back to the villa and drank his whisky. Neither the sun nor the sea nor the whisky eased his longing for Gretchen; his sleep was fitful; he woke at sun-up to the awful echoes of his last words to her. By October he was seriously considering the possibility of staying in France indefinitely, since nothing called him back to Ralston's Cove. But when he learnt that both the café and the restaurant were closed, off-season – that, by the first of November, he would have to fend for himself, buy provisions, cook his own meals – he resigned himself to a return.

For over a month in Ireland he was busy moving his books, his clothing, the leather chairs from his grandfather's library – and the portrait of his grandfather – from Ralston's Cove to the Christie house, where Jim Farquahar's cabinet-maker had transformed the gun-room with book-shelves from the floor to the ceiling, flanking the fireplace, flanking the door, flanking the north window on one wall and the east window on the other. He took a grim pleasure in the work of hands and drew some comfort from Mrs Trask, who never intruded on him, who – almost miraculously – materialised the instant he rang for her, who was a superb cook, and ironed his shirts, sewed on loose buttons, darned his socks to perfection. A week before he went back to his practice he stopped at his office and retrieved all of the letters, circulars, catalogues which waited for him and sorted them out at his leisure in the Christie house. A week later, on a Monday, he walked into his office at two o'clock in the afternoon. At three o'clock he summoned Mrs Mullin.

'How many more of them are out there?' he said.

'Twenty-five to thirty, I'd say,' said Mrs Mullin. 'There wasn't a thing wrong with them all those months you were away. But now that you're here again every one of them's at death's door.'

'I'll see ten of them today,' Donovan said. 'The rest will have to wait until tomorrow.'

Throughout the winter, throughout the spring, he accepted no invitations, he invited no one to come to him. The Christie library was stocked with complete sets of virtually every nineteenth-century writer of note and, in the evenings, he read Trollope or George Eliot or Thackeray until well past midnight since, knowing how difficult it was for him to sleep, he preferred to stay awake over the fire in Mr

Christie's library than in his cold bed usptairs. By June he could sit in the gardens, drink his whisky, eat his dinner on a tray which Mrs Trask brought out to him, and see Gretchen kneeling by a rose-bush or racing up the cliff. He could hardly believe that he had survived for a whole year without her, tormented night and day by his memories.

One morning in June Miss Nellie sent for him. The message was so urgent that he went at once to the Hall. He had not been near Dufresne Bay since he had brought Gretchen back to it after she had seen the Christie gardens. As soon as he had crossed the threshold he knew that Miss Nellie's had been no idle summons. Seamus, unconscious, already in Cheyne-Stokes breathing, was lying on his bed in the entrance hall, Miss Nellie was sitting in a chair beside him. Immediately Donovan took Miss Nellie outside, some little distance from the front door.

'It's never been my policy to talk about a patient within his hearing,' said Donovan. 'Not even if the patient is unconscious.'

'He's dyin', isn't he?' said Miss Nellie.

'Yes,' Donovan said. 'I'll take his blood pressure, his pulse, listen to his chest but, you understand, those will be no more than formalities. There's nothing anyone can do for him now.'

'Quentin's comin',' said Miss Nellie. 'I rang him after I rang you.'

Donovan rapidly examined Seamus, then sat down in a chair on one side of the bed facing Miss Nellie on the other. Twice, in half an hour, Seamus stopped breathing for well over a minute. Three quarters of an hour later he stopped breathing forever.

'Do you want Rob McCormack to take charge of him?' said Donovan.

'He's the only one close at hand,' Miss Nellie said.

'I'll give him a death certificate and send him down immediately,' said Donovan. 'Is there anything else I can do for you? Do you want a sedative?'

'No,' said Miss Nellie. 'But there is one thing you could do for me.'

She walked into her library and came out with a small package in her hand.

'The girl forgot her alarm clock,' Miss Nellie said. 'Mary spotted it after she'd left. I've had it wrapped up and ready for the post for months and months. But I've always meant to post it from Ralston's Cove. Millie, up on Dufresne Hill is fine for a letter but parcels are too much for her. At all events I never remember to take it up to town with me when I go. Could you deal with it for me?'

'Of course,' said Donovan, well aware that Miss Nellie never went to Ralston's Cove any longer, that Mary and Ben Daly did all of her shopping and paid in the cash which Ryan's and Haskell and all the others demanded.

That evening, when Donovan got back to the Christie house, he undid the small package in the library, being careful with his scissors. Neatly he clipped off the little square of brown paper on which Miss Nellie had written Gretchen's name and her address in Pennsylvania. That he folded and put in his wallet, beside his credit cards. The new knowledge of precisely where she lived, of her exact address was a solace, the scrap of paper he had saved was precious to him. The rest of Miss Nellie's wrappings he threw on the fire before he went upstairs, put his own alarm clock in the back of a drawer, and set Gretchen's on his night-table.

It was a compact, rectangular clock with a simple dial, plain, easy-to-see-at-a-glance numerals and, as it was battery-powered, it was still going. He remembered it perfectly, standing by Gretchen's bed in the hotel, in the Hall and, on *his* night-table, as it ticked, it was almost as if he were listening to Gretchen's heart-beats. Consulting his watch he saw that the clock had neither gained nor lost a minute in the space of a year – clearly it was a clock to be proud of – and, while he watched the second-hand circling past each numbered hour, he rejoiced, abjectly, to have the sturdy clock which had told Gretchen's time to tell his own.

That summer he took no vacation for, months earlier, he had sold his grandfather's house to the township of Ralston's Cove – with a clause in the bill of sale which stated that a given portion of the ground floor was to remain at his and at Reilly's disposal during their lifetimes and was to be made over into waiting rooms, examining rooms, offices to their specifications. He and Reilly met with the architect and with the contractor two or three times a week, indignantly protesting about shoddy workmanship and insisting on higher standards in the execution of the architect's designs.

'You and I'll be pretty good on the harp before this job's over,' said Reilly.

'I'm tone-deaf,' said Donovan, in jest – but by that time the possibility of taking his own life was often uppermost in his mind.

'You make me feel like Elizabeth Barrett,' said Gretchen, the morning after her home-coming when, once she had bathed and dressed, her mother had arranged for her to lie full length on the sofa in the parlour, with two pillows behind her shoulders to keep her head slightly raised.

247

'Mrs Isaacs said you were to have rest, quiet, and comfort,' her mother said. 'What would you like to read?'

'I might read *David Copperfield* again,' said Gretchen. 'It's easy to get along with Dickens.'

'A little later I'll bring you a glass of milk and a slice of last night's apple pie,' said her mother. 'Right now I'm going to start on the first batch of Christmas cookies.'

In two days Gretchen had done no more than hold the book in her hands. On the third day she had read three or four pages when the postman came by.

'You have a letter from Ireland,' her mother said.

'Give it to me,' said Gretchen.

By the return address on the envelope she saw that the letter was from Eliza Moore.

'Not a week after your departure I got your address from Miss Nellie at the Hall,' Eliza wrote. 'Ever since then I've been meaning to write but I've never quite got around to it. As a matter of fact I might never have known you'd gone, were it not that Arthur Flood broke his wrist. Harry took care of the fracture and, for some reason or other, Arthur told him that he'd taken you to the airport in Port Ferris.'

Gretchen bore with Eliza while Eliza dwelt upon how much she hoped that Gretchen's thesis had been well received. She kept on reading while Eliza touched on herself and her work, on Harry and the vacation he desperately needed, on Seamus' death, nearly six months earlier. Then, at the top of a new page Eliza – apparently – took a breath and wrote:

'No doubt you've been in touch with Clement Donovan. He must have written to tell you about the four months – or more – he spent in France last year, and about the sale of his grandfather's house in Ralston's Cove, and about the offices he and Reilly are hoping to open there when the workmen have finished cutting up some of the ground floor into small rooms – if the workmen *ever* finish. It's impossible to get *anything* done in Ireland these days. I myself haven't seen Clement Donovan since he came back from the Continent over a year ago. Harry runs into him from time to time, of course, and finds him much changed, brusque and withdrawn. We've invited him here on every imaginable pretext but he never comes. Ever since he moved into the Christie house, which he did immediately he was home from France, he's kept to himself. Surely he's written to you that he's bought the property –'

'Gretchen, where are you going?' said her mother.

'To Knightstown,' said Gretchen.

'But your father needs the car this morning,' said her mother.

'He can have it when I come back,' said Gretchen.

'He needs it *now*,' said her mother.

'Then he'll have to wait,' Gretchen said.

'How much do I owe you?' said Gretchen.

'I'll have to count the words,' said the clerk. 'Do you want this to go as a straight telegram or as a night letter?'

'As a straight telegram,' said Gretchen.

'You must lie down,' said Gretchen's mother. 'You went up to Knightstown this morning, you've spent the whole afternoon trimming the tree. Mrs Isaacs said you were to rest.'

'Let's forget about Mrs Isaacs,' Gretchen said. 'It's hardly a week until Christmas and there are so many things to do –'

In Ireland, the next day, in the late afternoon, Mrs Mullin accepted a telegram addressed to Donovan, whose last patient was scurrying away. She walked down the narrow corridor, knocked on the door of his office, and entered the room.

'I don't know why they put themselves out to deliver this by hand,' said Mrs Mullin, laying the sealed telegraph form on Donovan's desk. 'They could just as well have phoned the message.'

'Is anyone else waiting for me out there?' said Donovan.

'Not any longer,' Mrs Mullin said. 'There were four or five of them here not a quarter of an hour ago. I daresay they decided to get home before the storm could break.'

'What storm?' said Donovan.

'There've been warnings on the wireless since noon,' said Mrs Mullin. 'All small craft have been urged to put in to the nearest harbour without delay – if possible. Or else to make for the open sea. All motorists are urged to get off the roads. I'd be much obliged to you if I could call it a day myself.'

'Go, by all means,' Donovan said.

For a few moments he sat at his desk listening to her retreating footsteps. Then, wearily, without interest, he opened the telegram. The words, written in capital letters stupefied him so that he read them several times, as though he were searching for an error in the brief text. When he lifted his head he found himself looking at the wall-clock over the examining table. Suddenly it occurred to him that the post-office would be closing in five minutes. He grabbed his overcoat and, since there was no time to start his car, fight the traffic in the High Street, battle for a parking space, he put his faith in his feet and ran. Still running he took the six steps up to the entrance of the post-office and shoved the door open.

'Daisy,' he said, 'I must send a telegram.'

'Just let me lock the door behind you,' said Daisy, 'whilst you catch your breath. Now then, sit down over there. You'll see the forms in front of you. Take your time. I'll go to the back room and tell May not to skip out before she's sent your wire.'

His fingers clumsy in his haste, Donovan managed to open his wallet, take out the small square of brown paper he had cut off the little package which Miss Nellie had asked him to post to Gretchen. All too rapidly he scribbled her name, her address, his message, his signature on a form, read over what he had printed, and concluded that it would be illegible to anyone but himself. Doing his best to be calm, he took out a new form and painstakingly copied what he had written on the first.

'Have you it ready, Dr Donovan?' said May, coming out of the back room with Daisy.

'Yes,' said Donovan. 'Here it is.'

'Let me get it out on the instant,' May said. 'Then we can take it easy reckoning up how much is owing.'

Donovan folded the scrap of brown paper and put it back in his wallet. Then he folded the first form, too quickly completed, and put that in his breast pocket. Presently May reappeared.

'That's done, so,' she said. 'Storm or no storm it's safely on its way.'

Donovan had to fight a rising wind to get back to the car. Forgetting his black bag, forgetting to lock the front door to the office, he thrust himself into the driver's seat and turned on the ignition. Once clear of Ralston's Cove he made good time until he veered off onto the lane that led to the Christie house and to no other. Then, with each ascending curve, the wind seemed to whip at him from sharply changing directions. The car bucked, swerved, shuddered as it rounded each bend, while his fingers began to ache from the ferocity with which he gripped the steering wheel. Only a little while earlier he would have put no value whatsoever on his life; now he prayed to the God in whom he had never believed to rescue him from the fury in the darkness. For an hour he fought the tempest and then, just as he was starting on the driveway which would bring him home, a deluge of rain hurled itself against his windshield. In spite of the windshield wipers, in spite of the headlights, full on, he could hardly see the hood of the car, he could only rely on instinct to keep the wheels on the gravel.

'You're soaked to the skin,' said Mrs Trask.

'I know,' he said. 'And the car's not three yards away. It was those three yards on foot that left me drenched.'

'As you can see,' said Mrs Trask, 'we've no electricity. The wires must be down everywhere. But we've an abundance of candles and I'll be doing your dinner on the gas cooker tonight.'

Docile, trusting – for the first time in his life – Donovan, at Mrs Trask's bidding, draped his sodden coat over the newel-post and took the stairs. In the *niches* on the wall, rising with the staircase, Mrs Trask had lit candles and when he came to his bedroom that, too, was illuminated.

'If you'd be so kind as to empty your pockets and take off every stitch of clothing on you,' said Mrs Trask, 'you could slip into your bathrobe and give me all your dripping things. I'll put your jacket and your trousers and your shoes by the kitchen fire. The other things I can wash tomorrow.'

Donovan followed her orders to the letter.

'When you've had a good, hot bath,' Mrs Trask said, 'you'll find your whisky waiting for you in the morning-room. The fireplace in that room is one of the few I trust with the wind as high as it is. So you'll find the fire lit and drawing nicely.'

No small luxury had ever been so grateful to Donovan as the bath he took that evening. Dressed again, in a clean, dry shirt, dry socks, grey flannels, a smoking jacket, and a pair of leather slippers, he left his keys and his wallet on the top of his chest of drawers. But the telegram which Mrs Mullin had given him and the first form he had scrawled in reply – and rejected, sure, that no one could have deciphered what he had written in such a hurry – he took down to the morning-room with him.

'This is the book you were reading, isn't it?' said Mrs Trask. 'I found it by your chair in the old library.'

'That's the very book,' said Donovan. 'Thank you.'

'I think there's enough light in here,' Mrs Trask said, looking around the morning-room. 'There's your bottle, there's your glass, and there's your soda water. And the fire's going well for you. Would you like time to relax before your dinner?'

'I would,' said Donovan.

'Will I call you downstairs in an hour?' said Mrs Trask. 'Or will I bring you a tray up here, by the fire.'

'Bring me a tray,' Donovan said. 'That would be splendid.'

For some little time he sat by the fire, watching the flames and drinking his whisky slowly. What he had done in the post-office in Ralston's Cove was done. For better or for worse there was no turning back. Nor could he suppress the surge of a happiness in which he could not – quite yet – believe.

He rose, crossed the room, laid the telegram addressed to himself open on the writing table, and read the message over and over again. It ran:

'You will never find me in the Christie house if you won't let me in. Gretchen.'

At last he opened the rough draught of his reply, already speeding – even on such a night – across the Atlantic. The twisted handwriting mocked him even while the words restored his soul and brought him an ineffable sense of peace. Holding the wrinkled form up to the candle-light he read the answer which he had so urgently composed, the absolutely final answer to the only person he had ever loved since his mother had turned her back on him. It ran:

'Gretchen, I will let you in.'

Virginia Moriconi
Ferr' agosto, 1984
Dordogne